MATING HABITS of FIREFLIES

MATING HABITS of FIREFLIES

A Novel

M.C. St.Clair

CuR-StC Fine Art

Copyright © 2024 by M. C. St. Clair

All rights reserved.

Printed in the United States of America

No part of this book may be reproduced in any form or by any electronic or mechanical means, including information storage and retrieval systems, without written permission from the author.

This is a work of fiction. Names, characters, places, and incidents are a product of the author's imagination or are used fictitiously. All resemblances to events or actual persons, living or dead, have been fictionalized or are entirely coincidental.

ISBN: 979-8-9905438-0-5

Published by Cathee vanRossem-St.Clair Fine Art
Cover Design by Cathee vanRossem-St.Clair
www.catheestclair.com

*For the sensitive ones
and for those who love them.*

What is life?
It is the flash of a firefly in the night.

— Crowfoot

Author's Note

Though *Mating Habits of Fireflies* was inspired by true events, the story is fiction. So are the characters. As soon as I named them, they doggedly dragged me into scenes I resisted and pushed me into situations I didn't expect.

David Foster Wallace, an author who astounds me, wrote:

> *"In dark times, the definition of good art would seem to be art that locates and applies CPR to those elements of what's human and magical that still live and glow despite the times' darkness..."*

Writing this novel has helped me, in Wallace's words, *"find a way both to depict this world and to illuminate the possibilities for being alive and human in it."*

May our remarkable journeys on this planet continue, and may we do our best to step gently on her surface, offering kindness and light to every being we meet.

Mating Habits of Fireflies

2006
Italy

The artist sees what others only catch a glimpse of.
— Leonardo da Vinci

Sunrise

Italy's daybreak tasted like a warning.

Emily Rowan wrinkled her nose against the sensation, shifted gears, and climbed into the mountains of Umbria. After driving all night, guided by the glow of the third-quarter moon, she expected the morning to be more welcoming.

The rental car balked as she shifted again. She willed herself to stay calm.

Nothing looked the same. A row of warehouses filled a valley that used to be alive with vineyards and farms. Barbed wire fences barricaded the hillsides.

The last time she was here, Italy was on the brink of ruin, the Vietnam War was raging, and she was at war with herself. No wonder she felt disoriented. She slowed down to gather a stack of old photos lying on the dash, hoping they'd help her remember the route.

No such luck.

She tossed the pictures against the windshield. A tattered Polaroid edged toward the instrument panel. Tightening one hand on the wheel, she lifted it to take a closer look.

Floppy camo hat. Rifle on his back. Danny. The boy she'd loved and lost back then.

He was a grunt in this picture. Humping through the jungle. Holding a firefly in his hand. His unmistakable eyes. Haunted. He was just a kid back then, fighting for his life in a foreign country. At the same time, she'd been fighting for her sanity—right here, in this foreign place. Helpless to save him.

The memory shot shrapnel through her brain. She glanced at her husband, asleep in the seat beside her. As if in response, his lips parted, releasing a whistle of air.

The sour taste in Emily's mouth intensified into an alarm.

Focus! On the road!

An eagle owl startled from the shadows, its wings flashing in the headlights' beam. Rattled, she swerved to avoid it and gently skidded the car to a stop on a patch of dead grass.

The photo landed in the footwell. She picked it up, pushed it into her pocket, and waited for her heart to stop pounding.

Her husband didn't stir. His body had surrendered to dreaming, and his face looked peaceful for a change. It felt unreal to see him so relaxed. Even the swathed painted chest sitting next to his feet hadn't moved.

She sighed, gathered the rest of the fallen pictures, stuffed them into the console, and checked her map. There must be a landmark close by, a clue—anything to help her find the place where she'd once lived.

After downshifting, she pulled out, steered into the climb, and stifled a sneeze while squinting against the glare.

Around the next hairpin turn, as if on cue, the sun's rays vanished behind a row of Italian cypresses, revealing a scene straight out of a Renaissance painting. The evergreens stood at attention as she feathered the brakes and turned onto a dirt road. It didn't take long before the countess's tower came into view, surrounded by a grove of young olive trees.

At last.

The owl's cry echoed through the mist as she backed the car alongside the courtyard wall. She killed the engine and lifted the visor to get a closer look. Again and again, she'd painted images of this castle and its sprawling estate. She'd found her voice here. As a college student. As a budding artist.

"As a survivor," she reminded herself.

Now Emily was a middle-aged woman with an apology to make. Bringing a handmade chest she'd painted especially for the countess's heir. A gift to make amends.

It takes courage to turn a gut feeling into a work of art.

Danny's young voice still lived in her head. His words had guided her as she worked on the hinged box, coaxing her brushes to flatten and surrender to each stroke. Ultramarine. Vermilion. Umber. Naples yellow. Even now, she could feel the colors rumbling on her palette like excavators after a storm. Beneath gilded layers of pigment, washes of underpaintings, and carefully sanded primers lay an invisible foundation holding together the fragments of her past.

This was what she'd carried across the ocean to deliver to the count—a container of forgotten dreams.

And courage.

Emily stepped from the car.

She lifted a handful of soil and felt its texture. She'd been nineteen in 1970, the last time she stood on this sentient mound of earth.

She sprinkled the living dirt in an arc around her feet. Staccato visions flashed through her fingers, sending a rush of energy into her arm, her torso, her throat.

Suits of armor.

Etruscan screams.

The shattering of wine bottles against farmhouse walls.

Strikes.

Tanks.

The Huey.

The Firefly.

Danny.

His body. Face down.

From thousands of miles away, on this very hill, decades ago, she'd heard his panicked cry.

Inside the car, her husband ran his fingers through his hair.

Emily puffed her cheeks and exhaled hard.

Her memory had a shape. Like a boot, it kicked.

1969

California

I would like to paint the way a bird sings.

— Claude Monet

1

HOLDING A SMALL SKETCHBOOK IN HER TEETH, eighteen-year-old Emily Rowan climbed out the window of her rented room and stood on the roof balcony of the oldest Victorian on Eighth Street. She lifted all ninety-five pounds of her body onto the nearest limb of the oak in the yard and crawled to the part of the trunk where two branches intersected, creating a small nest. After steadying herself, she settled into the arms of the surrounding boughs. The tree's support would help her brainstorm ideas for the artwork she was about to create.

Dr. Charles Finn, her favorite professor, had asked his ten seminar students to assess their teenage lives and submit an essay reflecting their findings. Specifically, "If you had only six months to live and could travel back in time, what would you change?" It was a typical college writing assignment, but Emily wanted to come up with a series of illustrations rather than a bunch of stapled pages cluttered with clichéd text by a girl who had little to offer. A comic strip seemed appropriate. It might even amuse her teacher. With his hangdog face and brown pipe, he reminded her of Pat Paulsen, the wry comedian on *The Smothers Brothers Comedy Hour*. To her surprise, Dr. Finn's response to the idea was exactly what she'd hoped for. With a nod and a chuckle, he'd scribbled a star across the front page of her illustrated proposal.

Finn was the head of Scholastics in Letters and Science, an experimental academic program housed in a Tudor building in the middle of the quad at San Jose State College. He relished quoting the classics, from Aeschylus to Wordsworth: *He who learns must suffer... and in our own despair... comes wisdom* and *Come forth into the light of things. Let Nature be your teacher.*

Exactly. That was why Emily chose to do her homework in a tree.

She pulled a few colored pencils from a drawstring pouch hanging from her belt loop and drew the leaves turning, like her mind. Then she painstakingly rendered the Scholastics building with brown leaves scattered across the shingled roof. She leaned back. The school in the drawing looked nothing like the Ivy League institution her father expected her to attend. Not because he wanted her to be a lawyer or doctor, of course. Women had their place. A teacher might do, but never an artist. If Emily didn't accept an invitation from Brown or Cornell, he wouldn't pay a nickel of tuition, especially for a lowly state college. Clare, Emily's best friend, had insisted the perks of Scholastics were worth it. They included a no-grade, no-test, two-year degree policy and an opportunity to study in Italy during sophomore year. But the idea of living abroad didn't impress Emily. Her father's tedious slideshows were mind-numbing enough. He insisted his trips were "strictly business." Who was he kidding? Especially when he focused his camera on the Sabine woman being taken by a Roman soldier. And Perseus strutting around with the decapitated head of Medusa. Did he think snapping those pictures would impress his Italian mistress?

Men.

Clare had suggested Emily fake some enthusiasm. "You can always pretend to like his boring pictures."

Emily already pretended too much.

She'd applied to San Jose State simply to defy her father. Of course, he'd given her his horrid kind of grief when he discovered his only daughter was willing to disobey him. Now she was dealing with the consequences. Working at Mrs. Martin's downtown gallery after school and most weekends allowed her to cover rent and make payments on the loan her mother had secretly secured by forging her father's signature and eliciting the help of an empathetic bank official. Emily made $1.50 an hour and earned great commissions, and Mrs. Martin liked her—who could ask for more? The biggest reward of all? Getting away from her dad.

The Great Escape. A perfect title for her project.

She elaborately embellished the three words on a blank page in her sketchbook. Her opening illustration would be a seedling hacksawing its way out of a terra-cotta pot and growing into a great tree overshadowing all the pretentious people in the world.

Emily fingered the bark of the tree she was perched in. *Let Nature be your teacher.*

Brown. Not the university. The pencil in her hand. The tree's trunk. The house, the yard, the dirt. Her memory.

Even the hair and dress on the Terri Lee doll she clung to as a child were army-umber dull. She pulled out another pencil and outlined in red her older brother, Walter, pounding on the bathroom door. Ignoring her distorted drawing of him, she positioned her doll on a 3D counter. Terri Lee, in all her plastic attentiveness, watched a hastily scribbled Emily practice her Oscar acceptance speech before the mirror. When Walter's banging morphed into unbearable jagged lines, Emily drew herself dancing on the tile floor and tiptoe-twirling until dizziness sent her forehead colliding with the doorknob.

She mapped out the doctor's office in green. A speech bubble surrounded the nurse's comment: "I put a butterfly on your forehead." It wasn't a butterfly at all. Emily drew a sad replica of an ugly strip, skinny in the middle with two sticky bands at each end. Then she rubbed a black cloud of graphite over the bandage—then over her entire face.

If you could go back in time, what would you change about your life? A mural the size of a city block couldn't contain all the lies.

She took a blue pencil from her pouch and transformed the black cloud into a storm of snickering quarter notes on a treble clef. She formed the number twelve and drew herself on the verge of becoming a teenager: sitting at the piano, closing the lid, and walking away. She locked herself in the bathroom and bound her breasts with strips of torn pillowcases. Under her big blue sweater, her dad and brother wouldn't notice. She refused to buy training bras. Bras her retired army-colonel father might finger in her dresser on inspection day, when he woke her to reveille, checked her room, smoothed her sheets, and lifted the blanket to see if she'd made her bed with military corners.

Emily clenched the pencil in her teeth and balanced her sketchbook on a flat spot of the limb so she could cling to the tree with both hands. She knew where her mind was taking her: to her safe place in the orchard.

She steadied herself and engraved the image of a gray wire fort into the page. She and Clare had built it together and covered it with leaves and branches so no one could find the entrance. Then she drew herself alone. After dark. Lowering her body through the narrow hole on top with her flashlight guiding the way. The leaves cast shadows that felt like moths brushing against her skin. She got chills but spent the night there anyway. Better than at home, where she could hear her dad, drunk and tripping on the hallway carpet. She darkened his silhouette and increased its size until it overwhelmed her bedroom doorway. She drew her spirit dissolving into stippled dots as he pulled her to him, lifted her nightie, and made her bleed.

That was when she discovered she could bend reality and touch time. Time crackled with static when her fingers grazed its invisible surface. Circular grooves sizzled into spirals as she closed her eyes. Images traveled through her fingertips, up her arm, and into her throat, filling her mind with narratives from the past and veiled visions of possible futures. Scenes overlapped, changing the quality of light as they folded in on themselves and unfolded back again. A Civil War soldier collapsing in mud. A hippie girl distributing food at a concert. Tanks rolling into a European town. Letters from a boy named Danny whipping and tearing apart in the wind. History was taking place all at once, even now, as she sketched. The past was enveloping the present, the future inlaid over it.

She scratched a pulsing heartline across the page. A stone-faced surgeon appeared next to its sharp angles. Then a crumpled car. Then her mummy-bandaged head. Electrocardiogram signals spiked when she faced the doctor in the hospital. She could tell what he was about to say before he opened his mouth. She drew a speech bubble in concentric circles surrounding his diagnosis: "simple partial seizures." Not the grand mal, twitchy kind of epilepsy. Rather, a quiet, semiconscious type of seizure that triggered a heightened sense of awareness. During those states, Emily could leave her body and move through several dimensions at once. Sometimes at will. Frequently without any warning except an amber-toned, light-shifting aura of aliveness. In these unnamed realms, she could read thoughts. She could travel through time. She could hear the night breathe. Shadow memories came with that breathing.

"Am I insane?" She'd turned to her grandfather, the only person in the room she trusted.

You're a gift, he answered without voicing the words.

She drew his thought bubble with shining yellow suns.

Her mother materialized on the page, eyebrows askew. A diamond bracelet circled the slender hand stroking Emily's hair. "You've always been special, dear."

Delusional was the kindest word her father used.

Emily didn't draw that.

Instead, she penciled her parents' house in the shape of an aerosol can. There had been no safe places to hide in that house after her grandfather died. She'd sprayed hairspray into the holes in her bedroom and bathroom walls and ceiling to flush her spying father from the attic. She'd cringed when he backed down the narrow stairway, clutching his stinging eyes and swearing revenge. After plugging all the holes with toothpaste, she ran outside, climbed her favorite tree, drew pictures of eyes looking through peepholes, and willed herself to disappear.

Then she'd quit eating.

She outlined a skeleton cowering at the bottom of the page.

Emily jerked awake from the picture.

She could have stopped drawing, then and there. She could have thrown away her sketchbook. Forever. Trying to be an artist: what a waste of time.

But she didn't.

Be strong. Go deeper. Her grandfather's words.

Emily inhaled and sketched herself diving into leaf memories, tossing them high, and giggling as they defied the wind. She picked a leaf and threw it, but it turned rigid before reaching the ground. It had her father's face. She pushed the image aside. Something else surfaced. She closed her eyes.

She saw herself walking across the playground with Clare, inventing stories. They took turns sharing chapters at lunch. They wrote fantasies about unicorns, princesses, and boys rescuing them from hurricanes. They did this daily from third grade until high school, their imaginations shaping their worlds. In the middle of their eighth-grade history class, the intercom announced that someone had shot the president. She and Clare braided their fingers together and filed across the quad to the cafeteria to wait for more terrifying news.

At home, on the oval screen of her family's black-and-white TV set, Oswald said, "I'm just a patsy!" The minute he fell, Emily knew. Telling the truth could kill you.

She drew her father opening the utensil drawer in the kitchen, pulling out a spatula, and ringing it against the heel of his hand.

The sound sent an orbit of sharp colors through her ears. That spatula became a weapon against the truth.

Emily drew a needle and a spool of thread. Then her mouth. Sewn shut.

A calendar came into view. She roughed out *1968* in hippie calligraphy to introduce a scene at the dinner table. She drew herself annoying her Nixon-loving brother by waving a "Bobby Kennedy for President" lapel button in front of his face. Walter sneered at her, noticed a zit on their dad's ear, reached over several plates of food, and popped it. Emily wanted to barf. She drew her hands, large and formidable, throwing dishes into the sink.

She hated her brother and father for their disgusting relationship. She hated them even more because they'd forbidden her from disturbing her mom while she was resting upstairs. Emily didn't know what the doctor meant by congestive heart failure, but she figured the car crash must have contributed. Nobody wanted to talk about the accident anymore. Nobody seemed to care.

She drew a TV. Six o'clock news. April fourth. She circled the date and embellished his name: Martin Luther King.

Then she drew another name and another year.

Malcolm X. 1965.

She silhouetted her body in white and outlined it in black. In the center of the form, she wrote a word: *Chiaroscuro*.

She drew an assassin. A gun. Then a human brain in the shape of a globe. She engulfed it in flames.

Without notice, an alarm clock materialized in the upper left corner of the page. Four a.m. She sketched herself stumbling out of bed. Piles of homework on the dining room table. Final exams. More cramming. Radio blaring.

June sixth.

Bobby Kennedy.

Another assassin. Another gun. Another globe. Ash. Her brain. Nothing but ash.

Emily stopped drawing, grabbed the nearest branch, and looked down. She'd forgotten where she was. An orange street sweeper roared down the road, stirring debris and paper fragments. Fallen leaves swarmed for an instant before the monster truck ran them over. A different memory fluttered toward her face. She tried to brush it away, but it darted and returned.

She followed the image back to her parents' house. Clare was to pick her up at noon for their first semester at San Jose State.

At eleven thirty, her mother glanced up from her magazine and whispered, "Now! Let's go! The guys are in the garage. We can do this before they notice we're gone." She tossed the magazine onto an unruly pile of old letters, clippings, and notes she habitually left there. After adjusting her oxygen tubes, Emily's mom turned on her new electric wheelchair and spun around. "I have something to show you," she said, eyes charged despite her labored breath.

Emily untangled the tubes behind her, helped her into the stair elevator, and supported her while transferring her to the manual chair upstairs. Her mother orchestrated with her hands; then she pointed to her bedroom.

As soon as Emily wheeled her through the door, her mom said, "It's in my closet. Go ahead. On the left."

Opening the angled door beneath the eaves of that closet was like entering a crack in the universe—a sacred place filled with the scents of wild roses, lilac, and wool. A pastel garden of powder blue sweaters, ivory-colored sandals, pink robes, and patterned tops. Silk. Velvet. Lace.

"To the left, Emily. Behind the nighties."

Emily closed her eyes and inhaled. She wanted to stay in that closet forever, to fall asleep in her mother's secrets and dreams. But they only had a few minutes, so she rummaged behind slips and pin-tucked nightgowns until she touched something large, narrow, and weighted. She wrapped her fingers around the middle of it, lifted it over hatboxes and shoe trees, and carried it into the light of the room. She fell to her knees and set it on her lap.

It was her dream box. She and her grandfather had painted it together when she was little and decided to call it that to give her hope in hard times. It had been hiding in her mother's closets for years—from the East Coast all the way to California.

Emily stroked the smooth texture of the wood.

"Rowan," said her mother. "Mountain ash. A tree of protection and vision."

"I never knew that."

"Your grampa did. He chose this wood for a reason."

"To protect me? Is that why Rowan's my middle name?"

Her mother squeezed her eyes. "He loved you a lot, dear. So do I."

Emily lifted the lid and pulled out a small stack of envelopes. "What are these?"

"Samuel's letters. Grampa read them to you when you were little, remember? You were the only one interested."

Of course she remembered Sammy, her great-granduncle. The plucky farm boy who left New York to fight in the Civil War. She used to call him her long-lost brother from another time.

"He meant a lot to my family. Anyway, I thought you might like to keep them safe."

Emily carefully lowered the hinged chest to the carpet. At that moment, she became a fragile little girl again. A girl who desperately missed her grandfather. A girl afraid to lose her mom.

"San Jose's close by. We're not losing each other, dear."

Wiping her eyes, Emily was about to get up and hug her mother when a loud thud alarmed them both. Her father's fist. Hammering the downstairs wall.

"Goddamn it, Emilia, where are you?" His military voice. "I've told you a million times not to disturb your mother. Clare's here to take you to that god-awful schoo—Christ Almighty, why did you make her go upstairs?"

"Put it away. Hurry! You can get it later," her mom whispered like a conspirator.

Emily shoved the box beneath her mother's favorite robe in the closet and began to help her to the lift.

"Emily, honey, I'm okay. I've done it hundreds of times. Get downstairs before your father destroys our eardrums."

"*E-m-i-l-i-a!*" This time, it was Walter. "Get the hell down here. Shame on you. What are you doing up there with Mother, anyway? You're not supposed to bother her!"

"Ignore them," her mother said. "Go, now. I'll meet you downstairs. Hurry! Before they blow up even more."

Emily believed her, of course. Her mother could get herself down in one piece.

Now both her father and brother were shouting. The volume of their curses grew louder.

It was hard for Emily to keep her balance. She couldn't feel her feet as she flew to the bottom of the stairs.

In the living room, Clare yelled to anyone willing to hear, "It's okay! We've got lots of time. I'll take her bags to the car."

"Where are your suitcases? Didn't you even pack? Goddamn it, Emilia. What's gotten into you?" Emily's father again.

"I have them here," Clare said as she carried the luggage out the front door.

Before Emily knew it, she was in the passenger seat, and Clare was backing her new red Mustang down the driveway toward the street.

What happened next came in slow motion: Walter waving them back, Clare pressing her foot on the clutch, shifting gears, returning to the house. The shocked look on her mother's face as she wheeled her way out the door.

Emily exploded from the car and raced to her arms. She and her mother rocked and cried and rocked, acutely aware that it might be for the last time. Then she overheard Walter, his voice false but firm, saying to Clare, "She ran out of the house without even bothering to tell her mother goodbye."

Emily dug the pencil into her palm to bring herself back to the present. "Eve of Destruction" blasted from a turntable in an apartment next door. Heart racing, she tore the day's drawings from her sketchbook, crumpled them one by one, and tossed them onto the balcony outside her room. She released the pencil and covered her ears with her hands.

She could still hear her mother's voice assuring her that she'd gotten downstairs okay but nearly fell while climbing into her other wheelchair. Then the darn thing was so slow. She couldn't get it to go straight. She tangled her oxygen tubes and had to back up several times, banging into walls down the hallway and into corners through the dining room and kitchen. Finally, she'd forced her way through what felt like a barricade of bodies to get to the doorway.

On the phone, her mother had said she sent angels to help Emily stay safe on all her journeys, short or long, from then on. Angels to let Emily know she would be in her heart always, even after she was gone.

2

A CRAYON IS A POWERFUL TOOL.
    Several days later, back in her room, Emily opened a palm-size box and touched the waxy memories of color. Her grandfather had given her his old Crayola Dream Stories Color Set No. 501 as soon as she could hold a spoon.
    "Little Bird," he'd said. "These colors will help you stay in this world."
    As a starry-eyed child, she used to sleepwalk and awaken to awkward images scribbled on the living room wall. Her grampa would scold her for using his favorite peeled-back nub of Celestial Blue in such an inexcusable way. One morning, to her surprise, he complimented her drawing of a hand reaching for a rectangle of sky. Pulling Lemon Yellow from the tin box, he drew a brilliant orb with rays circling the hand—connecting his drawing with hers on the wall.
    That was the day she tasted sunlight for the first time.
    Every morning after that, when the sun's rays awakened her, a strange flavor would prickle her sinuses—butterscotch infused with citrus. It usually made her sneeze. Sometimes, though, the flavor would turn sour. An omen.
    "My, my," her grampa said. "So you're a sun sneezer."

Exhausted from her convulsive spasms, Emily wiped her tiny nose with her sleeve. "What's a sun sneezer?"

"A little girl who sneezes when sunlight hits her eyes."

"Does that mean I'm allergic to the sun?"

"Just the opposite, my little friend. It means the sun sends you messages in special ways. Do you know what else you are?"

She shook her head.

"A dreamer. Like your great-grandmother." He opened his arms and gestured toward the constellations he'd painted on the ceiling of her childhood room. "You're about to discover what's out there." He handed her a tissue and tapped her on the temple. "And in here. So pay attention, Emmie. Your gifts might come in handy one day."

The morning sun had broken through the clouds a while ago, and its soft glow filtered through the curtains. Emily selected the same Lemon Yellow of her grandfather's sun and pulled the crayon from the tin, hoping it might help her tackle Dr. Finn's assignment once more. After peeling the paper from its blunt nib, she pressed sunlight into the frayed page of her exhausted sketchbook, emptied the remaining crayons onto the table, and sorted them by temperature.

At first she thought it was snow, but the icy flakes of color morphed into a flurry of fireflies flickering in the sunlight. She added more images. Trees shaped like women raising their arms to worship the sky. Blurred handwriting. Frowning portraits. Murmurs of music floating from cracks in stone walls. As if from the other side of time, she heard ancient voices echoing through the thinning page. *Remember us,* they sang as they broke apart and disappeared. Then her drawing rebelled. The center of the page tore, and the citrus flavor of sunlight morphed into a warning. Emily shuddered against the chill curling up her spine and closed the book.

Visions like this had been happening more frequently lately. She glanced at the handwritten Georges Rouault quote she'd pinned to the wall as a reminder to stay present: "Painting is a way to forget life. It is a cry in the night, a strangled laugh."

A wash of panic came over her. She lifted the alarm clock beside the bed.

She was late. She hated being late, especially for her weekend job at the gallery. She dropped the clock onto the pillow, hopped to keep her balance while pulling on her pantyhose, zipped into a cotton dress, buckled her sandals, snatched her pack, and ran down the staircase to the front door. Lurching forward, she caught herself and bit her lip to keep from swearing. She should have known her toe would snag on a sidewalk crack. It happened every time she rushed. She dug a vial of clear nail polish from her pack and dabbed it on her nylons to stop the run. Now she was in a full-blown sprint.

Mrs. Martin, the owner, welcomed her at the gallery with a knowing smile and a tap on her wristwatch.

Emily nodded in greeting, took another breath, and apologized as usual. She shook her head as Mrs. Martin placed a box of donuts on the front desk where the *San Jose Mercury* lay open with the headline blaring: "Berkeley Student Killed by Police at People's Park."

Emily skimmed the article. The headline was misleading. He wasn't a Berkeley student at all. He was just a boy on a rooftop, trying to get a better view of police aiming their shotguns at demonstrators protecting a community garden.

A boy from San Jose.

He had a name. James Rector. Did his family call him Jimmy?

"Hippies protesting the establishment," the article continued. Emily drummed her fingertips on the table.

James Rector.

Not wanting to forget him, she whispered his name aloud, tucked her pack into the bottom drawer, and flipped the desk calendar to May 17, 1969.

A play of light tickled her hand. She folded the paper, pushed it aside, and sat behind the desk.

"The artist had to work fast to catch this sunlight."

Emily startled. She always startled.

She looked up and squinted at a man's silhouette. He leaned into one of the paintings. "I like this one." He turned toward her. "Do you mind if I ask—what kind of art do you like?"

His low voice vibrated through her. She stood and assumed a proper salesperson posture. "Loose," she said, shrugging at the concept as she pictured her own painfully tight paintings.

He returned to the artwork. "This guy's good. I love how he makes everything fall apart as you look closer."

The light behind him inflamed her sinuses. She pulled a tissue from her dress pocket and sneezed into it.

"Bless you," he said, moving away from the wall and blocking the glare so she could finally see his face.

"Are you James Rector?" She immediately regretted her whole life. Once again, she'd surfaced from her dreamlike thoughts and blurted the wrong words.

"Don't think so." His cheeks creased into crescent moons as he smiled.

It was contagious, his smile. It made him look much younger than he sounded. One front tooth angled slightly to the left. His nose cast a slender shadow on his upper lip. She wanted to paint his dimpled chin so she could place where she might have seen him before, but he was saying something about poking a stick through the ice in the Delaware—the way George Washington's men used oars in that famous painting—the sensation of solid yielding to liquid, how the original artist must have felt the same give beneath his brush. Like time turning into itself.

She listened, mesmerized by more than his voice.

"The old painting," he said. "Emanuel Gottlieb Leutze. The artist. Remember how he put terrified horses into rowboats in the background?"

"He did?"

"Nobody could do that without the boats sinking—"

Like she was sinking, faint from his gaze. She didn't hear what else he said before he eventually walked out the door. When he glanced back at her through the window, she tasted a sweeter kind of warning hiding behind the sun.

After work, she climbed the narrow stairs to her rented room, tiptoed past the colorful doors of anonymous housemates, slipped a skeleton key into her antique lock, and turned the crystal knob. As soon as she switched on the light and shut her door, she closed the outside world behind her.

Her entire life barely fit within this cramped space. T-shirts, thrift store jeans, skirts, a couple of blouses, a sweater, and a denim jacket all hung from a single row of hooks on the wall behind the door. Lining the floor beneath were moccasins, boots, sneakers, and a worn pair of flats. A makeshift bookcase held textbooks and favorite novels. Overworked paintings crowded the gap behind it. Everything smelled like sage.

Emily threw her pack next to the alarm clock on the bed, stepped to the window, and opened the lace curtains. Pinks and oranges filled the sky, casting a pastel glow across the drawing table in the corner. After pulling down the shade, she walked to her palette and squeezed a pool of alizarin from a tube. She replaced the sketchbook and crayons with a freshly stretched canvas, rotated it sideways, and dipped her largest brush into a paint-stained jar of water.

Crimson. The color of blood. Pulsing through her temples, her fingertips. She swiped the pigment across the center of the canvas. Her brush spoke in bold strokes.

Don't tell me you're falling for that guy.

The chill in her spine muted her hand. She wouldn't allow herself to fall for anyone, especially someone she'd just met—not now, not ever.

She hesitated, then squeezed ultramarine across the red-tinged bristles and covered the entire surface with a thick layer of blue streaked with rufescent lines. It was a risky choice, but she felt compelled to do something to cool her thoughts of him.

Feeling nauseated, she stood back.

It's all wrong.

She swirled her brush in a jar of clean water, set it aside, and wiped her hands on a towel.

The painting lacked any potential for truth, except this: She knew it now. Her whole life was about to change.

He returned to the gallery the following morning. From the back room, Emily recognized his voice. Baritone with a steel-drum lilt, its thrum mimicking the thump beneath her breastbone.

She stepped out as soon as he asked Mrs. Martin about a small salesgirl with long dark hair. He smiled when he saw her and extended his hand—a smooth hand, brown, with a fan of intricate bones.

"Danny Jackson."

Nice name.

"You're Emily, right?"

She wanted to speak but couldn't seem to open her mouth, so she nodded.

He buried both fists in his pockets and cleared his throat. "I was wondering. Emily? Do you—I mean, would you like to go for a walk after work sometime?"

Mrs. Martin gave her an exuberant nod from the back room.

Emily swallowed, searching for a flavor to tell her what to do.

As soon as the gallery closed the following Sunday, she waited on the sidewalk. Mrs. Martin had told her this Danny Jackson sometimes came into the showroom on weekdays to sketch.

"Polite," she'd said. "And quiet. He's a good artist, too. He carries this big sketchbook and asks permission before he opens it. But he doesn't draw the artwork—only the gallery. Mostly the light. He uses it to add drama to the people gazing at the paintings."

Chiaroscuro—light vs. dark. Now she remembered. She'd seen his name written in cursive in her own sketchbook.

She bit her lip and sat on the curb.

Before long, he pulled up in his baby blue VW Bug. "I call her Beulah," he said after climbing out. She stared at him while he ran his fingers along the chrome visors shading the car's headlights.

His ponytail was the color of blackened copper. Loose white shirt, mushroom-shaped belt buckle, torn jeans. Tan Birkenstocks on his tawny feet.

He opened the passenger door and asked her where she wanted to go. She couldn't think of anything except his clear eyes and the way the sunlight tasted of butterscotch the minute it defined his cheekbones.

"Big Basin? Do you mind the long drive?"

She tugged the hem of her skirt. "I love Big Basin."

"Warm enough?"

She showed him the sweater she'd stuffed in her backpack.

Neither of them spoke as Danny drove.

Emily tightened her skirt around her knees. Ignoring the odd taste in her mouth, she tried to lose herself in the lyrics of "Crystal Blue Persuasion" as the song played on the radio. "Universal Soldier" only reminded her of the war, but Otis Redding's voice heartened her in "Dock of the Bay."

Danny seemed to be mesmerized by the nonstop music as well. The rolling hills twisted and turned into heavily forested switchbacks leading to a parking area near the Redwood Loop trail. It was one of her favorite places.

They walked a path that meandered around Opal Creek. Each giant redwood had a name: Mother of the Forest, Father of the Forest, the Animal Tree. The Santa Clara Tree was the largest: fifteen feet around, maybe more. She'd wandered this route a million times, but everything seemed new to her next to this guy. It was nearly impossible to mimic his stride. His feet barely made a sound as they contacted the earth.

"How do you do that?" she finally asked.

"Do what?"

"Walk like you're floating."

He raised his eyebrows and looked at his toes. "I guess I get it from my grandfather."

"Your grandfather?" She shifted from one foot to the other and nearly lost her balance on a twig.

He caught her arm. "It's all about stillness. Want me to show you?"

She nodded, and he stepped behind her. A pulse quivered up her spine as his hand guided the small of her back.

"You can be still even when you move."

"You can?"

"Here, try this." His finger pressed into her backbone.

She recoiled.

"It's okay. Just draw your belly button toward my hand, like it's about to reach your spine."

His voice. Could she lean into it?

"Yes, like that." He touched her crown. "Now imagine a vertical thread through your body, out the top of your head. Feel it as I pull the thread upward into the sky."

She straightened like a puppet and slumped when he released her. His touch unnerved her. At the same time, she wanted to fall into his arms and let him carry her.

He placed his hands on her shoulders and turned her to face the creek. "See this stream? Imagine it flowing down through your head and into the soles of your feet. Let it rest there. Then let it flow from your feet into the core of the earth."

A tremor rippled through her veins.

"Now move the current back through your body, out the top of your head, into the clouds. Connect sky with earth. Earth with sky. This is how my grandfather taught me to walk."

His mouth grazed her ear. His words made no sound. Instead, they surged in waves through her body.

Do you hear it? The wind? That's what gives us life. We share the air with everything. We're all common, like a breath. One step inhales. The next sighs. Fill your lungs with walking.

She was in the breath of something stronger, older, deeper.

"Walk from that place," Danny whispered.

Emily and Danny walked, defying gravity with each step, until they found themselves back at the trailhead where they began. Beulah welcomed them in the parking lot.

Danny drove to a nearby field and pulled to the side of the road. Reaching in the back, he grabbed a grocery bag and a blanket. He patted Beulah's roof before opening the passenger door. They removed their shoes and walked through the grass, his flashlight guiding their way. They sat near a boulder and waited for the stars.

He took a peach from the bag and gave it to Emily before pulling out one for himself. She watched him take a slow bite. Juice spilled from his mouth and trickled through fine down on the exposed part of his chest. She bit into her peach. Its sweetness overcame her, and she slumped against the rock, satiated and in awe.

3

EMILY DIDN'T FALL IN LOVE WITH DANNY. SHE TRIPPED. All her life, she'd wanted to meet someone as magical as her grandfather—someone who talked like him, who moved like him, someone she could trust. Soon after her grampa died, she'd gazed at the constellations he'd painted in her room and asked for this kind of love. In a dream, he'd told her she would find it.

Today was Danny's twentieth birthday. September 14, 1969. She decorated the date in her sketchbook and drew him playing music at a remote rock and roll bar in the Santa Cruz Mountains. He had a gig tonight. She'd known this for weeks, but the deadline loomed for Dr. Finn's assignment, and she decided not to go. Her frowny cartoon face reflected her chagrin.

It was late. She closed her book and waited in her room. She lit incense. She paced. She placed the Moody Blues' *Days of Future Passed* on the turntable and arranged pillows on the floor. She knelt beside her small mattress, smoothed the Indian bedspread, and immersed herself in the music. Nearing the album's end, she scrutinized the painting she'd started the day she first met him. It had morphed from a brash succession of red-and-blue strokes into a winged woman sitting inside the curve of a crescent moon, spreading her feathers and arms. Emily had intended to capture a magical feeling: how her body throbbed after Danny kissed her on the night before the moon landing in July. Thinking about it sent every nerve within her flickering like the stars. But the painting didn't work. Instead, it felt strained, like this night. Rather than hide it behind her bookcase, as she often did with her failed artwork, she decided to be courageous and mount it on the wall.

She pounded the nail and jumped.

"It's just me, Emmie," Danny said, tapping on the door and opening it.

He set his gear on the floor, hugged her from behind, nestled his nose in her hair, and nudged the door with his heel until it clicked behind him. He took her hammer and set it down next to his belongings. After twirling her around, he covered her mouth with his, then abruptly released her.

"Did you feel that?" he asked.

"You mean all the planets in the universe colliding?"

"That's what I like about you. An earthquake becomes a celestial pileup."

"Earthquake?"

"You didn't feel it?" Danny surveyed the room. He removed the skipping needle from "Nights in White Satin" and lifted Emily's winged-lady painting from a clutter of baskets on the floor. "At least this wasn't damaged," he said as he hung it on the nail. "Glad it was only a small one."

How could she miss an earthquake that size?

Tremor. This is what you do to me.

Papers from last week's seminars littered the room. Her alarm clock lay on its side. Roger Zelazny's latest book, *Creatures of Light and Darkness*, had inched toward the edge of the shelf.

Danny began to tidy odds and ends. While he wasn't looking, she dug into her backpack for a package she'd wrapped in a map of Santa Clara County.

"What's this?" he asked when she stopped his fussing and placed the package in his hands.

"Go ahead, open it." She flattened her voice, pretending to be aloof.

He pulled the crocheted string and lifted a stout candle from the folded paper.

"I rolled a million sheets of beeswax for you."

"You're kidding." He rotated the candle.

"It wasn't really a million sheets. More like fifty. Actually, fifteen. There's this cool little shop in town where they show you how to trim sheets of beeswax and wind them around a piece of string dipped in a huge pot of melted wax. I thought you might like—"

"I do." He held the candle to his nose, closed his eyes, and inhaled. "Wildflowers." His voice drifted before he opened his eyes again. "I love this smell. I always wanted to be a beekeeper. My grandfather taught me how to catch their swarms and keep hives and all. How'd you know?"

"I didn't."

There was so much about Danny she didn't know. Shortly after they met, she learned he was not only an artist but also the lead guitarist for Wave, one of her favorite Bay Area bands. She'd had no idea until he climbed onstage after inviting her to one of his gigs. The setting, it turned out, made all the difference. Now this thing about his grandfather and bees. It was intimidating how cool he was. Maybe too intimidating.

She picked at her fingernail.

He sat cross-legged in the center of the floor, pulled a match from a tiny box in his pocket, and lifted a slate coaster from the bedside. His eyes became gazing globes in the flickering light as he secured the candle on the coaster and set it on the rug.

Emily adjusted her skirt and settled across from him. "Your grandfather's still alive?"

Danny nodded. "He loves the land. Plants. Bees. Fireflies."

"Fireflies?"

Leaning on his hands, he glanced at the flame, then at Emily.

"They talk to each other with light, did you know that? But only the males flash while they're flying."

She pictured cartoon insects tossing sparklers back and forth.

Danny arched his back and looked up at the ceiling. "Okay, imagine a female sitting in the grass like this. She's watching the flash patterns all the males are making overhead. Say she likes that one, over there." He pointed to a spot. "So, she flashes to him. Just once. That male firefly gets so excited he lets loose a bunch of fireworks." His smile widened. "But she's cool, so she flashes again. Only once. He gives her another light show, and they keep dancing like that all night."

Emily laughed. "Do that again."

He shook his arms while twisting his shoulders.

"You're too much. You know that?"

"Grandfather tried to teach me how to use a flashlight to try to get a female to light up. We'd be out there all night, clicking past midnight, but nothing ever happened."

"I always thought fireflies were like fairies."

"Beautiful beings of light. Like you." Danny reached over and tucked a wisp of hair behind her ear.

His touch softened her.

They spent the rest of the night talking about things that had never surfaced before and discovered that both of their families came from different parts of New York. She told Danny how her parents had moved to Saratoga, California, partly because of her dad's job, but mostly because the name had reminded him of his favorite upstate horse racing track. Unlike her dad, though, both their grandfathers loved animals. Danny's grandfather was a naturalist. Her grampa was a storyteller and an inventor.

When they finally ran out of words, Danny lit a cigarette and immediately crushed the glowing cherry on the sole of his boot. "Really need to quit these things."

The candlelight cast a shadow across his face. He suddenly looked faded and old.

Emily fiddled with her bracelet.

The candle flashed, making a hissing sound. Several ages seemed to pass as they watched the flame.

In a low voice, she broke the silence.

"Once, I asked my grampa about reincarnation."

"Yeah? What'd he say?"

"Nothing at first. He just licked the salt off a potato chip and returned it to the bag. I told him, 'No, that's recycling.'"

It was a stupid joke. Danny laughed anyway.

She bit her lip again, trying to fight the sensation that she'd been with him like this before. This night—the hissing candle, his affectionate smile, the glimmer in his eyes—had all happened eons ago. Or yesterday. The same shifting light, the same amber aura, the same shadowy sighs of a thousand souls merging in the darkness. The feeling made her shiver the way a tiny bird shivers.

Danny rested his hand on her knee. The fluttering candle cast more shadows that quickly turned into wings.

"Grampa was always rescuing birds," she whispered. "Once, we found a dazed sparrow behind a rock. He cradled it in his hands and carried it inside while I ran to get a shoebox. I poked air holes in the top of the box, and we placed the little bird inside with my mom's favorite towel."

"Her favorite towel?"

"Grampa said, 'Shh! If we don't say anything, she might not notice.' Then we spent the afternoon building the bird a proper home. One that didn't need a fancy towel. Grampa made a wooden box—a dream box, he said. To save the fragile ones. He drilled air holes on top—"

—and you painted the back of it with moons and stars and planets and put the sun and a few clouds on the sides. A constellation of time. A creation myth.

Emily swallowed. Her grandfather had said something similar.

Sorry. Danny lifted his hand from her knee. He seemed to be speaking, but his mouth wasn't moving.

The shadows twisted inside her. She grabbed her cramping stomach and willed the episode to disappear. She focused on her grampa, the one man in the world she trusted, and all the bluebirds, thrushes, and chickadees who trusted him. They'd sit on his shoulders while he filled the feeder.

Then her vision turned dark.

Time. Static. Spiraling grooves. She cradled her head.

Danny didn't seem to notice.

She did her best to speak. When her tangled tongue began to unsnarl, her voice accelerated into near panic. "He didn't know what his inventions would do—machines mostly. Paper pulpers. Incinerators. Things like that. They spewed pollution everywhere. He didn't know he was sending millions of his beloved birds to their graves. I guess that's why I asked him about reincarnation. I guess I needed a name for not letting things die forever."

Danny shifted his weight. "What are you talking about?"

"I don't know. Chips in a bag, dream boxes. Grandfathers, grandmothers. Mothers—"

"Mothers?" He leaned toward her.

"Maybe reincarnation is another word for making up stories to save poisoned birds, so they never have to die?"

Danny frowned. "Your mother died?"

"The opposite of a creation myth, if you ask me."

"When did she die?"

Emily tried to force her head to clear. She couldn't remember the date. The day itself, however, was fused in her bones. Every jarring detail of it.

"Just before I met you, I guess." It was the best answer she could come up with.

Danny curled next to her and folded her hand in his.

She shrugged. "When I was little, Grampa told me death is a mystery to the living, that's all. To everything else, it's a creative force. He never spoke those exact words, but I can still hear his voice saying something like that."

"Emmie." Danny pressed her knuckles to his lips and whispered through her fingers. "Tell me about your mom."

She fought the flood in her throat. "I miss her, that's all."

He released her hand and gently squeezed his arm around her shoulder.

"She loved angels. I asked if she wanted to be one. She said she didn't have wings. She didn't want wings. What she really wanted to do was run."

Run. That was what Emily wanted to do. How had this conversation turned to her mom dying? She hated her tongue. She wanted to rip it out and become a mute forever. Maybe a deaf-mute, so she wouldn't have to listen to all the rubbish in her head. She'd ruined everything. She'd made this night about her stupid self instead of Danny.

The beeswax buzzed as he kissed her forehead.

She stiffened.

He traced her cheek, her nose, and her chin with his lips. He slipped her blouse off her shoulder and kissed her collarbone.

She clutched his wrist.

Danny's eyes softened as he backed away and held her to his chest. His pulse was steady, his breathing even.

Emily had never in her life felt so broken. She wrinkled her nose. If only she could say something, anything, to make the shadows go away.

It's okay, Emmie. Danny pressed a finger to her mouth.

His voiceless message echoed inside her head. She pulled away to take in his face, his transparent eyes, and the competing scents of citrus and butterscotch in his hair. A wave of familiarity merged with the chill quivering up her arms.

She knew him, deep in her bones. She'd known him for ages. But could she trust him like she trusted her grandfather? They both carried the same glow. She could tell by the way the candlelight fragmented and contracted and flattened and shifted before finally streaming in a glimmering beam.

What is it when you recognize someone the same way you recognize the sun?

"It's love," Danny whispered.

"Did I say that out loud?"

"You didn't have to."

4

"I don't want to smoke anymore," Danny told her a few weeks later. He stopped, just like that. His Chesterfield Kings habit ended when he tossed all his half-empty packs into the trash, and his roasted peanut addiction began. *Goober peas,* he called them, cracking the shells and popping the kernels, one after the other, into his mouth.

Mrs. Martin had given Emily the weekend off. To celebrate Danny's decision, they piled sleeping bags into Beulah's trunk and hummed their way to North Lake Tahoe. Danny's brother, Ben, was staying in a cabin above Donner Lake, near Truckee. He said they could sleep on the floor that Saturday night.

Danny chose to take Highway 80 over the summit instead of the old Highway 40 she remembered from childhood. He was familiar with the route, but she'd never traveled that way before. The road was gigantic but not as scary as the old one that swerved down nauseating switchbacks with heart-stopping drop-offs.

Emily adjusted her sunglasses. "I always hated Truckee."

"Yeah?"

"I remember seeing the Donner Party monument when I was a kid. It gave me the creeps. I thought only cannibals lived here."

"Still think that?"

She laughed. "There's something about this place. You know, something weird."

Danny reached over the stick shift and squeezed her knee before changing the subject. He said Ben was smart, a year ahead of him in school. He'd always been a trickster, a bit testy, but he was also the kindest guy you'd ever meet. After he and Danny had followed friends to California, Ben joined the marines on a dare, went AWOL during his R&R from Vietnam, and somehow found his way back to the States. He'd been hiding out in secluded places ever since.

Sure enough, Ben's cabin came into view at the end of a dirt road shrouded in aspens, pines, and firs. Squirrels dropped cones all around them, and strange sounds echoed through the trees. It was October and bone-chillingly cold. Emily pulled a knit hat over her ears and watched her footing as they unloaded the car. They climbed a million steps to the door, which opened before they knocked.

Standing before them was a slender boy-man with black hair. He hugged them both together, gear and all. They stumbled over each other into the dark interior of his home.

Emily removed her hat and sunglasses and inspected the front room. Braided oval rug on a plank floor. Link Wray poster on the wall. Tattered sleeping bag draped across a well-loved sofa. Log pitch snapping in the wood stove.

Ben and Danny thumped each other on the back. Danny took off his boots and socks, wiggled his toes, and settled into the warmth of the couch. Ben, also barefoot, straddled a folding chair next to Danny. Emily set her bag on the rug, slipped off her sneakers, and joined Danny on the sofa. It felt like a ritual, this orchestration of bodies. Tim Buckley's surreal voice accompanied their movements with "No Man Can Find the War."

"So, Emily, tell me who you are." Ben's smile seemed too large for his face. And his question confused her. She was expecting the usual "Tell me what you do."

"It's okay not to answer," he said before she could respond. "Some things aren't meant to be spoken in words."

"I warned you, Emmie." Danny reached over and cuffed his brother's arm. "Lighten up, man."

"Sorry." Ben shook his shoulders and head. He reminded Emily of a puppy shaking off water. The heaviness in the room dissipated. "So—what do you have to say about yourself?"

"She's a cool chick, Ben. Give her some slack."

Ben leaned forward and studied her face. "Do you walk in the woods?"

"Stop, Ben," Danny said.

"It's a valid question. You know that, Dan."

Emily raised her head and jutted out her chin. "Yes, but not as much as I'd like."

Let Nature be your teacher.

Ben folded his arms and leaned back. He had that *I thought so* look on his face.

After a long pause, he nudged Danny. "Hey—got some good stuff."

"Yeah?"

"Get your coat. We'll smoke it outside."

"I'll make dinner," Emily called, chastising herself under her breath as Danny and Ben stepped onto the back porch. Why couldn't she tell him straight out how trees kept her sane?

She located the turntable and adjusted the volume so she could make out Buckley's lyrics. He was moaning about never asking to be your mountain. After turning the album over, she placed the needle on "Once I Was," a ballad about soldiers and lovers and wondering why. She switched to "Goodbye and Hello" and peered out the window. The two brothers were huddled in down jackets, smoking doobies and stomping their naked feet. She retreated to the kitchen and washed her hands before assembling what she could find to create a meal.

Ice-cold water flowed from the faucet—a sign of autumn. The

week before, she and Danny had broken the earth beneath a pile of yellowing leaves in the Santa Cruz mountains to dig for his favorite chanterelles. Ben's button mushrooms weren't as exotic, but they'd still taste good after sizzling in the pan with onions, garlic, and herbs.

No herbs or garlic. Salt and pepper, then. Frozen peas. A carrot. She'd make something delicious to prove she was worth at least that.

Outside, Ben raised his voice. "You damn well *should* worry about Nixon's scam. You're a lucky SOB, you know? Shoulda been drafted by now, that's for sure."

"Fuck, Ben. I don't want to talk about it anymore."

Emily leaned against the sink. The volume, the tone of their voices. They were arguing about everything wrong in the world.

She boiled water for rice.

After a while, Ben and Danny returned to the kitchen with silly grins on their faces. Emily filled Ben's tin soup bowls with white rice and veggies.

"How'd you know we'd be hungry?" Ben joked, cradling one of the bowls in both hands. Then he looked surprised. "Why didn't you cook the hamburger in the fridge?"

"She doesn't eat meat," Danny said. He seemed eager to defend her.

Ben pinched Emily's ribs. "Little girl. You need meat on your bones."

"This looks great, Emmie." Danny nudged her away from his brother.

It felt good to feel the heat of his protection as she nestled beside him. Lifting a tarnished fork to her lips, she watched the sun slip away and imagined spending her life cocooned in Danny's warmth. Then emerging. With powerful wings.

After helping with the dishes at Emily's request, Ben and Danny brought out Go, a war game much more demanding than chess. Emily placed a bowl of goober peas on the table. Hours passed as the boys clicked black and white stones onto a gridded board. They cracked peanuts while strategizing their attacks and capturing each other's territory. Sometime after midnight, Ben swept the remaining stones from the grid. He punched Danny's shoulder and retired to the upstairs loft.

Emily closed her copy of *Slaughterhouse-Five* and crawled into a connected sleeping bag with Danny.

"I like it here," she said, taking on his strength as they snuggled before the fire. "Something about this place feels safe."

Danny pulled back her hair and kissed her neck. "You? Safe in Truckee? Where all the cannibals live?"

"You got me there."

"Yeah, I'll eat you alive if you let me."

She giggled as he nibbled her ear.

"Shh," Danny said after she nearly screamed. "We'll wake Ben."

"Tell me more about him."

"Ben?" Danny pulled away, sat up, and gazed at the glow in the window of the wood stove. He paused to watch a couple of logs collapse into each other as the flames consumed them. "He used to come to our place after his parents died. Ma liked to feed him because he was so skinny."

"I thought he was your brother."

"Ma and Grandfather sort of adopted him."

"Adopted? Sort of?"

"He was just a kid when it happened. Motorcycle accident. Both parents gone in an instant. Ma took it hard. She couldn't hold back her crying like Ben did. I think his ma was her best friend."

Emily couldn't imagine losing her best friend. She shifted to keep the sadness from overwhelming her. "Your dad? Did he help?"

"Nope." Danny slid down beside her and pulled the sleeping bag over his chest.

The ceiling and walls flickered with the stove's light, casting mysterious shapes everywhere.

Danny lowered his voice. "Ben stayed with us because nobody

else cared. Became part of us. Smart guy. Got to the point where I could hardly keep up with him."

"How in the world could they not care?"

"Just the way it was."

She didn't know what to say. When the silence became too heavy, she changed the subject. "How'd you learn to play Go? From Ben?"

Danny looked puzzled for a moment. Then he laughed. "Go? Guess my roommate got us into that stuff when Ben and I left our land and came here to check out the music scene."

"Your land?"

"Doesn't matter. That was a long time ago."

She nestled into him and kissed his cheek.

"Oh, so now you like cannibals?" His dimples deepened as he smiled.

She jabbed him hard. He exaggerated a crumpled pose and gasped. They tickled each other to near exhaustion, stifling their giggles.

"Why did Ben go AWOL?" Emily asked after they calmed down.

"His way of playing games, I guess."

"Games?"

"I'm joking." Danny turned toward her, leaned on his elbow, and twisted her hair around his finger. "But games are all we know. The whole human race plays games. It takes skill and courage to be able to play a game intelligently. Sometimes that's the only thing that keeps us alive."

"Are we just a game, you and I?"

"That's not what I said. But if we are a game, then we're a good game, and I don't want it to end."

"Ever?"

He laughed. "Ever. Okay?"

His eyes flared. In them, she saw stars, galaxies, and a universe of fireflies. Then cloudiness. And dread.

She touched his chin. "Danny?" She hesitated, searching for the right words. "Do you ever get scared?"

He tilted his head.

"You know, like Ben? He must have been scared when he lost his parents. But your family took him in. They protected him and gave him what he needed to survive. Then he went to Vietnam, and the war took everything away from him again. It's so tragic."

"Ben's not tragic, Emmie. He's here, alive and well. And he beats me at Go every time. Even before we finish a game."

"I'm serious, Danny. I can't help but wonder why the human race is so cruel. Everywhere we go, we step on something alive. We don't even notice, and no one seems to care. That's the problem, isn't it? No one cares. Just like those people in Ben's life." She pointed to the crescent outside the window. "The moon must think we're idiots."

Danny opened her fingers and slowly kissed each one. "You're brighter than the moon. More significant than you know."

"Nothing changes, though. Because we don't change."

"We do change, Emmie. We have to in order to survive."

"But what if survival isn't enough?"

"Look, as long as there's a moon out there, someone will see the light and feel a little hope. That will inspire new beginnings, right? Which leads to action. That's what changes things."

"But what if you have to go to Vietnam? Is that the kind of action you want? Is there any hope in that?"

Danny rolled onto his back and stared at the ceiling.

Emily watched the fire slowly flicker to blackness. The refrigerator stopped humming. The room carried an inaudible weight.

I'm scared, Danny.

He turned to her, his eyes filling.

Without thinking, she unzipped the bag, straddled his hips, and kissed his mouth. Softly at first. Then with a force that surprised her. Fighting to stay in her body, she tried to let herself come alive with his touch, his lips, his tongue, the brush of his skin against hers as he removed his shirt, then hers.

Emerging. With powerful wings. She could do this. Her circular dial of pills would protect her, right?

Still, she refused to fill her head with fairy tales, castles, and all the happily-ever-afters that never happened in the real world. Not the Roger Zelazny world where an Egyptian god hides his wife in a secret place to save her from the Thing That Cries in the Night. Not the kind of world where birds sing after a massacre. The only world she wanted was the one she was living in right here. In Truckee. With this boy who was surprisingly patient. This boy who understood the value of moving with care. This boy who was gently reaching into her, awakening all the forevers she thought she didn't need.

5

"Turn your shoulders a little to the left. Good. Now, look at me."

Emily sat as still as she could.

"So fine," Danny hummed while dipping his brush into a palette of zinc white, barium red, cobalt blue, and yellow ochre. He dabbed pigment on the canvas in staccato strokes.

TJ—Danny's roommate and best friend, Wave's bass player, and a blond groupie magnet—was away for the weekend, which meant the apartment was free of swooning girls and screeching amps.

It was sunny out. Danny had opened all the windows in his paint-splattered room and arranged jars of stained brushes, linseed oil, turpentine, and paint tubes on a card table next to his easel. He'd curtained the window and two speakers with gray bedsheets and tacked another neutral backdrop to the wall. "I Shall Be Released," Emily's favorite song on *Music from Big Pink*, played in the background. Danny had arranged a stool for her with a box of tissues on a nearby table in case any leaking sunlight might make her sneeze.

She smiled as he wiped his brush with a rag and walked toward her. He kissed her head and unbuttoned the top of her cardigan with his free hand, pulling it down just enough to reveal her shoulders. She never thought she'd be able to trust a guy like this. A musician. A musician who could paint.

Wave was one of the coolest bands around the South Bay. Everyone she knew was in love with their sound.

The Memorial Day holiday came to mind. That was the weekend she realized Danny was the lead guitarist of her favorite group. It still embarrassed her to think she was dumb enough not to recognize him when they first met. The gig had taken place at the Aquarian Family Festival, a three-day be-in on San Jose State's football field. Clare and Emily's other friends in Scholastics—Matt, Ryan, Larry, and two girls named Spider and Holly—were part of Dirt Cheap Productions, a local organization that helped put the festival together. The show was sponsored by the Institute for Research and Understanding, a nonprofit that promoted services like drug crisis intervention and draft resistance. A free rock concert, everyone thought, would be an excellent way to protest the nearby pop festival that charged an insane amount for admission at the Santa Clara County Fairgrounds.

Spider—all legs, arms, and smiles in her rainbow headband and cutoffs—helped Matt and Ryan find generators for the gig. They'd convinced the best bands to play. Of course, the local DJs also contributed. Musicians came from around the world to jam nonstop all weekend.

Holly helped bake over a hundred loaves of bread to feed the crowd. She floated in a gossamer dress, calling out "Hungry?" in her breathy voice as she distributed her bounty. The local 7-Eleven opened its refrigerators to store food from Friday morning through Sunday. Larry silk-screened an armload of psychedelic posters. Clare volunteered to create light shows. A dude with crazy hair gave away thousands of donuts. Another guy paid for a row of portable johns with his own money and hauled them to campus in the back of his pickup. Because Spartan Field was off limits to the city police department, a local branch of the Hells Angels acted as security.

Mating Habits of Fireflies

Hendrix, Jefferson Airplane, Big Brother, Steve Miller, Led Zeppelin, Eric Burdon, Canned Heat, Chuck Berry, Muddy Waters, Taj Mahal, Ace of Cups, Flamin' Groovies, Joy of Cooking, Weird Herald, and Sons of Champlin headlined the gig. About fifty bands in all. Several, including Hendrix, never played. But Wave did. They came in after the Greater Carmichael Traveling Street Band and before the Crabs.

"There he is," Clare said, nudging Emily as Danny stepped onstage. The strongest vise in the world couldn't close Emily's gaping mouth. Clare snorted with laughter.

Danny was like a god up there. His voice. His eyes. His ostinato riffs. He radiated like the sun.

Nearing the end of the be-in, Danny took Emily to the fairgrounds. He wanted to purchase tickets to the pop show so they could see Jimi play, but the ticket guy recognized Danny and returned their money. Danny escorted Emily to a spot next to the stage, and, to her delight, Jimi nodded and shook his sweat right on top of them during an extended rendition of "Sunshine of Your Love." When the song merged into "Voodoo Child" at the crescendo of the crowd's cheering, the promoter pulled the plug. Speakers fell silent. But Hendrix didn't miss a beat. He kept singing while he arced his guitar strap over his head and walked away. Danny nudged Emily through a fence behind the stage before the stunned crowd realized what had happened.

They made it back to the be-in just before Hendrix appeared at Spartan Field. He'd hoped to close the free show, but the crew was already dismantling the stage. Emily, Holly, and Spider circled Jimi. He smiled, took Holly's hand, drew her to him, curled his other arm around her waist, and dipped her in a backward bow. Holly could hardly contain herself. When he picked up his axe and turned to leave, Ryan stopped him. "Come to our party at the Eleventh Street House, okay? It'll be fun. It's where we live. The Dirt Cheap folks." He gestured to the girls. "That's us."

"Okay."

"Really? Yes?"

Hendrix never showed.

That evening, Emily sat on the kitchen counter, sipping tea with Holly while the party raged in the big room. The smell of booze and pot drifted in the air.

"C'mon! Why do the sweetest girls always wind up hiding in the kitchen?" TJ asked when he wandered in with Danny.

Danny hopped on the counter beside Emily. "Dance with me? Please?" He jumped down, offering his hand.

Emily shrugged at TJ and fell into Danny's arms. TJ stayed in the kitchen with Holly.

Someone was playing the blues harp. A group in the corner was laughing and singing. Clare tossed her thick braid over her shoulder, threw back her head, and howled to the music. Emily and Danny twirled around the living room as Larry offered a bottle of Southern Comfort to a couple necking on the couch. The night rotated with them.

The next morning, Matt and Ryan poured black coffee into a confusion of mugs and mason jars and passed them out to all the bodies stirring in the room. Holly and TJ emerged from a bedroom. "For What It's Worth" played on the turntable. The chilling lyrics hushed everyone.

When the song was over, Ryan straightened his wire-rimmed glasses and announced that the Grateful Dead might be working with them on another free concert at Spartan Field. With the Rolling Stones as surprise guests.

"Did you hear me? The Stones! Sometime in December. All we have to do is get permission from the town."

Danny dipped his brush into a pool of pigment and coughed to bring Emily back to the present.

"Emmie, lift your chin. Now, look into my eyes. Yeah, like you did before. I love it when you smile like that. A little more to the left. No, the other left. That's it. Hold that for a while?"

Meditation. That was what Emily needed. A couple of Wave's band members were into it. The more she thought about it, the more she realized she'd rather gaze at constellations than sit in the lotus pose all night only to wake up stiff, grumpy, and far from enlightened. Then again, her buzzing brain confirmed she was in no position to judge people for wanting to quiet their minds.

Then she thought of Clare, the one person in the world who knew Emily better than Emily knew herself. Clare always scoffed at her for spending so much time in her head.

"You're too passive. That's your whole friggin' trip in three words."

"So? You're too bossy," Emily would retort, knowing full well Clare was right.

She'd met Clare in the third grade at an elementary school in Los Gatos. Their mothers were both teachers, and she and Clare often noticed each other on the playground after school while waiting for their moms to take them home. One day, Clare walked over to Emily and announced she was about to buy a pack of gum at the Candy Shack across the street.

"It's against the rules," Emily said. "We're not supposed to leave the playground."

Clare's curly pigtails bounced as she spoke. "That's during school time, silly. It's playtime now."

She took Emily's hand and bolted across two paved lanes onto the tanbark path leading to the door with the bell. Right in front of Emily and everyone, she lifted her dress and pulled a dime from a pocket in her frilly underwear.

Emily never knew underwear could have pockets.

"I'll have two Juicy Fruit gums, please," Clare told the man behind the counter.

She handed one of the packs to Emily and stashed the other in her panties. They ran back to the playground and right into the angry arms of a second-grade teacher.

Emily was the one with gum in her hand, so Emily was the one the teacher sent to the principal's office. As she smoothed her jumper and folded her fingers over her knees, she knew it wouldn't be long before Mr. Thompson would take her into the room where he hid the spanking machine. She'd heard it was as big as a pirate ship, with metal and paddles and chains. She kept looking at the door behind him. She nodded as Mr. Thompson asked questions her ears never heard. The important thing was this: he didn't open that door. And he let Emily go without telling her mom.

Clare said she was sorry and gave Emily three of her five sticks of gum because the teacher had taken Emily's.

"Don't ever do things you don't want to, especially if somebody you don't know tells you to do them."

"Like you?"

Clare unwrapped yellow paper from foil. "Like me."

"Does that mean I shouldn't be your friend?"

"Probably." Clare wadded the gum into her mouth.

"What if I want to be your friend?"

"Then that's okay," she mumbled. "It's only not okay if you don't want to."

That was the moment Clare became Emily's best friend. When they played Barbies, Clare showed Emily how to use her mother's clean Kotex as beds and cover them with handkerchief sheets and facecloth blankets. They giggled as they rubbed bald spots onto the fuzzy heads of their Ken dolls. When they were stuck inside because of bad weather, they compared each other's faces in Clare's hand mirror. Emily couldn't find adjectives stunning enough to describe her friend's thick hair and olive eyes. Clare said Emily's eyes looked like mud.

Clare threw the mirror onto her bed. She pulled two harmonicas from Marine Band boxes and demonstrated how to suck and blow to the rhythm of rain. They took turns plucking colorful percussions from their stretched shoestrings. Emily taught Clare how to draw. She posted pages of crayon dogs and chalk horses on Clare's bedroom walls. Clare showed Emily how to howl like cartoon coyotes and dance like rainbow fillies. Clare understood celebration.

Danny cleared his throat and set down his brush. "Come see what I've done so far." He brought Emily to his side of the easel, then backed her away from the canvas until she was in the perfect viewing spot.

The painting surprised her. He'd made her look beautiful. Her skin, her eyes. Diaphanous. But when she stepped closer, fragments of paint replaced her image, and the girl who was supposed to be Emily began to fall apart and disappear.

Is it possible to be beautiful if you disappear?

She struggled with the concept.

Her great-grandmother's beauty inspired men. Emily's father would snicker at this. "She had money. That's why all the fellows followed her everywhere."

"Oh, George," her mom would say, dismissing him with her hand. "Must you ruin everything?"

According to her mother, this handsome man (all the men in her mother's stories were handsome) had asked the lovely Lila Rose to marry him. "She loved him so much," her mom said. Then there was this other guy (who was not so handsome) who stole Lila Rose away and made her marry him because, in those days, you had to marry a man who got you pregnant. It turned out he was after the large dairy farm Lila Rose had inherited from her father.

"So it was true, after all, what Dad said about the men?"

Her mother frowned at the military picture of Emily's decorated father on the table. "Ruthless men will use beauty for their own means."

Emily thought that was the end of the story. She wasn't sure what had prompted the private conversation with her mother a few days later.

Emily's mom had grabbed a nightgown from her closet and turned toward a painting on the bedroom wall.

"My grandmother was a dreamer like you. She also listened to trees and sang with birds. When no one was looking, she swam naked in the river. She painted the place. There." Her slender arm arced toward the framed watercolor, a painting Emily had seen so often she took it for granted. "It was the last painting your great-grandmother did before she died." Her mother's voice trailed as she slipped her nightgown over her head.

"How did she die?"

Her mother put her fingers to her pale lips to remind Emily this wasn't a topic they should discuss.

There were other difficult stories. Emily's mother had starved herself in an attempt to abort her pregnancy, weighing slightly over one hundred pounds the day Emily was born. Immediately after Emily slipped out, two months early, her mother asked to go home so she could get back to teaching.

"Oh, no, you don't," said the doctor. "You have a baby to take care of."

Emily was isolated for several months in the incubation ward of the hospital. When she was strong enough, her grandparents fostered her in New York because her mother was too depressed to have anything to do with a baby. To escape her pain, her mom spent more time with her kindergarten kids than at home with her own family. After Emily's gramma died, her grampa sold his upstate residence and brought three-year-old Emily with him to California. They moved in with her parents. It turned out her grampa was the only sane member of her family. Then everything changed when his heart failed.

Emily couldn't understand why her mother let her father invade her room the night after the funeral. Had her mom wiped reality from her brain, replacing it with delusion so she could go to school and pretend everything was okay? How in the world could such a beautiful person function so blindly?

Emily closed her eyes. *Am I blind too?*

"Do you like it? The painting?" Danny asked.
"What?"
"You're deep into it, aren't you?"
Emily sighed.
"Name one thought if you can."
She shook her head.
"Go ahead, say it."
"I guess it's hard to have you paint me."
"All I want to do is paint you."
She buttoned her sweater.
Her mind had already retreated to the day the phone rang.
"I need you."
It was her mother.

Emily had arrived at her parents' house early that morning. She found her mother resting on the sofa bed in the living room. Her big brother was giving her painkillers and chasing them with blackberry sherbet to help her get them down. He looked surprised when he saw Emily. He set the bowl on the end table, forced his elbow around hers, and led her out of the room.

Emily yanked back her arm.

Walter pushed her into the kitchen, where their father was stirring brandy into his coffee.

From the bed, her mom yelled in a loud kindergarten-teacher voice, "Goodbye!"

Her brother and father sipped their spiked coffee, divided sections of the newspaper, and ignored her mother's call. "She cries like that all the time." Walter's comment was deliberately loud.

Then they began to argue. "Why do you always get the first page?" They were acting like the cartoon characters she'd illustrated in her sketchbook.

Emily tiptoed back into the living room.

Her mother's forehead was hot. Emily ran out, moistened a washcloth, ran back in, and bathed her mom's face and neck.

Her mom opened her eyes, placed her hand on Emily's cheek, and smiled. Her forehead glistened with sweat. It wasn't fair how beautiful she was.

"You look like Venus," Emily said, close to tears.

"What are you doing in here?" It was Walter. "Don't you get it? She needs to rest." He pushed an armload of bedsheets and towels into Emily's belly, nearly knocking her over. "These need washing. Do something useful for a change."

"I'm not Cinderella."

"No, you're the family's fucking *dreamer*."

Around noon, Emily's mother flailed her arms, then dropped them, letting them land wherever they landed. Then she gasped and picked at her blankets.

Walter promptly entered to administer more pills with the blue-black sherbet and a tall glass of water.

Emily grabbed his wrist. "Don't."

He shoved her away.

She marched into the kitchen and begged her father to call Dr. Moore. He shook his head. She lifted the phone and dialed. Her father grabbed the receiver, but not before she heard Dr. Moore's voice: "George, is that you? How's Betty? Is it time?"

When the doctor arrived, Walter—dramatically, of course—allowed Emily to join them in the living room.

"We must get ahead of her distress and make her as comfortable as possible," Dr. Moore said while injecting morphine into her vein.

Her mother relaxed for a moment, then looked terrified. She cried out, "I take it back! I don't want to go!"

The doctor sighed and gave her another injection.

"No!" Emily screamed. She fought her brother's hold.

Her mom threw her arms toward the ceiling, her face a question. The doctor grabbed her wrist and checked her pulse. Each time she gulped for air, he filled the syringe and gave her another shot.

Emily broke free and seized his arm. "You're killing her!"

Walter grabbed her around the waist and hauled her to the other side of the room.

Her mother cried "Help!" again.

Her father pulled up a chair by her mother's side and said, "Don't worry, dear, I'm here. I'm always here for you. Dr. Moore is here too. He's here to help you."

Her mother turned her head and mumbled something to the doctor.

Emily strained to hear. "What did she say?"

"*Some help you are.* That's what she said." Dr. Moore squeezed her mother's hand. "Feisty to the end, aren't you, Betty."

Her mother smiled.

The same creep of sarcasm and disdain grew within Emily as her own lips began to curve. Her mother's mockery ruled.

Dr. Moore rechecked her mother's pulse and looked up. "Not long."

Her mother's jaw slackened, and her chin sagged toward her neck.

The doctor nodded. "She's gone. I'm sorry, Emily. She won't suffer anymore. You have to understand, your mother cried out because the human body is hardwired to survive."

"Fuck you."

Walter sank his fingernails into Emily's shoulders. "Don't be a bitch."

Furious, she jerked away, suppressing the urge to slug him.

The priggish doctor picked up his bag. Walter and her father followed him out the door.

Her mother's tiny shape lay motionless on the bed. Fighting back tears, Emily walked to her side. She touched her cheek, lifted her head, and tucked wisps of hair into her pink hairnet.

"I'm sorry, Mom. I didn't fight hard enough." Emily choked on the words. "They always win, don't they?"

Her mother's mouth dropped open.

Blackberry sherbet coated her teeth. Arsenic black.

The color reminded Emily of the time she'd given her mom a copy of *Madame Bovary*. She'd told her what a great book it was, but her mother thought Flaubert was a pervert. Emily had warned her. They laughed about how her mom had read it anyway.

Emily couldn't get the image of Emma Bovary's poisoned mouth out of her mind. She turned to a cluttered end table laden with pill bottles, washcloths, lotion, tissues, and other personal items. Emily found a toothbrush, squeezed toothpaste onto it, and dipped it into a nearby glass of water. She gently pulled back her mother's lips and tried to clean off the stain. When it didn't work, she grabbed a washcloth and scrubbed her mother's teeth. Carefully. Then not so carefully.

She lifted a clean cloth from the table and rinsed her mother's face. "There," she whispered. While straightening her nightgown, she thought about ancient rituals of caring for loved ones after they died, anointing their skin with scented oil and saying goodbye for the last time. She placed her mom's hands with their tapered fingers and perfect nails on the lacy bodice of her nightgown. Then the song of the blind man outside Emma Bovary's window came to her: *Often the heat of a summer's day / Makes a young girl dream her heart away.*

Her mother had done just that—she'd dreamed of a better life and died of a broken heart.

"Did you ask to die?" Emily whispered.

She felt a chill down her neck.

Walter's breath.

"Nobody's going to see her except the people at the morgue," he said. "Quit being creepy and get out of here."

Emily squeezed her mother's hands, released them, and raced outside.

A choke of expletives constricted her throat. Disgusted with herself for not standing up to those cold-hearted men, she wiped her eyes and raised both fists to the clouds. She searched for a sign, any sign, that her mother was okay.

The sky grew dark. Slowly, the clouds drifted apart.
There she was.
Venus.
Above the Cheshire moon.
Winking.
Emily sank to her knees.

After a long while, she composed herself and walked to the nearest phone booth to dial the local police. Taking a deep breath, she reported what she believed were suspicious circumstances surrounding her mother's death. The voice on the other end of the line sounded familiar. One of her dad's buddies, no doubt. He asked who was calling. As soon as she said her name, the man cleared his throat and hung up.

It was unmistakable now—the corruption in her dad's world. Her mother had tried to warn her, and so had her grandfather. Why hadn't she understood?

The secret river in her great-grandmother's painting? It was an artery connecting her to all the women on the planet who'd slipped into the age-old stream where cruel currents drowned them. *Speak the truth,* her great-grandmother's painting said. *Speak the underwater truth, the surface truth, the truth only mountains and rivers know. Ask the sun, the moon, the stars for it. Ask the rain, the snow, and the droughts. Face the tides and question their power to build as well as erode.*

An elusive presence surged through Emily's body. *Let Nature be your teacher.*

If she couldn't save her mom, she could at least save herself.

But I don't know how to live these things out loud.
"You just did," said Danny, wiping her eyes.

6

"You gotta go back to school, man. Either that or move to Canada." Ben was talking to Danny at the table in his Donner Lake cabin. All the makings for a traditional Thanksgiving meal sat in paper bags on the counter.

Ben lit a doobie and passed it to Emily. She shook her head and offered the joint to Danny, who took a long hit.

"Canada's a cop-out," Danny said after exhaling.

Ben cleared his throat and handed the doobie back to Emily. "Ma says she could—"

"I know what you're thinking, Ben, but I'm not going to allow Ma to work another five jobs to get me into college just to avoid the draft. And if I quit the band, I won't have any money to go to school anyway."

"So, what're you gonna do?"

"Hope I get a high number."

"We could go to Canada together," Emily said, holding the joint above her head like a question.

Danny fiddled with a packet of Zig-Zags before placing his hands on the edge of the table. He pushed back his chair.

Emily returned the joint to Ben, who sucked hard until he burned his fingers, then dropped the ashes into an abalone shell.

Mating Habits of Fireflies

His voice tightened as he tried to hold in the hit. "She's right, you know."

Danny rose, grabbed his jacket, crossed the living room, and nodded to himself before turning the knob. He stood on the threshold for a moment before clicking the door behind him.

Ben exhaled smoke.

Emily, unsure if she should have followed Danny, traced the grain of the table. The *Reno Evening Gazette* yelled from the counter beside her: "Lieutenant Accused of Murdering 109 Civilians." The story was everywhere. Pinkville. A Vietcong stronghold where American GIs massacred a village of civilians, including women and children. The headline made her shudder.

"He does this," Ben said, brushing the ashes of the spent joint from his shirt. "Whenever things get heavy, he walks." He shoved away the seashell. "There was this hill where we grew up. Danny would climb to the top on his birthday. Every year. Always alone. He'd spend the entire day there. No one could convince him to come down. That hill was sacred to him. Every mountain is. The higher, the better."

The light shifted. Emily looked up. Ben's eyes were intense, like a crow's.

He leaned forward. "Danny's stubborn, like his dad. White guys like that split the scene when things get tough." Ben slumped against the chair. His voice seemed distant, as if he were talking through a veil. "Ma and Grandfather? They're the real deal. The coolest family anyone could ask for."

The room contracted around Emily. She fingered a line of amber light on the table.

Ben spoke about a New York town called Red House. "Jóë'hesta'," he called it. "Ma and Grandfather moved us out of there. The truth is, we were forced out. By the army. For a stupid dam. Money. It's all they ever care about." He picked at his fingernail.

Emily nodded, recognizing the gesture. She did the same thing whenever she was nervous or wondering if she should say more.

But Ben kept talking. It seemed he might burst if he didn't

release everything he'd been holding inside until now. His crow's eyes narrowed. "Our people fought hard for the river, the trees, the animals. The government made promises. Then they broke those promises and burned everything down. All that was left were the steps to our old school."

"Your school?" Danny had mentioned that school.

"But they didn't stop with fire. They used water too. Flooded our neighbors' towns. Hydropower, they called it. Broke Ma's heart, so she made sure we never forgot our language, our traditions. Grandfather was smart. He became a biologist so he could learn the vocabulary of scientists to teach them the importance of honoring the land. They didn't listen. They never do." He studied her face. "You didn't know that, did you? Danny's right from the roots of our tree. His. Ma's. Grandfather's. Mine. Onöndowá'ga:' roots."

A wave of embarrassment curled up Emily's spine. Her throat tightened. How could she not have known?

Danny's connection to the land had been evident on their first date when he showed her how to walk without making a sound. Then there was the way he drummed his heartbeat on the side of his guitar between riffs. Life's pulse beneath the surface of the earth. Since the beginning, hadn't she known—

"Emily?" Ben flattened his palm next to hers. "You've got to understand one thing. Danny's different. He lives in worlds only he can understand. His white half separates us. But this we share: We fight for this country because we believe in its possibility. But the government keeps double-crossing us." He leaned back and looked out the window. His voice trailed. "But he won't tell you any of this. He keeps his stories to himself."

Guilt. Emily shuddered under its weight. Throughout history and every possible future, her visions had shown her the same cruelty endlessly overlapping and repeating. Colonization. Genocide. War. Her family was on the wrong side of that equation, and there was no way she could grasp the depth of Ben's words. After all, she was the daughter of a white man with guns in his closets and medals on his uniform.

"We fought in the Civil War, you know. For the Union. And guess what? The government washed its hands of us after we helped them win." Ben turned to face Emily. "That's why some of our ancestors joined the Lakota when they came east and boarded a plane to Europe with this crazy killer of sacred animals. The guy had the gall to name himself Buffalo Bill. But he was good to us. Our great-grandfathers wouldn't have survived if they'd stayed in America."

Emily closed her eyes against the sting of his words.

"I have no idea why we keep fighting for values we hope the government will one day honor. But you'll never convince Danny to do otherwise. He's proud of who he is. I doubt if he'll tell you any of this because—" Ben glared at her for a second, then picked at his fingernail again. "Anyway, I'm not so polite." He looked up. "So, Miss Girlfriend of My Dear Brother, you have to promise me something."

"Okay."

"Don't hurt him."

She opened her mouth to reply, but Ben interrupted her.

"Danny's way too sensitive for your world, Miss Emily. If you decide to stay with him, you gotta look out for him. You can't let him—" He bit his lip, clutched the back of his chair, and turned away.

"Let him what?"

He sucked air through his teeth. By the time he turned back again, his expression had changed. His mouth curved into a slight smile. "That turkey you brought? Time to dress it up pretty and put it in the oven, don't you think?"

He walked to the record player. After lifting the needle from "Salt of the Earth," he replaced *Beggars Banquet* with *Aoxomoxoa*. Rick Griffin, one of Emily's favorite poster artists, had created the cover.

"Check it out," he said, showing Emily. "If you blur your eyes, it reads 'We Ate the Acid' instead of 'Grateful Dead.'"

He placed the needle on a specific groove, just after the first few chords of the first song. Animating the rhythm, he waltzed her into the kitchen. "I said too much. Sorry." He released her when the music's tempo changed. "My brother likes you. What's good for him is okay by me. As long as you know where you belong." He squeezed her shoulder before opening the refrigerator and grabbing a beer. "Let's get this dinner going."

Emily knew where she belonged—in the kitchen, with her mouth shut—but she wouldn't have it.

She unloaded the contents of the grocery bags. "May I ask something stupid?" Of course she'd use that word.

"Be my guest."

"Why do you celebrate Thanksgiving?"

"We do it for you. Everything, we do for you."

While Ben worked the bird, she struggled to process what he said. The more she thought about it, the more she realized he was right. About everything. Even her stupidity. She focused on the Link Wray poster in the living room. Danny loved the opening chords of "Rumble." She took a knife from a drawer and stupidly played a little air guitar with it while Ben wasn't looking. Then she dug the eyes out of the potatoes, chopped celery, scraped carrots, and washed lettuce. "Stupid," she muttered to herself.

As soon as she heard the haunting sounds of "Mountains of the Moon" playing on Ben's turntable, her anxiety returned. "You think he's okay out there?"

"Danny? For sure. He has some shit to sort out."

"Just the lottery—or something else?"

"*Just* the lottery. Jesus. You didn't hear anything I said, did you?"

Emily's head throbbed. She fought back tears. Generations of secret rivers bubbled up from the canvas of her past. A weathering of shame. Was she too shallow to comprehend?

Ben stuffed the last bit of dressing into the turkey's cavity and opened the oven. After shoving the roasting pan onto the rack, he shut the door, wiped his hands on his jeans, and leaned against the counter.

"One more thing you've got to understand. Danny's scared. When you're scared, you have to open your guts and face yourself. That's what he's doing right now. But he'll be back by the time we have this food on the table. I guarantee it. He loves turkey. As soon as the aroma gets to him, he'll be sprinting for home." A grin took over Ben's face. "Too bad you're not into meat."

Emily swallowed his comment. She cleared the table and billowed Ben's bedspread onto it. He handed her a stack of blue tin plates speckled with white. She placed an odd assortment of forks and spoons on paper towels beside each. He poured beer for Danny and himself. She stopped him when he got to her glass. He clicked his tongue and shrugged as she took the glass to the sink and filled it with water.

"Cosmic Charlie" played as the bird cooked. Ben closed his eyes and mouthed the lyrics. Emily stirred potato slices into boiling water and tore a head of lettuce for salad. At the end of the song, Ben took Emily's shoulders and turned her to face him. "You're better than you think you are, kid. Whatever you do, stay good. Remember that, okay?"

The earth must have revolved around the sun a million times before the meal was ready. Sure enough, the moment he transferred the turkey to the platter, the sound of heavy boot steps on the porch signaled Danny's return.

A crisp breeze followed him as he entered. He closed the front door, strode across the room, scooped Emily up, twirled her, and kissed her until she felt dizzy. He set her down and nodded at Ben. "Smells good."

Emily brought the rest of the food. They settled in. Ben grabbed Danny's hand. Danny took Emily's. Emily completed the circle with Ben. No one said a word until Ben released them and unfolded his paper towel in his lap.

"I thought about that comic book you made for your school

assignment, Emmie. The one for Dr. Finn." Danny handed her the bowl of mashed potatoes. "How even if you only had a short time to live, you wouldn't change anything about your life. Even your past. Especially your present. Because everything you've experienced shapes your future. Remember?"

"All I drew was an angel trapped inside an egg." She plopped a wad of white onto her plate and passed the metal bowl.

"One of the many scenes you illustrated."

"And the last."

"Which says everything. Your angel, teetering on the edge of her shell, getting ready to fly. I love that image." Danny briefly took her hand before turning to his brother. "Just like you, Ben. Big Brother might easily knock on your door, court-martial you, or send you to prison. But here you are, living in paradise. You didn't go to Canada. You did what you believed was right. It's what you always do. I honor that, brother."

"You gotta be kidding," said Ben. "You're just going to wait and see?"

Danny smiled.

Ben set down his fork and squinted into Danny's eyes. "None of this makes sense. I get it, though. It's easier to be passive. But goddamn it, dude. You gotta wear a pair of gloves before you go picking roses. If you don't put 'em on, you'll bleed."

"Roses? Really, Mr. Poetry Man."

"I just hope you're not the idiot I think you are," said Ben.

"Life's a gamble, man. You, of all people, know that."

Ben rolled a line of peas across his plate with his middle finger. Emily took a long sip of water.

"My advice is this," said Ben. "Run. Get out of here. Better to find out you're free and clear in Vancouver than up shit creek in Nam."

Emily nodded. "Why don't we all move to Vancouver?"

"Because I like it here," said Ben, deflating her burst of enthusiasm.

Danny shook his head. "No, Ben. It's because you're a lazy son of a mule."

"Lazy? Mules are hardly lazy, bro. I gamble with my life, yes. But lazy? No way."

"So? I'm a gambler too. Why do you object to that?"

"Shit, Dan. Because I don't want them to do to you what they did to me."

The two brothers glared at each other.

Emily picked at her fingernail.

They finished the meal in silence.

Emily finally set down her fork and scooted back in her chair. "Anyone want pie?"

No response. Not even a nod.

"How about if I clear the table and make coffee, then?" she said. "Maybe open a can of beer for myself for a change. It's apple pie, by the way."

Ben shifted his weight. "I'll be okay. Promise you will too? Dan?"

"Yeah, man, I promise."

"Okay, then." Ben patted his heart and placed his open palm against his brother's chest. *"Nya:wëh."*

Danny managed a smile. "You're welcome."

7

December 1. The dreaded day. Danny, Ben, and TJ went to Wave's drummer's place to watch the draft lottery on the news.

Long after midnight, Danny appeared in Emily's doorway. Patched jeans, sandaled feet, tangled hair almost to his waist. The only thing missing was his guitar.

He shook a torn piece of paper at her. She downed the last drop from a can of Tab, stepped over scattered homework pages, sidestepped the portable record player sitting on a crate beside the door, and took the note from his fist.

It was the slightest move, really, but sudden. The side of his hand sliced needle across vinyl. Robert Plant's voice zipped off Led Zeppelin's second album. "Whole Lotta Love" ended just before the last verse.

Shaking, Emily unfolded the paper, the reason for Danny's blue mood—as blue as the Mayall-Butterfield LP next to the record player she used to take to the beach in high school—as blue as Danny's eyes. Hollow blue.

Scrawled in his backhand was a number. A number that would take him away. A number that would wring him out until he was surreal. Voided. Done. A number.

8

Danny peered inside the fuselage of the Japanese Zero littering the postage-stamp lawn. Emily steered him away from the fighter jet's dented wings, twisted propeller, and faded red bull's-eye behind the cockpit.

The warplane belonged to her new professor, William Steele. He and Freya, his wife, had painted every shingle, every window frame, and every sideboard of their San Francisco Victorian in rainbow colors—the epitome of funk and fashion in the Haight. A local artist had sculpted a life-size papier-mâché Nile crocodile that scaled the second story. Everyone in the bohemian world called this a place a work of Art with a capital *A*. Emily's friends called it the Carnival House.

Inside, Country Joe's music blasted from the stereo system. Steele slouched in a psychedelic chair, pushed his black-rimmed glasses up the bridge of his nose, and fingered his guitar to the cadence of "Flying High." His moodiness settled like smog.

Emily had seen this new professor hanging around the Scholastics building at San Jose State, but she'd never met him formally. Now she understood why: there was nothing formal about him.

She spotted Clare in the kitchen with Matt and Ryan.

Crossing the room to join them, she stumbled over an orange-purple-green papier-mâché cat slurping painted milk from the floor.

"Hey, girl, watch out! This whole place is a trip," Clare said, giving Emily a welcome hug. "No wonder the college hired this guy. He and Freya are trendsetters."

Ryan lifted a square of ceramic bread from a Dada-inspired toaster. He rotated the polka-dotted slab, replaced it, and cleaned his glasses to make sure he was seeing correctly.

Matt exploded with laughter.

It was hard to miss lion-maned Larry. He seemed to be escorting Holly and Spider around the house. When he noticed an old tennis shoe, now a glittering beast, hanging from its laces in the hallway, he said, "Damn, what a scream!" and swung it against the wall. More strange beasts teased Holly from their paisley corners. Larry caught her in a fit of giggles. They both disappeared through a curtain of beads.

In the living room, Danny prodded a latex rock mounted on tiny wheels. It jerked across a moon-shaped table and bumped into a bowl of food-colored slime. Ceramic frogs popped from the bowl and made burping sounds before disappearing into the ooze. Several onlookers squealed.

Larry burst through the beads again. "This is a fucking amusement park."

Holly laughed behind him.

Spider brushed her hair away from her face. "Wait till you see the bathroom. Eyes painted everywhere."

The last thing Emily wanted to see was a bathroom filled with eyes. She fell into the arms of an overstuffed chair, its tie-dyed lace catching her skin. All the details of the room dissolved into a patchouli haze.

She startled from her daze when the back door slammed.

Freya Steele strolled in, stroking her mink stole. Red lipstick, red earrings, red necklace, red dress, red fingernails. Her red hair flamed around her neck and down her arms, accentuating her green eyes and porcelain face.

Danny approached her in the kitchen. "Do this all yourself?"

Freya smiled, removing her mink and tossing it on the counter. "Like it?"

"Everywhere you look—genius."

"This place wastes my senses," said Larry. "She calls these things Faunas, you know?"

"Hey, this is cool," Danny said, admiring one of her primitive paintings on the hallway wall.

Emily understood the appeal of this animated chaos. It evoked cartoonish wonder. But something beneath the surface tasted sticky. The kind of energy she didn't want to mess with.

Clare sat on the arm of Emily's chair and nodded toward Steele. "Check out ole Wanna-Beat."

"Kerouac was also a Wanna-Beat, Clare. But this guy seems sad." Emily gestured to the professor's corduroy slacks, which rose as he crossed his legs. He scratched the blue veins on his creamy ankle, plucked a few guitar strings, and paused to take another hit on the joint.

She and Clare exchanged glances.

"Hey, man," said Matt, scooting a mosaic stool before their teacher. He had to shout over a song about kryptonite and LBJ blaring in the background. "So, what's the deal with Italy?"

Steele surveyed the room.

"Want me to round 'em up?" Matt asked.

Steele shrugged.

Matt cupped his hands around his mouth and yelled, "Meeting! Guys! Over here!"

Someone turned down the music.

It took time to gather everyone. A few people lowered their voices and coughed to quiet the others. They dragged Fauna-painted chairs across the carpet. Some sat on the sofa. Danny settled on the floor between Emily's feet and draped one arm over her knee.

There must have been twenty Scholastics students there—maybe thirty—and at least three seminar groups. For the first time, Emily realized how homogenized they were. Middle-class white kids, every last one of them.

Except Danny. Steele slowly eyed him up and down. "You one of us?"

"Yeah, but I'm not a student, if that's what you mean."

"What are you, then?"

"Here with me," Emily said.

Steele continued to scrutinize Danny. "Live around here?"

"You don't know about Wave?" said Ryan. "He's their lead guitarist, man. And Emily's boyfriend."

Matt changed the subject. "What's up with the trip and all? You know, logistics? Like where in Italy is this place?"

Steele eyed Danny one last time before turning to Matt. He announced how he got a fucking address from his ex-girlfriend, who was dating a fucking Italian count whose mother had a fucking villa in Umbria. "And we'll study art and literature with a little *fucking* anarchy thrown in for kicks. I've arranged accommodations in the *fucking* castle, no less."

He struck Emily as immensely entitled and crude. Like her father, whose dicta were winning at all costs, taking advantage without penalty, bulldogging your way. What better place to practice that ethos than in a castle with a bunch of captive students?

She wanted no part of this scene. Besides, Danny was going to the Oakland Induction Center soon. Then basic training. She'd considered what Ben had told her and begged Danny nonstop to change his mind. Arguments followed. Some had grown heated, especially when she repeated the usual: Become a conscientious objector. Play the insanity card. Do everything to flunk the physical. What about Canada?

Danny rose from the floor. Rubbing his leg, he limped to a row of paisley-painted shelves next to the art hanging in the hallway. He ran his fingers along a series of Dada books and asked Freya to show him more of her work.

"So, where is this place?" Matt repeated his question.

"Umbria," said Steele.

"How're we going to find it?"

Steele stroked his beard and followed Freya and Danny with his gaze. "It's somewhere between Florence and Rome." His voice trailed when his wife and Danny disappeared into another room.

"I think Matt wants the address," said Larry.

"Sure."

Matt took a small notebook and pen from his shirt pocket. Steele returned his focus to Matt. "You'll get specifics later."

"What about now? We're leaving next month."

"Date's been bumped." Steele adjusted his glasses. "To the sixteenth. Logistics, you know."

"Of *December*?" asked Matt.

Larry frowned. "What logistics?"

"You're messing with us," said Matt.

Steele grinned. "December sixteenth. San Francisco Airport."

"Fucking A," said Larry. "That's before Christmas. We've already got flights. My parents have already paid for my flight."

"What luck." Steele lit a blown-glass bong and handed it to Freya, who had wandered in, explaining to Danny how she cut oxtails for oxtail soup. Freya took a hit and passed the bong to Matt and Ryan.

Danny settled into the beanbag chair Larry had vacated on his way out the door.

"Where's Larry going?" asked Holly in her wispy voice.

"Outside to scream or something." Emily sucked in a gurgling trail of fog and gave the bong to Danny.

After a long silence, Steele slapped his hand on the arm of the chair, rose, and followed Freya as she, too, made her way out the front door.

"That's it?" Ryan rubbed his ear. "This was supposed to be a meeting, and they're leaving? This is their house!"

"Okay, then," said Matt. He snatched his jacket from the back of a chair and walked out.

Spider unfolded her legs and stretched them in a long V across the rug. "Well, cool. I guess that means the house is ours. Where's that bong?"

"Here," Ryan said, handing it to her. He walked to the turntable, placed the needle on Country Joe and the Fish's "Section 43," and turned up the volume.

Spider inhaled, squinted at the fused glass, and crinkled her nose. "What's in this stuff?"

Spider's words bounced against Emily's skull. She was losing track of the bizarre Steeles, her departing friends, and the chill in the room. She drifted into the song while staring at the hundred eyes of Argus stitched into the fabric of Freya's cloud chair.

One hundred eyes.

Her father invaded her thoughts. Drunk out of his mind, spying on her from his attic lair. And here she was, stoned out of hers, trying to erase his vileness from her head. She thought of the peacock tattoo on Danny's shoulder. "For vision," he'd said when he first took off his shirt for her. Above it were two words: "For Ma."

She wanted to brand her own mother's name in her flesh.

Throughout his second tattooing, she'd watched the needle thread together two throbbing words crossing his heart: "For Emily." They joked about his body becoming a visual poem, a tapestry of images and letters fused into his skin.

He'd cut the third tattoo himself on the night of the lottery. Snatching his draft number from Emily's hands, he'd crumpled the paper and tossed it into the trash. He crawled to the bed, set his notebook on his crossed legs, and refused to let her touch him. She sat on the floor, her back against the wall, and pressed her ballpoint so hard it curled the paper in her worn sketchbook. Page after page of fantasy spiraled around renderings of women playing with ravens and adders. She drew toad-like frogs shooting wart guns at heart-shaped targets.

Danny filled his journal with illustrated plants and notes about the mating habits of fireflies.

The male firefly flashes his light for a split second, at intervals, waiting for the female's reply.

He'd scribbled those words on a torn-out page, folded it, placed it into an envelope, and left it on her bed. She'd been sketching his face in her journal at the gallery that day. The envelope was waiting for her when she got home, but Danny was gone.

It had been raining outside. She was half-asleep when he walked through the door just before dawn. She heard him set down his guitar and take off his boots. He encircled her body with his and kissed her ear.

"Emmie," he sighed.

She startled awake.

Danny was no longer there. She must have been dreaming.

She stumbled into the bathroom and found him curled on the floor.

"Who in hell gets number *one* as a draft number? Who in hell?" He was sobbing and pounding his fist on the linoleum.

Blood everywhere. Broken glass. His birthdate slashed into his thigh.

She'd gasped, grabbed a towel, tightened it hard around his wound, and rocked him.

Jolting back to the present, Emily awoke to Danny humming in her ear. Her lips crusty, her eyes swollen. He lifted her from Freya's bulky chair—the chair Emily had thought was a multieyed cloud monster, but now it was only a blur of shadows, like the burping frog on the table, the slurping cat in the kitchen, and the torture in her heart.

"Let's get out of here," he said, favoring his right leg as he carried her out the door of the Carnival House. Past the crocodile clinging to second-story shutters. Past the wreckage on the lawn.

9

Outside the window, Emily's landlord wobbled on his ladder, stringing Christmas lights beneath the eaves of the old Victorian. She cringed. It felt too soon. Too soon for decorations. Too soon for Vietnam. Everything was too soon.

Yesterday, Clare had said Italy was a go for her.

Matt's new girlfriend, a dancer named Vicky from one of the other experimental programs at school, told him that living with a countess in Renaissance country was a fairy tale worth stepping into. But Matt wasn't into fairy tales. He wanted to be with Vicky the same way Emily wanted to be with Danny.

"Vicky's looking out for you," Clare told him. "She wants you to go for your own good."

"What good?"

"So you'll write about it—Steele's brand of anarchy. It could be your thesis."

"Anarchy? My thesis?"

"Why not? Isn't political science your major?"

"I hope not."

Ryan couldn't wait to go. Spider was always game for new things, so she was in. If they were on board, Emily wondered if she should give it a shot. Then the thought itself disgusted her. So what if everyone else's parents had paid for everything at the beginning of the semester? Talk about privilege. There were more pressing things to worry about. War, for instance.

Danny didn't want to discuss any of this. Instead, he wanted to sit in on the free concert their friends at Dirt Cheap Productions had talked about in May.

"It'll be good for us," he said, mopping the last puddle of spaghetti sauce from his plate with a hunk of garlic bread. He set his dish on the cluttered counter in the communal kitchen at Emily's place.

"It'll be good for us," Emily repeated under her breath. She frowned while filling the sink with suds. "I don't know. There's something hit-and-miss about the way all this went down."

It would have been one thing if Dirt Cheap could have pulled off the event on campus as planned, but Ryan and Matt washed their hands of it as soon as the city politicians said no. The Airplane thought it would be cool to have a West Coast Woodstock take place in San Francisco. Then the Dead apparently took over. And the Stones? Ryan said the band wanted to make a movie of the show to improve their image.

Dirt Cheap thought the Stones would give a surprise performance. So did the new promoters, or so Ryan thought. He'd heard the Stones got restless around Thanksgiving, and they told the press they were headlining the concert—for free—to make up for the exorbitant prices they'd been charging for their regular concerts. This meant the new promoters had ten days to organize a different venue. Golden Gate Park bailed because of "scheduling." Then Sears Point came on board. Everything was a go. The new promoters built the stage on a hill at Sonoma Raceway, but lawyers freaked over the possibility of an unruly crowd. Panic. They had to find a fourth location. Maybe they twisted arms. Maybe they didn't. Just two days before the gig, the promoters chose a barren speedway in the middle of nowhere. December sixth. Emily remembered circling the date in her sketchbook next to a stick-figure Jagger dancing with an oversize mic.

"Holly says the moon's in Scorpio." Emily dried forks and spoons and slipped them into a drawer. "Not a good sign."

Danny shook his head while scrubbing the pots.

Emily eyeballed him. The night he cut himself, they'd both evaded an earful of questions while the doctor at the free clinic stitched his thigh. Going to a big rock concert while he was still healing was the last thing they should do.

"Can't we just curl into bed and read?"

"Emmie, you don't understand. I've been looking forward to this for a long time. It's a last chance to have a bit of fun. Come on, one final show before we both head to paradise?" Danny tickled her ribs, sudsy hands and all, and kissed her until she felt faint.

"You're not going to paradise," she said. "And neither am I."

"So you've decided. If you're not going to Italy, then, all the more reason to go to the concert. I mean, it's 'Satisfaction,' you know?" He twirled her around the kitchen.

Emily sighed. No use fighting this.

As soon as they put away the last dish, their quiet evening at home morphed into a scramble. Emily ran upstairs and gathered pillows, flashlights, toothbrushes, and a change of clothes. Danny was already bringing Beulah to the curb. They dropped their sleeping bags behind the driver's seat and piled potato chips and a couple of sodas on top of their gear. Before long, they were on the highway, heading toward the mountains of Livermore.

On the horizon, the slightest lunar sliver penetrated the sky. A waning crescent. Emily squinted her eyes, barely making out the craters and shadows along its razor edge.

The moon gentles strong feelings. Her grampa's words stung with Scorpio's energy. Even the stars seemed out of place tonight, blinking in and out of the clouds, struggling to claim what little light they could. "White Bird" played on the radio. Emily imagined the clouds turning into doves opening a gateway to the stars. It's a Beautiful Day, one of her favorite bands, offered some hope.

In a little more than an hour, they followed a line of cars to the Altamont Raceway. Every so often, someone would honk or lean out a window to wave. It took forever for Danny to find a place to park.

It was crazy cold. They pulled their jackets tight as they hiked up a small hill. Emily stopped to pluck sticker burrs from her socks before they claimed a spot for the night. They set up camp, zipped together their sleeping bags, and hugged each other for warmth. In her dreams, Emily watched spotlights and massive speakers materialize from white-bird clouds. Then the scene disintegrated into darkness.

It seemed a lifetime before Danny nudged her awake. "Emmie, you gotta see this."

He unzipped her from the bag and helped her stand. An ocean of people engulfed the small stage below them. They surged in unison, impatient for the concert to begin. Freaks, a vibrant array of them, climbed a flimsy scaffolding surrounded by a maze of equipment and haphazardly parked vehicles.

"I can't believe it's so low," said Emily.

"What?"

"The stage. Look, people are climbing all over it."

"Must be the one they built at Sears Point. It doesn't work so well in that sinkhole down there."

A loud roar turned their attention to a line of Hells Angels entering the scene. Not the friendly guys who'd safeguarded the stage at Dirt Cheap's free festival. Cameramen filmed them dismounting their hogs and motioning for the crowd to stay back. Several settled on the edge of the stage and popped open beer cans.

Speakers screeched. Roadies scrambled to check wires. They were still tapping microphones when Carlos Santana wove his way to the stage. Black-and-white static drowned out the band as soon as they started to play.

Danny steadied Emily beside him.

A random guy approached the stage. Leather-chested giants stormed after him. Roadies followed. Yelling. Pushing. Muddled voices echoed over the PA. Feedback squealed. Emily clenched her teeth against the coppery taste in her mouth. Discordant pigments of chaos splattered inside her skull.

It's all wrong.

She glanced at the sky, then at her feet.

Connect earth to sky. Sky to earth.

When the Airplane finished setting up, the crowd roared. Gracie stepped forward. Then everything unraveled. Someone started cursing. It looked like Balin dropped his mic and jumped into the audience. An amplified voice penetrated the feedback loop: "Oh God! Someone fucking punched Marty!"

In a flash, one of the other band members came to the rescue. It sounded like he was arguing onstage with one of the bikers.

Danny curled his arms around Emily and pulled her close. "Stay with me," he whispered, as if she'd consider wandering off. They rode the wave until things settled down.

When the Flying Burrito Brothers began to play, the crowd miraculously returned to normal. Emily could hear actual songs instead of static and shouting. Their upbeat music inspired a couple to dance next to her.

The interlude didn't last long. At the end of the set, another scuffle. Danny pressed his lips to her ear. "This whole scene is cursed."

The crazy drugged-up throng pushed and pulled. Garcia and the Dead were nowhere to be found. Bodies squeezed in on Emily and Danny. They had no choice but to ebb and flow with them.

Crosby, Stills, Nash & Young approached the stage. Mayhem overwhelmed them.

Danny looked for an out, but there was no place to go.

Night collapsed around them. People up the hill burned garbage for warmth. Everything smelled like vomit.

The Scorpio moon vanished behind a cluster of clouds. Jagger strutted into view, twirling a Halloween cape around his body. He flashed black and red into the crowded spotlight and ordered the bikers to make room for him.

Emily clenched a strangely dismembered howl in her gut.

As if in response, the Stones stopped playing. Jagger said something, but a frenzy devoured his voice. The band continued again. Speakers screamed above the belligerent fans.

"This way!" Danny yelled, pushing her through a narrow opening to the left.

They wove through a labyrinth of arms, torsos, and gaping mouths. When they finally reached the road, they slowed to a walk and caught their breath.

"What happened?" a guy alongside them asked.

"Looks like someone got hit by a car," his girlfriend said, pointing to the blood-splattered van roaring by. Or was it mud-splattered?

It took forever to find Beulah. Danny and Emily climbed in. Then they noticed they'd forgotten their sleeping bags.

Danny rubbed his sore leg. "At least we still have our packs."

The road glowed red from a stalled line of taillights. Long-haired freaks spilled from their vans and passed whiskey bottles through the open windows of neighboring cars. They danced, whooped, and beat their chests, stirring up followers. Soon the pavement disappeared beneath the feet of all the hippies twitching toward madness.

"I should have listened to you. You know when things aren't right." Danny squeezed Emily's knee.

She was too spent to reply.

"Guess we'll find out what happened when it hits the papers in the morning."

Emily took a breath. "If it hits the papers."

"You know it will, Emmie. They'll do anything to bad-mouth free concerts. They'll shut us down for good. Just wait."

She gestured to the rowdies. "Drunks like those should be shut down, not the concerts."

Danny stuck his head out the window and coughed from the exhaust. "Booze. That's the problem. If everyone smoked pot, they'd have the grins so hard they couldn't possibly fight." He rolled up the glass. "Maybe calling it quits would be a good thing. All these cars, all this smog, all these hammered people. The scene isn't what it used to be." He turned Beulah's wheel right and left. "Everyone should ride a bicycle. Get high that way."

Emily pictured the highway crowded with stoned cyclists, Danny among them, straddling a ten-speed, guitar strapped across his back, singing to the gentling moon while pedaling home from a gig in the wee hours of the morning. The image made her smile.

Then again, everything she believed, everything she felt was just and kind and civil in the world, was turning in on itself. This was the dark side of America. Born in hubris. Buried in slaughter. Slavery. Deception. Cruelty. War. An interplay between order and chaos, beauty and insanity. In such a world, how could any vulnerable person survive?

Earth to sky. Sky to earth.

10

"You two are coming with us," Clare said after she burst into Emily's room with Matt and Ryan. She threw clothes on the bed and ordered them to dress as fast as they could.

Danny pulled the blankets over his head.

"No sleeping allowed. Up! Up!" Clare shook the mattress.

Before they knew it, Emily and Danny were sitting in the back seat of Clare's red Mustang. Ryan sat with them, looking dapper in his English newsboy cap. From the passenger seat, Matt helped Clare navigate the switchbacks.

Stars winked through the windshield.

Clare parked her car halfway up a winding road above the city. She and Matt opened the back doors and gestured to the view.

They all huddled against the breeze, looking down on San Jose. One by one, lights flickered on the east side, the west side, the north, and the south. Darkness slowly morphed into a glow of awakening. Emily imagined mothers making coffee, fathers shaving, and kids padding around in footed pajamas. Five friends watching suburban America from the top of the world while the sun crested the horizon.

Normalcy. Emily had no idea how that felt. She couldn't find it in her past. Nor in her present. It probably wouldn't be a theme in her future. She wrinkled her nose against the depressing taste in her mouth and pulled out a tissue to catch her sneeze.

"Whatever happens," Clare said after a long silence, "whatever we face today or tomorrow or the next day, let's remember this sunrise."

They all agreed, making communal pacts to take care of each other in every way possible from now on. They linked pinkie fingers to honor their commitment.

Below them, Monday morning launched another smoggy workweek. Woody station wagons, trucks, buses. Honking, roaring, exhaust. Clare threw her arms above her head and howled. Matt glanced at Ryan. Ryan threw his cap in the air, caught it, folded it inside his jacket, and grinned. He, Danny, and Emily opened their throats to their own untamable noise.

Soon they were laughing and running so fast they couldn't feel the ground beneath their feet. At the top of the next hill, they stood like fools, gasping and breathing hard. It took about an hour to get to the creek. Everyone collapsed on the bank and watched Danny fashion a sailboat with a large piece of bark, a stick, and two leaves. He launched it into the stream, and it floated away.

Minutes passed. Then more. Ryan unfolded his cap from his oversize pocket, adjusted it on his head, and broke the silence. "About this Italy trip—"

"I can't wait," said Clare. "It's going to be a scene, that's for sure."

"Yeah," said Ryan. "But I can't shake the idea that it's going to be a little weird."

Clare sat up and tied her unruly hair into two braids. "Of course it's going to be a little weird, Ry. That's the whole point!"

"Steele's clearly a jerk," Matt said, eyes closed, arms crossed behind his head. "But he's a great musician. Did you know he used to be a classical pianist or something? Maybe he'll surprise us. If not, Larry's big enough to scoop him up and eat him alive if we need a good bouncer."

Emily shifted to her side and supported her head with her hand. "I don't trust Steele."

"So?" said Clare. "You don't trust anyone."

"You have to come with us, Em," said Ryan. "We need you. Besides, it's part of the curriculum."

"I'd rather go to Canada." Emily avoided Danny's *not Canada again* look. "Why don't we all go to Canada?"

"I tell you what," Clare said. "We can do this together. I mean, living in a castle with a countess in Italy? C'mon!"

"Maybe we can sneak Danny into our suitcases." Ryan turned to Danny. "What about it, dude?"

"I can't. You know that."

Ryan shook his head. "My old man was a career officer, like Emily's. War messes you up, man. You come back all redneck and uptight. My dad got so paranoid he built a bomb shelter in our backyard."

Danny laughed. "No chance of that."

"What about objecting?" said Clare.

"Just makes you a medic," said Ryan. "In a war zone without a way to defend yourself, it's not worth it."

Danny squinted and turned away, the same way he blocked Emily when she tried similar worn-out arguments.

"They'll make you cut your hair," said Matt.

Danny was silent for a moment. "Maybe I wouldn't get the finger so much if I had a flattop."

Emily leaned into him, her heart pounding. He was already slipping away. Beyond her reach. Beyond anyone's reach.

It was well into the afternoon before they returned to the Mustang. Danny limped into the back seat.

"How's this for the last hurrah?" he said as Ryan and Emily settled on either side of him. "Maybe I won't pass the physical after all. Feels like I split these stitches."

Emily touched his thigh.

"Cool," said Ryan. "Great way to get out of it."

"No last hurrahs allowed," Clare said.

"First things, then?" Danny turned to Emily. *I'm fine.*

"I'm game for firsts." Clare turned the ignition and headed down the road toward campus.

"Okay, Danny." Matt turned around to face him. "Question time. Ask anything."

Danny smiled. "Where're we going?"

"Wherever you want, handsome. My treat." Clare winked into the rearview mirror.

"How about to Italy with all of you?"

Ryan and Clare hooted. Matt and Emily stomped their feet and cheered. Matt reached back and high-fived everyone before clapping Clare's hand.

"Thanks, guys," Danny said.

"Any chance? There's time. Larry convinced Steele to put off our departure until January," Ryan said.

"He did?" Emily perked up.

"Didn't you get the letter?"

"Maybe I tuned it out."

"Or your dad got ahold of it," said Clare.

Danny turned to Ryan. "Sorry to tease you like that. It takes money, my friend. Airline tickets. Food. Not to mention bribing customs to let me through. I don't want Big Brother after me."

"AWOL's different. There are a lot of other ways to scam the system."

"Ryan, you're as much of a dreamer as Emmie. You know that, don't you?"

"How 'bout the coast guard? Navy? Shit, even the air force is better than the army." Ryan frowned. "You have a death wish, you know? Wish my dad was still around. He could've pulled strings, let you off the hook."

Clare flashed a look at Emily in the mirror.

Sure, Emily's dad had connections too. Would he help Danny get out of serving like he had for her brother? No way.

"Fortunate Son" played in her head as she pressed her nose against the window and fogged it with her breath. The landscape didn't speak. It continued in an endless blur as if none of this mattered at all.

11

The thought of going home for the holidays didn't appeal to Emily, but Danny convinced her it was the right thing to do. He wanted to say goodbye to his ma and grandfather before boot camp. His grandfather might be able to heal his leg. Emily joked that he should let it fester so the army would refuse to take him, but he didn't think that was funny.

Danny took American Airlines to New York. Emily took the bus to Saratoga. She hitched a ride home from the station.

Her dad and brother were oddly civil to her. Soon the reason became clear. Since childhood, her usual Christmas gifts had been pajamas, slippers, soap, and socks. This year was different. One large package contained everything she needed to know: a Super 8 movie camera, the latest Kodak Instamatic, a generous check, vaccination appointment dates, airplane tickets from San Francisco to New York, a hostel card, a Eurail train pass, and a Christmas card stating that her father had chartered a private flight to take her and her friends from New York to Iceland to Luxembourg. The final destination, of course, was Italy.

She glared at him. "What's this about?"

"It's to get rid of you, stupid," said Walter.

Her father was silent.

Emily refused to join them on the couch to watch Christmas specials. Instead, she retreated to her old room and blasted her journal with curses that morphed into sketches of an owl preening in the tree outside her window. As she detailed the bird's feathers, the idea of going to Italy grew on her.

The following morning, she sneaked into her mother's bedroom, slipped her grandfather's dream box into a laundry bag, shoved cameras, tickets, and passes into a framed pack, and crept out of the house while her father and brother were asleep on the couch downstairs and the TV crackled with static.

She hitched a ride to San Jose.

The following week, she and TJ took Beulah to the San Francisco airport and waited for Danny's flight.

He looked taller as he descended the steps and walked in a firm line across the tarmac. "Hey, man." Danny set down his bags and cuffed TJ's shoulder. "Haven't seen you since last year."

TJ held Danny at arm's length. "You haven't changed a bit, joker."

Danny turned to Emily. "Hello, beautiful." He lifted her and held her for a heavenly moment.

Beulah purred to the apartment while "White Room" played on the radio. When they arrived, Danny opened the little Volkswagon's trunk. He and TJ carried everything into the living area, where Danny unearthed two small bundles from his pack. Both were wrapped in soft leather tied with kite string. TJ came up with two gifts of his own. Emily dug into her bag for hers. They sat on the floor, presents waiting on the rug.

"Heard about the storm," said TJ.

"Yeah. Great way to travel." Danny winked at Emily as if to say *It's okay. We'll have our time alone soon.*

TJ took a package he'd wrapped in brown paper decorated with drawings of snowflakes. "In honor of winter," he said as he handed it to Danny. "And late Christmases."

"Thanks, man." Danny nodded. "In honor of friends," he said as he gave TJ the smaller of his bundles.

TJ opened an envelope of guitar strings for his new 1968 Fender Precision Bass. Danny opened a package of strings for his 1963 Gibson Firebird III.

They thought alike. TJ grinned. Danny frowned.

"It's okay, Dan. We have gigs lined up to keep you playing forever."

"That's not long."

"Shithead. There'll be more when you come back."

Danny pocketed the strings. "I'm keeping these with me. You know, luck and all."

"You're just like your Firebird there. Legendary. As long as you've got music, you're cool."

"Thanks, man."

Emily pictured Danny in the jungle, securing guitar strings across his knees and plucking them the same way she and Clare used to strum their shoelaces. The thought made her smile.

She looked at the remaining presents on the rug. "Here," she said, offering TJ a felt pouch she'd made.

When TJ reached for his gift for her, she interrupted him.

"Open yours first."

He grinned, searched within the pouch, and retrieved a small prism hanging from a silver chain. It caught the lamplight as he spun it.

"Rainbows for rainy days," Emily said.

TJ was quiet. He walked to the window, hooked the prism to the latch, spun it, and sat back on the rug. "Gonna need a lot of rainbows when you two are gone."

Danny shot a puzzled look at Emily. "You're going to Italy?"

"Maybe."

She'd intended to tell him but hadn't known how to reach him in New York. Think-talking with him hadn't worked either. She sampled the colors rotating around the room. Berry-flavored reds and sharp sunlight. Plus rainwater. Mixed with mud.

TJ hesitated before handing her his gift.

Emily tore the tape from the snowflake package. Within the

folds of paper, she found a painted bead knotted in the center of a leather cord.

"You made this?"

"Yeah."

She turned it in her palm and admired the simple pen-and-ink designs. "Wow. I can't believe you did this. It's beautiful." After tying it around her neck, she knelt over to give TJ a quick kiss.

He shifted his weight away from her.

Danny gathered up the remaining packages. "I'd rather give Emmie her present when I get to her place. Kinda tired. After the flight and all, you know."

TJ winked. "See you in the morning, then?"

"Afternoon. No, wait. Monday. You didn't book any gigs, did you?"

"Why would I do that?" TJ's smile faded. "See you Monday, then. Don't forget that drive we're taking on Tuesday."

"Yeah. To the bus station."

"You can still back out, you know."

"Out the driveway, onto the road. It'll be cool, TJ."

"Fuck, yeah. If you say so. I still don't get why you forced your way into Fort Ord. This early, man. How'd you do it? Most people have at least a month."

"Get home sooner that way."

Emily cringed. Danny hadn't forced his way in. It had been forced on him by Alexander Pirnie, the ranking Republican on the House Armed Services Committee. It was all over the papers the moment he pulled a blue plastic capsule from a gigantic glass bowl and handed it to General Lewis B. Hershey, who unrolled the number inside and, in a proud military voice, announced, "September fourteenth. September fourteen, zero-zero-one." The first letter of Danny's last name, Jackson, was also deemed zero-zero-one for induction.

Doomed from the start.

Danny grabbed his jacket and a small duffel of clothes. He helped Emily slip into her coat and swung her pack onto his shoulder. They were almost out the door when she doubled back and hugged TJ again for a final goodbye.

He squeezed her hard and buried his face in her hair. "It'll be okay, Em. Italy will be good for you. Wish I'd gotten that number instead of Danny. But he'll be okay. Don't worry. I'll take care of that painted box you brought from your dad's place. I'll miss you. You know that."

"I'll miss you too."

Beulah seemed impatient to get going. Danny and Emily waved before getting in. Beulah puttered to the other side of San Jose.

By the time Danny had opened the door to Emily's room and dropped their bags on the floor, they were already entwined, lips joined, rolling onto the bed. She memorized every molecule in his body. After tracing the line of his jaw, she kissed the nape of his neck. She ached for him.

They awoke in the morning to the chirping of a song sparrow outside. "Little Bird," Danny nicknamed Emily.

"Grampa used to call me that."

Danny smiled. He pushed up the window, climbed onto the roof balcony, took her hand, and helped her step over the sill. Wrapping a blanket around themselves, they sat in the chill of dawn and watched the birds chatter in Emily's favorite tree. Clouds overwhelmed the sky. They crawled back into the room as soon as the rain began, rummaged through their bags, and snuggled into the warmth of the covers with their presents.

"I want to see it before we get into those," Emily said.

"See what?"

"Your grandfather's work. On your leg."

"You didn't notice last night?"

"It was dark, remember?"

Danny opened the blankets to his thigh. No sign of oozing or puffiness. No red anywhere. The scar was healthy and clean. What had earlier been a wound was now a stark tattoo.

"How did he do it?"

"Magic. And herbs. He knows them all. He made me rest, of course." Danny replaced the blanket. "Here," he said, handing her his gift.

She stroked the suede rectangle and mouthed a silent "thank you" before pulling the kite string until it released. Inside was a cardboard sleeve. In that, a downy feather.

"From an owl. My grandfather gave me two: one for each of us. For wisdom and vision. They're small, so we can carry them everywhere."

"An owl?"

"I know. A lot of people are superstitious about owls. They think they symbolize bad luck. But these feathers are different. My grandfather gave them to me for our protection." Danny put his arm around her as soon as she drew in her breath.

It's okay, Emmie. We'll be okay, you and I.

"I saw an owl outside my window in Saratoga."

"Yeah. I saw her too. She landed in a tree right above my head." He held her closer. Then he pulled away. "Why didn't you tell me you decided to go to Italy?"

Emily sat up. "I didn't decide. My father decided for me. Like he always does."

"You could have told him no."

"How? He'd make my life miserable. Anyway, where would I go?"

"Back to school?"

"*Regular* school? You're kidding." Scholastics in Letters and Science had spoiled her with its intimate seminar groups.

"I'm glad you're going. It'll do you good."

"Why is everyone telling me that?"

He tucked her hair behind her ears. "You know what Grandfather said about the owl? He saw her, too, in a dream. He said she came to teach us how to see in the dark, to help us navigate obstacles, and to remind us to use vision wisely. That way, we can survive just about anything—as long as we're alert and aware of our surroundings."

Emily rubbed the chill from her arm. "Isn't that a little naive? I mean, especially where you're going?"

"Look at it like this, Emmie: owls can turn their heads almost all the way around, right?"

"Yeah."

"Flexibility keeps them alive. If we stiffen, we're no longer alert. If we're not alert, we're dead, right? You know what I'm saying?"

"I'm not sure."

"Emily. Be straight with me."

"About going to Italy?"

"No. About your visions."

She stared at him.

"You know what I'm talking about."

"They're seizures, not visions."

"Think so?"

"I have medicine for them. Somewhere around here." She glanced around the room, knowing full well she'd thrown away the pills.

Danny took her hand. "Want to know what I think they are?"

"Hallucinations? Signs that I'm crazy?"

"You're what I call One Who Slides on the Wind."

"Sounds about right. Slipping and sliding everywhere. One Who Slides off the Edge is a better definition."

She was pissed. How could her visions define her when she couldn't define herself?

"It's called perception, Emmie. And yours is unique." He pointed to the feather. "The owl started coming to you a long time ago, didn't she?"

Emily nodded. It first happened soon after her grandfather died. A strange light had filled her bedroom. When she looked up, a woman with black hair stood beside the window. Then the woman vanished. Emily dropped her book, stumbled to the kitchen, searched the fridge for something to eat, and plopped on the living room couch. She needed grounding when visions like this took hold, but nothing could settle her for long.

Talk to her, the oak tree in her yard whispered a few mornings later. *Ask for her name.*

Emily turned to her sketchbook the following day. A name flowed effortlessly across the page. *Homa.* The same name her great-grandmother, Lila Rose, used to sign her paintings. Then a woman's voice: *Go to the stream where the flow is greatest. You'll see me there. You'll know what to do.*

A magnificent white oak used to stand halfway down Emily's favorite walking path. It had split when it was a seedling, two trees from the same trunk. She named it the Kissing Tree because it grew back into an embrace. She would sneak out of the house and sit with her spine against its base. When she closed her eyes, she could feel sap running like blood through its core. If she put her nose to the bark, the fragrance was so sweet it gave her vertigo. Music swirled in yellows and greens within the aroma. She could taste the colors the same way she tasted the sunlight filtering through the trees. She drew strength from the old oak. Yet if she stayed too long, she was afraid she might slip through a portal to another world.

One day when her brother was out, her father was on a business trip, and her mother was resting upstairs, Emily followed the path to the stream's bank. She chased leaves in the rushing water and rinsed her hands in the small waterfall spilling over a favorite boulder. She turned over rocks, played with sticks, and tiptoed across mounds of spongy earth. Hours passed. No sign of this Homa. No tingling. No shifting light. No aura or déjà vu. Rotting acorns crunched beneath her boots. As soon as the sun dipped below the horizon and the sky grew gray, Emily became discouraged and headed home.

Then this: an invisible weight had borne down on her, so hard she had to duck to protect her head. The edge of a wing grazed her hair. The Kissing Tree glowed. A great horned owl landed on a low branch and turned her head around to focus on Emily's face.

She stretched her wings and folded them, but never broke her stare.

Emily fell to her knees.

No owl in her right mind would be so close to a human, especially a terrified girl attempting to rise on wobbly legs.

I have to go home. Sorry.

The owl continued to stare.

Emily looked up *Homa* in her school library. The card catalog guided her to the Homa bird, a creature of fortune known for rising above the troubles of the physical world. She lived in the sky and laid an egg in the air. Because it was so high up, it took the egg many days to fall to the earth. As it fell, it hatched, and then the chick fell. As the chick fell, her eyes opened. As soon as she could focus, she realized she was falling. And if she hit the ground, she knew she would die. So she strengthened her wings and learned to fly.

"Like the mythical Firebird," the book said, "the Homa bird cancels negative energies and ensures a long and healthy life."

Emily savored this fable. She found similar ones in her great-grandmother's storybooks. She listened in awe when her grampa read the Sufi myths inside. Legends from around the world graced her grampa's bookshelves, and he shared each one with her.

Visions like this, however, scared her.

From then on, Emily had dreams of owl eggs tumbling from the clouds. Her great-grandmother sang lullabies to lull Emily to the safety of the stream where the owl families gathered to catch the emerging owlets. *Courage,* her songs urged.

It took several weeks before Emily could turn to her sketchbook again. She needed proof of this ghost woman's existence, so she asked the blank page for an object. Something she could hold in her hands. She'd heard somewhere—from her grampa?—that a rock with a natural hole through it would offer protection and good luck.

Show me this rock, she'd written to Homa.

On a day when the sun rose without making Emily sneeze,

she'd followed the path to the bank. She threw sticks in the water. She sat on the boulder near the waterfall and practiced her sighing mantra: *Sigh. Inhale. Sigh.* After a while, she began her hunt. *This rock?* No. *That one? Or this?* No. And no.

She needed to trust the voice in her dreams.

Never trust anyone or anything. Especially a vision.

Emily dragged her feet as she navigated her way home.

Maybe this one?

She doubled back to check the rock she'd just tripped over, half-buried in the hard-packed earth.

Nothing.

The path narrowed a bit. A gnawing within. Emily turned and retraced her steps to the place where she'd tripped. She took a stick and dug the rock from the ground.

Back in the room with Danny, Emily snuggled closer and handed him the velvet pouch she'd made. Navy blue exterior. Red interior. Dream sky. Blood earth.

Danny pulled the cord, lifted the rock, and peered through the hole. He turned the rock around in his palm and thrust his little finger through the opening in the center.

According to her grampa's stories, a rock like this was called an adder stone. In times of danger, it protected the person who carried it. In the Celtic legends he'd shared, it was referred to as a fairy or holey stone, which gave the owner the ability to see into other realms. In Scholastics, Dr. Finn's mythology lessons gave her another name for her rock-with-the-hole-through-it: an Odin stone. It held the wisdom of the ages. Vision. Awareness. Protection. A gift from Odin's ravens. A gift from Emily's owl.

"It's yours now," she said, holding Danny's feather to her heart. "It will bring you back."

12

Beulah wouldn't start. Danny opened her back hood.

"Sorry, ole girl," he whispered under his breath.

After he adjusted what he thought needed to be fixed, Beulah began to sputter. She continued to shiver and spit as she carried Danny and Emily to the airport.

They were late. They'd missed the plane everyone else had taken and were counting on a standby flight.

Emily wanted to hold Danny every second from then on. She wanted to listen to him complain about arthritis and white hair and age spots. She wanted to break him free from glassy-eyed stares. Better to grow senile together than to lose each other to a stupid war.

Danny slung her pack over his shoulder as they approached Gate 2. White plastic letters wedged between the ridges of a black cloth sign spelled "Departures: New York."

He lowered her bag onto a nearby chair. Before he could sit, she grabbed the bronze mushroom on his belt buckle and drew him to her.

"You'll be okay," Danny whispered.

She should have said that to him. As soon as she opened her mouth to voice the words, something else slipped through.

"How do people do this?"

Danny held her back so he could see her face. "What? Fly?"

"No, you know, *leave*."

"Don't worry, Emmie," he said again, pressing her knuckles to his lips. "Everything will be okay."

Sure. Worry was her world.

A uniformed man announced four vacant standby seats. Danny and Emily kissed, hugged, and kissed again.

Long before she was ready, she squirmed into the pack frame, followed a line of suitcase-lugging strangers out of the terminal, climbed the cold metal stairs, turned, waved, turned back, and ducked into the gaping mouth of the bolt-ridden dragon about to eat her alive.

She unwrapped a stick of gum. Across the aisle, a pigtailed girl turned the knobs of a red Etch A Sketch. The guy beside her sighed and stretched his denim-covered legs. She ignored her sinking gut, pressed her nose against the pane, and gazed at the diminishing landscape below.

No support but a mantle of clouds.

Then she heard the Homa bird sing: *You must fall before you can learn how to fly.*

1970

New York / Italy / Greece

One eye sees; the other feels.

— Paul Klee

13

A BLACK ROLLS-ROYCE PULLED UP TO THE CURB AT Kennedy Airport with Emily's stockbroker uncle at the wheel. She and her friends had gathered at the baggage claim and were waiting outside.

Her uncle frowned as he opened the trunk and tossed in a load of metal-framed packs. His current wife stayed in the front seat. She adjusted the tight curls hugging the nape of her neck, revealing the ornate clasp of Emily's mother's diamond bracelet.

Emily bit her lip and looked away. Her father had summoned these wealthy relatives to check on Emily and her friends because, well, of course he had.

Matt, Ryan, and Larry climbed into the back seat, gang-like, wearing dark knit caps and army jackets. Clare, Spider, and Holly settled on the boys' laps. Emily had no place to sit except on the door's armrest. When they pulled up to what her friends called Fat Cat Tower, the concierge bowed low as her uncle led everyone into the lobby. Before saying goodbye, he tipped the bellhop in loose change.

After entering a large suite, Emily wandered to her allocated room. Featherbed. Flocked wallpaper. Gilded picture frames. She dumped the contents of her pack—toothbrush, T-shirts, jeans, a dress, a harmonica, a new sketchbook—and surveyed her belongings as they spilled across the bed.

The following morning, she found Clare in the suite's sitting room, sifting through pages from the New York *Daily News*. Used coffee cups and leftover muffin wrappers cluttered the table.

"Check this out," Clare said without looking up from the comics section. "Lucy and Linus. They're choking on snowflakes. Ever done that? Stick out your tongue and catch snowflakes?"

"No."

"Me neither. And look at this. The Museum of Modern Art is having a light show."

"Nice."

Emily scanned the room. Two sets of double doors lined what looked like a baroque parlor. One set was closed, and the other revealed an additional bedroom with clothes and toiletries piled on an ornate chair.

"Where is everyone?"

Clare crumpled the paper into her lap. "They had a sudden urge to explore the hotel."

"Sounds like a load of fun."

"That's why I'm here."

Emily leaned against the wall, feeling jittery from a dream about looking for her mother in New York City. Then she realized she'd been searching for Danny all along. She'd noticed him for an instant before he vanished behind a bus. He'd materialized again, only to disappear across the street. Like a ghost, he was constantly appearing and fading away. She'd awakened to his voice.

Don't worry, Emmie. I'm still here.

She flattened her tangled hair and sank into a chair upholstered in white-and-green-patterned silk. An art print on the wall caught her attention: Benjamin Franklin reading at a table, his right thumb resting on his chin. But it looked like his hand was clutching at his collar for air.

A sudden pressure tightened her chest. The ceiling and walls began to close in. Fighting to breathe, she grabbed her own throat and imagined a gust of wind giving her life. She gasped, only to find herself submerged and drowning in a different painting, the one Danny had referenced the day they met. Washington crossing the Delaware with those poor horses thrust into distant rowboats. In the frigid waters, she could hear panicked people flailing and clawing at slabs of ice. Like them, she felt desperate. How could anyone survive the undertow of greed and broken promises?

Emily shuddered in an attempt to release herself from the vision.

"I hate this place."

Clare folded the paper and set it on the table. "Em, it's nice. Your uncle paid for it. It's comfortable, warm."

"You like the fuzzy wallpaper?"

"We won't be living here, silly."

Emily fidgeted with a doily on the armrest. "I have to leave. Now."

"Sure you do. Here, have some coffee." Clare pointed to a white carafe and an empty cup. "And eat." She handed Emily a muffin.

Emily shook her head.

"Then get dressed, for god's sake. We're going shopping."

A sickening flavor puckered Emily's mouth. Ghosts. The room was filled with them. She clutched her T-shirt and took a breath. "Tell everyone I'll be back before our plane leaves."

"What do you mean, *before our plane leaves*? Shit, Em. I like you because you're odd, but this is insane. What will you do out there? Walk the streets like a tramp? For two days?" Clare's gestures flared in red-orange streams.

The shadows were now gossiping about tête-à-têtes by politicians who silenced women, took advantage of workers, and sent other people's sons to war. Abusive secrets whispered through the walls.

Emily's tongue tangled as she tried to explain all this to Clare, who shook her head and said, "You're crazier than I thought."

"Screw you." Alarmed, Emily covered her mouth as soon as the words escaped.

Clare threw up her arms and walked away. Midstride, she turned around. "Okay, you flaming idiot. If you're going to be a jerk, have at it. I'll even help."

Close to tears, Emily ran into her room and packed her stuff. Clare followed. Emily placed her passport, her driver's license, and all her money into Clare's hands. Clare sighed and slid a wad of bills and several dimes into the back pocket of Emily's jeans. Emily fished it out and handed it back. Clare crossed her arms and shook her head.

"Seriously, you could die out there," Clare said a few minutes later. She pulled Emily's hair from the straps of her backpack, turned her around, and tied her new sleeping bag to the frame. "Phone me, okay? And meet me at the museum—Modern Art—tomorrow, ten o'clock. Have a watch?"

Emily lifted her sleeve to reveal her bare wrist.

"Shithead." Clare unbuckled her Mickey Mouse timepiece. "Take this."

Out the door, down the hallway. Emily stepped into an empty elevator. She nodded at the doorman in the lobby and sauntered outside, projecting an air of confidence to prove to herself that she knew what she was doing.

She walked to the end of the block without looking back. She walked to the end of the next block. And the next. Step after step, she walked until the salmon sky sank into a cloud of gray. She turned a corner, crossed at a light, and rounded another corner. She had no idea where she was or where she was headed.

She wiped away tears. Clare was right. This was no way to escape her demons. Her feet kept walking.

She found a diner where a small group of people slid into one of the booths, eager to eat the abandoned food. Fingerless mittens, missing teeth. Emily tried to imagine the details of their lives. Were they running away, like she was, desperate to squelch a sucking gnaw in their guts? She saw her face in theirs as they dropped soiled napkins across their laps, checked bread baskets, licked saltines, finished fries, and slurped final drops of soda through crumpled straws.

How did these people stay warm? What if they got sick? How long would it take before they turned liver-yellow, starving, without friends, without names?

Time was twisting her own life like this.

A honking fury of cars startled her. The sound of screeching tires rippled beneath her feet, wrenching her nerves from their endings. A crumpled cab stalled in the middle of the intersection. The driver emerged, all arms and mouth and nervous legs. Crowds appeared from nowhere, as if the crush were a bottleneck flushing an array of humans in all shapes and sensibilities from the safety of their worlds.

Emily grabbed her pack and left the greasy spoon.

She walked until streetlights cast shadows across her path. She walked until she could no longer feel one foot step in front of the other. She tried sleeping on a wooden bench inside a bus stop shelter. She couldn't settle. She walked again. Several blocks. Several more. Nobody seemed to notice her.

Flashing neon lights surrounded giant Broadway billboards: *Promises, Promises*. A taxicab pulled alongside the curb. A minked lady stepped from the back seat.

I wouldn't trust those cab drivers if I were you.

Was that Danny's voice in her head? Or hers?

She squeezed her eyes. The crunched cab. The Polaroid her dad had taken of her mother's crunched Buick after the accident all those years ago. She tried to blot the images from her mind. The attempt only encouraged more images. Metal. Blood. Danny, burdened with a pack, an ammunition belt, and a heavy rifle, running for his life from ghosts in the jungle.

Someone tapped her on the shoulder. She turned. A Hare Krishna disciple offered a comforting smile. She zipped up her jacket against the cold and followed his orange robe to a nondescript building with a nondescript door.

Could she trust him?

He invited her in.

Clouds of incense filled the room. Tapestries embellished with tiny mirrors hung from beams in the ceiling. Oriental rugs insulated the floors. Orange-robed teens chanted while coaxing brass bowls to sing using wooden mallets. The young man offered her rice and saffron. Hungry and exhausted, she swallowed her doubts and accepted. He led her to a secluded corner where she could eat without being disturbed. She chewed slowly, placed the half-empty bowl on the floor, and fell asleep beneath a blanket he'd left on a bamboo mat.

At dawn, the bowl was gone. She bowed to the sleeping disciple, whispered an ardent thank-you, and tiptoed out the temple door.

A sprinkling of snow dusted the street. She lowered her head. Fifth Avenue. Saks. Sequined mannequins. Window-shoppers. A photographer focused his lens on a waifish blonde wearing white patent leather boots and modeling a navy peacoat against the backdrop of winter.

She checked Clare's watch.

Too soon.

She wandered in circles, not knowing which way to turn.

Here. A bench. A place to think.

She closed her eyes.

Her mother would be shocked to find her like this: swearing at her best friend, fleeing screeching tires, following strangers, and rummaging through garbage cans—all because Danny wasn't around to save her from herself. Then it hit her. The disciple. Had her grandfather sent him to help her "stay in this world?" Or had Danny? Or was he one of her mother's angels? Or was she just sitting on a freezing bench in New York City, flipping out? Going bananas? Losing it?

Flaming idiot. Clare had nailed it.

She rose to her feet.

From here on, nothing would be easy.

It was a wonder she found the Museum of Modern Art. Clare paced outside the entrance. Matt, Spider, Ryan, Holly, and Larry were with her. No one said a word as Emily shed the burden of her pack, sat on the cold cement, and handed Clare her watch. Matt offered a thermos of coffee and dropped a fistful of jelly beans into her hand. Emily took long sips between bites.

Clare bought everyone's tickets with Emily's money.

The museum was well heated. Inside, they settled on a leather-covered seat. Emily studied the bold green rectangle in the center of Matisse's *Memory of Oceania*. The profile of a desperate woman materialized in the upper left of the painting. Emily looked away.

They entered a white room void of sound and then a black room lit only by bouncing lights. They climbed a flight of stairs and examined Reinhardt's *Newsprint Collage*, Pollock's *Animals and Figures*, O'Keeffe's *Banana Flower*, and Stella's ominous *Street in Allegheny*.

They sat on a pew-like bench facing a mural-size painting titled *Hide-and-Seek*, by Pavel Tchelitchew. In the heart of the image was a frightened girl. Lost. Reaching past a butterfly fluttering around her. Biomorphic figures floated before her. A surrealistic tree morphed into knobby hands turning into dozens of children crying out. All with translucent skin. All revealing root-like veins of blood and horror.

14

The Icelandic propjet taking Emily and her collegemates from New York to Reykjavík was a belly of nuts and bolts. Everywhere, raw metal. She and Clare slid into a pair of what felt like iron maidens in front of the left wing.

"Whoa, baby!" Clare said during the rattletrap takeoff.

It didn't take long before the propellers hummed like bumblebees. Clouds disappeared. Emily pressed her face against the oval window and gazed at the Atlantic below.

Clare pulled out the student identity cards they'd claimed at the UN after they left the museum. They'd stood in line like storks, shifting their weight from one leg to the other. She joked about how they puckered their mouths and mimicked the stone-faced bureaucrats standing before them in the building. She reenacted the dramatic ways she and Emily squinted as they posed for an even more unreadable man crouching behind a stilted Polaroid camera.

"You look pissed," Clare said of Emily's picture.

Emily snatched her ID card. She leaned into her friend and slowed the word until it slid off her tongue, emphasizing the sizzling sound as she pointed to the half-moon eyes in Clare's photo.

"You look sssssstonnnnnned."

They were a giggling mess when a head popped over the seat in front of them. It was Matt, kneeling to hand them a bag of magic brownies Vicky had made for the trip.

"Don't think you need these, but I know you want some."

Magic brownies weren't new to Emily. She'd made them once before in Danny and TJ's apartment, at TJ's direction, to help them get ready for a party. TJ had been hunkering around the stereo system, all stubble, sweat, and shredded T-shirt, trying to hook up something important. He'd opened the cupboard above the fridge, grabbed a box of Betty Crocker's, and set it next to the stove. "For tonight? Please?" He tossed a lid of Acapulco Gold on the counter. "Only put half of this into the mix." She'd spilled more than three-quarters of the ounce into the bowl before recalling TJ's instructions. Shrugging at the mass of roughage she'd already stirred into melted butter, eggs, milk, and powdered chocolate, she'd poured everything into a pan. What Emily had pulled from the oven made her think of lichen buried in a rectangle of earth. The last thing she remembered after masticating one brownie was the enormous paper moon spinning from the light fixture on the ceiling.

She took a hunk from the bag and passed it to Clare.

"The biggest of the bunch!" Clare thumped her before taking a clump and handing the bag across the aisle to Spider.

Emily loved Clare. Her lace-trimmed jacket. Her faded jeans. Her dare-me grin. She smiled at her best friend.

Clare stuck out her tongue. Their stony mirth cracked into side-stitching hysterics. Emily pictured all twenty-five Scholastics students as an asylum of loons. It was a good thing they were the only ones on her father's cheap chartered flight.

The sun greeted them the following morning as a spectrum of colors swirled through the propjet window. Then she saw them— entire mountains hiding beneath the ocean with only white tips appearing above the blue.

Icebergs.

Emily didn't remember the descent. Someone must have helped her climb down the steps when they landed in Reykjavík. The rest of Iceland was a barren blur.

It was well past midnight when they arrived in Luxembourg. Walled city. Cobblestone streets, wet with rain. On her way to the hostel, Emily posted a letter to Danny. She mentioned the constellation-filled sky.

We're not that far apart. We're looking at the same moon.

The next day, on a train traveling through fog in the middle of France, an Iranian boy in their compartment asked about the least expensive way to tour America. They thumbed through guidebooks and discussed possibilities, from hotels to hitchhiking and camping, and came to the disappointing conclusion that it was impossible to see America on less than five dollars a day. When they pulled into the station at Lyon, they sadly parted ways.

Larry, Spider, and Holly decided to hang out in France for a few days. Emily, Clare, Matt, and Ryan took the next train south. They shared a sleeping compartment. Two tiny bunks. Girls on top, boys on the bottom, traveling in their sleep, following a line on a map from Lyon to Geneva to Bern to Milan. Emily dreamed of bending the lonely wail of the rails on her harmonica, of Danny harmonizing, of Danny lulling dreams into rainbows. She sneezed herself awake as dawn ignited Switzerland in yellow and orange. Storybook scenes came to life outside the square-foot window. Stucco-and-wood chalets, colorful blankets draped over balconies with cutout balustrades, brass bells around the necks of sheep, firewood piled in carts guided by men wearing rubber boots and wool knickers.

"Look! A postcard," she said to Clare, who handed her a pack of tissues to catch her inevitable sneeze. Noses pressed against the windowpane, they watched a steady stream of panoramas roll by.

While changing trains in Milan, the four travelers learned about a bomb that had destroyed a bank inside the same station only a month before. Then another bomb had exploded inside a different bank in Piazza Fontana, killing and maiming an alarming number of people. Yet another was discovered near Milan's La Scala opera house but was safely detonated by police.

Clare, Matt, Ryan, and Emily clung to each other and made their way through chaotic crowds to board the train to Florence.

Michelangelo's *David* stood before them in his glory—not the fake David in the Palazzo della Signoria or the offensive sculptures her father loved—this was the real *David* in the Galleria dell'Accademia. Her friends discussed how this new chapter in their lives might help them face their own Goliaths.

While gazing at Caravaggio's *Sacrifice of Isaac* in the Uffizi Gallery, Emily felt the angel of God halting Abraham's hand and tapping her on the shoulder.

Matt steered her away from the knife, the father, the ram, and the terror reflected in Isaac's eyes.

15

Eight gates allowed access to Perugia. Trapezoidal towers stood guard on either side of the Etruscan Arch, an intimidating structure. In the fifth century BC, the city had become an ancient stronghold overlooking the Tiber River in central Umbria.

Matt closed his guidebook and gestured to the daunting wall that had survived the barbaric invasions after Rome had seized power over the region.

"You only have to remember a few things about Perugia: It has a chocolate factory and two universities. And it's Umbria's capital. Not to mention that it's a headquarters for the Italian Communist Party." He showed Emily a picture of the building in the town square.

Italian Communists? In a country where Fascism was born? "I bet those Communists were artists," Emily said.

Matt thumbed through the book. "Here's an artist you'd like: Perugino. He has frescoes in Collegio del Cambio and paintings in Umbria's National Gallery."

"Apolitical humanists, not Communists," Emily whispered, more to herself than to Matt. She wanted to believe artists were more ethical than politicians.

"What's with all the griffins?" Ryan asked, cleaning the film from his glasses and adjusting the cowboy hat he'd purchased from a street vendor in Florence.

Griffins appeared to grace every corner and occupy every square. Part lion, part eagle, they were icons of strength and intelligence, and guardians of the human and the divine. Humanism merging with classical mythology—Emily preferred this view of Perugia's artists. She liked this place. She could learn something here.

She and her friends parked their belongings at the nearest youth hostel before looking for a place to eat. They found a perfect little café with a Coca-Cola sign out front.

The next day, they scouted the countryside for La Contessa's estate. Two Chilean med students drove them to San Marco, where Matt assumed the castle was. They didn't realize they were in the wrong place until after the students dropped them off in the tiny village. It took all of Emily's dictionary Italian to find out which road to take to Montealina, where Clare thought the castle was. Their next ride returned them to the hostel because the driver got lost.

"Bummer," said Ryan as they collapsed in the room he and Matt shared. They spread a local map on the table. "We should have hog-tied Steele until he gave us directions." He tipped his hat and imitated a nasal John Wayne drawl: "Somewhere in the boonies over there—between Perugia and Gubbio."

"I still think it's around here." Clare pointed to a dotted line representing a dirt road.

"Great," said Matt. "We'll all have to pile on the back of an ass to get up there."

"You're the perfect ass," said Clare.

They hitched up and down the same road for two more days. None of the locals could tell them anything about a castle, let alone where this one was.

They returned to Clare's suggested road the next morning and crouched by the shoulder, hugging their knees.

"Tuesday," said Roundup Ryan, donning his cowboy hat. "Already."

"Where's everyone else?" Emily asked.

"Spider's probably in Amsterdam smoking gold," said Clare.

Matt sighed. "I'd like to do that right now."

The wind picked up. Clouds gathered.

Ryan returned to his fake Texan drawl as he pointed to the sky. "What luck. We're in the middle of nowhere, man, and a storm's a-brewin'." He pulled his thumb back and aimed his forefinger at the clouds.

"And someone's coming our way," said Matt.

In the distance, a giant blob grew into an even larger blob of backfiring metal.

"Must be Americans," said Clare, standing and extending her thumb.

Ryan's wrangler facade dropped. "Jeezus."

Emily looked around.

Sure enough, the approaching blob evolved into a beat-up gray van with Freya's Faunas painted all over it. In hippie calligraphy, she'd scrawled "Low-Flying Manatee" across one side.

Matt elbowed Clare. "Woohoo! Crazy coincidence day! We're keeping you with us, Clare Voyant."

A couple of Scholastics students motioned for the foursome to climb into the back. There were no seats, only a corrugated metal floor with nasty bolts sticking out everywhere.

Clare whispered to Emily, "Remind you of anything?"

"Icelandic Airlines on wheels?"

Clare exploded with laughter.

Huddled with maybe ten other kids in the moving bunker, Spider looked around to see what was so funny.

"We were just talking about you," Matt said to Spider.

"Yeah?"

"La Contessa's having a dinner party," Holly interrupted in her breathy voice. "At her castle." She shrugged and folded her paisley shift around her thighs. "We've been staying at this cool hotel in town. Then Steele found us wandering around the bus station and picked us up." She motioned to the man sitting low at the wheel.

The one and only William Steele, greasy hair and all, started bragging about the deal he'd gotten when he bought the van in Germany several days before. And how, in Day-Glo colors, Freya —who presently turned around to smile at everyone from the passenger seat—had painted its new name along the entire length of the left side.

Spider and the others shared colorful globe-trotting stories. Their voices faded into the background as Emily watched Steele take an unmarked road to Montealina, exactly where Clare had predicted. They traveled a few miles on dirt lanes through farmland until they climbed into the mountains and turned onto a narrow drive lined with a row of Italian cypresses.

"Look at the top of the hill. Within those trees are the castle walls." Steele had become their new tour guide.

Emily cleared a fistful of smudges and fingerprints from the window. Below the road, she spotted vineyards, olive trees, house-size haystacks, and a small frog-shaped lake. Rounded women stooped to seed the fields. Farmers lifted layers of burlap and shoveled mounds of composted soil from wooden wagons hitched to a pair of fidgety oxen.

Steele cruised past bare fig trees and parked before a stone wall. As soon as he opened the metal gate, everyone piled out, and he walked into the courtyard like he owned the place.

Faint voices echoed through the air. Emily recognized their cries. She'd heard them before. In her visions. In her dreams.

Before her stood a real castle with turrets and gates and a medieval well in the center of the courtyard. It was a fairy tale straight from her grandfather's books, with ghosts—always with ghosts.

Giovanni, La Contessa's son, greeted them with a flirty grin. "*Benvenuti!* Welcome!"

He sported dark sideburns and wore a formfitting shirt and brightly polished shoes.

"*Seguimi!* Come. Let me show you something." He spoke in heavily accented English. "Do you see? The passageways in the well?" It sounded like he was resuming a previous conversation about secret escape routes.

Emily and her friends leaned over the opening and peered into the darkness. A dank odor rose from the depths.

"Corridors. Do you see them? At the bottom? The Etruscan tombs?"

"In the well?"

"In the passageways. There are tunnels everywhere beneath this property. For centuries, we fought our wars underground." He opened his arms and gestured around him. "To protect the vineyards, of course. This is how much we love our land."

Whispers. Cloak-and-dagger plots. Farmers trapped in the shadows with soldiers. Somehow, Emily knew this story.

It began to rain.

Giovanni shepherded everyone through double wooden doors accented by lion-shaped knockers.

Emily lingered in a hallway lined with medieval armor. She reached toward their hilted swords.

Giovanni's sultry voice shooed her from behind. "Quickly now, through the library. Dinner is waiting."

Secretly, she ran her fingertips along antique volumes posing on one shelf and again along the top of a Savonarola chair sitting next to a row of antique bookcases.

Musty. The taste of history.

"Illuminated manuscripts. Twelfth century," Giovanni said, scooting her along. "Do not worry. You will have plenty of time to look at them later."

In the dining room, tapestries and portraits decorated the walls. Polished silver. Etched crystal. Everything had been neatly arranged on a feasting table. Giovanni introduced white-gloved Vittorio, who pulled out a chair and motioned for Emily to sit.

He announced the aproned lady as Perlita, who lifted Emily's glass and poured a small amount of ruby liquid into it. Smiling, she moved to Clare's setting, on Emily's right. She'd filled every glass by the time La Contessa entered, wearing a teal suit and pearls. Her hair was streaked with gray.

Emily fingered the grommets adorning her denim pockets and regretted wearing jeans.

Following Vittorio's lead, everyone stood as La Contessa took her place at the head of the table. As soon as La Contessa sat, everyone else sat. The students looked pleasantly polite while unfolding starched napkins and placing them on their laps.

Only Steele inspected the stemware.

La Contessa spoke in Italian. Giovanni translated.

"I am happy to welcome you to our home."

La Contessa seemed at a loss for further words, so she smiled and nodded again. Then, she motioned for her guests to sit down.

Perlita disappeared into another room. Emily's imagination followed her. She visualized Perlita rising before dawn, opening a sack of flour, and measuring cupfuls into a large bowl. The scene unfolded like a documentary in Emily's mind.

> *She mixes the flour with yeast and water, rolls the dough with a thick pole, kneads, and lets it rest.*

Emily's daydream took hold.

> *Perlita asks Little Maria to help her flatten the pasta. Her husband, Vittorio, enters with freshly harvested vegetables. He instructs ten-year-old Lorenzo to prepare them for sauce. Vittorio and Angelo, Lorenzo's grandfather, light pipes. They sit back and talk about last year's late harvest, hoping the wheat and grapes will make good bread and wine for the meal.*
>
> *Perlita tends to the animals. Little Maria feeds the chickens and helps her mother gather eggs. Maria is afraid of the rooster and runs whenever she sees him. Lorenzo and his grandfather*

look after the trees, the vineyards, and the gardens. Vittorio lets them think they do most of the work. Perlita grinds the lamb, butchered by a neighbor, and prepares the crepes while Little Maria samples the cheese. She yawns when her mother gives her a bowl of peas to shell. Perlita slices potatoes and gently touches Little Maria's hand with the tip of the knife to keep her focused.

Clare nudged Emily's arm to bring her back.

Perlita announced Course I: "Fettucine with bread and Chianti. Grain from La Contessa's fields. Grapes from La Contessa's vineyards. Tomatoes and carrots from La Contessa's garden."

Emily lifted her fork. Course II arrived before she could finish the last bit of pasta.

"Crepes polpette with lamb," Vittorio declared. "Lamb from La Contessa's sheep. Vegetables from La Contessa's garden. Eggs from La Contessa's chickens. Olives from La Contessa's trees. Cheese and milk from La Contessa's goats."

Emily stared at the lamb. The thick potato chips, peas, hard cheese, and milk would be easier to swallow than this poor creature. She sliced a small portion and placed it on her tongue. It tasted gray, like a pending storm. She discreetly spit it into her palm and hid it under the largest chip. Then she disengaged. Her vision resumed.

Angelo tends the hives while Lorenzo, afraid of bees, hides behind the shed. Lorenzo and Little Maria pick pecans with their grandfather. Little Maria slips a few into her pockets. Perlita prepares the pastry in advance while Lorenzo and Little Maria lick the spoons.

Course III arrived, as if on command.

"Honey-pecan pastry served with special dessert wine." Perlita sounded especially proud. "Honey from Angelo's hives. Pecans from La Contessa's orchards. Grapes from La Contessa's vines."

Emily covered her mouth with her napkin. Her imagination

was becoming predictive, and it scared her. But she was curious. She took a breath and re-entered the scene.

Early in the morning, Lorenzo, Little Maria, and raven-eyed Angelo pick oranges. Perlita and Little Maria slice the fruit while Lorenzo and Angelo shell pecans and almonds.

Course IV, served on individual platters, felt like a manifestation. Vittorio lowered his voice. "Blood oranges, pecans, and almonds. Fruit and nuts from La Contessa's trees."

Emily stopped eating. When no one was looking, she slipped the nuts and orange sections onto Clare's plate.

Perlita delivered Course V in crystal carafes. "Orange liqueur, a gift from Giovanni, La Contessa's son."

Perlita and Vittorio bring dishes to the kitchen and remind their children to wash them. Lorenzo scrapes sticky honey while making faces at his sister. Little Maria cleans the plates and complains that the water is too cold. Vittorio ignores her, mentioning the demonstrations in town. He grabs a towel, teasingly snaps it at Perlita, and says he's glad she's safe at home. She giggles, kisses him, and puts the dishes on the shelf.

Little Maria and Lorenzo roll their eyes when their parents ask them to wipe the kitchen counters. Perlita switches off the lights. Vittorio latches the door.

Vittorio, Perlita, Lorenzo, Little Maria, and Angelo pull on shawls and jackets. Along the way to their farmhouse, the males gather fallen olive branches for firewood.

Once home, Perlita and Little Maria boil potatoes harvested that morning from La Contessa's garden. They fry a bit of ground lamb from tonight's meal at the castle. Little Maria scoops a handful of pecans from her pocket and gives them to her mother. Vittorio and Angelo drag wooden chairs across the floor to the table, fold their hands in their laps, and nod at the family to pray. Pray for the workers demonstrating in town. Pray for the union members on strike. Pray for the family of Giuseppe Pinelli, the revolutionary railway worker murdered by Milan police. Pray for the safety of everyone in the room.

Perlita pulls a flask from her apron and nudges Vittorio. Orange liqueur, a gift from Giovanni, La Contessa's son.

"Giuseppe Pinelli," Emily whispered. She'd retreated to a nearby balcony after the meal.

"I love the smell of rain after a storm," said Clare, joining Emily and taking her hand. And here we are in an Italian castle—better than all the stories we made up when we were little."

Clare was right to promise new beginnings, but the haunting in Emily's head remained.

16

It had been several weeks since the Scholastics students first arrived in Perugia. They'd dined with the countess. They'd moved into one-half of Vittorio's Little Farmhouse below the castle—fifteen college kids squeezing into three small rooms because La Contessa didn't know where else to house them. They'd cleaned eels from the market, thrown them into a large pot, and added carrots and onions. They'd choked on this, Freya's slippery fish soup, while watching Perlita and Vittorio's two children chase chickens around the building.

Further down the hill, the Big Farmhouse was undergoing construction. Emily winced at the distant sound of pounding nails. This shell of a structure that once housed chickens and goats would soon be their home. According to rumors, humans hadn't occupied it in over three hundred years.

She shook the image from her mind and opened Danny's letter under a tree near the frog lake. He wrote about GIs shooting seagulls and seals in the Monterey surf.

It's cruel, Emmie. Even the first-aid stations are filled with gore. Mannequins of wounded soldiers lie on the ground, peppered with bullet holes. They keep us on the move nonstop. I fall asleep before my body hits the bed.

His words blurred.

The day she stepped off the Icelandic propjet and shuffled into the Luxembourg airport with her friends, Danny was marching in formation at Fort Ord. He'd traded his T-shirt and jeans for fatigues and left his dark ponytail in a mound on an army butcher's floor. As she'd marveled at the sound of her boots tapping on cobblestoned streets, Danny was pulling on combat boots and wriggling into his new uniform.

Danny had transferred early to Fort Benning, Georgia, for Advanced Individual Training. Military Occupational Specialty: 11 Bravo 40, Light Weapon Infantryman.

No one smiles. We're completely alone. It doesn't matter that we're surrounded by men wearing medals on their shoulders. I won't allow them to make me this callous.

The irony burned. She ate gelato in Florence while Danny ate "shit on a shingle," chipped beef and gravy on toast. She and Clare sang Beatles songs to annoy Matt. Danny was forced to chant "I want to go to Vietnam. I want to kill a Charlie Cong. Here we go, here we go."

She folded his letter.

His whisper in her head: *I'm okay, Emmie.*

She wiped her eyes and forced herself to descend the dirt road to the construction site.

A small group of workers swarmed the Big Farmhouse. Ryan and Matt distracted them with Frisbees while Larry targeted the chickens with trowels of plaster.

Emily located an abandoned brush and joined Clare. "Who knew we'd be restoring an Italian farmhouse instead of going to school?"

"C'mon, Em. This is way better." Clare deliberately splattered Emily with paint.

Emily detailed a line of brown pigment across the toe of her friend's sneaker.

"Neat freak." Clare cleaned her shoe with her sleeve. "Who cares if our clothes get ruined out here?"

Emily reloaded her brush and laughed. "If you say another word, I'll cover your face with this."

They'd completed the trim around two windowsills when Clare dropped her brush into the can and wiped her hands on her jeans. Pointing to a crumbling cornerstone, she questioned the building's age. "Which came first? The farmhouse or the castle?"

"The farmhouse, of course." Emily glanced at Vittorio and an older man—Angelo?—who were busy mixing cement. "They do all the work. Without them, the castle wouldn't exist."

It was true. Vittorio and several other farmhands had spent the last few weeks fashioning a makeshift kitchen, reinforcing ceilings, walls, and floors, grouting tiles, and hauling an old cooking stove, striped button mattresses, cots, and weathered dressers up the stone steps. All this for the benefit of Emily and her friends. A wringer washer waited on the landing. No one knew what to do with it.

During their first week at La Contessa's estate, Emily and Clare had shared a room overlooking the castle courtyard—until Steele invited a group of his San Francisco buddies to help him claim the castle's first floor by kicking out "all the kids."

Emily missed the castle room where she used to stay. She missed its white plaster walls and high ceiling. She missed the tiny arched window above her head that allowed the morning light to cast particles of hope across the room. She missed the nightingales singing about that hope. She missed the metal bucket chained to the top of the well outside, the bolted iron doors, the lanterns, the lichen, the climbing ivy, the pottery vases, the strange trees—even the haunted hallway leading to what she used to call her bedroom. She missed it all.

So far, none of the farmhouses had restrooms. Cranky-dirty and in dire need of a bath, Emily grabbed a towel and climbed the hill to the castle's facilities. There, the claw-foot tub only offered enough tepid water for two baths a day or two loads of laundry. By the time she arrived, it was clear Steele's friends had used the last drop. T-shirts and underwear covered every surface. Thick hair circled the drain in the old tub. Leaking faucet. Cold water.

Back at Vittorio's place and feeling grungy, Emily settled on a wooden bench installed within an enormous fireplace. Wrap-around fireplace benches—who'd have thought? Apparently, they were commonplace in this region. This one faced a large cauldron hanging over the open fire. Emily cracked walnuts and tossed the shells into the flames.

She'd already helped to clean Freya's squid and, with the other girls, finished setting up cookware in the Big Farmhouse kitchen. She'd even gathered firewood. All that was left was wiring, plumbing, and heavy lifting—guy stuff.

She pulled her sketchbook and pouch of colored pencils from her pack. Nightingales trilled from the page. Roosters appeared, strutting around and crowing at noon. Mockingbirds imitated the roosters. On the next page, she covered a dark-blue sky with winter constellations. Danny's smiling face morphed into the full moon. The nightingales flocked around him, repeating their morning calls. Musical notes followed them. A uniformed Danny leaned against the castle well and mimicked the birds' songs on his guitar.

She closed her book, returned everything to her pack, and removed her shoes. Walking barefoot might help her connect with the earth's calming energy. Outside, she danced in place to warm her feet on the snow-dusted soil.

A short distance away, Matt and Ryan hoisted topped-off fuel tanks into a creaky wheelbarrow. They struggled to push the wooden cart from Vittorio's place to the Big Farmhouse, where they hooked the tanks to the cooking stove. Emily followed them, shifting from one foot to the other, and volunteered to help.

"Here," said Ryan, scowling at her naked toes and leading her back outside. He reached into his pocket and pulled out several coins. "Why don't you put on some shoes and buy socks at the market?"

Emily grabbed the camera hanging around her neck.

Click: her mocking friend.

She turned around.

Click: a strutting chicken. Click: a Frisbee in a tree. Click: dirty wine bottles in the bushes.

She turned again.

Click: William Steele, strumming his guitar beneath an olive tree, doing none of the work.

She looked down.

Click: her purple feet.

She looked up.

Click: her third finger in the frame.

17

Emily wanted to blot out her worries and focus her camera on the sky, the castle, the farmhouses, and the Van Gogh haystacks. She plodded up the hill to photograph a new sunrise. As soon as she looked through the lens, she tasted the light, lowered her Instamatic, and let her sneeze fill the air.

The Low-Flying Manatee sputtered by with Steele at the wheel and Freya sitting in the lap of a large man in the passenger seat. Emily kept her eye on the van as it coughed exhaust, disappeared into the trees, and headed toward town. She grabbed her pack and rushed to the courtyard.

The doors to the castle hall seemed heavier than usual. She banged the knocker ring against the wood. "Anyone here?" No answer. The bathroom door was ajar. She tapped on it several times before peeking inside. No one there either.

A kettle sat beside a portable hot plate next to the tub. Twisted toothpaste tubes and hairbrushes littered the pedestal sink. Emily closed the toilet seat, pulled the chain to the wall-mounted tank, and flushed its contents.

She boiled water and carried it to the claw-foot tub. A sizable gray spider waited in the silver soap dish. If she approached him quickly, he'd scatter, leaving his web behind, so she moved with care while quietly addressing him as Oggi, meaning "today" in Italian.

"Will you bring me something curious today?" She used her softest voice and smiled, feeling like Alice in Wonderland.

She swore Oggi was watching her while she mixed hot water with cold. He didn't move when she squeezed in a bit of Freya's shampoo for bubbles. She undressed and stepped into the lukewarm lather. As soon as she reached for the cracked bar of soap, however, he disappeared.

After bathing, she dripped to her former room in a sun-stiffened towel. Instead of a nightingale wonderland, she found a disaster. Shirts and unzipped jeans cluttered the two cots. Freya's Faunas had taken over the walls, the wardrobe, and the opened shutters. Paraphernalia littered the unclaimed surfaces.

Repulsed, Emily returned to the bathroom and looked for Oggi. He didn't answer her calls. She scrubbed her laundry in brown tub water. After tidying up her mess and dressing, she draped her wet clothes over the whispering well. "Drops of water to hydrate you," she said to the ghosts below. When her laundry was dry enough to transport, she grabbed her pack and walked outside the courtyard gate.

A large tow truck motored up the drive, followed by a red Ferrari with Giovanni at the wheel. La Contessa waved from the passenger seat. They paused in front of a pair of open doors on the far side of the castle and waited for Emily to reach them.

"Emi-lee!" said Giovanni, helping his mother climb from the car. "I see you have finished your laundry. Is there anything we can do for you?"

Emily lowered her belongings to the ground and motioned to the antique wagon strapped to the flatbed behind the truck.

"Forgive me for asking, but what is this?"

Mounted on top of the wagon sat a large gray box, about the size of the Ferrari.

Giovanni grinned. "Aah, it is our treasure, of course."

La Contessa nodded and gestured to the box. *"Una macchina leggera."* Her face glowed with pride.

"I will tell you about it later," Giovanni said, pointing to the open garage. But first, we must get it ready for an exhibit."

La Contessa took Emily's arm and led her beyond her son's earshot. "These men," she whispered. "They keep their secrets close. But I will tell. It is my grandfather's light machine."

"A light machine?"

"Per illuminare i sogni."

"For dreams?"

"You will understand one day." She flashed a knowing smile before joining Giovanni in the garage.

A jolt of energy charged Emily as she watched workers remove the wagon from the flatbed and roll it into the garage. She wanted to see the magical light machine hiding inside this featureless box. Giovanni and La Contessa closed the doors.

Emily sighed and strolled downhill, past the frog lake, the olive trees, the grapevines, and the haystacks.

Inside the Big Farmhouse, she spotted Margherita, their soft-hearted cook, stirring soup in the cauldron. Her muscles strained as she lifted the iron pot with her bare hands and set it on red coals. She removed her apron and squeezed Emily's shoulder before going home for the day.

Margherita had been teaching Emily kitchen Italian. Together they grated *parmigiano*, sliced *carote*, cracked *noci*. Whenever Emily shared her journal sketches, Margherita would smile and nod.

Emily lifted a food box from the floor and set it on a chair beside the table. The least she could do to thank Margherita was to learn how to cook like an Italian.

"Incoming!" Giovanni's voice echoed up the stairwell. A loud scraping noise followed. Emily dropped the tomato she'd pulled from the box and ran to him.

"It is okay, Emi-lee. I have this."

He dragged a heavy wooden cart into the main room. On it

sat two demijohns of the week's wine. The guys appeared out of nowhere, bears after honey.

After Giovanni left, Larry fastened a siphoning hose to the wicker-covered vessel. He, Ryan, Larry, and Matt took turns filling dozens of liter Chianti bottles, sipping long and hard between each one. It didn't take long before their drunken bodies lay scattered across the floor.

Emily cleaned up the splattered tomato and returned to the food box. *Carne di cavallo.* The clearly labeled packaging confirmed what she didn't want to know. She untied bloody white paper from a slab of horse meat. Flies moved from the dead chicken on the cutting board and gathered around the new treat. In the shadows beneath the table, her knee brushed against the edge of Oggi's new web.

"Gross, isn't it?" Clare said, sneaking behind her.

"Who in the world would buy horse meat?"

"And who in the world would unwrap it? Emily the vegetarian, that's who. The one who plucks the chickens."

"This isn't chicken."

"But that is." Clare pointed to the poor bird someone had left at the other end of the table.

"No one else will do it. Except you, Clare."

"And Margherita."

"Mostly Margherita."

"Martyrs everywhere." Clare poked Emily's rib. Put it away. We'll deal with the corpses later. Mayonnaise is on our to-do list now. Superstition tells us," she said, parodying Dr. Finn's Pat Paulsen voice, "that it's best to have a male and a female straddling the bowl. One fork-whisking the yolks, and the other pouring olive oil in a thin stream. But the girl can't be on the rag. That's the trick."

Emily had heard this story before. "You add the oil super slowly and beat the yolks furiously to keep everything from separating." She repeated the words "slowly" and "furiously" while pointing to the curdled endeavors that filled the shelves of their soaked-burlap fridge.

Clare lifted the chipped porcelain bowl. "None of the guys want to do this."

"Lord, let them bring us an eggbeater, then!" Emily laughed, spilling oil everywhere.

The mayo failed three times, but the fourth attempt inspired cheers. They ripped several large pieces of the region's bland bread for dipping and gathered strength to face the chickens. Emily and Clare wielded pliers. Feathers flew.

Emily glanced out the window. In the distance, she spotted the boys tossing Frisbees to each other. Larry's hair was getting longer, like all the guys', but his fuzzy mane grew more away from his head than down his back. Suddenly everything about him felt like a contradiction.

"Pity, isn't it?" she said, ignoring her thoughts and clicking her tongue at the display. "Little kids stumbling on the playground after siphoning wine." She set down the pliers and led Clare to the window.

Ryan leaped, missed, turned midair, and landed in the grass. He retrieved the Frisbee from the field and launched it toward Matt. They rotated, twisted, dove, bounded, reached, soared, and somehow managed to avoid Holly sunbathing beneath an olive tree and Spider sharing smokes with the wind. They circled around the girls and hurdled over the makeshift garden.

A group of farmhands leaned on their shovels and watched. Ryan motioned them over and demonstrated his skills. Soon the workers were awkwardly tossing brightly colored disks back and forth.

Emily imagined Danny supporting his back against the farmhouse wall, warm and safe in the afternoon sun.

Clare chopped the horse meat into cubes and dumped them into a pan. "Should we tell them this is horseshit?" She was referencing Steele and his friends, who'd been complaining about not getting enough beef for protein. "Or bullshit?"

"Both would be too kind," said Emily, still at the window. Steele was now invading her thoughts. Earlier that morning, he'd cornered her in the stairwell. She couldn't see his beady eyes behind the fog in his glasses or his mouth beneath his heavy mustache and beard, but she could feel his intentions. Especially when he deliberately brushed against her before continuing down the stairs.

18

Posted on the wall in typed caps:

ENCOUNTER GROUP AFTER DINNER.

The fourth one since they'd arrived in Perugia.
"A meeting to settle scores," Larry said.
"Fat chance," Emily muttered to her sketchbook.
Keeping their usual vitriolic meetings from becoming physical had proved to be a hopeless task.

The first gathering had incited arguments about the unfinished showers in the Big Farmhouse. Using her travel set of watercolors, Emily had splashed red and orange around two facing pages. She was too angry to draw. She'd added these words:

Oh, someone promised to hook up the plumbing but forgot? What about the washing machine? Nobody knows how to operate it? So now what? Find someone who does? You think? Is anyone in charge here?

The following encounter group had focused on the missing textbooks.

Someone forgot to order them? Who might that be? Not true, you say. They're sitting in your room, and you haven't opened the boxes. Oh, off to Florence again with friends? Didn't have time, did you, Steele?

The latest addressed the issue of seminars.

"Frisbee for Health." "Haystack Photography." Only two silly lessons so far? Why not literature and art as promised? What about learning Italian? Go to the University for Foreign Students in Perugia, you say? Sure. We'll take you up on that. Just pay our tuition there. Oh, yeah. Why not pay your share of rent and food while you're at it? Hello? Steele? Are you listening?

Emily closed her sketchbook when she realized she was part of the problem. Then she absent-mindedly opened it again, turned to a new page, and dipped her brush into a tin of water. Impressionistic wine bottles cluttering the kitchen and yard. Piles of laundry in the hallway. Chicken heads tossed atop a mound of dirt named "Vegetable Garden." She underscored the pictures with captions and embellished two gigantic words:

NOBODY CARES.

Tonight's encounter group began with the usual small talk after the girls cleared the dishes from the table.

It didn't take long for wild-haired Larry to confront Steele.

"According to Spider, everyone but you has paid up for room and board. How can we afford to keep everything going if you don't pitch in?"

Steele cocked his head. "What's Spider got to do with it?"

"She's our treasurer." Ryan cleaned his glasses, as he often did when things got strange.

"Spider? Treasurer? You're kidding." Steele glanced at his middle finger and chewed on a hangnail.

"All of us appointed her. Including you. She's responsible for paying the countess and arranging all our market runs."

"Spider? That airhead?" Steele put his middle finger into his mouth and sucked.

Emily cradled her sketchbook.

"What do you mean, *airhead*?" said Ryan. "She's a lot smarter than you are."

Spider sneered and threw a dish towel over her shoulder.

"You're changing the subject," Larry said to Steele. "Point is, you're stiffing us."

Steele pulled his wet finger from his mouth and pointed it at Larry. "I'm the reason you brats are even here. Look around: castle, nobility, all the wine you want. You'll be thanking me for this when you finally grow up."

"Bastard," Larry mumbled.

"What did you call me?"

"Bastard," said Clare, wiping a spot of stew from the table.

Steele's eyes lit up. "Little sissy Larry doesn't have the balls to say that directly, but Clare does?"

Larry grabbed a wine bottle. "You prick."

Steele folded his arms across his chest and nodded.

"You got it." Larry threw the bottle at the pseudoprofessor, who ducked before it crashed against the plaster wall Freya had recently covered with Faunas.

Steele stood, assuming his full height. "Would you like to borrow my glasses?" He took them from his face, spit into his fingers, and cleaned the lenses.

Larry started to lunge, but Ryan stopped him. "Get out of here, man," he said to Steele. Ryan's face was the color of the Chianti pooling on the floor. "We're done with you."

Steele exaggerated the weight of his folded arms. He had no intention of going anywhere. He grinned and surveyed the room. "You're all blind to what's going on here. A little hardship in your bourgeois lives, and all you do is whine like babies."

"I beg to differ, Mr. Know-It-All," said Larry. "You're baiting us. Your friends, by the way, are just like you—freeloaders. You're trying to turn this whole experience into mayhem so you can write about it and become the next William Golding."

A chill spasmed Emily's back. Shuddering away images of Simon and the pig's head, she opened her book and drew Steele as a hog, which she titled "Lord of the Flies." Then she regretted disparaging innocent hogs in such a thoughtless way. She closed the book and tried to stand, but fell against the bench in the fireplace instead. She tried to stand again, but wavered.

Matt caught her elbow. "Change of scene," he whispered. He took her sketchbook and helped her to the landing, down the stairs, and onto the back of the communal Vespa outside. "We're out of here," he said, pocketing her book in the sidebag and kickstarting the bike.

They traveled past La Contessa's vineyards, along the cypress-lined way, and onto the dirt road. Emily felt the divide of the waxing moon in her chest, light versus a thin void of darkness carved from the left side.

She focused on the sky to keep from vomiting.

Gubbio was stark and gray. Matt slowed the bike to a quiet hum as they entered the medieval town. They crossed an arched bridge above the river and navigated serpentine Etruscan alleyways. Shadows transformed cobblestones into knobby monsters, their spines rising from the walls of buildings. Several houses had a narrow second door, bricked up about a foot above the main entrance. Matt stopped the bike and pulled out his guidebook and a flashlight. *"Porta dei morti,"* he said. "Door of the dead. For the passage of plague coffins so Death won't be able to find the real door to the house."

Emily clutched her deathly cold shoulders and surveyed the Palazzo dei Consoli towering in the distance. Matt started the bike and headed toward it. They circled a silhouetted structure in the square. "If you ride around this fountain three times, you'll go insane," he said.

I'm already insane. Emily's verdict hollered in her head.

They journeyed past flower-lined staircases and negotiated a labyrinth of cobbled streets climbing into the hills and down again. It took a while before they found a different bridge out of town. When they rumbled into the foothills of Mount Ingino, Emily felt like they'd been making their way through the Dark Ages, fleeing plagues, thieves, and predatory kings. She envisioned a brigade of knights, fresh from battle, raising their swords and urging them forward.

Hours later, an eagle owl led them back to the Big Farmhouse. They followed its ghostly form beyond silver haystacks in silver fields and up the hill to the castle before the raptor disappeared into the woods. Matt circumnavigated La Contessa's keep several times, then headed toward the Big Farmhouse.

"Em, do you have a place to sleep tonight?" he asked as they dismounted the bike.

"With Clare."

"Good." He handed back her sketchbook.

They tiptoed up the steps of the Big Farmhouse and peered around the corner into the main room. Larry sat on the fireplace bench, nursing a bottle of wine.

"It's cool, man," he said. "Godzilla's gone."

Matt settled beside Larry.

"We got him stupid drunk and pushed him out. All of us. Even Holly. Nearly made him fall down the stairs, but Ryan caught him before he lost his balance. Too bad. He should have let him hit bottom."

Emily sat next to Matt. "Think he has a good side?"

"Nah," Larry said after taking another chug. "Steele's a bastard through and through."

Emily fell asleep on the fireplace bench. In the morning, she awoke to Matt and Larry snoring in their chairs. They regained consciousness just before Ryan and Spider entered the room. Nobody said a word about what had happened the night before.

Freya and a small group of students appeared out of nowhere, followed by Steele and a gaggle of his friends. A man they called

Otto trailed behind, carrying a stack of William Blake books. Emily recognized him as the guy who steadied Freya in his lap as Steele drove the Low-Flying Manatee toward town on the day the mysterious gray box disappeared into the castle garage.

She watched the checkered parade march into Clare's room.

"Finally, a lesson," said Ryan.

Larry laughed. "That's a lesson?"

"Hey, Blake's cool, man. Straight from the Romantic Age. What more can you ask?"

"Then why aren't you in there with the other groupies?"

Ryan shrugged and buried his face in *Etruscan Places*.

Matt paused between paragraphs in *Man and His Symbols* to fiddle with the flames he'd reignited in the fireplace.

Emily doodled in her journal.

Yesterday, while Emily's friends were raiding the box of books Steele had neglected, Margherita had spent the morning cooking and sweeping the floor. Now nearly all the tiles were littered with broken glass and stained with red wine. Emily showed Matt her drawing of shattered bottles before grabbing a broom.

He stopped her midstride. "Steele should clean this up."

"It's glass. It might cut someone's foot."

"That's precisely why we wear shoes." He grinned, snatched the broom, and leaned it against the wall.

Emily moved to a spot at the table and away from the fire. Holly strolled in, grabbed an orange, and sat beside Ryan.

Margherita entered, noticed the floor, and lifted the broom. She raised her palm against Emily's attempt to help.

Chicken steamed. Goulash simmered.

"Someone must set the table," Emily said after a while.

"*Someone*? *Must*?" Matt clicked his tongue. He was now sitting in Emily's place on the fireplace bench.

"Demonstrations are happening all around us, and you're worried about domestic chores?" Larry mimicked Matt's tongue clicking.

"I'll get the dishes," said Emily.

Margherita looked up. She gathered an armful of dishes and grabbed a mop. Emily rose to help, but Margherita stopped her. "I do it. You sit."

"What demonstrations?" asked Matt.

"In Florence," said Ryan. "Last week. The fascists brought in tanks to disperse the communists and socialists—"

"—mostly to hassle the student activists," interrupted Larry. "They're the ones rooting for the workers, the disadvantaged, the poor. Not those corrupt rich guys."

"The locals were demonstrating, too," said Ryan, gesturing to Larry. We were there."

Emily pulled up a chair. "They brought in tanks?"

"Yeah," said Larry. "They're afraid of a Russian Revolution here. They don't want the common people disrupting their double-dealing lives."

Emily glanced at Margherita laboring in the kitchen. Her father looked down on good people like her. Companies over employees. Bankers over professors. He was the problem. So was she. So were her friends. Margherita did all the work while they sat around and argued about injustice. She rose to join Margherita, who was wiping her hands on her apron and smiling at the clean kitchen.

Margherita gestured to the dirty windows muddling the scene outside. Freezing fog swept over the valley. Two days ago, the bread man forecast snow while delivering his weekly bounty in his flour-dusted coat.

"I clean windows tomorrow," Margherita said.

Emily shook her head. "Let me do it."

Margherita nodded and pointed to the simmering goulash. Emily was happy to keep an eye on the pot. Margherita stuffed her apron in her bag and headed down the stairs.

"Where's Clare?" Holly asked.

"Rats in her room," Matt said. "She's in town getting traps."

"We heard them gnawing on her pack all night," said Larry.

Holly looked surprised. "Steele's doing a Blake seminar in Clare's room, where there are rats?"

Larry twiddled his pencil. "Rats attract guys like him." He rose, spun his chair around, and left the room. He returned with the entire carton of books and chose a copy of *A Portrait of the Artist as a Young Man*. Matt, Ryan, and Emily walked away with Herbert's *Dune*, Brautigan's *In Watermelon Sugar*, and Krishnamurti's *Freedom from the Known*, respectively.

A door slammed. Heavy footsteps down the hall and into the main room. Laughter.

The Blake seminar had ended.

"Everyone's getting fat," Steele announced as he walked to the stove.

"Or fucking skinny," said Otto, the big guy who followed Steele everywhere.

"What you put next to things is important," Emily whispered to Matt, who was now sitting beside her at the table. "You can't tell which people are transparent until someone opaque enters the room." She thought she was saying something profound.

Matt shrugged.

Steele checked the pot. "Not quite ready."

"I'll wait," said Otto.

19

Nationwide labor strikes had frozen the postal service, closed the local museums, and caused uprisings all over town. Emily hadn't heard from Danny for almost two months, and she wondered if he'd received any of her letters. Ryan was also waiting for word from home, specifically, a present and an envelope with an American Express check inside. Holly was expecting money from her parents as well.

Ryan's twentieth birthday celebration would be a welcome escape from the anxiety.

Emily, Ryan, Holly, Clare, and Matt climbed into the gangster-black Topolino Larry had purchased a few weeks ago. Larry drove. Elbows to shoulders, hips to laps, they held their breaths as the Fiat puttered up and down several hilltops before reaching Parco delle Stranezze, an amusement park near a nondescript town. A rare place not on strike.

Emily dug into her pack for her Super 8 movie camera. She filmed Ryan modeling the Italian felt fedora Giovanni had given him for his birthday. Then she focused on Larry offering a jug of La Contessa's wine to a llama. Its velvety nose twitched when he uncorked the bottle, but as soon as the llama touched the lip of the glass, it recoiled. Larry laughed. Emily spun around and refocused her camera to catch Holly waving from a windmill balcony. She panned down and filmed Matt snapping his Kodak at a yellow backhoe with "Perugia" stenciled on the side. The group of friends walked through a pseudo-African village where a Coke machine leaned against a thatched hut. Clare inserted a coin, pulled out a bottle, popped the cap with the machine's opener, and took a long sip for the camera. Beyond the village was a park where bumper cars careened around an oval track. A tan-suited man and his toddler gave Emily's camera a backhanded wave as they flew by in a canopied dodgem. Two cute guys in navy blue sweaters did the same, swerving their miniature cart until it ricocheted off the tire barricades.

At Fort Apache—or as the locals pronounced it, "Fort Ah-pah-*shay*"—Clare mounted a cannon and pretended to shoot Spider. Spider surrendered with her arms in the air. Then Clare gave Emily a sorry look before leaning down and burying her head in her hands.

A woman with beehive hair and a sophisticated pink suit distracted Emily. She filmed the wealthy-looking lady wrestling her five-year-old out the fort gate. The mother's hostile hold on her child's arm and her biting look at the lens convinced Emily to press the off button and lower the Super 8.

"Emi-lee!" It was Paolo, Larry's new friend from Fontana, calling from the parking lot. He was with his buddy Umberto. "We're off to my place to get albums for tonight. Come, I take you there. Not far."

Ryan, Holly, and Clare squeezed into the back of Umberto's Alfa Romeo. Larry and Spider settled into Mickey Mouse, as Paolo called the Topolino. Paolo motioned for Emily to hop on the back of his orange Lambretta.

She clung to his waist and hugged the gas tank with her knees as he leaned into the narrow dirt roads. They passed thick-ankled crones plucking yellow-green drupes from olive branches and tossing the fruit over their shoulders into baskets on their backs. Emily persuaded him to stop the bike. She picked a red poppy from a green wheat field. A sudden wind snatched it from her fingers when they rounded the corner and headed toward an olive grove surrounding his family farmhouse.

Paolo supported his motor scooter against the stucco. She followed his lanky hips up a set of cement steps. Inside, jars of golden oil waited on the kitchen sill. A saw rested by the fireplace. On the hearth sat an antique wine barrel containing several pieces of split wood.

Emily peered out the window at the freshly cut stump out front. The tree next to it had taken the shape of a woman. Breasts here. Thighs and hips there. Gnarled elbows rose away from her twisting trunk. Skeletal fingers combed her leafy crown. She seemed distraught. Her sibling must have spent a lifetime driving roots deep into the rich soil only to become a stack of firewood in the end.

While Paolo searched for LPs in another room, Emily heard voices in the distance. Below, a group of oxen drivers were pumping their fists in the air, shouting at the Alfa and Topolino skidding into the driveway.

Laughter entered the kitchen with Holly, Ryan, Umberto, and Clare. Larry and Spider followed.

Umberto swept back his hair and poured a stream of oil into a cup. He broke a corner from a loaf of bread on the table and saturated it. "It was funny at the time," he said while chewing. "But none of us dropped out of school, Ryan. The police evicted us only after we occupied the university."

"But you said you took it back." Holly sat down, dipped a hunk of crust into the oil, and gave Umberto a sultry look, as if she thought occupying a university was sexy.

"It was dangerous, Holly." Umberto's smile suggested both pride and pity. "Thousands of us against hundreds of them. Brutal. But they had batons. Tear gas. Guns. We tried very hard, but we did not take back the university."

Holly sighed and took another bite from her dripping bread.

"Now all students are labeled extremists," Larry said. "Even

I'm considered a revolutionary because I joined them last weekend to protest through-the-roof tuition fees and lousy teachers who don't bother to show up to class."

"Like Steele?" said Ryan.

Larry chuckled.

Umberto leaned over Holly to tear another hunk from the loaf. "Everyone is on strike. Even my dad. He's a doctor at the medical center." He nodded as he sat, scooting his chair next to hers. "Hospitals, bars, hotels, shops. Everything is closed."

Ryan placed his hands on Holly's shoulders, as if to claim her. Emily wished she had her sketchbook to catch the drama.

"It's working, too," Umberto continued. "After the postal service went on strike, we started getting better wages and a forty-hour week for laborers across the country—"

"—except the people who are right now cleaning up after us at Parco delle Stranezze. Of course, you think about them, no?" Paulo had emerged from the other room, his arms loaded with music that was sure to last all night. "Berto. No more politics. Let us have fun." He handed the albums to Umberto.

The postal strike was all Emily could think about as she rode behind Paolo on the back of his Lambretta. The price of revolution: keeping loved ones from communicating with each other. She hugged Paolo's waist and tightened her legs against the bike.

They returned to the Big Farmhouse at four in the afternoon. Emily's pocket mirror revealed millions of freckles covering her sunburned face. Instead of running to the frog lake to soothe her fiery skin with mud, she joined Clare to face the snap of brittle necks. Two more chickens for Ryan's birthday dinner.

The gory task almost felt normal now. She and Clare wrenched feathered roots from slippery carcasses and cooked the poor souls, one by one, in the tiny oven. They scrubbed the graffiti-carved table, lit broken candles, and set an odd assortment of forks and knives for Ryan's party.

Paolo, Umberto, La Contessa, Giovanni, the village doctor, a neighborly marquis, several lords and ladies, and countless townspeople ushered the cold night into the room. Defying Emily's impressions of restrained aristocrats, many of them drank too much wine, ripped flesh from the chicken bones, and wiped fat from their lips. La Contessa appeared curious as she fingered Larry's hair. The marquis teased about spying on the students' nefarious deeds from his nearby castle tower. And Steele—he belched, rubbed his belly, lifted his guitar, and played discordant tunes.

Emily retreated to the bench in the fireplace and nursed her sunburned thoughts with a glass of Chianti. She opened her sketchbook and wondered if it was morning where Danny was. She drew the sun rising over an imperfect horizon and forced herself to render the scenes she'd witnessed in last night's dream. Peasants. Foot soldiers. Medics. Innocents. Not-so-innocents. Cannon fodder, all of them, splattered across two opposing pages as terrified faces watched from behind the clouds. In a flash, she realized she'd just drawn Danny among them, face down in a pool of blood.

"You missed a good seminar the other day." William Steele settled beside her. "Did you know Blake was an artist like you?"

Emily jumped. She slammed shut her sketchbook and shifted to the other side of the bench.

Steele chuckled. "You have a vivid imagination." He picked up his guitar, plucked a few chords, and nodded at her book. "What else are you working on?"

"Nothing."

"All artists say that. The real question is whether you want your art to be seen." His smile revealed a softness she hadn't witnessed before. "Letting people see your work might make them feel good. Ever think of that? But that would make you a Pollyanna, wouldn't it? Not a real artist. Real artists reveal the truth, no matter how hard it is to bear. Like you're doing with that sketch." He strummed the open strings, then abruptly palmed them. "If you want to get the truth out, Miss Emily, you might benefit from learning from a visionary like Blake."

"I don't really—"

"He was way ahead of his time. *A visionary revolutionary.* I like the ring of that. It'd make a great mantra." He fingerpicked a few more chords. "Seriously," he said while still playing. "Being a good artist isn't everything. Getting your work seen is most important." He nodded at her book again.

"My art is none of your business."

She shouldn't have said that. Still, her work spoke a language only she could understand. It was a deeply personal practice. She needed it to push toward verity. To cope with realities beyond her control. She'd never share it with a person she didn't trust.

"What good is art if you hide it away?" Steele stopped to tune a string. "Art is fiction, you know. But people get more truth from it than anything in the history books. They can see things they've never noticed before."

Exactly. Emily placed her palm over the doodles on the cover of her sketchbook.

"Have you ever thought of your life as a work of art?"

She considered this for a moment. "Maybe."

"Then it's fiction." He leaned into the guitar as he adjusted another string. "Hear this? It's the wavering sound of Miss Emily-Who-Does-Not-Know-Her-Life-Is-Art." He played the fifth fret on the fourth string along with the open third, adjusting until they sounded identical. "Now, this is Miss Emily-Who-Becomes-the-Hero-of-Her-Own-Story."

"Heroine."

"Want some?" His laugh was oddly kind. "No, you don't. Heroin isn't the answer for you." Tucking his guitar under his arm, he closed his hands around an invisible ball. "You've got to shape your life like a clump of clay. That's the lesson you missed. Don't depend on anyone, even that boyfriend of yours. Do whatever you want, whenever you want. Be the protagonist of your own story. Illustrate it. Paint it. Write it. I don't care. Just make a lot of noise, even if you lie, cheat, or jump off a cliff to get yourself seen. Create endless quantities of repetitive thoughtless crap and get the ego boost of making your life interesting. That's all you have to do. Emily, it's the only way you'll come out of your shell."

"What are you talking about?"

"You."

"You're telling me to lie and cheat to get what I want?"

"Everything's a lie. That's the truth. Something you must come to terms with if you want to get ahead in this world." Steele strummed the open strings again, knocked twice on the side of his guitar, and stood. "Think about it and find a way to become the powerful woman I know you are. Then get back to me."

Emily got up before he took a step. She nudged him aside and descended the steps. Sketchbook in hand, she settled in a hollowed-out haystack outside.

She forced herself to reflect on Steele's words. Strength and power through art. No. Art with a capital *A*. He was right. He just had a bizarre way of showing he was on her side.

But cheating? Was that on her side?

"Nothing Is Easy." Jethro Tull said it all. Emily mimicked Ian Anderson's finger positions as the breathy sound of his flute blared through the windows of the Big Farmhouse.

"You in there?" Clare ducked through the haystack's opening and collapsed next to her. She handed Emily a bag. "Morning glory seeds. Mellow, easy high. Something to keep your mind off—you know—Danny. They're not poisoned here, like the ones in the States."

"Like our minds," Emily said. She wasn't joking.

Clare stuffed a handful of tiny black seeds into her mouth. "You're supposed to chew them until they liquefy." She garbled the words as her teeth worked the wad. Her cheeks bulged. "Then swallow in one gulp."

Emily hesitated for a moment. Then she reached into the bag. The gelatinous seeds congealed in her mouth.

She and Clare held their stomachs and resisted the temptation to hurl clear across the vineyards. Emily crossed her watery eyes and rolled them back. They clutched each other's shoulders and choked it down.

Hallucinations came slowly. Moonlight into starlight. A meteor flew past Venus. Another through Lyra. Clare took Emily's finger and pointed to remote galaxies.

"Swirling psychedelic flower heads," she giggled.

From the farmhouse, Donovan's voice was now ringing out. Faded colors from his ballad about Guinevere wove through Emily's brain. She envisioned a tapestry featuring Danny—first as a jester, then as Lancelot—standing before a large easel. He was painting himself surrounded by a congress of ravens while trapped inside a bottomless well. In the sky above him, fireflies sprinkled the darkness with light. Then she swore she heard Donovan sing these words: *Art will save him. Art with a capital* A.

20

Above the clang of dishes, Emily heard the mail lady's car choking up the potholed road to the castle. She stopped washing silverware, dried her hands, and ran up the hill. Her bare toes were frozen by the time she reached the well in the courtyard.

She found Holly and Ryan thanking the bespectacled woman for a small group of letters. Several *grazie*s and *prego*s later, the mail lady climbed into her vehicle and rumbled down the hill.

"Strike's still on, but the postal lady found these for us at the countess's request." Ryan shuffled through the envelopes. "Let's see, one for Spider. One for Larry. One for Matt, and"—he bowed to Emily—"for you, my dear."

Emily snatched at the letter. Ryan moved it away.

"Stop it, Ryan. Come on. Please."

He winked at Holly. "How long should I keep it from her?"

"That might be long enough."

Emily could see her name beside Ryan's thumb, scrawled in Danny's cursive. She squealed and danced when he finally handed it to her.

Clutching the letter to her heart, she watched the pair skip down the hill, holding hands and balancing with their free arms to keep from stumbling. When she could no longer see them, she searched for a secluded spot to read. She finally settled on a large rock overlooking the frog lake.

She ripped the airmail envelope and opened the folded page. A black-and-white photograph fell from tissue-thin paper. She lifted it from the ground.

Long hair, guitar at his feet, dimples in his cheeks and chin as he smiled. One of her favorite pictures. Sometime after Thanksgiving, TJ had taken it at the Chateau Liberté, the rock and roll bar in the Santa Cruz Mountains where Wave used to play. Surrounded by redwoods on that outdoor stage, Danny looked like a holy man.

She pulled out another photo. Polaroid. Taken at night. Was this Danny? Wearing fatigues? Floppy khaki—was it a hat? With a kind of rod sticking out of his head?

A radio antenna, Danny wrote in ballpoint on the back of the picture. *Trying on my buddy's equipment.*

Emily checked the postmark. Unreadable. No date on the page either. It was already April, and this was only his second letter. She still carried the first, from boot camp way back then, folded in her jeans pocket. Were there others buried in the local postal building?

She studied the picture again. Rifle slung over Danny's shoulder. She couldn't see his hair—but here was his face and his unmistakable eyes: scary now. Dark. Flat. Expressionless. Illuminated by the camera's flash. She could make out a river behind him. He was holding a tiny light in his hand.

> *There are thousands of them where we are. This one landed right in my palm. My buddy happened to be snapping pictures, so here I am, living proof of the existence of fireflies. You won't believe how they light up entire trees like it's Christmas.*

Emily couldn't believe it. Instead of tanks and exploding bombs, Danny sent her fireflies. Not only that, he went on about plants, of all things.

Staghorns! Enormous. There are all kinds of species here, hanging like monkeys in the trees. And orchids. I couldn't help it, Emmie. I stashed one in my pack. Not sure what I'm going to do with it, but I'm saving it next to your picture. You know, to remind me of beauty in this world. And it is beautiful here. Spectacular waterfalls, rapids. And orchids. Did I mention that? Can you feel me nudging you? More kinds than you can imagine. Cymbidium, cattleya, even dendrobium. Grandfather learned all the Latin names, and he'd go crazy if he could see the real plants growing wild like this. If you open the small envelope I made, you'll find a neatly pressed Paphiopedilum. A lady's slipper. For you. I'm keeping the rest of the plant next to my heart.

A flattened rice paper sleeve had stuck to the side of the outer envelope. She used the tips of her fingers to open it. Fragments of a flower fell onto her jeans. She gathered as many pieces as possible, returned them to their container, and continued reading.

I won't tell you about the leeches and bamboo vipers. Don't want to give you nightmares. We've set up what we call hooches. Huts to most locals, but ours are canvas sheets held up by sticks. It's getting dark, so I can't write much longer. I just want to tell you how much I love you. I dream about you every night. Did I tell you I love you? I love you.

Emily kissed the page. She turned it over, hoping for more. Lifting the photos from her lap, she held them side by side. The first revealed a beautiful young man. The other, a changeling—kidnapped and taken to another world.

Before, when Emily felt a wave of emotion surging like this, Danny would cradle her until her shaking would stop. He'd sing. Whatever it took to calm her. Now, she had only herself to do the soothing. She squeezed her arms across her chest, clutched her sleeves, and rocked until it came: the storm, dark and cold, streaming down her cheeks. She cupped her eyes after moving

Danny's photos out of the way so her tears wouldn't ruin them. Her lungs shuddered. The tempest rose from that moonless place that carried all her fears.

Danny's voice: *Inhale to your toes. Yes. Okay. One more breath.*

She waited for her pulse to calm. Then she pulled a wrinkled blue postal note from her pack and clicked a pen.

Dearest Danny,

Below me is Vittorio's Little Farmhouse. On the ridgeline, the marquis's tower juts from mountainside trees. To my left, Gubbio. No fireflies here—not that I know of, anyway. But there's one in my heart. You. Always you. And a lady's slipper and an owl feather to remind me. Thank God you're okay.

She chewed the pen's metal clip and glanced at the confusion vehicles down the hill.

I'm living in the castle again. Way too crazy at the Big Farmhouse. I managed to co-opt an empty room next to Steele's and the first-floor bathroom. It's only a cot, a table, and a wooden cupboard where I can hang my coat. But it's a luxury. All the rooms in the Big Farmhouse have been taken. I've become someone with no claim to a place to sleep, so I was bunking on one of the benches inside the fireplace. It's true. They actually have benches inside gigantic fireplaces. We all have ashy gray jean-butts from sitting on them. I usually wind up sketching all night and getting up to nap by the frog lake at dawn. Last week, Clare and I spent three days plucking chickens, cooking, and cleaning for the whole gang. Once I grated an entire pound of Parmesan and half my thumb. Then I helped Clare and Margherita, our cook, make three dozen wine cookies. We ended up baking five loaves of bread, tossing three huge salads, plucking two more chickens, washing, drying, and putting away a kitchen full of dishes—all within four hours. I'd have done more after Margherita left if

Larry hadn't given me a jug of La Contessa's Chianti to slow me down.

What was she saying? Danny was discovering magic in the jungle despite the war, and she was complaining about being domestic. He was so careful about what he shared. Shouldn't she at least try to do the same? She crumpled the page and pulled out another.

So far, I've only gone to the town doctor to act as—get this—translator for the group. The girl with long legs, the one we call Spider. Remember her? She can't walk. The guys take turns carrying her. The doctor says she has arthritis. Too much pasta. Clogs everything. But I think it's gout. She laughs about it. Good sport. She'll be back on her feet in no time with all the pain pills he's given her. Clare has a bladder infection. Not enough water. Too much wine. "Drinky, drinky, drinky," says Doc. Everyone else has crabs.

And Holly—you know, the pretty one? She got busted for shoplifting because she needed toothpaste and shampoo and hadn't received the money her parents had sent. She blames the mail strike, and so do I. Anyway, she asked me to translate at her hearing. Picture an entire row of Italian judges wearing robes and powdered wigs. Surreal. I'm not that good at Italian, so Ryan volunteered to join us and act as moral support. He suggested Holly wear her shortest skirt and cry a lot—and it worked! She got off free and clear.

Then Clare told the Bread Man we were going on strike because his unsalted bread got stale before we could eat it. He told all the townspeople that Americans don't like bread. Before we knew it, all the wives in the area came over to scold us. They were worried we'd get sick because we didn't eat bread. Clare, of course, set them straight. "We're not sick! We're on strike!" Thanks to Clare, we're making our own bread now—and adding loads of salt.

Emily couldn't believe she'd written all that. Why was she telling gossipy stories about her friends and the townspeople without their permission? And how could Danny forget Spider and Holly? They were his friends too. She covered the entire page with a dark drawing of the marquis's hillside.

Out of nowhere, Margherita appeared, bringing boots for Emily's naked feet. She draped a shawl over her shoulders and gestured to the darkening sky. Emily handed her Danny's pictures. Margherita grabbed her heart, nodded, and waved her gnarly hands toward the heavens. She cradled Emily's face and kissed her forehead before giving back the photos and hobbling down the hill.

Emily tore up her letter. On another postal note, she thanked Danny for telling her about orchids and ferns and for sending the lady's slipper. Then she thanked him for the pictures. She tucked them into her undershirt and described the Umbrian landscape, the olive trees supporting grapevines, the nightingales, and the frogs in the frog-shaped lake. *Thank God you're okay,* she added. Then, in capital letters, she embellished the three words she longed for him to hear.

That night, with the Steeles and their cohorts away, Emily slept alone in a closet-size room next to theirs. She hung her jacket in the small wardrobe and placed Danny's owl feather on the table beside her. She shook out her sleeping bag and watched it settle on the thin mattress.

Clare had shown her how to create cockroach traps. "Fill these rusty tins with olive oil. See? Like this." She'd lifted the cot and lowered each leg into its can. "That way, the buggers'll smother and drown instead of climbing into your sleeping bag."

Emily stripped to her underwear and crawled inside her bag. When she was afraid of the dark, Danny used to tickle her until she'd curl like a sow bug and laugh. Then he'd carry her to bed, make tender love to her, and whisper, "Sweet dreams, Little Bird."

She pressed a fragment of Danny's lady's slipper against her skin. He was right about the magic. A sea of fireflies filled the space behind her eyes. Danny stepped into the night. On a mountaintop overlooking pools of water—stars above him, stars reflected below—flickering insects linked sky to earth, earth to sky. For a moment, he looked like a tiny planet whirling.

Then her dream changed. Fire-red sky. Sunrise? Sunset. The edge of darkness. A crowd of moaning people forcing Emily into a field. They slogged through a meadow of sucking sludge. Danny shoved her away from the swampy mire toward an opening in a mountain. A cave. A grandfather clock guarded the entryway. Danny stomped ooze from his boots and sank to the ground at the base of the clock. Emily collapsed next to him. Danny rose and followed a glowing figure down a hallway. A second diaphanous being came for Emily. It led her down a light-filled corridor into an unseen room. Emily sat on an invisible examination table. The being tapped her feet. Everything below her ankles vanished. It tapped her knees. Everything below them dissolved. Then her shoulders and neck. As soon as the being touched her head, Emily evaporated into light. Mirrors of her former self floated everywhere, and she became a universe of holograms.

One of the holograms reflected details of the car accident she was in when she was a girl. Navigating switchbacks in the Buick, her mother had swerved to avoid a shadow. The car fishtailed, crashed into a guardrail, and dangled over a cliff before the guardrail caught the bumper and threw the moving vehicle back onto the road. The Buick kept going with forty feet of metal buckling through the interior.

Emily remembered the light. The being touching her head. She dissolved into a million stars, and her visions took hold.

Did you review your life? It was Danny's voice.

Snippets. Frames in a movie. A black-and-white movie.

But you didn't die.

No, not then.

You're a visionary, Emmie. You know that, don't you? As I said before, you're One Who Slides on the Wind.

I don't know what that means.

You're dreaming now, aren't you?
I guess so.
And I'm here with you. And I'm talking with you. And you can hear me?
I'm happy about that.
That means you have the power to help me.
I do?
I need you to do something for me, Emmie. Please.
I'll do anything, Danny. You know that.
Emmie, dream me alive.

21

Rattled about Danny's terrifying request, Emily sequestered herself in the tiny castle room. She hadn't had one of her normal déjà vu seizures in a long time. Only these strange dreams.

When the Steeles returned, she wandered back to the farmhouse and discovered a room recently abandoned by trekking students. She rendered a "Do Not Disturb" sign and closed the door behind her. In her sketchbook, she drew angels to rescue Danny. She scribbled images of his face across several pages. She wrote to him. Asked stupid questions. Crumpled her fears and threw them across the room. She asked for specific dreams. Dreams of Danny alive, happy, living at home with her in the States. They didn't come.

A week later, Clare burst into the room with a rescue bottle of La Contessa's Chianti.

"Come with me, Em." She was out of breath. "Steele's having a midnight seminar about ghosts. It's going to be good, and I need you with me. You like ghosts, so let's go." She turned Emily around and prodded her out the door.

"No," said Emily as she stumbled down the steps.

"Darn it, Em. Be a soldier for a change. I dare you. You can't stay in that room forever."

Emily's glare should have convinced Clare to go on her own, but Clare didn't take the bait. Instead, she seized Emily's arm.

"I can't believe I have to force you to have fun."

They climbed up the hill, surrounded by full-moon shadows. An eagle owl soared overhead. Emily imagined him hunting for scorpions. She stopped to brush Clare's hand from her arm. "This doesn't feel right."

"Nothing feels right to you." Clare sat on the ground next to the well and gestured to a spot beside her.

Emily obliged. She leaned on her hands, crossed her ankles, and adjusted her weight. A flash of gray caught her eye. She thought she saw La Contessa's light machine resting on the far side of the courtyard.

"There it is!"

"What?"

Emily pointed, but the wagon wasn't there. She squeezed her eyes.

"What is it?"

"Nothing."

Clare shook her head.

Steele and his friends threw open the castle doors.

Emily bolted upright.

"Chill out, Em. They're only stories." Clare opened the bottle of Chianti and passed it to Steele.

He took a long sip, handed the bottle to Otto, and launched a particularly good tale about shrouded phantoms tormenting the streets of San Francisco. His buddies laughed and volleyed anecdotes. They'd heard this story before.

Emily sat across from Steele. The castle tower loomed behind him. Emily heard a muted cry coming from its highest window. She slipped down the throat of the sound.

Giovanni said a murder had taken place in that tower. Under the strap of an ancient count, the workers' sweat polished those rocks. Peasant blood buried in mortar held the walls together. Fractured bones sealed the cracks. A cardinal had been killed in that room. For a special relic to bless the castle's chapel. His knucklebone would do.

No. For the ring on his knucklebone.

What really happened that night (it had to have been night) when the murderer sliced the cardinal's finger through the bone and pocketed the ring? Ruby, gigantic, set in gold. Maybe the murderer approached him in the shadows? Was there a candle? There was surely a scuffle—or was the cardinal asleep? When the murderer realized what he'd done, he might have turned without looking, tripped over the table, and accidentally knocked the burning candle to the stone-cold floor. Did the servants hear? Did they tell?

What became of the servants?

It was Danny's voice. He seemed to be speaking from the other side of night.

They changed into owls.

Emily scanned the sky for the owl she'd just seen. A few days ago, she'd sketched a group of them releasing their smocks, donning feathers, and flying from their graves to alert her of their presence. They winged against the arched window in her old castle room. They kept her turning in her cot. They gathered in the hallway and whispered their stories. Eagle owls guarded the Etruscan corridors below the well. Passageways opened by their kin, the servants who joined the ghost soldiers still battling beneath the ground to preserve the vineyards.

She glanced at the place where she thought she'd seen the wagon with the gray box, half expecting a parliament of owls to have gathered around it.

Darkness overwhelmed the area.

Danny's voice again: *What became of the owl-people, the ones who fought?*

Emily's response was immediate.

Their descendants keep their memories safe in their hearts.

She respected these descendants. They cooked for her and her friends. They wired the Big Farmhouse with electric light. They plumbed the cistern to flush the toilets. They carried the wringer washer up a thousand steps to the landing so a bunch of American loadies could clean their clothes. They scrubbed the floors and struggled to catch Frisbees. Descendants, Margherita especially, who sat on the stairs and helped Emily mend her broken Italian.

"Whores!"

The decibel level startled Emily back to the seminar.

Steele was reading aloud from a draft of his latest novel. The words sounded like dialogue, but nothing made sense. Syllables collided, bumping from one side of her brain to the other. He seemed to be reading several stories at once, mixing scenes at whim. Emily heard him say their names: *Holly*, then *Spider*, then *Clare*. Certainly not the Holly she knew, nor the Spider. Not the same Clare sitting next to her, in this lurid scene. Mantled men haunting the castle hallways. Stalking them. Abducting them. Handcuffing them. Sodomi—

"Stop!" Emily went cold. A dark shape entered her, shivered up her spine, and chilled the thoughts in her head. Adrenaline pumped. Her fingers twitched. The fist in her gut said, *Run!*

Steele didn't stop. Instead, he read her own name. In his hands and out of his mouth. Her name. In his seedy book.

"Emily," he read, eyeing her. "The fragile one. The one her perfect boyfriend can't protect. She wants him to cradle her tits, kiss those dark nipples, open her legs—"

"You bastard!" Emily yanked herself out of her frozen fear. "Bastards, all of you!"

"Oh yeah, sister!" Otto grinned. "You love it, don't you? Makes you wet, doesn't it?"

She grabbed Clare's arm and dragged her out the gate. She stumbled over shadows, blinded by images of her father, his hands large and terrifying, holding her down as he pushed into her, ripping away her dignity, her sanity, her soul.

Outrun those thoughts!
Otto's yipping laugh followed her.

"Pathetic assholes," said Clare after they slammed the door of the Big Farmhouse.

Emily collapsed onto the bench in the fireplace, clutched her chest, and gasped for air.

"I'm sorry," said Clare, putting her arm around her.

Emily shoved her away.

"I get it, Em. They're filthy pigs. But you can't run like that. Every woman on this planet deals with jerks like Steele. You have to show them who's boss. Even if we hadn't gone up there tonight, they'd have found another way to get at you because you're so oversensitive and such easy prey."

"I don't need this right now."

"It's true, Emily. I love you to bits, but shit. You have friends right in front of you who are trying like hell to support you, even when we know you're expecting us to pick up all the pieces after you fall apart."

"Look, I'm trying to process all this, okay?"

"What do you want, then? For us to abandon you so Steele and his friends can carve you like a piece of meat?"

"Cut it, Clare," Emily hissed through her teeth. "I'm not helpless."

"What are you, then?"

Emily kicked herself upright and stormed to the table. "Have you ever stopped to think about what men like this *do*? Salivating through peepholes. Fantasizing about rape. There, I said it. It's all about power, don't you get it? They think they're special. Avant-garde artists, of all hilarious things. They pretend they're helping us learn something important. Then they do stuff like this and pat themselves on the back for making us wilt and fall apart. They think they're teaching us how to be strong. Bullshit. I told you it was a bad idea to go up there. But you thought they were just telling stories. Don't you see? We're their pawns. Token pieces. It makes my skin crawl." She bit her lip. "Fuck it, Clare. I'm sick of all the garbage men keep shoving down our throats."

"Wow."

"Don't wow me. You have no idea what I'm going through right now. How could you?" Emily reached under the table, grabbed her pack, charged downstairs, and sat at the bottom of the steps.

Victim. Her father had branded her, and she had to scrub off the sticky label. So much for being her mother's daughter, conditioned by generations to be sweet, demure, silent.

No more.

After that night, she avoided Clare. When Steele and his gang were at the castle, she slept in the fireplace. When Steele was away, she returned to her tiny castle room, where she found Ryan and Holly co-opting it for their lovemaking. When Larry offered a pipeful to soothe her, she shook her head, plodded down the steps to the heavy door at the bottom, and surrendered to the stars.

Something else, however, lurked in the darkness. She could feel it. Something ancient.

22

"Ready to take that trip to Greece?" Matt faced Emily in the kitchen. "Don't worry about Danny's letters. Clare will forward them to the Athens American Express. We can check every day if you want. No more excuses, okay?"

Emily packed her rucksack in less than ten minutes. All she had to do was remove it from the aluminum frame to lighten her load. She threw in her toothbrush, her sketchbook, several pencils, her movie and still cameras, and a small case carrying other odds and ends. She added a couple of books, hoping to find a moment to open them. What else? She scanned the room and spotted her T-shirt and underwear on a drying rack inside the fireplace. She wadded them into her bag.

She trusted Matt.

They hitchhiked to the Perugia station, took the train to Rome, ate lunch in the Colosseum, took another train to Naples, and spent the night in a hostel before hitchhiking south along the coast. By the middle of the week, they were picnicking near the ankle of Italy's boot.

Paestum. A desolate place. Two ravens played tag in the thermals above the Temple of Hera.

Matt pointed to one of the birds. "Huginn," he said as an orange peel slipped from his hand.

Emily picked it up and handed it back. "Huginn?"

"The raven on the left. He represents thought. Muninn, on the right, is memory."

"Where'd you learn that? From your guidebooks?"

"You don't remember Huginn and Muninn? The two ravens who brought Odin information? You were there." He flicked a burgundy wedge into his mouth. "Norse mythology. Dr. Finn," he said, chewing.

Emily shrugged. "Maybe Muninn forgot about my memory."

Matt smiled and handed her a section of blood orange. It tasted like the sun.

Huginn and Muninn argued above the Temple of Poseidon. Emily sketched the birds between citrus bites.

"How did Greek temples get into Italy? Thought you'd never ask." Matt thumbed through his travel guide. "This ancient city used to be Poseidonia until the Romans conquered it and renamed it Paestum." He closed the book, pulled a pair of black leather gloves from his pack, and stretched the right one over his hand. A wide gap opened in the fabric between his index finger and thumb.

"Here, give that to me," said Emily.

He removed the glove and tossed it to her.

She held it to the light. It looked like a raven's wing.

"I think I can fix this."

"Really? I knew you'd come in handy one day."

She threw it back to him. He flattened it between his palms and spun it like a Frisbee. She caught it midair.

"Here's the deal," she said. "I'll mend this if you find us a nice place to stay tonight."

"Okay." Matt opened his guidebook to the section on lodging. "Looks like there's a hostel nearby. We can walk."

When they arrived, the building appeared empty. They rang the bell on the counter and waited. A balding man shuffled out.

He raised his eyebrows and looked Emily up and down. She shifted away from his bulging stare.

They handed the man their passports and hostel cards. He nodded at Matt and pointed to the left: the boys' wing. Then he walked around the counter and took Emily's elbow. He started to escort her to the right, but Matt stopped him.

"We can find the rooms on our own, thank you."

The man shrugged and walked into a back room, closing the door behind him.

"What's with his bug eyes?" Emily whispered.

"Something to do with his thyroid."

"How do you know?"

"My uncle has the same thing." Matt paused for a second. "Sure you're okay by yourself in there?"

"Are you kidding? This is luxurious. Almost as creepy as Fat Cat Tower."

He cocked his head.

"Honest. I'm fine."

"Okay, then." Matt led her to the entrance of the girls' wing and surveyed the hall. "Holler if you need me. The way this thing's built, I'm sure I'll hear you." He squeezed her shoulder. "See you in the morning."

"Wait. Are we the only ones here?"

"Think so. Why? Want to come with me?"

"It's okay. Thanks, though."

Rows of empty bunks cluttered the first room. Emily chose the one closest to the window. She threw her rucksack on top and pulled up a chair to face the view.

Temple of Hera. She remembered now. Goddess of fertility and the arts. Zeus had turned the maiden Io into a white cow so she could be safe. And Hera had recruited Argus to guard Io. The hundred eyes of Argus. She shuddered. Always a hundred eyes. No wonder she tried to erase the story from her mind.

She took Matt's glove, pulled a needle and thread from her bag, and began to mend the hole. The right glove. Muninn's. She wished she could be like that old raven and use her memory wisely.

When she finished, she found Danny's owl feather and the tiny envelope housing his lady's slipper. She also pulled TJ's bead pendant from her bag and tied it around her neck. The last thing she recalled before falling asleep in the chair was the sunset: reds, oranges, and purples flaring behind the temples.

In a dream, she saw herself sitting on a peak called the Keeping Still Mountaintop. She was flipping a silver dollar with her thumb. Danny was strumming his guitar and singing a song she'd never heard:

Can you call a raven with a silver coin,
rolling it over your knuckles, flashing it up your sleeve?
Can you call a raven?
You play a magician's game for the restless clouds
in a raven's domain. Silent power in your hands.
Magic so strong, it's hard to believe
the cry you hear. Tiny voice in the distant blue.
Can you call a raven?

Danny stopped singing and set down his guitar. He spoke with a whisper so soft it sounded like a zephyr:

You twirl the coin.
It vanishes.
Reappears.
Attracts the sun with its dance.
The voice forms wings.
The cry grows louder.
Giant feathers pump the wind.
Raven eyes catch fire.
Shadow devours.
Beak opens. Talons stretch.
Can you call a raven with a silver coin?

He lifted her chin. Cobalt eyes burned into hers. His lashes brushed her brow. She assumed he was about to kiss her when he raised his voice with an urgency that surprised her.

Don't blame the raven for coming too close!
Toss the burning coin high.
Watch him swerve.
Catch the flash of lightning in his claws!

Danny nudged her hand. The coin rotated in slow motion as it flew upward. The raven cawed, swooped, reached, grasped. An indelible cry rose within her like an ancient song. The raven's eyes linked with hers.

She jolted awake.

Foul breath covered her nose and mouth. Bulky arms tightened around her.

"*Carina,*" he whispered.

Emily wrenched her face away, but the hostel owner used his hand and his hook nose to get her to look at him. All she saw were two protruding eyes.

"*Chi tace acconsente.*" Silence gives consent.

He folded his wet mouth over hers and pinned her to the chair with his legs.

Emily tried to vomit him away. Each time she struggled, he increased his grip and kissed harder. Then she attempted to do what she'd done with her dad: leave her body, feel nothing, greet the morning with all those shadow memories stuffed in a little compartment, tucked away in her bones. No blame. No harm. Nothing happened. New day. Smile.

"Shit! You're hurting me!" She couldn't believe she was able to speak. "Damn it, man. Get off!"

An edge grew in her. On her back, a pair of wings lifted her to an intimidating height. She opened her mouth, now a sharp beak. Her throat released a guttural clicking, then a harsh, grating caw.

She widened her eyes. She stretched her hardened lips away from her tongue and let out an undulating, earsplitting alarm.

She had turned. Her mouth-beak became a black hole with daggers. She struck his balding head, leaving a bloody streak across his skullcap. She struck the vile man again, this time in his right eye, Muninn's eye, so he would remember this moment for a long time.

He fled the room, cupping his face, crying, *"Oddio! Oddio!"*

Emily thrust her jaw in determination as she checked her body for wounds. No longer a feathered beast, she pulled the chair upright and searched for her jacket.

Here.

She buttoned it over her ripped shirt and touched her neck. TJ's pendant was still there. She searched the room for Danny's owl feather and lady's slipper, finding everything intact next to Matt's glove. With the help of her Odin stone, Danny was protecting her. She was sure of it. He was dreaming her alive, not the other way around.

After buckling her boots onto her pack, she tiptoed in stocking feet to the open door and peered out. The last thing she wanted was to find that wretched man waiting for her in the hallway.

Thank goodness the moon was nearly full, so she could see where she was going. Still, she avoided the light, hugging the wall as she crept past the office where the hostel owner had confiscated their IDs. She took care with each step as she inched toward what she prayed was the boy's wing and opened the door to a maze of bunk beds.

"Matt?" she whispered.

Nothing.

Emily followed the moonlight, scanning the room for an occupied bed. When she found her friend, she lowered her pack to the floor, climbed to the top bunk, and shook him.

"Matt, wake up! We have to leave. Now!"

His long moan grew into a series of slurred words. Then he

rolled away. She tried to rouse him again without success. Finally, she backed down the ladder to the lower bunk. The mattress was hard and cold. Just as well. She shuddered beneath her jacket and hugged her rucksack. There was no way they could steal back their passports and bust their way out of a locked hostel.

When the morning sun didn't make her sneeze, she understood the meaning of possibility. Pinks, lavenders, and yellows entered the room, erasing the fog from her head. For the first time, she felt clear inside.

Matt was leaning on the sill of the dorm window, watching her.

"You okay?"

"Let's get out of here." That was all she intended to say.

Matt rang the bell at the front desk. Again. Several times more. He threw his army green jacket over his shoulder and said, "Sound sleeper."

Emily's nod was measured. She was trying to find the words, the right way to tell him about wings, how she'd noticed one of them in his glove, how her own wings and beak helped her defeat the predatory hostel owner. But before she could open her mouth, a buxom matron came through the door behind the counter, arms flying, expletives spilling from her lips. Her husband hunched behind her, his fingers unable to hide a swelling field of red, yellow, black, and blue around his right eye, Muninn's eye. The woman pushed him out in front of her, toward Emily and Matt. He fumbled with a key and unlocked the file holding their passports and hostel cards. After he threw the documents on the counter, he shuffled out the back, his wife screaming at his heels.

Matt glanced at Emily, his eyebrows nearly reaching his hairline. Then he smiled. A knowing smile.

An assortment of feelings surged within her. She didn't need to name them. She pocketed her documents, slung her bag onto her back, and walked away from the ruins.

The first ride they secured was on the open bed of a farmer's truck. They settled with their backs against the cab. She pulled the mended glove from her bag and handed it to Matt. He separated the thumb and index finger to inspect where the hole once was and marveled at her handiwork.

"I didn't know you could sew like this. Thanks, Em." Matt unbuckled his pack, pulled out a hunk of bread, and offered it to her. She was grateful—and starving.

Matt was her quiet ally.

Her mind carried her back in time to a perfect little cottage hidden in a fairy-tale grove in the Santa Cruz Mountains. White siding, green shutters, and "Cassiopeia Oaks" neatly carved on a sign above a handmade door. A woodland bungalow from the pages of Grimm. She and her friends had discovered it on a retreat Dr. Finn suggested they take. He'd wanted them to create a cooperative community—a week in the woods without an adult—fodder for an essay on social systems. Emily loved that about Dr. Finn. His seminar students could do what kids do: write about their experiences and get credit for their discoveries.

Cassiopeia Oaks became their code for freedom. It didn't matter that the cabin was boarded up. They camped in the yard surrounding the tiny house, Emily, Matt, Clare, Ryan, Spider, Larry, and Holly. Plus TJ. Since Danny was sick with the flu, TJ had offered to tag along in his place.

Typical college kids on a sabbatical from their studies, they spent most of the week playing. They skated through autumn leaves and ran down slippery slopes. They caught as much air as possible in a makeshift "ski jumping" contest to see if they could clear a small stream and land on the other side without breaking any bones. Because she was so light, Emily almost won in the Most Spectacular Jump category, but she splashed right onto her tailbone in thigh-deep water. TJ rescued her, carried her to shore, and wrapped her in his jacket.

They'd spent two icy nights in separate sleeping bags. Then they held a vote: zip their bags together or freeze. Everyone chose to stay warm except Emily and Matt. Matt had recently met Vicky

—instant love—but Vicky hadn't been able to join them. Emily agreed with Matt, but TJ didn't want her to sleep alone. She was too small, he said. Someone had to keep her from hypothermia. Emily didn't say yes. She didn't say no either.

Thank god TJ was a gentleman. Cozy cocoon for two nights.

Then Larry surprised everyone with several jugs of wine he'd stashed in his oversize pack.

"Have a s'more." TJ offered the treat he'd just singed over the fire. "Wash it down with this—Red Mountain." He handed her a jug.

Before she knew it, the faces, the fire, the burning marshmallows, the flashing sparks, and the background of shadowed trees—all were spinning around her. TJ? What was it about him? So innocent looking and cute by the snapping fire. She was floating, dancing with fireflies, Danny's fireflies, swirling in a galaxy above the oak grove, the fairy-tale cottage, and the black night. TJ was on top of her, and Emily knew what she didn't want to admit. She'd let him in.

Matt had taken her under his wing a few days later.

She couldn't defend herself. It was the first time she'd ever been drunk, and she'd done this terrible thing. She did it. It was her fault. She was the girl. She should have known better. She was supposed to stand up for herself, to fight, to set boundaries. Why hadn't she shoved him away? Was she just full of wine, or was she afraid? Afraid he wouldn't like her? She wanted everyone to like her. That was her problem, wasn't it?

Matt had sat beside her and listened to her jumbled thoughts.

"I have to tell Danny," she'd said. "I need to be straight with him. He deserves it. I deserve it."

Matt nodded in slow motion, like he was absorbing more than her pathetic words.

To Emily's surprise, Danny dried her eyes and wrapped his arms around her. He didn't say anything. He just held her and rocked her like he always did.

Countless discussions followed. Danny, Emily, and TJ called

them their personal "triangle encounter groups." They talked about friendship, betrayal, victimhood, boundaries. And love. They spoke of possibility, existence, and the wonders of the universe. They discussed music and art. Then they talked about seduction and deceit—and the mating habits of fireflies.

Danny was fluent in firefly. He knew their language. How they danced. How they were driven to survive.

"It's easy to talk to them," he'd said. The three of them sat in a circle on the living room floor of the apartment he shared with TJ. He told TJ how, when he was growing up on the East Coast, his grandfather showed him how many blinks per minute it would take for a flashlight to attract the glowing insects. "Did you know there are hundreds of male fireflies and only about two females in an acre of land? It's intense, man. The competition." He turned to Emily. "There's a code to their blinking. It's the female who starts the dialogue. She's the one who signals first. She communicates with up to ten males in a single evening. She can even keep several conversations going at once." Danny smiled. His eyes were large and clear. His dimples widened. "But she mates with only one. The male she connects with best."

"Em, wake up! We're getting off here."

Emily was still thinking about Danny's words when she and Matt entered a strange, isolated town. He opened his map and pointed to a region called Puglia, southeast Italy, outside a hamlet called Alberobello.

It felt like they'd been dropped off on another planet. All the buildings looked like upside-down funnels—conical drystone huts. Something Lilliputians or Munchkins might have lived in. After questioning a few fellow travelers, they found out the buildings were called *trulli*. Each *trullo* was made of hundreds of small squared-off stones with no cement or mortar of any kind. A tourist from Germany said that in the 1700s, people were taxed according to the size of their homes. The villagers designed these odd dwellings so they could dismantle them at a moment's notice before the inspectors came around.

Emily imagined the ancient people of Alberobello singing their land into existence while rebuilding their homes. The same way Australia's first people created their birth lands through songs to entice the ground to come alive and support each step they took. The ancient ones gave her hope. She wanted to dream a place into being where she could walk with Danny after the war. Few people gave credence to such unlikely stories because no one seemed to fall off the edge of the earth. Perhaps this was because, somewhere in the world, the wise ones were constantly singing and dreaming the world into existence.

Matt shook her shoulder. "Let's go. We have to get to Brindisi before the last ferry leaves."

They thrust out their thumbs for what seemed like hours. Finally, a family in a white pickup answered their prayers. Then they got caught in traffic. More stop than go. The father climbed from the cab, pulled a massive tarp from the cargo bed next to where she and Matt were perched, and whispered a string of Italian phrases punctuated by a finger to his lips. He threw the canvas over them and tied it to the sides. Emily and Matt sank to the bottom of the bed. The engine started. The truck jerked forward. Stopped. Moved again. It did this a few more times before coming to an abrupt halt.

Angry voices. *Chk-chk* of cocking rifles. The driver's matter-of-fact reply. A shuffling. The taut tarp above Emily's body gave only slightly beneath a pair of hands pressing on it here and there. She and Matt lay prone on the bed's floor and didn't dare move. Emily willed herself to stay focused. She wanted to be present in case she needed to block a bullet or dodge one. She must have been trembling because Matt's foot pressed against hers ever so slightly. The ringing in her ears intensified. The blackness of that hole threatened to swallow her.

Suddenly the truck lurched forward. Nervous clutch work

stuttered them away from the checkpoint. Soon they were on the open road.

Emily dozed as they made their way toward the sea. When they eventually reached their destination, the father removed the tarp, clasped his hands in prayer, thanked the heavens, and bowed. He helped them find their footing on solid ground. His gestures seemed to imply that, to the military, all college-age kids were dangerous revolutionaries. Umberto and Larry had warned them.

Before long, she and Matt were boarding the ferry at Brindisi. They climbed onto the top deck of different ferry at the port of Piraeus.

Their destination: Crete. The land of bull jumpers and monsters. The place where ancient stories helped people make sense of their fears.

.

23

It was already May. Emily and Matt had traveled to Crete and back. No Minotaur. No labyrinth or mythological kings jumping off cliffs in despair.

They'd spent over a week sleeping in a mountaintop cave on the hippie-occupied beach of Matala. While Matt settled on a boulder overlooking the sea, absorbed in the pages of *Dune*, Emily ate cucumbers and watched the locals gawk at scantily clad flower children dancing in the surf.

She and Matt had attended an impromptu wedding and joined turban-headed hippies baptizing themselves in an open well at the mountain's base. Emily lounged on the beach with Matalan mothers and grandmothers who hid red Easter eggs in the sand and coaxed their children to find them. Several generations of families shared blood oranges with her and smiled as she savored the refreshing juice.

Day after day, the sun supported Emily's sense of freedom. The moon engulfed her in the realm of dreams. She walked along the Milky Way until she found Danny, face down again in the mud. She turned him over and cleaned his mouth and eyes. He smiled. She helped him stand. Together they made it to twilight, only to be ambushed by morning. It was a recurring dream, and

Emily would wake with a start. She'd crawl onto the lip of the cave and beg the dawning sky to show her how to dream Danny alive. Then she'd sit on the beach and empty her mind of thoughts.

Sunburned and somewhat renewed, Emily and Matt were now standing in line at the Athens Red Cross building. They'd already been to American Express. No letters waited for them.

"Holy crap," Matt said as he wrestled with the *International Herald Tribune*. "Look at this."

"Open Combat on American Campus," the headline read. Four students. Murdered in cold blood by the National Guard in Ohio. Four kids just like them. Kids who happened to be hanging around, gawking at fellow students protesting America's invasion of Cambodia. Kids shot down because they had the gall to walk along an exposed road at Kent State University. As if they were the enemy. They weren't even carrying signs.

"Damn Kissinger," Matt whispered under his breath.

Emily snatched the newspaper and folded it in thirds. She turned him around, unbuckled his pack, and stuffed it into the main compartment. If this had happened at San Jose State, Matt could have been Jeffrey Miller or William Schroeder. She could have been Allison Krause or Sandra Scheuer.

Did their friends call out their names? *Allie? Sandy? Jeff? Bill?*

It seemed like only yesterday that James Rector had been gunned down by police at People's Park in Berkeley. His name was forever etched in her memory. Then Giuseppe Pinelli, the railway worker murdered by Milan police. Now, four American kids. Emily whispered their names, but all she could think of was blood.

She wanted to donate hers to the Red Cross to honor those kids. She wanted to give blood for Danny. She wanted to offer it to all the grunts and jungle dwellers targeting each other on the other side of the world. She wanted to sacrifice her cells so every living creature could continue their journey on this planet.

Matt wanted to give blood because they needed ferry money.

They stood in line to be weighed. Nearly all the kids inside the

Athens Red Cross building were travelers—backpackers, long-hairs, American soldiers on leave, and students of various nationalities. One after another got the nod, the signed papers, the hand pointing to waiting-room chairs. But when Emily stepped on the scale, the Red Cross nurse frowned. She slid the top and bottom weights over notch after notch. The nurse shook her head, scratched a number across the line on the form, and handed the document to Emily. She said something in Greek and looked past Emily's eyes into those of the person behind her. No nod. No gesture telling Emily where to go.

Matt pulled Emily out of line. He took the paper from her hand and scanned the page. "Looks like they don't want your blood."

"Why?"

"Let's see. According to this, you weigh thirty-six point eight kilograms."

"Which means—?"

He squinted as he calculated, then sighed. "Em, you need to eat more. You weigh only eighty-one pounds."

Emily sank into a nearby chair and studied the reception room. White plaster walls. Black-and-white checkerboard floor. In her mind, the entire place dissolved into a conglomeration of rusting metal file cabinets separating medical histories from the truth that pumped through her heart.

Wasn't this what she'd always wanted? To disappear?

Matt followed a white-capped nurse down a hallway into another room. Emily imagined it containing a bed, a large needle, and a bag filled with his offering.

Her tears flowed from a well beneath her ribs. They traveled up her spine, surged through her chest, choked her throat, and escaped her stinging eyes. She wanted to drain all the cells from her body and give them back to the gods.

There was no way she could help Danny now. Or the college kids face down in pools of blood. Or the guys struggling to survive in a maze of vines and crosshairs, where orchids grew like

Mating Habits of Fireflies

weeds, fireflies shimmered like constellations, and the jagged jaws of the earth threatened to devour anyone who bushwhacked into a trap.

Doodlebugs.

Danny used to get down on his knees to inspect the ant lions' snares. Scribbly trails surrounded the pits the insects would build. He'd point to the carefully constructed earth funnel.

"This is where the lacewing larvae wait, at the root of a slippery slope. Soon, an unsuspecting ant will stumble in."

Emily was that ant, teetering on the edge and slipping away. Did *One Who Slides on the Wind* really mean *One Who Passes into Oblivion*?

Emily thought of Stavros Melissinos, the famous cobbler who'd made sandals for the Beatles. Earlier that day, she and Matt had located his shop near the Monastiraki Square flea market, across from the Acropolis. She'd been walking barefoot since her right boot had lost its sole on the Matala beach. She'd left it and its mate with a hippie chick who said she could make the proper repairs with embroidery thread.

The cobbler was as modest as his shop and had a poet's voice. He held Emily's feet, one and then the other, measuring them with his fingers. When he released them, she pulled a crocheted pouch from her pack, spilled a pile of coins into her left hand, and offered them to him. He shook his head and closed Emily's palm over her tiny fortune. He moved her hands toward her heart, nodded, and then passed from sight behind a beaded curtain. In a few minutes, he returned with a simple pair of lace-up leather sandals. He pointed to a picture of Sophia Loren on the wall. The legendary Stavros Melissinos tied his creations onto Emily's feet.

"For you," he said, smiling and turning her toward the door. "Walk into the sun, young lady. Remember, Sophia Loren walks with you."

Emily swung her feet as she waited for Matt at the Red Cross. The chessboard tiles became harlequin jesters dancing beneath her new sandals. She wiggled her toes.

Sophia Loren. Strong. Beautiful.

Ever since she was young, Emily had willed herself to hide her hips and breasts, to stop the flow of blood. Disappearing would keep wicked men from noticing her. Oddly enough, it seemed to lure them even more. She saw herself falling apart in Danny's portrait. If he'd painted Sophia Loren's likeness, the result would have been bold. Intimate details would have magnified her strength. Why was Emily so afraid of this?

It felt like a century since the day she couldn't tear herself away from the *Sacrifice of Isaac* in the Uffizi Gallery. The angel's finger pointing to the ram. The quiet *No, not me!* look in the sheep's eye. The care Caravaggio took to render Isaac's face, the panic it revealed. Emily wanted to be like that boy, breathing his way to courage.

Matt coughed, money in hand. They walked from the Red Cross building, across the square, and down several blocks to the sea. They grabbed the first ferry to Italy and, from there, caught a series of trains. Sunlight streamed through the train window as they inched their way toward Umbria. Emily let herself sway with the car as it tapped through fields of green wheat and bloodred poppies, Sophia Loren sandals on her feet.

24

Emily and Matt stood outside the Perugia train station and stuck out their thumbs. To their surprise, Larry, Umberto, and Paolo picked them up.

"Great timing, you two," Larry said. "We just dropped off Ryan and Holly. They're being initiated into Transcendental Meditation by the Maharishi himself. In India."

Matt half-jokingly asked why in the world they would do such a thing. Emily dismissed the conversation and leaned most of her body out the Topolino's passenger window to take in the view, her movie camera rolling. Larry skidded the Fiat into the driveway in front of the Big Farmhouse. From the back seat, Matt grabbed Emily's legs so she wouldn't fall out.

"You're home!" Clare yelled from the steps. More words danced with her as she feather-stepped to the car door and into the frame of Emily's camera. "Good news! Danny's alive!"

Emily nearly dropped the Super 8.

After Clare untangled her from the car, she circled her with hugs. Then she seized Matt by the shoulders and shook him hard. "What took you so long? We missed you guys." She rocked him back and forth. Soon, a confusion of friends followed them into the farmhouse, where new faces greeted them. Emily, anxious to hear more about Danny, tugged at Clare's sleeve to no avail.

"This is Nicolas, and this is Irene. And here is little Penny," Clare said, lifting a wriggling child in her arms. "She's only three."

"Penny belongs to us," said Nicolas, a Lincoln-like man with large eyes. He gestured to Irene, who seemed to be brooding from behind the table. She sucked on a cigarette.

"They're living here." Clare nodded as if she were getting used to the idea. She released little Penny and gave Emily her *I'll tell you about it later* look.

"What about now?" Emily insisted.

Clare slipped her elbow around Emily's. "Let's go outside," she said.

"Yes," Clare affirmed when they reached the landing. "Danny's okay. He sent some letters."

"How many?" Emily clutched her friend's forearm. "Do you have them?"

"No. Steele has them."

"Steele? Why in the—"

"It's like he was waiting for them—"

"What?"

"Em, he has something against you, I swear. As soon as the mail lady came, Steele took them."

"Why would Steele take Danny's letters?"

"I have no idea, Em. We couldn't do anything about it. We tried, but you know how Steele is."

"*You know how Steele is*? That's all you can say? You tried? For God's sake, Clare. I have to get those letters. Now!"

"You can't, Em. He doesn't have them anymore."

"You just said he did."

"Damn it, Emily, I don't know how else to tell you. He cut them up for his collages. He even bragged about it."

It was a dead-on strike. A dizzying, all-consuming sensation devoured her, and she spiraled through a multitude of dimensions to answer its call. Emily's core rose out of her torso and hovered over the clouds covering the earth.

Nicolas's voice, deep and loud, echoed from below. "What's wrong with her?"

The sensations before a seizure were always the same: the amber aura, the prescience, and the overlapping dimensions of time. Usually, she was gone only for a minute or so, but eternities separated her from everyone else's clock.

Danny came into view, surrounded by light. Mud covered his boots. He groaned, holding his bleeding flesh. As he fell, other men came out of the shadows. Black shapes surrounded him. A blinding light from above cascaded overhead. A man yelled, and his shoulder hit Emily's hand. Her index finger scratched across the scene and landed on an adjacent groove, revealing a small girl hiding beneath a kitchen table. A scrubbing sensation traveled through her fingertips and up her arm, igniting all her nerve endings. Her great-grandmother's washboard. Her great-grandmother hummed while working the clothes. A brown-and-white dog hid under the table with the girl. The dog morphed into a boy, his moonlike eyes filled with horror. Hands outstretched, he planted his palms next to hers on the rear windshield of a car careening off a cliff. He was shrieking, as clear as her own voice was shrieking.

It wasn't the night that troubled her. It was what tore at the edges of morning. Emily thought of the sun, how it would soon move through Clare's room. She laced her fingers together and pulled them apart. In the back of her mind was a painting, a pulsing membrane of color and line. Web. Rock. Lichen. A tree rooting down.

Sunlight filtered through the window. Emily pinched her nose against her sneeze and imagined a woman whose future was in her breath, in the veins of her eyes as she closed them, in the dark places within her cells where all her worlds met. She imagined a man. His fate was shadowy, yet he embodied the sun.

Opening to a blank page in her sketchbook, Emily drew soft whisperings to shape the woman's hair and strong angles to construct the man's nose. A swift stroke curved around slender hips. She listened to the textures and tasted the light scratching through her pencil. She pressed darkness into the folds beneath the woman's breasts and moved her hands forward.

Emily noticed how the twilight in the man's eyes contrasted with the intensity of his chin. Squinting to consider the space between the two forms, she sensed warmth. Still, she feared if she wasn't careful, a cool distance might grow between them.

She thought about the English language and how it had only one or two words for *love*. The Greeks had at least three words, maybe four. Her grampa had told her that ancient Persians had more than eighty.

Art didn't need words. Neither did love.

Using a second pencil in her hand, she connected the figures with a crimson line. Easy. The way breath followed breath. Red joining two hearts. She searched her backpack for the crayon that created her grandfather's sun. She pressed yellow into the page, haloing her drawing with energy. Heat to bring the couple together.

Pinching away another sneeze as the sun grew brighter, she noticed she was still wearing her jeans and T-shirt. Clare and Matt must have placed her on Clare's cot. They were kind to have brought her pack and belongings. She recalled Matt telling someone to leave the room and Clare whispering, "Danny's alive. That's what matters. Danny's alive."

Emily tore her drawing from her sketchbook, folded it in thirds, and slipped it into an envelope from her backpack.

Danny, we've been together before. We've known each other for lifetimes.

She scribbled his name on the envelope and addressed it to his commander in Vietnam.

25

"Hey, you!" Spider met Emily outside Clare's room. "Missed you, kid. Good to see you back."

Emily dropped her bag so they could hug.

Spider pulled her away and held her at arm's length. "I heard about what happened. Did you know Clare slept on the floor next to you all night?"

Emily shook her head.

"She and Matt are up at the castle trying to get Danny's letters from Steele." Spider released Emily and spread her arms wide. "Soooo, since you need a place to stay, you can stay with me up at the Little Farmhouse. I'm there alone, can you believe it? So many people have split this scene. You can have your own space. And I can keep you company if you need it. We won't have any madness there."

Emily remembered the layout of Vittorio's Little Farmhouse. It seemed like a century ago when everyone climbed the exterior stairway, piled into the main room, and choked down Freya's odd-tasting soup.

"Oh, and I have to tell you about Matt—you'll never guess what happened to him last night. There was this party here."

Spider led Emily into the kitchen and pointed to a mash of dried spaghetti on the table with wine spilled everywhere. "Everyone was singing and dancing. I'm amazed the table survived their weight. Matt was so disgusted that he left. It turns out he slept outside, and Giovanni nearly shot his head off with a rifle. He thought our dear Matt was a thief or something."

"You're kidding."

"Time to go!"

Spider snatched Emily's pack, took her hand, and marched her down the steps. They were halfway to the Little Farmhouse when they noticed Matt and Clare tromping toward them from the castle.

"What a candy-ass wuss!" Clare waved her hands as if trying to shake leeches from them. "Steele split again, with Freya and Otto, of course. The bastards."

Matt shushed her. "No sign of the collages," he said to Emily.

"What happened to you last night, Mr. Cat Burglar?" Emily asked.

"Me? Nothing. I was just keeping an eye open for the mail lady."

For a second, Emily was confused. Then she realized Matt was evading her question.

Spider led everyone to the Little Farmhouse and unlatched the door. Dead cockroaches littered the floor. She ignored the crunch as she strode, long-legged, across the entrance.

"My room's over here." She pointed to the right. "Ryan and Holly were staying in this other room before they went to India. It's all yours now." She opened the door to the left.

All the basics were inside: a cot, a weathered bureau, a table, a shuttered window with used candles on the sill. Emily's empty pack frame rested against the wall.

Clare opened the hinged panels to air out the room. Spider lowered Emily's bag to the cot. Emily picked it up and placed it on the floor to prevent hitchhiking critters from invading her new sleeping space.

"The view's not bad." With her finger, Clare lifted one corner of her mouth into a clownish grin. Then, in a deliberate movement, she pulled up the other corner to make Emily laugh.

Emily rolled her eyes.

"Okay, then. Let's get to the castle before the mail lady beats us to it," Clare said, leading everyone out the door and down the steps. On the way out, Emily fished a flashlight and jacket from her pack.

A skin-and-bones dog greeted them at the bottom of the stairs.

"Etrusco!" Clare circled the hound with hugs. "We found him wandering around the Big Farmhouse, so we took him in. We've been feeding him nonstop for about two weeks now. Look how fat he is!"

"Fat? You've got to be kidding." Matt opened his arms to the pup's kisses.

"Clare also rescued a rabbit she named Peter," Spider said. "And you know what happened to him?"

"Shut up," said Clare.

"What happened?" Matt was still receiving kisses.

Clare's eyes welled up for a second before she composed herself.

"The guys renamed him Dinner," said Spider.

Matt curled his lip. "I don't want to hear any more."

Etrusco followed them up the hill to the gate, his bobbed tail spinning with each step. He stopped to twist his body and lick his privates before jump-stepping back in line with everyone. He was the first to enter the courtyard, gathering scents everywhere.

They spent most of the afternoon sprawled around the well. Matt picked dried grapes from a climbing vine. "Raisins," he said.

"So, what'd you two do in Greece?" Clare asked.

"Slept in caves," said Emily.

"A mountainside hippie hotel," said Matt. "Quite the scene."

Emily nodded. "Matala. On the coast of Crete."

"You went to Crete?" Spider looked surprised.

Matt rolled up his sleeve. "That's how we got so tan."

"And all hell broke loose here," said Clare.

"Because we got tan?" asked Matt.

"She's talking about the bonfire—"

"Spider, I'm not talking about the bonfire—"

"What a night that was. Larry poured gasoline on a pile of olive branches. They flared like a mother. Lucky we didn't burn the place down. It got so hot the guys took off their shirts. So did the girls. Then everyone was dancing naked around the fire—"

"Enough!" said Clare. "I'm talking about us nearly getting arrested. Don't you remember?"

Matt raised his eyebrows. "Because you were naked?"

"No," said Clare. "Because we've been living here illegally. We thought the immigration cops would bust us all."

"Oh, that," said Spider.

Clare nodded. "Yeah, that."

"But that wasn't the bonfire night. It was a few weeks ago. And they didn't bust us. They tore up the paperwork—"

"—because Steele and Otto insisted on smoking a couple of rounds with them, and they got so high they forgot what they were here for."

Spider leaned into Matt. "Then there's the thing Larry said."

"What thing?"

"Steele blackmailed the countess to get cheap rent here. Maybe he blackmailed the cops, too. That's why they didn't arrest us."

"Blackmail? Why?"

"Someone must have balled someone they weren't supposed to," said Spider.

"Oh, brother." Matt wrinkled his nose. "This sounds like a soap opera."

"Remember when Steele said his ex-girlfriend used to date the count?" said Clare.

Spider plucked a raisin from the vine and made a toasting gesture before dropping it onto her tongue. "Giovanni's cute enough to make Steele good and jealous," she said, chewing. "Maybe that's why our dear professor has it in for Danny. Have you seen Freya's painting of Danny as a centaur? Pretty racy if you ask me."

This perked Emily's attention.

She recalled Steele singling out Danny at the Carnival House after Danny showed interest in Freya's work. Of course, Freya would bask in his compliments—perhaps too much. Back then Emily had thought it was amusing, but not anymore.

The conversation continued. They rambled on about the pros and cons of Holly and Ryan going to India. They discussed the weather and the benefits of rescuing strays. They shook their heads at the sorry number of books they'd read while abroad.

Hours passed. The mail lady never showed.

Emily stayed behind long after her friends had returned to the Big Farmhouse. It was nearly dark, and she zipped her jacket against the sudden cold.

An eagle owl sounded an alarm. Emily listened. The owl called again. Moonlight illuminated the outer castle doors.

Closing them behind her, she clicked her flashlight, walked down the hall, and entered Steele's unlocked room.

Papers littered the unmade bed. A confusion of shirts and jeans looked like they'd been purposely drop-kicked across the tile floor. Scissors and an open can of rubber cement sat on a nightstand.

Emily stepped over the mess, made her way to the bedside table, twisted the sticky brush back into the can, and cast a line of light over the rest of the room.

There were no collages or centaur paintings on the wall, and nothing leaning against the furniture. On top of a small desk, however, sat a column of standard postcards.

She sidestepped towers of books as she moved across the

room. While shuffling through the cards, she looked carefully at the torn pieces of paper glued to both sides. Steele had scrawled cryptic poems over pasted fragments of airmail letters. Freya's Faunas obliterated nearly all traces of original handwriting. Emily examined the postcards again, hoping to decipher even a few of Danny's words.

She sighed and stacked the cards back on the desk. When she looked up, she noticed a collection of large cardboard signs in the corner. On closer inspection, she saw that they were covered with scraps of envelopes revealing her friends' names. Ryan. Holly. Spider. She riffled through the placards. Unlike with the illegible postcard collages, she could read a few words here and there, but nothing made sense.

She tidied the mess she'd made, returned to the desk, and stuffed a couple of postcards into her back pocket, making sure nothing else had been disturbed. She was about to leave when she spotted a canvas bag beneath the desk.

Clenching the flashlight between her teeth, she knelt on the floor and rooted inside the bag. She pushed aside makeup containers and empty candy wrappers until she located a large envelope containing a bundle of letters and a framed photograph. She gasped after she turned the picture around.

It was of Danny in Freya's room at the Carnival House. Did he know she'd taken this picture while he was admiring one of her paintings?

Shaking, Emily placed the photo on the floor and shuffled through the opened letters. She found birthday cards and notes from parents to various students, each referencing enclosed American Express checks. She searched for the checks. None. Anywhere.

"What are you doing?"

She dropped the letters.

Bootsteps on terra-cotta tiles. A weighted stride, approaching from behind.

"I thought better of you," he said, removing the flashlight from her mouth and shining its light onto the mail scattered across the floor. He lifted the framed photo.
Recognizing his voice, Emily clutched her chest.
"Oh, my God," she said. "I'm so glad it's you."

26

It had been a long night of negotiations. Giovanni urged Emily not to tell anyone about the stolen letters and missing checks. He wanted them both to work behind the scenes.

    The following morning, she sat before her travel mirror and released her hair, pin by pin. Thick sections streamed past the waist of her cotton dress. She took a pair of scissors and snipped. Dark mounds fell to the floor.

    She imagined Danny resting on the bed in her old room, watching her unfasten the front of this same dress from the first button to the last. His gaze gave her confidence. He raised his eyebrows as she slipped pin-tucked cotton down her hips and gently stepped out, folds of fabric pooling to the floor. She pretended not to notice when he lowered his book. Instead, she went about the business of her slip, catching the hem like a net and pulling it over the swells of her breasts, allowing her hair to gather static and cling to her face. She'd long abandoned abusive bras and pantyhose. She dropped her shoes and sat at her drawing table, the length of her back teasing him. She let her legs move freely. Her toes savored the cool wood beneath torn braids in the rug. Her mother's silver brush flashed in the lamp's glow as she unsnarled her hair a hundred times. Pulling a porcelain jar from her canvas bag, she twisted its lid, took the satin puff, lifted her right breast, and powdered beads of sweat there. All the while, Danny waited on the bed. His smile, those dimples, the way his eyes slightly widened. She knew as the scent of lavender reached him, he would stir. He'd stretch his toes and uncross his legs. His belt would click as he unclasped it. His salty lips. His warm hands moving her—

"Emily?"

She jumped.

"Emily? Are you in there?" A woman's voice.

She put down the scissors and opened the door only far enough to see who was there.

The girl was about Emily's size, maybe a bit taller, with wavy hair to her shoulders. She hesitated, then rallied with a slight smile.

"I'm Irene. Is it okay if I talk to you?"

"Sure. Come in."

Emily vaguely remembered her.

Irene scrutinized the room before sitting on the edge of the cot. Her face was softer than her voice. Hazel eyes, narrow chin.

"Cutting your hair?"

Embarrassed, Emily gathered her uneven ends behind her neck.

"Here, let me help you."

Irene stood and rested her hands on the back of the chair. After Emily sat, Irene pushed the chair forward to face the propped-up pocket mirror. She placed one hand on Emily's crown and took the comb in the other. Her touch was gentle.

"How short do you want it? To here?" She held her palms face up near Emily's shoulders.

"Maybe a little shorter."

"To your ears?"

"Maybe halfway down my neck."

Irene began by trimming sections Emily had already cut. She knew what she was doing.

"Cut hair for a living?"

"Oh, no." She laughed. "I just practice on my family."

"That's right—you're Nicolas's wife."

"Yeah, if you can believe it. He'd rather I didn't cut his hair. He likes it long and scraggly. My three-year-old, Penny? She just squirms. This will be a lot easier."

Emily smiled. Irene was not at all the wraithlike woman she thought she'd seen when she returned from Greece.

"Why are you here? I mean, what brought you to this place?"

Irene sighed. "We were living in this commune in Perugia for a while. They wanted us to share everything—clothes, money, even Penny, our daughter. It was too much, so we left."

"Wow." Emily audibly exhaled.

"Forgive me for saying, but it's weirder here. Everyone in town is talking about this place and how strange it is. A bunch of American hippies living in a castle—"

"We don't exactly live in the castle."

"I know."

Emily nodded.

They were both silent while Irene continued to work. Finally, she set the scissors on the table and ran her fingers through Emily's hair.

"What do you think?"

"Oh, I like it." Emily resisted the urge to rough it up a bit.

Irene beat her to it. "The windblown look." She laughed.

Emily turned this way and that before her reflection while Irene gathered chunks of hair and tossed them into a paper bag in the corner. She wiped her hands on her jeans.

"Emily." She backed to the edge of the cot. "I have something to tell you."

Emily didn't like the gravity of her voice. She hesitated before turning around and studying Irene's expression.

Irene creased her brows as she sat. She sucked in her cheeks as if she were hunting for words. After a moment, she relaxed. "I'm just going to say it." She reached into a large pocket on the side of her coat, pulled out a worn envelope, and stared at it for a moment before holding it out. "I have one of your letters."

Emily wanted to scream. It took a lot of effort to keep from snatching it from Irene's fingers.

"Nick and I were up at the castle when your teacher was in the middle of this art project. Nick gets along fine with Will, but I get a strange hit off him." Irene pressed the letter into Emily's hands. "Anyway, I saw this on the floor and slipped it into my pocket when no one was paying attention." Irene paused and twisted an earring with her free hand.

Emily traced Danny's backhand on the envelope. Her pulse raced. She stood.

Irene met her halfway.

They hugged each other for several seconds, then separated to wipe their eyes and noses.

"I wanted to give it to you as soon as I heard your name, but everyone surrounded you the day you got back from vacation, and then you were so upset, and then you fainted. And then I forgot about the letter until I put on this coat and found it in the pocket."

Emily fingered the seal. She sat on the cot, relieved no one had opened it. "Does anyone else know about this?"

Irene shook her head.

"Thanks."

"I'm glad you can finally read it."

Irene had a nice smile.

"I don't trust Steele," Emily said.

"Me neither."

Emily tightened her grip on the letter.

Irene rose. "I'll try to get to the mail lady before he does, and I'll keep an eye out for anything that belongs to you." She paused before opening the door. "I'll leave you with Danny," she whispered before leaving.

The envelope was postmarked on April 27, 1970, only a few weeks ago, from Binh Tay, Republic of Vietnam.

After all this, Emily dreaded spoiling her image of Danny playing with fireflies and orchids. Even the leeches and vipers didn't worry her. Danny could cope with the natural world. It was the human world that scared her.

She took her scissors, slipped one of its blades beneath the airmail flap, sliced the fragile seal, and pulled out a folded page.

Dear Emmie,

It's hot today. As if that's unusual. At last, I have a chance to catch my breath and write. We've been humping our way through the boonies so much that I don't know which way is up anymore. Everything has changed. Now we're at a fire support base where we can rest for a bit. I've never been so exhausted. I don't know how long we'll be here, maybe three or four days if we're lucky. Most patrols last twelve to fifteen days in the jungle, looking for enemy activity. Hopefully, not the enemy himself. We've already been through enough of that horror to last a lifetime.

Finally got a chance to have a beer. You can't imagine how good that felt. When we can get our hands on one, we spin the can on a block of ice to get it cold. Also got a shower. My buddies and I set up a tripod with a canvas bucket, a showerhead, and a wooden pallet to stand on to keep out the mud. No privacy, but hey. Haven't had that for a long time. My feet have taken a real beating, though. Find I'm hobbling a bit. This break will do me good.

But that's not why I'm writing. I want to let you know I still love you and dream about you. Write to me, Emmie. Please. I need to know you're okay. I hope you'll still love me, no matter what happens, what I've done, or what I'm about to do. I don't know who I am anymore.

Thank god for my buddies. They're the reason I can write to

you now. Every day, I send all my love to you—and more. So much more.
Yours forever, Danny.
PS. Write, okay?

"Emily? Are you in there? It's me, Spider."

"Shit." Emily surveyed the room for a place to hide the letter. *Here, under the pillow.*

Spider exploded through the door and gasped. "Your hair! What have you done?"

Emily had already forgotten about cutting her hair. She ran her fingers through it.

"Cute. It makes you look twelve."

"It'll be cooler for summer," she said as Spider turned her around so she could inspect the back.

Then Spider plopped on the cot. "I can't wait for summer. Been a little chilly lately. You know, a bunch of us are going to the open market on a food run. It'll be fun. Wanna come?"

"Not really."

"C'mon, Em. I insist. You gotta get out of this room, I swear." Spider grabbed the jacket from a pile of clothes at the foot of the bed and placed it over Emily's shoulders. "Where's your bag? Oh, here." She handed it to Emily.

"Spider—"

"Everyone's waiting outside."

Spider coaxed her out the door, down the outside stairs, and into the Topolino with Clare and Matt. After a million comments about Emily's haircut, they headed toward Perugia.

The daily market took place within a large building accented by several arched entryways. In the plaza across the road stood a statue of Emanuele II, the first king after the unification of Italy in the 1800s. A bronze mermaid bathed in a fountain on the other side of the same plaza. Emily and her friends lingered in the square, watching pigeons bob around the fountain as carp swam away from their shadows.

Emily retrieved the Super 8 from her rucksack and filmed two small girls chasing each other around the base of Emanuele II. As soon as the children noticed they were in a movie, they stopped to adjust their sweaters and skirts and ran to their mother for biscuits. Emily lowered the camera and waved. The girls shied away, peeking at her from behind their mother's skirt.

"Em! Get a shot of this." Matt gestured to a line of students carrying torches and marching toward the plaza. Emily turned the camera and focused first on the demonstrators, then on the crowd following them. Several people were chanting along with the students and pumping their fists in the air. A tank covered in fascist banners growled toward them. Most of the protesters moved out of the way. A few spit and kicked at the armored vehicle.

"Communist headquarters." Clare pointed to a structure on the right. Then she pointed to the tank. "Fascists. And there?" She opened her arms to the university crowd. "Socialists."

More students crowded around, crushing against Emily and almost taking Clare along as they advanced behind the torch-bearers.

Matt pulled hard on Emily's sleeve. "Let's go."

She threw her camera into her bag, grabbed Clare's arm, and yelled to Spider, who joined them. They threaded through the masses, taking pains to avoid the Polizia di Stato on the way to the marketplace. Turning back, Emily noticed a wild-haired guy chanting along with the crowd.

Larry. He was repeating every inflammatory word Umberto yelled into a megaphone. Steele and Otto pitched in, and Freya, too. All five brandished the collaged signs Emily had discovered in Steele's room. Headlining each were the words "Ode to Anarchy!" And across the backs: "Ode to Insanity!"

Matt pushed the girls into the safety of the indoor marketplace, where vendors were already packing up. Emily and her friends sidestepped a man balancing dozens of empty fruit boxes over his head. He smiled at them while teetering around the booths, indifferent about the demonstration outside.

Spider led the way to their favorite farmer, who grew the best *arance* and *cetrioli* in the region. He knew what they wanted and even posed for Emily's camera. She filmed him pulling burlap from his cache, weighing his oranges and cucumbers on a hanging scale, placing them in a crate, and adding a couple of free heads of lettuce—all while smiling into the lens.

Emily exhaled with relief when she finally climbed into the backseat of the Topolino. "What was that all about?" she asked her friends.

"Best to stay out of foreign politics," said Matt, more serious than ever behind the wheel. He steered into the mountains and followed a maze of familiar hilltop roads.

"Did you see Larry? Steele was there, too, with his little cabal, of course. But Larry? What happened to him? Is he part of Umberto's revolution now?"

"As I said, best to stay out of it, Em." Matt's face looked grim in the rearview mirror.

Clare seemed concerned when they dropped off Emily near the Little Farmhouse. "Sure you don't want to have dinner with us?"

"Not tonight."

Clare rummaged through the small crate in her lap and leaned over the passenger seat. "Here's an orange, then. You need to eat something, I swear."

Emily climbed from the back, orange in hand.

"See you in a bit," said Spider.

"Night," said Matt. His eyes gave Emily the hug she needed.

She didn't realize how dark it was until she lifted the door latch and searched for the nonexistent light switch. Night bugs ruptured beneath her feet. She winced and pulled her flashlight from the outside pocket of her rucksack.

The beam cleared a path to her room, and the armored insects fled. She shook out her bedding to ward off the creepiness and jumped when Danny's letter fell to the ground. She picked it up.

After igniting anti-cockroach candles around the room and making sure the cot's legs were immersed in the cans of oil, she settled onto the mattress with Danny's voice in her hands.

Dear Emmie.

She was eager for his words to silence the protestors' chants and the groan of tanks haunting her brain. Ignoring the shadows around her, she tried to bring Danny closer by imagining the jungle's heat. She felt his exhaustion, disappointment, and resolve. She closed her eyes.

Horror to last a lifetime.

She understood panic. And terror. Even dread. But she couldn't grasp horror. Or maybe she could? Was she insulating herself to come to terms with the unthinkable?

She shook away the darkness and pictured the familiar relief of beer and the deliverance of a shower.

She returned to the letter and reread the last part. She wasn't worried about how much he said he loved her. It was his phrasing that surprised her. His words suggested he hadn't received any of her mail. She narrowed her eyes and gazed at flickering candles. Was the postal strike still active? Or had Steele taken her letters too?

She squirmed in her sleep.

118 degrees.

Danny was speaking loudly in her dream. He nodded at a blanket of flies clinging to lamb carcasses hanging in makeshift gallows alongside an abandoned road.

They'd been traveling on a bus through the Moroccan desert. It seemed only oranges could save them from the heat.

Blood oranges, Danny confirmed.

They carried the fruit in fragile bags crocheted with frayed threads of purple, gold, and green. One orange escaped and bounced down the metal aisle toward the bus driver's foot. All ten passengers gasped as the driver released the wheel. Reaching to the floorboards, he caught the blazing orb in his right hand. A pitcher receiving a ground ball. He tossed it over his shoulder to the boy seated behind him. That orange traveled through ten sets of fingers before finally coming home to Emily.

She and Danny peeled their dinner in a Marrakech hotel. Citrus stained their fingertips. They found a thousand ways to take the orange apart, to chew each section so slowly, so completely, only sweet juice could slip down their throats. The full moon scattered shapes across the wall, turning their hands into date trees and bleating lambs. Danny spread his fingers wide. Images spiraled from his palms: blood oranges exploding on the bus; juice splattering across the dusty floor.

Emily tried to calm him, insisting there had been no explosion. She led him to a ballpark, handed him a bat, lifted her camera, and filmed him tapping the bat on the plate before cracking an orange sun over a barbed fence.

You've hit it out of the park, Danny. Only one more base to round, and you'll be safe. I'll make sure.

27

Several weeks had passed. Emily and Giovanni had accomplished what was necessary. Now, all they had to do was wait.

Meanwhile, springtime awakened with electric energy. Was it possible to dream Danny alive and the landscape as well?

"*Bravissimo!*" she whispered to the newborn vineyard grapes. She welcomed the bees, thanked the olive trees, and praised the opening flowers. After searching the countryside for the slightest hint of Gubbio on a distant hill, she murmured "*Tanti auguri*" to honor the residents there. More importantly, she called out "Best wishes" to the wind as a way to keep Danny safe and to celebrate her love for him.

There were days when she leaned against her favorite olive tree to watch her friends gather in front of the Big Farmhouse. They'd aptly named their dope-smoking, sun-worshipping gossip sessions "Euphoria Seminars." Irene and Penny played hide-and-seek around them.

It seemed a century ago when Irene had taken Penny to town to post Emily's letters to Danny, along with a package addressed to the dean of San Jose State College. In it, Emily had placed detailed notes about what had transpired under Steele's watch.

She'd added receipts, sketches, journal entries, photos, movie reels, and her footage of Steele and his friends waving their protest placards above the shouting activists in town. Giovanni had enclosed a handwritten cover letter detailing in English what he and Emily had unearthed in Steele's room that night. He'd used his Polaroid camera to document the evidence. From all appearances, Steele and his friends had no idea anyone had breached their quarters.

Emily joined Clare, Matt, and Spider at the Big Farmhouse table. Playing pick-up sticks with dried spaghetti was now their favorite form of entertainment.

Larry entered, out of breath, a mailing tube from the States tucked under his arm. Etrusco sniffed at the package. Larry shooed the hound, cleared a space on the table, and unrolled a Fillmore poster of a concert that had taken place back in April. It featured Jethro Tull and Fairport Convention with lights by Little Princess. David Singer, a Fillmore West poster maker, had added a miniature man to the corner of the image. The man was shrinking away from a larger-than-life woman placing a garland of flowers on her head. A Victorian woodcut formed the foundation of the collage.

"Cool poster," Clare said while calming Etrusco.

"A little too women's lib for my taste," Matt teased.

Clare jabbed him.

Larry shook his head. "You guys are missing the point."

Matt shrugged. "Yeah, we missed the gig, if that's what you mean."

The few remaining Scholastics students gathered, along with several hitchhikers the townspeople had sent their way.

"Is this it?" someone asked.

"Yeah," said Larry. "Check out all the hits!"

Clare leaned closer. "Hits?"

"You can't see them in this light. Let's take it over here."

Emily stood back as the others followed Larry to a window beside the stove. He rotated the poster toward the light in just the right way to reveal what appeared to be hundreds of transparent dots hidden within the illustration.

Spider pointed out a faint grid dividing the individual hits of LSD. "Where'd you get this?" she asked Larry.

"A couple of Angels in the Haight."

Matt sighed. "I thought you knew better than to deal with those guys again."

"None other than William Steele made the connection." Larry traced the address on the mailing tube. "He said to bring it down here. It's the purest stuff you can get, man. He thought you guys would be happy. Are we happy?"

"I thought you didn't like Steele," said Emily, echoing Matt's words.

Larry ignored her comment and rolled the poster into the tube. "Not today. We have to choose the right time."

The following week, Nicolas drafted everyone's astrological charts to see if they could drop acid as a group without any hassles. Emily accepted his offer to work on her horoscope even though she had no desire to take psychedelics, regardless of any celestial predictions—and definitely not if Larry and Steele were involved.

"I'll try it if you do," said Clare.

Spider chimed in. "Me too."

"Em," said Matt. "I'll look after you and make sure everyone else is cool. I've had this stuff before. It can be life changing in a good way."

Irene also volunteered to help. She wanted to be straight so she could mind Penny.

"Good," said Clare. "Take care of Etrusco too? Please?"

Matt and Irene promised to nanny Etrusco like he was their child.

"Guess we're going on a trip then. Em?" Clare poked Emily's shoulder.

"In bocca al lupo," Emily sighed on the morning of the big day. Into the mouth of the wolf.

Pin down the wolf. Danny's voice whispered in her head.

She climbed the stairs into the mouth of the Big Farmhouse. Larry greeted her at the landing with a torn-off square about half an inch wide. "Put it on your tongue and let it dissolve."

She wrinkled her nose. "Since when did you become a radical? Did Umberto influence you?"

"It's your choice, Em. I'm not forcing anything on you."

"That's not what I asked."

"I just took mine," said Spider, elbowing Emily toward the newly completed farmhouse washroom. "It's our day for showers. Let's do this before the stuff comes on."

Emily studied Larry's face. "I'm not sure I trust you if you're hanging around with Steele."

"We were picketing for the workers, Em. Of all people, you should understand that. We did it for Margherita. For Vittorio and Perlita. And for all the local students who are just like us." He took her hand, placed the LSD on her lifeline, and closed her fist around it. "This will open your mind."

Emily followed Spider to the communal shower area. Spider occupied one stall, and Emily took the other. The warm water felt good, and it helped her relax. Then she heard Spider shriek.

"Whoa, baby!" Spider slammed the wooden shower door. "Shit, that was fast!"

Emily shut off the water. She heard her friend struggling to dress.

"Need help?"

"Solid ground. Around here, someplace. Stuff's already kicking in. Sorry. Out the door."

Emily dripped across the room to a towel. Spider was gone. She scrutinized her image in the mirror before searching for the hit in her T-shirt pocket.

Crepi il lupo. Pin down the wolf.

She took a deep breath and placed the acid on her tongue.

She began to dress.

It didn't take long before unexpected details distracted her. The parchment texture of her jeans. The map of wrinkles in her shirt. She tied her Sophia Loren sandals around her feet and considered the meaning of consequence and the elusive nature of time.

Soon, the walls around her began to move. She opened the bathroom door and shuffled around midair musical notes until she reached the main room. She settled on a bench. Fibers in the wood quivered. She watched in awe as they loosened and flowed in a gentle stream. It reminded her of Big Basin's Opal Creek. Patterns rippled down the length of the table, circled the knots and knife cuts, and cascaded off the far edge. Waterfalls of bark formed burls when they reached the floor.

Out of the wood popped a tiny frog.

It's okay, Emmie. Ride this trip.

Were those Danny's words or the frog's? Or hers?

As if in response, the frog jumped on her shoulder. *Andiamo!* he said, making a clicking sound. He thought Emily was a horse.

"*Offro io!*" she said aloud, knowing full well the phrase implied offering to pay the tip for a meal. She was using "It's on me" to address an imaginary frog now kicking his heels into her shoulder to get her to move. The image amused her, and she started to giggle.

Irene entered the room, dancing with Penny. They sprinkled glitter everywhere. Clare followed, transforming into an earth spirit. And now she was a tree spirit, her branches morphing into invisible webs of color, embracing everyone with shimmering light. Etrusco trotted after her, an extension of whatever form Clare assumed. They moved in sync, a walking forest of two.

Emily's leapfrog guide announced with joy, *You're tripping, sister!*

"Outside!" This from ringmaster Larry, his red T-shirt glowing and adorned with gold buttons and epaulets.

Emily's own ever-changing top distracted her from Larry's

carnival-barking style. Her T-shirt grew into a dress and then became a hot air balloon. Gravity loosened, her toes lifted from the ground, and her altered attire ushered her outdoors. A chorus of colors led her into the wheat fields.

The frog leaped to the stem of a swaying poppy. *Volare!* Tiny owl wings sprouted from his back. *Find your wings! You can't dream Danny alive until you learn to fly!*

Emily gawked at her toes. Poppy blossoms tickled her skin as she beat her arms. The breeze elevated her. A palette of music surged below. Yellow was A. Brown was B-flat. Red was C, orange became D, green was E, and purple emanated a blaring F-sharp. Time became the harmonica note Emily could bend without trying. Her favorite harp—G, low and rich—sang Danny's songs. His music spiraled through the wheat, stained the earth a beautiful blue, and washed away her fears.

Do you hear it? The wind?

A whooshing sound.

She found herself standing before a door.

An opening.

No. It was just the shower room again. Graffiti shamed the walls, and Steele and Otto's curse words mocked her. She tried to gag them away. When that didn't work, she willed the obscenities to pool into an inky spiral. The letters gave in and gurgled down the drainpipe and into the holding tank below. Relieved, she slumped against the counter.

Silence at last.

But not for long.

In the distance, a new noise grew: cymbals crashing, clanging, shrieking. Emily groaned and covered her ears.

The frog had returned, conducting an earsplitting marching band in her brain.

Emily! You will need those words!

With a wave of his baton, the frog ordered the graffiti back up the drainpipe and onto the walls.

Emily shrugged him off and retreated to the stairwell. The wringer washer throbbed. *Slush and beat. Slush and beat.*

Time folded in on itself. She squinted at the anxious sky and tripped down the stone steps and into the twilight. Clouds swirled into shades of pink and orange.

Darkness dropped.

Out of the shadows slithered Steele, a creature from Mordor. His insides stained black, his essence off key. His voice spit tentacles into the night. Appendages grabbed living, swirling colors and sucked them into his mouth-hole.

Emily's tiny frog guide transformed into a toad. He donned a cape and twirled a wart-gun. *Dovrà passare sul mio cadavere!* Over my dead body! *NOW! Use the words!*

He aimed. Warty syllables penetrated Emily's skull.

She shrieked in pain. Then she screamed her professor's name. "Steele!" Her tongue caught, but she forced it to work. "You son-of-a-bitch thief!" She rammed against him and knocked him into the stairwell wall. More expletives escaped.

"Do you know what you are? A *motherfucking asshole!* You've been one all your life, and you know it, you *shit-faced bastard!*" The ugly graffiti consumed her. "Taking everyone's money and running away like a *lily-livered rat.* Coward! You're nothing but a *boneheaded* fraud! And a *pissy prick!*"

Steele laughed. There she was, waving her arms like a maniac while shrieking out his words, and the fucker laughed.

"You're finally learning, little girl," he said.

Matt grabbed her arm and danced her up the stairs, into the main room, and out of Steele's reach.

Emily figured the wannabe professor would follow her. She glared at him over her shoulder. His smirk taunted her. Unstoppable and flaming with rage, she broke loose.

"To hell with words," she muttered.

She snuck behind Steele and tapped him on the back. When he turned, she hauled off as if about to punch him but kicked him in the groin instead. The crack sent fractured bands of color through the air.

Emily winced.

"*JESUS!*" said Matt, pulling her off.

Steele moaned and rolled to his side.

"Sorry to offend," she said to Matt before stomping down the stairs and out the door.

The universe and all its particles energized her stride. She nearly flew, crossing the flattened fields to the frog lake. The sun's reflection revealed an astonishing dawn.

Finding strength in the morning, she hiked to the castle, through the gate, and into the courtyard. There, twisted on its side in the very spot where she thought she'd seen it over a month ago, lay La Contessa's wagon, still supporting the gray box. Freya's Faunas and Steele's graffiti spewed insults over most of its surface. Drugged-up stupidity must have convinced them to try to break open the padlock protecting the light machine inside.

She touched the damaged wood. A shock of brilliance entered her fingertips. Muffled voices electrified her shoulder. She jolted and almost fell to the ground.

Tears flowed down her face. She limped to her closet room, hoping to recover. To her surprise, Freya was there, painting Faunas on the clipped fabric of a jacket—Emily's jacket. She must have left it in the wardrobe during her last stay. Then something else caught her eye: the centaur painting of Danny. It was leaning against the wall. Freya had glued fragments of his letters to the margins.

The image was provocative—much more so than Emily had imagined. Freya had transformed Danny's nude body into that of an aroused stallion.

Livid, Emily snatched Freya's paintbrush from her hand and threw it against the wall. A bloom of color exploded against the plaster. Letting her middle finger speak, she grabbed the painting, poked a hole through the edge of it with her thumbnail, and ripped it down the middle. She booted it against the wardrobe and accidentally broke the door panel in two.

Freya grabbed a wine bottle and aimed.

Emily didn't even flinch. She plucked it like a rose from Freya's painted fingernails and hurled it against the castle wall. Without saying a word, she stormed into the courtyard and out the gate.

The sky wasn't purple-red anymore. Olive trees no longer danced in fluorescent hues. Red poppies stood motionless in the fields. The frog's incessant buzzing gave way to weighty silence.

The symphony had ended.

Breathless from carrying her rucksack and running up the hill, Matt found Emily stomping along the cypress-lined drive.

"We're leaving, Em. Come with me."

The Topolino caught up with them, Clare at the wheel. Matt squeezed Emily into the back seat with Spider and hopped into the passenger's side.

The Fiat sputtered down the switchback roads, past cypress trees and oxen drivers in the fields. It turned left toward the train station.

It was late. Emily closed her eyes. The frog's final warning echoed in her ears: *Morto un papà, se ne fa un altro.*

One father dies, but another takes his place.

There are William Steeles everywhere.

28

LONDON.

Emily opened a large parcel waiting for her at the American Express travel office. It contained Emily's belongings. At the bottom of the box, Matt had placed two envelopes: one from him and the other from Giovanni.

She summarized the first letter for Clare. "Matt went back to Italy to clean up my mess and make amends with La Contessa. And Steele's been fired."

"I don't believe it." Clare shook her head and snatched the page. After reading, she turned to Spider. "He says the college banned the Scholastics program because of Steele. And La Contessa filed a lawsuit against both Steele and San Jose State. Now Giovanni's counting on a settlement to reimburse him and his mother for the money they gave back to everyone who lost theirs."

"That's how I bought my guitar," said Spider.

Clare wrapped her arms around her friend. "And that's how I could afford to spend so much time goofing around in Morocco with you and Em."

"With those snake charmers."

"And Baba Outasight. Remember how he insisted on reading

our palms after serving us spiked mint tea?" Clare nudged Spider with her hip.

"I hope they can repair all the damage I did," said Emily.

Spider groaned. "You're such a bummer, Em."

Clare handed back the letter. "Emily wasn't the only one who wrecked the place, Spider. We all trashed the fields. And Freya painted Faunas all over the walls. We ate their chickens and left our stuff everywhere for Margherita to clean up. And Steele's gang broke into La Contessa's garage, wheeled out that wagon La Contessa liked so much, and vandalized it. We were Steele's perfect students. He wanted anarchy and chaos. He got all that and a lot more from us."

"It was true about the blackmail, wasn't it?" Spider asked Emily, who was now reading a letter from Giovanni's envelope. "Steele said his ex-girlfriend dredged up some ugly stuff about the countess's family. That's why Giovanni helped you take him down, isn't it?"

Feeling faint, Emily folded the letter and slumped against the railing in front of the building. "We have to go home," she said. "Now."

1970–1974
California

I am in a dream which I don't know how to recall.

— Edgar Degas

29

Four in the morning. Emily, Clare, and Spider stumbled off a Greyhound at the San Jose station. The driver took forever to retrieve their packs from the bowels of the bus. They hauled their belongings to a bench beside a phone booth where Spider dug into her pocket for a dime and deposited it in the slot to make the call.

"TJ lives in Ben Lomond now," she said after replacing the receiver. "He'll be here in about an hour."

Emily couldn't think, let alone speak. She pocketed the letter TJ had sent to Giovanni and dozed until Beulah stuttered around the corner.

TJ switched off the motor. He stared at the steering wheel for a moment before stepping out. He looked smaller, thinner. Blond strands clung to his slumped shoulders. He still had that beautiful face. His pale eyes filled when he opened his arms.

All three girls dove into him. They rocked and hugged and cried until everyone nearly lost their balance.

Nobody spoke as TJ drove along Highway 17 and into the Santa Cruz Mountains. Beulah's headlights revealed a surreal but familiar landscape. Emily rolled down the passenger window and inhaled the scent of coastal redwoods, firs, and oaks.

He lived in a place called Hidden Island Cottages, along the San Lorenzo River and overlooking a mounded island of land that supported a replica of a Scottish castle. The cabin closest to the castle was his—one room, not counting the thimble-size bathroom and kitchen with a tiny table next to the stove. The girls' gear took up most of the space in the living and bedroom area. He motioned for them to make themselves comfortable. The only place to sit was on a double mattress on the floor next to the window.

Speakers, wires, and cords tangled through the room. TJ's bass and Danny's guitar case leaned against each other along one wall. The entire place smelled of skunk.

TJ collapsed onto a pile of clothes draped over a wooden chair in the corner. "I'm not sure where to begin. I guess I'll start with this." He handed Emily a note.

Clare squeezed Emily's shoulder.

"I found it in Ben's kitchen. Not sure who sent it. I think it was his grandfather. Maybe his mom."

Every nerve inside Emily's body flared as she read. It was only a paragraph. Typed. No sentiment. No salutation other than Ben's name. An illegible signature was barely visible at the end.

DANNY'S MIA. RECEIVED A TELEGRAM FROM SEC. OF WAR SAYING HE'S BEEN MISSING SINCE SOMETIME IN MAY. THEY'LL NOTIFY US IF ANY FURTHER INFORMATION IS AVAILABLE.

TJ crossed to the bed. Spider moved over to make room for him. He unfolded Emily's fingers from the page. She looked vacantly at her empty hands. He gently slid next to her and curled his arm around her.

She must have cried herself to sleep.

The following afternoon, TJ took Clare and Spider to Matt's girlfriend's house. Vicky now lived on Eleventh Street in San Jose. Emily stayed behind. She wanted to be close to Danny's Firebird. She rested his guitar case against the wall in the kitchen and sat at the table next to the window. The prism she'd given TJ last Christmas cast a spectrum of light across the room.

After clearing a space to make way for her watercolor kit, she opened her sketchbook to a blank page. She lifted her brush and rotated it inside a glass of clean water. While contemplating the concept of red swirling into blue, she worried about values and prayed for luck in the wash.

Holding her brush just so, she spun it through a puddle of pigment. It knew how much it could take. It would tell her when to let go. One subtle movement, one stroke. Something simple like that could destroy an entire painting.

The brush spoke of rain in a jungle.

Yellow spiraled into the blue and red in the glass. She choked back tears and watched the sediment settle into a gray mass.

She used to know how to feel a brush. How to sense when it had enough pigment and water to release a fluid stroke. When it wasn't right, she had to begin again.

Just stay good.

Ben's words from long ago singed her brain.

TJ had been there the morning it happened. He'd knocked on the cabin door and called Ben's name. He thought Ben was sleeping, so he tiptoed in.

The walls were splattered with particles of Danny's brother, a spent rifle on the floor.

30

IN 1864, EMILY'S GREAT-GRANDUNCLE HAD FALLEN during the Third Battle of Winchester at Opequon Creek, Virginia. Her grampa said Samuel was tall with dark hair and blue eyes. Like Danny. Twenty years old, again like Danny. His brother, who was Emily's great-grandfather, also tried to commit suicide after Sammy's death but luckily didn't succeed.

When she was little, she begged her grampa to let her see her great-granduncle's letters. He hesitated at first, then tenderly read them like bedtime stories to help her understand the gritty side of love. Until now, Sammy's story had been the closest she'd been to war.

While spending Christmas at home last year, she'd made sure the Civil War letters were still in her grampa's dream box. She'd given the box to TJ for safekeeping, and TJ had brought it to San Jose, where Emily was now living with Clare, Spider, Vicky, and Matt, who'd recently returned from Italy.

Emily cherished Sammy's words. He felt like a brother to her. Like Danny, he'd been declared missing during the war. After the siege of Port Hudson in Louisiana, he'd spent three days in a ditch, bleeding from a chest wound. Someone eventually found him and took him to a makeshift hospital in Baton Rouge. In a weathered note, his mother described how she threw herself upon the bed and sobbed.

It took him months to heal before he re-enlisted and asked his mother to send him money, chewing tobacco, and shoes.

He composed his last letter while camped in the field near Berryville, Virginia.

Dear Parents and Brothers,
*   I received your kind and welcome letter last night, and I now take the first opportunity for answering it. I am well, and I hope that this will find you all enjoying the same great blessing. It is very near dark so I cannot write you a very long note. Everything is quiet along our lines except a little picket firing, although we are liable to be attacked at any time for there is a large rebel force not far from here. It is pretty cold weather to be on a campaign like this, and it rains almost every day, and they are keeping us on half rations. So, taking it all around, we are having pretty hard times. I guess if my brothers had been here even two days, they would wish themselves back home again. In my last letter, I wrote for you to send me five dollars. I thought you would send it as soon as possible, for I need it now. I have not received any papers from you lately, and I never received that letter that you spoke of. I wrote to you on my birthday two days ago. It is so dark that tonight I can see to write no more . . .*

The chaplain from his regiment described Sammy's death:

He fell in the first charge in which we were repulsed and had to retreat, giving the enemy the ground and our wounded. Else he would have received immediate attention. When the second charge was made in which we recovered the ground and much more, I found him lying on the field severely wounded. He was too weak to speak, having lain all day there. I secured an ambulance immediately to take him back to the hospital, but when I returned with it, he had expired . . .

His lieutenant, Charles Wolcott, wrote:

Samuel was wounded in the right leg just above the knee. When wounded, he turned around to me and with eyes looking upward and hands raised above him, he said, "Lieutenant, I am shot." He ran about ten steps and fell, thence crawled into a ditch and drank water therefrom while there he was taken with the Colic. One of his friends gave him water to drink and washed his wounds and endeavored to give him medicine, but without avail. If he could have been brought off the field before night, I think the chances would have been all in his favor. But as I mentioned in my last letter, we were repulsed, and he was not evacuated till too late to do anything for him, and he died at night, a soldier's death. That box you spoke of—he got it the day before the battle and made disposition of it the same day among his friends . . .

Danny had given her boot camp, fireflies, lady's slippers, and the sensation of cooling beer on blocks of ice. Sammy had mentioned his mother's biscuits and honey. Neither would have wanted their loved ones to know about terror and blood. But Danny might have shared those things with Ben. And Ben would have felt the blunt force of his brother's words.

A stark realization threw her backward. She caught herself. Still, she slipped, flushing now, pounding with panic, lightheaded, short of breath, counting on the wall behind her.

Danny's not coming back.

She didn't know what to do, so she rose and began to pace. Then she ran into the empty kitchen and called out.

Her echo responded.

Back to the main room. No TJ. No Clare. No Spider. No Matt. No ravens. No owls. No déjà vu seizures to rescue her.

At the kitchen table now. A glass of water. Blank paper. Brushes and twisted tubes of paint.

Burnt sienna mixed with crimson. The scorched colors of her broken dreams. The tint of Caravaggio's sacrifice. The pigment

Artemisia Gentileschi used to strengthen her paintings. Rage paintings of women rising against rapists and abusers and hucksters of war.

One broad stroke across the pebbled page.

Emily dropped her brush into the jar. She pushed it away and returned to Sammy's letters, as fragile as the brief moments she'd spent with Danny and Ben. Danny had asked her to dream him alive in April, maybe earlier. He was declared missing in May. Confused, she latched on to an explanation, any explanation—she didn't care if it sounded untenable or absurd. Perhaps he was talking about a different war in a different time? Could he have been Sammy in another life? After all, they shared the same birthday. If time overlapped, could he still be Sammy now?

She traced the faded calligraphy on the tattered envelopes and considered this. Shaken, she dismissed the idea of reincarnation and people suffering the same fate over and over again. She questioned her childhood experience of history taking place all at once. But if time folded in on itself, wouldn't an imprint remain?

She placed Sammy's letters next to Danny's inside her grampa's dream box. TJ's pendant and Danny's owl feather were also there, along with the rice paper sleeve protecting the spirit of a lady's slipper's dream.

Danny. Ben. TJ. Matt. Sammy. These were the good guys. So was Danny's grandfather. And so was her grampa. Especially her grampa. She recalled the day he'd opened a tube of midnight blue so they could paint the night sky on their dream box. He'd added translucent swirls of red and green to suggest distant galaxies. She'd used her first paintbrush to render the full moon and stars. She chose brown for the branches of her favorite tree. He chose raw sienna to paint an owl sitting in that tree. An owl to keep her dreams safe.

Her home economics teacher teased Emily about wanting to become an artist after spending the weekend creating a "silly" box of dreams with her grampa. Wearing heels and red lipstick, she lectured Emily about what a woman's role was meant to be:

"Mend your husband's clothes, darn his socks. Cook his dinner and have it ready on the table when he comes home. Wear nice makeup, new nylons, and a pretty dress. Open the garage door for him and hand him his favorite cocktail."

Then have his babies. Send them to battle. Watch them come home in flag-draped boxes.

Chiaroscuro. Reflected light. Cast shadow. Subtleties of relationship. A question of values.

At the kitchen table again, Emily squeezed a mound of black onto her palette. Crimped from sitting in the water so long, the brush hairs dragged across the page. Saw-toothed edges, silhouetted shapes. She needed light to add form to her images. But the light rebelled, refusing to reach her paper in a straight line. It bounced all over the place, gathering zest from the stars, its energy influenced by gravitational tugs. It moved faster and slower depending on the shape it was curving around or moving through. Then it hit full speed, instantly, finally free of whatever held it back. Emily had to grab it, to make it her own, because she knew, at any moment, without warning, she could lose herself in its blaze.

Until now, her grampa and Danny had been the light in all her paintings.

She dipped her brush.

Sometimes you have to make an abrupt transition to darkness.

31

Emily returned to San Jose State that fall, along with Clare, Spider, Matt, and Vicky. As far as she knew, Ryan and Holly were still in India. Larry, the last she'd heard, had stayed in Italy after teaming up with yet another group of revolutionaries. Steele and Otto had escaped to Canada to avoid the authorities. Freya left Steele and went back to her beloved Carnival House in Haight-Ashbury.

Quietly, TJ had asked Emily to return to Ben Lomond and stay with him. In truth, she wanted to. She'd been feeling alone, even while living with her friends. Thoughts of Danny created a relentless pull. She needed to be near him through Beulah and the Firebird and a few belongings that she and TJ had decided not to send to Danny's family.

She planned to move in with him a month or so after she'd enrolled in a couple of traditional classes at the college. She felt closed in there. And desperate. She missed the freedom Scholastics had provided. Removing herself from this unfamiliar scene seemed like the best way to counter the neatly ordered desks and tight-lipped professors straitjacketed in suits and ties. Ben's death made the gravity even stronger. Hendrix's passing was another blow. Now no one could believe Janis was gone too. On October

26, after attending Joplin's wake at the Lion's Share in San Anselmo, TJ drove Beulah to San Jose to pick up Emily. He parked in front of the Eleventh Street house. Once again, he sat motionless in the car.

Emily approached Beulah. "It's warmer inside," she said, opening the door and resting her hand on his shoulder.

He nodded and followed her into the house.

Matt slouched on the couch with a newspaper folded in his lap. "Glad you're here, man," he said, motioning for TJ to get comfortable in the chair beside him.

TJ lifted Vicky's orange kitten before sinking into the cushions. The bundle of fur curled into his lap and purred. His voice cracked as he tried to mutter something—then he shook his head and stroked the kitten's ears.

Spider entered with a floral teapot and a bag of Oreos. Vicky followed with several mugs dangling from her fingers.

"So, TJ," said Spider. "How'd it go tonight? You're so lucky you were invited. With that crowd, I thought the party'd last for days."

Matt shook his head at Spider.

Emily sat on the arm of TJ's chair. "You okay?"

He didn't look okay.

"Have some tea," said Spider. "Honest, it'll make you feel better."

Frozen grief. There was no way around it. Emily wanted to take reality, shake it by the shoulders, yell at it, slap it around a few times, and eventually embrace it. But inertia had set in, miring her in its spell.

Spider turned on the TV. Channel 4. The weather girl posed behind sliding glass panels, writing backward with a cigar-size grease pencil.

"And here is the weather for October twenty-sixth," she said, facing the camera and tapping the fat pencil on the glass before her. "High, sixty-eight degrees; low, forty-eight point nine degrees; wind speed, nine point six seven miles per hour." She drew a series of curvy wind marks after the waxy black numbers. "Maximum sustained wind speed, fourteen miles per hour."

"How does she do that?" asked Spider, forming backward symbols in the air.

"Practice," said Vicky, sitting on Matt's lap.

"Or she's a natural," said Clare. "She must be related to da Vinci with all that mirror writing."

"I love her pearls," Spider said, tracing a semicircle across her collarbone.

Clare frowned at her reference to Janis.

TJ stared at the flickering screen.

Spider continued to joke about the weather girl until she lost interest and changed the channel to *Monday Night Football*. She rolled her eyes and began another rant about the insufferable sportscaster.

"This is our cue to leave, Em," said Clare. "Ready for a walk? Let's go to the corner for more cookies at the market."

Stygian was Emily's initial thought as she glanced at the yawning sky outside. She detected a sliver of moon but no stars because smog ruled the Bay Area. The night's gloom suited her image of the underworld.

She studied the sidewalk as they headed to the store. Tufts of dandelion heads squeezed through cracks between the walkway squares, mimicking cement dominoes spilling in front of brown-spotted lawns and Victorian houses. "Watch your step," she said to Clare seconds before tripping on a kink of concrete that caught her toe. "Ow, ow, *ow*!" Her voice ascended to a feel-sorry-for-me whine.

Clare laughed while Emily hopped until she could support her weight again.

"Have enough money?" Clare asked.

"Me? I thought you were buying."

"I bought last time. Your turn."

Emily rummaged through the purse she'd bartered for in Morocco. Its texture summoned visions of an old woman spinning dog fur into threads strengthened with veins of carded wool. The weaver must have sat for hours, shedding and picking, battening and taking up yarn, creating a rhythm at her loom as she worked the warp, the weft, the shuttle, the heddle, the reed. Emily hummed the patterns as she sifted through wads of Kleenex and gum wrappers in search of her crocheted money pouch.

The store glowed. Halos of lights circled the night. Emily and Clare exaggerated squints, the backs of their hands to their eyes, turning away from the glare as they walked inside.

That was when Emily saw him—a man—lurking between two aisles, watching her. She pushed Clare to the counter and grabbed a random bag of potato chips.

"I don't trust the guy over there," she whispered.

Clare snatched the pouch from Emily and told the cashier to keep the change.

The croucher's leer penetrated, creating a wound in Emily's back. She grabbed Clare's arm and focused on a path out the door and onto the sidewalk. She tightened her grip and thrust her friend forward, away from danger. But there he was, in front of them. The thug slapped Clare aside like she was a fly and wound his arm hard around Emily's shoulders, squeezing her to his chest while grabbing at her purse with his other hand.

"Get the guys!" Emily screamed to Clare.

She could barely see Clare's face—the man was turning Emily from the sidewalk toward the street—but there was this image as she rotated: her best friend, a thin stream of blood spilling from the corner of her open mouth. Before she could register the peril, Clare was gone.

The man, the purse, the struggle—Emily clenched her teeth. A familiar rage surged from her throbbing toe through her bowels, her lungs, her heart, her throat. It exploded toward the vileness trying to contain her.

Her shriek, earsplitting and relentless, stunned him. He let go of her purse and tried to cover her mouth with his hand.

She broke free.

"Asshole!" she screamed. "You vile, disgusting motherfucker! How dare you hurt my friend! How dare you tear my purse, for god's sake! Don't you know how much time that lady put into this? In Morocco, for god's sake. On a loom, you bastard! Have you ever seen a loom in your life? It's bigger than you, you clueless fuck—bigger than this goddamn street!"

The guy's head tilted forward as if he were trying to make sense of what she was saying. Tiny neck, fish mouth gaping, one yellow tooth surfacing from the cavern between his lips. Emily wanted to note the color of his eyes, but he lunged, grabbed her by the waist, lifted her from the sidewalk, pushed down her face, and began to stuff her through the open door of a waiting car. He tore her purse again. As each thread gave and popped, Emily's fury grew. She became a superhero, arms and legs busting the car to shreds. Then she saw the other guy. At the wheel. Gunning the engine.

"Red car," TJ told the cop from the back seat of the patrol car.

"Camaro," said Matt.

Emily sat motionless between her two friends. Clare was with them. She handed the coin pouch back to Emily.

"Red," repeated TJ. "Like his hair. Curly. Close to his head. No beard. Freckles. Pointy tooth in front."

"TJ here got Emily out of the car after tackling the snaggle-tooth," said Matt, "but the guy leaped into the back seat, and the driver blasted away."

"Bald driver," said TJ.

Several intersections later, siren on, the officer pulled over a red Camaro. A woman at the wheel. No redhead or bald guy with her.

"My mistake," said the cop to the driver.

"Nothing we can do," the same tired cop told Emily and her friends. He left them on the curb of the Eleventh Street house.

Inside, TJ slumped into a chair and stroked his temple. Emily set the pouch and her damaged purse on the table.

TJ and Matt had just saved her life, and her excessive apologies and thank-yous felt repetitive and lame.

It was two in the morning. Beulah turned onto Old County Road and took a left toward Hidden Island Cottages. TJ got out of the car. He passed in front of Beulah's headlights to open the passenger door. Emily watched the flash of his form in the light, then his shadow, motioning her to step out.

"We're here."

She nodded.

He placed his hand on her shoulder. "Emmie, it's okay."

"Don't call me Emmie. Only Danny can call me Emmie." The words just slipped out, and she couldn't stop them.

TJ pulled back. He turned and walked into the house.

Exhausted and confused, Emily stared at Beulah's dashboard. In time, she entered the cabin.

TJ was curled in a sleeping bag on the floor, facing the wall.

Emily crawled into his empty bed. She paused before pulling crumpled sheets and blankets around her neck and covering her mouth with her hand.

It was only a word, only a kindness he'd been offering.

When she awoke, TJ and Beulah were gone.

32

Emily padded barefoot into TJ's kitchen and rummaged for something to eat. Crazy headache. She opened the tiny refrigerator. It smelled so bad she shut the door.

The bathroom was no better. Mold invaded the grout around every tile, and yellow-orange streaks crusted the toilet.

How long had she been away from this place?

Emily checked the cupboard under the sink. At least TJ still had Ajax. She grabbed a grubby towel, soaked it in hot water, shook the scouring cleanser over it, and scrubbed each surface. Then she tackled the rest of the house. Slowly, because her head was pounding.

A few hours later, she heard Beulah putter around the corner and into the drive. From the kitchen window, she saw TJ climb from the car.

She glanced at the clock. Dinnertime. She hurried to wipe the last spot of grease on the stove, combed her hair with her fingers, and entered the main room.

He opened the door and dropped his gear on the rug.

"Hi." She couldn't think of anything else to say.

"You're up." TJ looked around the freshly cleaned room and tucked his lips into his mouth.

"When did you leave?"
"About ten."
"This morning?"
"Yup."
"Have I been asleep that long?"
"Yup."
"Were you away the whole time?"
"Yes and no."
"What do you mean?"
"Just that."

So, this was how it was going to be. Nothing but a series of staccato exchanges.

Emily made macaroni and cheese from a box she found in the cupboard. TJ said he wasn't hungry and spent the evening smoking outside. Emily threw away her portion, crawled into bed, and read Danny's letters under the covers.

The next morning, after TJ left for band practice, she organized the contents of her dream box and added her journal and several rolls of undeveloped film from Italy. Before bed, she took a long walk along the San Lorenzo River.

The next night, she sketched in her journal while listening to a stack of albums: The Who, Buddy Miles, Leon Russell. The color changes in Poco's "Nobody's Fool" made her wonder what she was doing with TJ, a guy she hardly knew.

Going back to San Jose seemed pointless. At least when she was here, she had hope. For what? She didn't know.

TJ was the one who broke the spell after being away for several nights.

"Surprise," he said, closing the door behind him and setting down his guitar. He dug into his pocket and pulled out a plastic bag. "Good stuff. From Joseph."

"Who's Joseph?"

He ignored her question and emptied a couple of pills into his left palm. One, a tiny blue dot. The other, a black pentacle. He gave Emily the dot. It was about the size of a pinhead.

"What's this?"

"Not quite windowpane, but a nice, clean high. You'll like it."

She'd heard that before. "And the other one?"

"Kick-ass. I could use a little kick-ass right now."

She didn't think. The blue dot felt like air on her tongue.

Steppenwolf dominated the group of records TJ replaced on the turntable. "Sookie Sookie" introduced the night. "Born to Be Wild" filled a void in the room.

A sepia tone took hold of Emily's senses. It tasted like an illustration from one of her grampa's books. In a vision, she could see a pair of nightingales nesting on a castle turret. She peered inside the tower's smudged window. An old man wearing a robe and slippers read by the fire. A cat jumped on the sill, wiping away steam as it rubbed against the inside pane. Emily stroked the cat from the other side of the glass. As soon as she noticed TJ's reflection, she was back inside his cabin. He was brooding in the corner and fingering Danny's guitar. His mood weighted the room.

Emily escaped outdoors. She gazed at the stars' reflections in the river and pictured Danny flashing his light from the other side of time.

I'm at TJs. Can you see me? Danny?

A paddling of ducks rippled the surface. *Over the river and through the wood,* the river sang.

"To Grandfather's house we go," Emily answered. *Danny, are you still here?*

She walked back to the cabin. The rhythm of the song took hold with each step: *Oh, how the wind does blow. It stings the toes and bites the nose as over the ground we go.*

She opened the door. A cloaked monster flew through her into the night. She shook it off. Only darkness. She switched on the light.

TJ was horizontal on the bed, body jerking, eyes rolling back. He tried to mumble something that sounded like *Joseph* and *thorzine* before twisting his head against his locking tongue.

Emily turned to look at him from a different angle and stared for a long moment. His mouth was filled with suds. She thought of the dishes, how she'd washed them that afternoon, how the soap had foamed over the sink's rim. Her mouth fell open, the taste of lye mixing with saliva.

No-o-o-o! The muscles in her face cramped as she screamed. She ran to his side and shook him hard.

No response.

"Shit! Come on, man, wake up! TJ! Help me here! Shit!"

Over the river and through the wood. To Joseph's house—

She darted out the door and ran until her thighs caught fire. Somehow, she knew it couldn't be far. Time escalated to a frenzy. Branches grabbed her hair and scraped her shoulders as she raced through the woods. The ducks quickly overtook her, leading her to a thrown-together shack in the distance. Candlelight glowed inside. She banged on the door.

A tall guy in a black hood answered. He held out a plastic pumpkin filled with M&M's.

Halloween? Tonight? You've got to be kidding.

"Joseph? Are you—?" She could hardly release the words between breaths. "TJ! Foaming—mouth."

"What?"

"Thorzine—TJ, man! TJ's in trouble!"

The hooded guy slammed the door.

Shit—wrong house. Now what?

The stupid song wouldn't leave her head: *We seem to go extremely slow. It is so hard to wait! Over the river and through the wood—*

He opened the door again. Now he looked like Jesus: white robes, long hair and beard. In an instant, he was gone. Wings for feet. Wings for ears.

He wasn't Jesus. Or Joseph. He was Mercury. Hermes taking TJ to the underworld.

Her naked feet danced, crimson with cold. No way would she be able to keep up with this wing-footed man. Still, she willed her frozen feet to fly.

When Grandfather sees us come, he will say, "Oh, dear, the children are here, bring a pie for everyone—"

Or was it Grandmother?

A cackling behind her. She turned, expecting a demon. It was one of the ducks guiding the line of waddlers, forging a path to TJ's place.

Her mind skipped to a time when she and Danny were hiking to an alpine lake in Desolation Wilderness. He'd dropped his clothes and dived in, swimming to the first island.

"Come in, Emmie! It's not that cold."

"I don't swim," she'd called.

It wasn't that she couldn't swim. She swam like a mermaid underwater. But she sank whenever she tried to stroke through the surface. The lake hadn't been that deep, but it was filled with algae, and she didn't want to submerge herself. So, she dipped to her waist, leaned into the water, and attempted a sloppy dog paddle. Out of nowhere, this family of ducks appeared, a mom and maybe a dozen ducklings. They surrounded Emily's floundering form, chattering and pecking at her hair. *You can do it. We'll help you.* They'd led her directly to Danny.

Tonight's ducks quacked and waddled beside her, forcing her to focus. They'd helped her find Joseph, and now they were blazing a shortcut to TJ's.

Joseph was kneeling beside the bed when Emily entered. Candles flickered everywhere. Joseph hummed something while lifting a string of TJ's sweat-soaked hair from his forehead.

TJ's face was gray, his body still. The shadow Emily felt earlier crowded the room and choked oxygen from her lungs. She sank to the floor.

Not TJ. Not now. Please.

33

Emily must have spent the rest of the night with Beulah. The taste of death in her mouth. She was afraid to go inside and face the truth.

She climbed from the little VW and slid her hand along Beulah's roof. Autumn's energy filled the air. She stumbled down Old County Road. Big-leaf maples glowed within the oak forest. Banana slugs left shimmering trails in the duff. Sunbeams penetrated the canopy's shade. For a moment, a vibrant palette of color surrounded her.

Then she nearly stepped in it. It took a while for her heart to slow down. She bent to examine what she'd stumbled over.

A narrow tire must have crossed the squirrel's back. Red and yellow intestines ribboned out each side. Only the emptied pelt held fast to head and tail.

Courage. Emily needed it to take the rodent from the road.

Her fingers circled the delicate skull, near the half-closed eyes. With her other hand, she felt a rope of tailbone. The lift was clean. Entrails dragged behind.

She wanted to shiver away lingering diseases and cleanse her hands of what had soiled them. But something shifted as she sheltered the dead squirrel under a bush and turned her palms toward her face. She sensed pads. Fur. Somehow, she knew the way tree bark softened to sinking claws. The blur of leaves in a race to the canopy. How incisors found the perfect place to slice the acorn's stem. She understood stillness. Then a split-second bolt across the road. The taste of shock. Her pinned torso burned.

She spit out the metallic flavor and wiped her tingling hands on her jeans.

Danny? Is this how you're talking to me now?

She ran back to the cabin, fearing the worst.

Emily gasped with relief when she found TJ and Joseph sitting together at the kitchen table, Joseph's hand on TJ's shoulder. A bottle labeled Thorazine, not *thorzine*, rested next to his other hand. She assumed it was a drug to counteract whatever was in that pentagonal pill.

Joseph shook his head and motioned for her to leave as soon as she picked up the bottle.

Stunned, she returned the antidote to its place beside TJ's cigarettes.

Outside, she leaned against Beulah's body for support. Now she was angry. Angry at Joseph for selling the drugs to TJ and at TJ for buying them. Angry for letting TJ take that evil pill. Angry at herself for swallowing the pretty blue one. Angry at all the hallucinogens and narcotics that were destroying everyone's lives. Angry at the guy who'd tried to force her into that car. Angry at the bug-eyed hostel guy lurking at the Temple of Hera in the ankle of Italy's boot.

She clenched her fists. Just thinking about her father, her brother, and the doctor who'd allowed her mother to die made her furious. Not to mention Steele and Otto and all the men around the world who violated women.

Most of all, she was angry at Danny for going to that bloody war and for not dream-talking to her in a way she could understand. Then she was angry at herself again because the one guy in the world who was grieving as much as she was was just a few feet away, struggling to survive, and there was no way she could help him.

After Joseph left, Emily slid into the chair facing TJ. She folded her arms on the table and leaned forward. He sucked on a cigarette and stared out the window. He was a skeleton wearing the same jeans and T-shirt he'd worn for days.

"Thank god you're okay."

He continued to suck and stare.

"TJ?"

He exhaled. Smoke consumed his face.

It looked like the entire universe had imploded within him and debris was escaping through his mouth and nostrils.

"Remember when you gave me that pendant?"

His gray eyes penetrated hers for a second. Then he inhaled, pressed the cigarette butt into a plastic yogurt lid on the table, and looked away.

"It saved me at least once when I was in Italy. And when you pulled me from that car in San Jose? You saved me again."

His blond hair was caked and dull. His stubble was longer than usual, yellow at the roots and white at the tips. His eyes were glazed.

"I don't want to hurt you anymore," she whispered.

She'd intended to give him permission to call her Emmie, but the words jammed in her throat.

TJ rubbed his eyes with his thumb and index finger. The sun filtered through the trees, then retreated. He lowered his head.

Emily hated the cast shadow. She pushed back the chair, washed her hands in the sink, walked two steps to the stove, and ignited the burner beneath a pot of water. She was doing this all wrong. After she reached for a half-empty jar of instant Folgers, she heard him mumble. She turned. She didn't want to blurt "What?" or "Say that again?" She didn't want to do something stupid and shut him up forever.

TJ rocked his head in his hands and stroked his nose. He

looked up. A rush of tears flooded his eyes. Emily's heart surged. She walked behind his chair and cradled his shoulders in her arms.

Sex with TJ was a tangle of elbows and knees, tongue and teeth. It was bone against bone, fingernails at odds with delicate tissue. It was a confusion of sugary stickiness and acrid aftertaste. When TJ was spent, his body became an oppressive weight. He didn't notice when Emily crawled from the knot of his arms, padded to the bathroom, turned on the shower, and cleansed her flesh.

The San Lorenzo River flowed right in front of his cabin. She tiptoed outside, slipped underwater, and thought of her great-grandmother swimming in a similar river. While submerged in a shallow pool, she turned her face toward the flickering stars and longed for Danny to flash his light.

Danny once told her about a dangerous female firefly, the *Photuris*, who mimicked the flash patterns of the gentle fireflies. The *Photuris* watched the sky above her and waited for an unsuspecting male to begin his light dance. She imitated an answering female, tricking the male into coming closer so she could seduce him into her trap. Then she devoured him.

"Don't hate this girl just yet," he said that night. "It's not only the female *Photuris* who's deceptive. The males have their own ways."

Danny described how a *Photuris* male took advantage of his female by pretending to be one of the gentle fireflies she was hunting. Throughout the evening, he changed his altitude and flash patterns to copy the various males that became active at different times of the night. When she flashed her scheming signal to lure her meal, he returned an equally deceptive pattern, hoping to get close enough to mate with her. And then, with luck, he would escape alive.

Emily splashed through the surface, coughed out water, and shook the river from her hair.

She was never innocent. Her father had made sure of that.
Photuris male.
Photuris female.

34

THANKSGIVING. ALREADY. EMILY SPENT THE afternoon cooking a tiny turkey. After pulling it from the oven, she basted it with butter and stared at it while eating her salad.

The poor bird got cold. She wrapped it in foil and squeezed it into the refrigerator. It deserved a reason for sacrificing its life. Maybe she would give it to Joseph. Maybe later.

She wasn't dumb. She figured TJ was gone so much because he was with someone—anyone who didn't distress him, who didn't remind him of Danny, Ben, and everyone else they'd lost. He didn't offer excuses. She didn't ask.

She also knew the band had been busy auditioning a new guitarist to replace Danny. Rishi was his self-given name. He was a guru-disciple with wealthy parents. They owned land all over the country, including several acres near Summit Road above Santa Cruz. Rishi wanted to build a practice studio and create a commune where the band could live. He suggested the band's chicks stay home from all practice sessions and gigs. He didn't want girlfriends interrupting potential groupie action.

As soon as he became a member of Wave, Rishi took charge of the schedule because he was great at getting new engagements. He also dictated everyone's diet: no meat, everything natural from the health food store, fasting every Sunday, and fruit every Wednesday. Emily hated how controlling he was. Once, she argued with him about the kind of vitamin C he insisted they take. Acerola, the chewable kind? Or C from a drugstore bottle? Who cared?

"Why do you keep Rishi around?" she asked TJ one day.

"We need the money," he said.

Resources had been scarce until Rishi came along. Now TJ could afford to purchase Joseph's junker Dodge truck so Beulah and Emily could travel as a team.

Beulah enabled her to work two jobs in Santa Cruz. On weekends, she picked mushrooms at the mushroom factory. Wearing a lighted helmet, she crawled into compost heaps beneath the building, whacking emerging buttons from their stems with a curved knife.

Her weekday job was gluing Supersuits for a famous surfing mogul who'd designed a unique line of wetsuits that inflated like beach balls. The female supervisor insisted this ballooning effect was for deep-sea decompression.

One morning, the supervisor sneaked a few of the finished wetsuits to the beach, where six giggling young women squeezed into the corset-like contraptions in the freezing air. They blew into the chest nozzles until they bloated like giant ticks bobbing in the surf. Emily finally had a chance to experience buoyancy in water, but it took her forever to right herself from an accidental face-down flip. It was the supervisor who rescued her. An experienced surfer, she seemed dismayed by Emily's clumsiness. All the girls sat on the beach, teasing Emily for not knowing how to swim. Emily weathered the sting of their words. She even laughed. Somehow, this odd group of girls made her feel included. After that day, they worked together, gluing neoprene strips over wetsuit seams and fusing the rubber using General Electric irons. The girls supported Emily's desire to remain on land. She cheered them on from the beach as they surfed.

Back at the cabin, however, Emily's mind atrophied. She struggled to paint. Even the thought of digging into the small stack of boxes in the corner for her art supplies felt like a chore. All her material possessions lived in that kitchen corner. She wanted nothing to do with most of them. They were just *things*.

She considered visiting Clare and Matt on occasional days off, but one look in the mirror negated that idea. Clare would only comment on the dark circles under her eyes and scold her about how gaunt she looked. Maybe they wouldn't be home? They'd be doing something constructive, like attending seminars or having an intense dialogue about Maurice Nicoll's *Psychological Commentaries on the Teaching of Gurdjieff and Ouspensky*. The Fourth Way system, how to come out of yourself, be human again, and finally transcend into a universe of stars.

Of course, the inevitable happened: TJ's rent tripled. He could no longer justify the cost of Hidden Island Cottages, even with her income and the band's profits. Rishi's family plot was to become their home.

TJ bought a camping tent and two cots. He found an asbestos sheet at the dump and secured it behind an old woodstove he'd hauled into the tent. He cut a hole in both the asbestos and the tent and threaded the metal stovepipe through it. From the wetsuit shop, Emily salvaged discarded cardboard tubes that once supported yards of neoprene. She sawed them into logs for the stove and stuffed them with newsprint. Luckily nothing caught fire except the paper logs.

After work, she rummaged through bins of free moldy bread and fruit from the Santa Cruz natural food store. She planted Jerusalem artichokes that never sprouted. She bathed in a large tin tub, using water she'd bottled in gallon jugs at her supervisor's house in town. Because she couldn't sleep, she added another job to her routine: delivering newspapers from midnight to three in the morning.

Things got bad. Then worse. The band argued. Their music suffered. They erased a few gigs from the calendar. They erased even more. It reached the point where Emily was the only one making money, and the band's disagreements were countering any efforts for them to find work.

To help with expenses, TJ invited Joseph, now one of the roadies and a cash-rich dealer, to move in with them in the tent. Three cots, one gigantic woodstove, two guys, and a girl.

After delivering papers, Emily and Beulah spent most nights under the stars at the beach. When TJ and Joseph decided to join her on her route, TJ insisted on driving the Dodge. The beat-up green truck and the guys' long hair attracted trouble.

One night, cops pulled them over and ordered everyone out of the cab, hands up. They patted unspeakable places on their bodies and threatened them if they so much as sighed. More cops searched every inch of the truck.

"Fucking pigs," said Joseph after the authorities let them go.

The following week, the *Santa Cruz Sentinel* reported the arrest of three members of the Manson gang: two long-haired men and a small woman in a Dodge pickup. The pictures gave Emily chills.

She saved enough money to rent a one-bedroom cabin nestled in the redwoods of Felton. She moved out of the tent and settled into her new home. A small stream flowed beneath a footbridge leading to the front door. Woodpeckers hammered the trees. Owls called at night. She and Beulah finally had a place to heal.

Months later, TJ showed up.

"I missed you." That was all he had to say.

35

Two years lost. Two years smoking dope, dropping acid. Two years making wetsuits. Two years picking mushrooms. Two years wasted. Two years gone.

Valentine's Day. Emily and TJ watched the six o'clock news on a television Joseph had given them. Peter Jennings turned the mic over to Lem Tucker, a reporter who was narrating a film showing military officers carrying men on stretchers and loading them onto a plane in North Vietnam. It was a newsreel of 143 POWs landing at Clark Air Force Base in the Philippines; 116 came in from Hanoi.

Emily leaned into the black-and-white TV set. All she saw above the swaddled bodies were patches of hair and maybe an ear or an arm. Soon the men who could walk came into view. Vacant expressions, even though several were smiling. None of them had Danny's eyes. The camera cut to the interior of the plane. Only the backs of heads. Bald spots. Each one. They interviewed a guy from Santa Clara. Wrong face. One man clutched a dog. His fingers were too short. Peter Jennings took over the narration when the film turned to the landing at Clark. Most of the men stepping down from the first plane were officers. Older-than-Danny officers. Dark pants, light shirts, ragged faces. Way too old.

ABC played footage of the men arriving from South Vietnam. They looked as tired as the rumpled khakis they wore. A few were limping. Others staggered down the steps. Uniformed men supported them as they walked across the tarmac.

TJ pointed. "Is that him?"

A young man with a wadded jacket under his arm steadied himself on the railing. An officer grabbed him by the elbow to keep him from falling. The boy smiled. There were no crescent moons in his cheeks, no dimpled chin. Emily bit her lip. Jennings said all the POWs had called their friends and loved ones as soon as they'd arrived at Clark.

No one had notified her. Or TJ.

TJ brought home a handful of peyote buttons and showed Emily how to clean out all the fuzzy stuff before chewing. Bitter chewing. Forever chewing. He took her to the beach, where they silently watched the sunset.

Weeks passed. Months passed. Emily knew. TJ knew.

Danny was gone.

One night while TJ was at a gig, Emily sat on the sagging couch and stared at her dream box, which she'd placed on the hearth in the corner of the room. Danny's guitar case leaned against the adjacent wall. A twitch of life entered her fingertips.

She'd never touched Danny's Firebird. It was sacred, off limits to anyone who didn't know how to play it. Danny had never told her this. She just knew.

She walked across the room, placed the case on the floor, clicked the latches, and lifted the lid. Nestled in the gold-velvet interior was a masterpiece. Danny had once told her the man who designed the Firebird had worked for the Packard automobile company. The curve of the guitar's body flowed like a wave. It had a white insert that reminded her of a dolphin's tail. A small engraving of a red firebird graced the top. The neck ran the length of the body. It looked like a boat paddle with sails added to each side. Even the wood was breathtaking—mahogany and walnut burnished to a delicate shine.

Emily sat cross-legged on the floor and placed the guitar on her lap. It was lighter than she'd expected. She imagined Danny's long fingers caressing the neck, a small chrome cylinder covering his fourth finger so he could slide Johnny Winter riffs along the strings. She pictured him dancing across the stage as he played an improvised version of Link Wray's "Rumble." She remembered how he'd stay up all night practicing Chicago blues like Muddy Waters. His voice mimicked the wind as he whispered lyrics to the chords.

His music was magic.

She was about to return the Firebird when she noticed a narrow door in the case. Taking a deep breath, she pulled the brown leather tab. In the hidden compartment was the packet of strings TJ had purchased for Danny at Christmastime, so long ago. Next to the packet was a velvet pouch. Navy blue. Handmade. She lifted the pouch, released the cord, and opened the bag. She freed it from its bloodred interior, held it to the light, and peered through the hole in the center. She turned it over and examined the back.

Her Odin stone. The one she'd given to Danny to keep him safe. Why had he left it behind?

Then she noticed something else—airmail envelopes. In the case's inner chamber beneath the guitar strings packet, a cracked rubber band choked a small bundle of them.

The first was from Danny and addressed to Ben.

Clutching the letters in her trembling hands, Emily returned the Odin stone to its pouch and replaced it beneath the secret door. She settled the Firebird in its nest, clicked the case closed, and leaned it against the wall.

It was almost one in the morning. Who knew when—or if—TJ would return home?

She pulled on a pair of jeans, a sweatshirt, a jacket, and boots. She grabbed her pack and Beulah's keys. She held the letters to her heart for a second before walking into the night.

Emily kept track of the splintered moon as Beulah escorted

her through the trees. She intended to go to San Jose. To Clare, Spider, Matt, and to the comfort of friends. But Beulah had other plans. They headed to the coast and stopped at the end of a remote street facing the sea. She switched off the engine, pulled the brake, cranked open the window, and stepped outside.

The sky, alive with stars and the sound of rumbling surf, offered hope. She looked for Orion, but it was late, and the constellations were turned around. She rotated with them until she found the Milky Way. Searching the skies for a single point of light in the galaxy's center, she discovered the impossible. Capella, a baby goat that Auriga cradled in his arms as he drove his chariot across the sky.

This was what she wanted. To be cradled like that.

In the glove box, she found a flashlight and a Swiss Army knife to slice the rubber band holding together the bundle of letters. To her surprise, none of the fragile papers tore.

They were in chronological order, all addressed to Ben, beginning with Danny's experiences at Fort Ord. His descriptions were brief, even abrupt—not what Emily was looking for. She put those letters aside. She upended the pile and opened the most recent envelope. It was written by a guy named Blink.

May 12, 1970

Dear Ben,

I've heard a lot about you—all good, that's the reason I'm writing. You've been through stuff like this. Danny trusts you, and you're the only person I can talk to now.

Danny and I were Cherries together when we landed in the country. I was the RTO. Danny loved my gear—he was fascinated with radios, I guess. Danny was the point man on and off in our old platoon. Everyone liked him. We called him Cougar because he walked so quietly and noticed everything. He was a good man to have as point. He and I got transferred to support the 4th Infantry because they needed fresh bodies. Then they took my radio away and made me fight.

Mating Habits of Fireflies

Danny might have mentioned in his last letter that we're in Cambodia now. We CA'd from Camp Radcliff at An Khe for a short bird ride to our landing zone. We humped out late in the afternoon, and that's when Cougar saw this kid, but he ran away. The next day we set up an ambush. Nobody came. The rest of the platoon gave up and returned to the perimeter, but Cougar, me, and a few snipers. We stayed behind because Cougar smelled trouble. I guess we weren't supposed to split up like that. Then we got word that two other platoons had made contact somewhere close. Cougar and I and this guy Norris humped over to them and found our CO dead, and everyone else was into some real hot stuff. We worked hard to get the wounded out and tried to save the rest of the guys who were pinned down. The enemy shot up the medivac dust-off place, so the Huey flew off before they could load everyone. We were out there, just Cougar and me and Norris and a lieutenant we didn't know—for hours—with a bunch of dead guys and a lot of wounded and Doc frantically trying to keep everyone quiet while we waited for another medivac to come. This kid—looked like he was about ten—a goner. Moaning and in a lot of pain.

Doc was our friend from the old platoon. Coolest guy you'd ever meet. He'd already given our guys morphine, so he went over to give the Cambodian kid a shot of tranquilizer. I guess that's when the lieutenant snapped. He'd been in a lot of shit before this, and he was a short-timer, and I think he was done with "gooks," as he called them. He told Doc not to give the guy morphine. Doc said it was his job to help people. "Not dinks," said the lieutenant. Doc said, "Look, he's just a kid. His guts are all over the place. All I want to do is take away the pain." So, what did the lieutenant do? He cocked his gun to Doc's head and threatened to pull the trigger. Doc ejected the syringe into the kid's thigh, and Cougar tackled the lieutenant right as the gun went off. There was this big scuffle, and before I knew it, Doc was dead, and the lieutenant had Cougar pinned under him, his gun pressing on Cougar's cheek. That was when Norris shot the lieutenant.

Thing is, the dust-off saw it all. The Huey's Firefly lit up the scene like a circus. I got scared, grabbed Cougar and Norris, and the three of us ran.

We tried to make it to the perimeter, but we were surrounded. We put up a damn good fight until the rest of the company came. When all the dust settled, the enemy was gone, and so were Cougar and Norris.

When we got back to the perimeter, the acting CO pulled everyone into the CP and formed a position for the night. He requested an aerial reconnaissance to look for Cougar and Norris. He said there was nothing more we could do for them because it was getting dark. The dust-off with the searchlights had already evacuated the wounded.

Next day the company made a sweep into the area. We came to this ghost town. We figured they took Cougar and Norris elsewhere, so we burned the hooches, dropped grenades into the bunkers, and moved forward.

I'm telling you all this because Cougar would want you to know. And make sure you understand the truth about what went down. Your brother's a sharp man. He seems to know the jungle, so we're all hoping he has a chance. He gave me a letter to send to you. I guess he was afraid he might not come back or something. Like all of us. He wrote it on May 6th when we waited for the choppers to pick us up at New Plei D'Jereng and take us over the border. I'm posting it today. You'll probably get it when you get this.

Sorry.

Your brother and Doc were my best buddies. I feel it with you, man.

Blink Johnson

Emily couldn't stop shaking. She folded the page into its envelope and set it on the passenger seat. Fumbling through the rest of the letters, she searched for one dated May 6. Nothing. The last was dated May 3.

Dear Ben,

We finished our last mission on the 29th. CA'd to LZ Hard Times and then convoyed to An Khe. It was great to have a standdown. Finally. Gave me a chance to take a few pictures and write another letter to Emmie. I'm worried about her. Don't hear from her much. I did maybe once or twice, but she was vague about what was going on. I hope she still loves me. More than that, I hope she's okay.

I know. You warned me.

It looks like we're leaving for a new mission tomorrow. Tonight, everything changed again, and no one knows what our AO is. Rumors say we're headed north and west of Pleiku, which means Cambodia.

They're setting up lots of ammo supplies, including mortar tubes—more than the basic load. Our packs are twice the normal weight. Pray for us, Ben.

As always, hug those trees for me, dude, okay? And take a good dip in the lake. Snow should be melting by now, and the water'll be cold enough to shrink your balls big time. I'll write again as soon as I can.

Love you, you know that.

—D

The moon had vanished, and the stars were shifting again. She couldn't bear to read the rest of the letters.

After a numbing crater of time, she placed the envelopes into her bag and hesitated before turning the ignition. Beulah shuddered back to the cabin.

TJ was slumped on his stomach, arms and legs splayed across the couch. Emily tiptoed into the bedroom, crawled under the covers, and curled into a ball.

36

Emily's existence felt more tainted and obscure with each day. How could it be Christmas already?

TJ nudged her shoulder. "Wake up, Em. I made coffee." He held the steaming cup at the perfect angle for the aroma to seep into her dreams. She opened her eyes to the sun and pinched her nose. Her sneeze came anyway.

"Bless you, Merry Humbug," he said, placing the cup on the orange crate she used as a nightstand. He handed her a tissue from the box beside the bed.

She took a sip. "Whoa." She felt instantly alert. "Where'd you get this? It's fantastic."

TJ's grin took over his face. "From your new Max-Pax coffee maker." He rose and closed the curtains to block the light.

"Coffee maker?"

"Your Christmas present. Let me show you." He helped her out of bed and led her to the kitchen. A shiny percolator sat on the counter. "Look," he said, lifting a filter. "You put these paper rings in this basket here, like this. No measuring or anything. And you don't get any grounds in the coffee. All you do is plug it in, and voilà! Fresh coffee! No more instant. And it's easy to clean."

"You sound like a commercial."

"I was hoping you'd like it. I have something else for you."

"Wait." She grabbed his elbow. "Let me get your present first."

"You've already done that."

"No, TJ. I hid it in Beulah's back seat."

"That's not what I mean."

TJ walked her to the chair in the living room and sat her down. He lowered himself to the floor in front of her. "Before we get into an argument, I need to come clean."

Emily stared at him. Was this about Danny's letters? She'd replaced them in the Firebird case but couldn't shake the feeling that TJ knew she'd found them. Then she thought there might be others. She'd even checked the boxes under the porch but didn't dare to rummage around in TJ's Fender case or underneath any of the amps.

TJ sighed and reached for her hand. "Danny told me to take care of you, but I haven't done a very good job." He was close to tears, alarming her even more. "Okay," he finally said. "Em, get dressed. We gotta go. Put on something nice, okay? We only have an hour to get there. That means we should leave in about half an hour or so."

"What are you talking about?"

"I can't tell you. A surprise. Please. Something nice, okay? I have to take care of something. I promise I'll be back soon."

Before she could protest, TJ was out the door and backing out of the drive in his truck.

Disoriented, she pushed her hair away from her eyes and circled the room. Catching her breath, she ran to the bathroom, stripped down, and showered. The tiles were shining like the percolator TJ gave her. He must have spent all night scrubbing them. The plumbing shuddered when she turned the knob. Cold water spurted from the showerhead. When she mixed in enough hot to balance the temperature, all the pipes squealed. Brand-new towels hung from the rack, tags still attached. Emily looked more closely before taking one. "Merry Christmas, Em" a tag said. "Sorry I've been such a slob" on another. "I thought you'd like these" on a third. Matching washcloths and hand towels sat on the hamper. All pink. Her favorite color.

Beads of towel fuzz stuck to her body as she dried herself. In the bedroom, she lifted a denim miniskirt from the back of the chair, slipped it on, and zipped the side. She searched the closet for underwear and a cardigan. She buttoned the front and grabbed the embroidered jean jacket Clare had given her years ago. She'd found her bag and was walking out the door just as TJ returned.

They climbed into Beulah. TJ recited directions as Emily drove. Beulah hummed down several winding roads, took the ramp onto the highway, and headed toward Santa Cruz. After getting off on one of the main streets and making a series of turns, she finally pulled up to the curb. She knew exactly where they were.

"Thirsty?" TJ asked as they climbed from the car.

"The Catalyst is open on Christmas?"

TJ winked. "Just for you."

"Wait, here's your present." She reached for the package on the back seat.

"Not yet, okay? It'll be here when we return."

Emily opened her mouth but couldn't find the right words, so she shrugged. She patted Beulah's hood and followed TJ to the front door.

"Is the band playing or something?"

"I just thought it'd be nice to have a drink together and listen to someone else for a change."

"Why don't you want my present?"

TJ took her hands in his. "I do, Em. There's something we have to do first—it's important. You'll see."

He was trying too hard. Emily needed to regroup.

"Will this something wait a minute? I need some fresh air. It won't take long."

"Sure." TJ studied her face. Then he disappeared inside.

It felt too warm for Christmas. The sunlight tasted vaguely familiar—sweet butterscotch with a slight citrus tang. She shaded her face with her hands to block the glare, but it was no use. A series of sneezes escaped into the tissue she'd retrieved from her pocket.

She sat on a nearby bench and swung her feet to admire her Sophia Loren sandals, still favorites after all this time. She hadn't polished her nails—she didn't even own nail polish anymore. Maybe she should have curled her hair.

Emily pinched her nose to stop another sneeze and rose to escape an approaching stranger.

"Please." The man held out his handkerchief. "Don't get up. There's plenty of room."

The sun blinded her. She clutched her pack and moved to the other end of the bench. It groaned as the guy threw himself next to her. A little too close. She could feel his heat.

"It's okay," he said, pushing the handkerchief back into his jacket pocket. "You can look at me."

What a joke. Emily stood and walked as fast as she could toward the door.

"Wait! Emmie!"

He knows my name?

The guy grabbed her elbow. She turned.

The sky was all over him. His smile. His dimples. His chin. His voice resonated like the timbre of drums.

"Emmie," he said.

The tone vibrated through her body.

"Emmie," he repeated. He wiped her cheek with his very-much-alive knucklebone. He opened his arm. She fell in.

What is it when you feel a man's pulse beneath his jacket, passion rising from his body and filling your own? What is it when you notice he's hugging you with one arm, the other limp at his waist? What is it when you press layers of loose fabric against his jutting ribs and release everything you're made of—good, bad, ugly, beautiful— into his wounded body and feel all your traumas merging with his?

"It's love," said Danny.

Did I say that out loud?

"You didn't have to."

37

SHE WAS ALL QUESTIONS.

When? How? Why wasn't he with the other POWs getting off those planes? Why hadn't he contacted her? How did he find her—of all places—at the Catalyst?

Emily wanted to ask what happened to Danny's arm, but she didn't know how. Besides, she was too upset, afraid, bewildered, and elated to want those kinds of details.

TJ brought her a glass of white wine to calm her down.

She searched for a clue in TJ's eyes.

He and Danny sipped their beers. Both were smiling.

Danny swallowed and put down his glass. "I came in the other night."

"What other night?"

"Day before yesterday," said TJ. "Danny showed up after our second set."

"And you didn't tell me?"

"I needed a little more time," said TJ. "I convinced Danny to stay mum until today. You know, Christmas and all."

Emily turned to Danny. "Why didn't you call me? You've been in the States for how long? Why in hell didn't you ca—"

"Em, it's okay." TJ reached for her.

Emily's chin quivered. She pushed away her wine.

"Let's get out of here," Danny said.

TJ nodded. "I know the perfect place."

Beulah took them to an isolated street near the beach. TJ set the parking brake before a small house. It looked a little like Cassiopeia Oaks from the old Scholastics retreat, only with peeling paint and a spotty lawn.

Emily tried to make herself invisible in the back seat. She watched TJ walk to the passenger door and open it for Danny. When he returned to pull Emily from Beulah's womb, she buried her head between her knees.

"I thought you'd be ecstatic. Come on, Em. I'll be back tomorrow. Joseph will follow me in my truck so Beulah can be with you and Danny." He stood awkwardly outside the door. "Look, I didn't know things would work out like this. Not this fast, anyway. I only had a day to find this place, and I just signed the papers this morning. I hope it suits you. It's the best Christmas present I could imagine giving you."

She glared at him.

"I'll bring the coffeemaker. And the towels. I already put a few of your things in the living room. I'll explain more tomorrow. You two deserve a chance to catch up."

He helped Emily climb out.

"Rent's paid for two months," he said. "That'll give you time to figure out if you want to stay here. It's close to town. I thought it might be easier for Danny to get around for now. Everything's paid on the Felton house, too, if you'd rather stay there."

"Don't forget your present." Her voice was flat.

TJ smiled. "I won't. I definitely won't."

Beulah didn't want to start at first. On TJ's second try, she relented and puttered away.

Danny smiled from the front porch.

Emily smiled back.

"Wish I could carry you over the threshold," he said before opening the unlocked door and switching on the light inside.

When she reached him, she touched his clean-shaven face to make sure he was real.

His shoulders relaxed. He took her bag in his good hand and kissed her cheek. "Sorry about this." He pointed to his arm. "Army ruined it."

"What happened?"

"You don't want to know."

Inside, the scent of sage greeted them. The living room held a beanbag chair, a duffel, and a few boxes TJ had brought from the Felton house. To the right was a delft-tiled kitchen with an electric stove and a full-size refrigerator. Down the hall, a bathroom with a claw-foot tub. And to the left, a wallpapered bedroom with a dresser and a mattress on the floor.

Danny placed Emily's bag next to the bed.

She'd dreamed about this moment for as long as she could remember. She'd pictured Danny in this very scene, ripping off her clothes and rolling with her, all tongue and breath and skin. Rose incense. Rose light. Jorma's "Embryonic Journey" playing in the background. Gracie's mellow recorder. Balin singing "Comin' Back to Me."

But that wasn't how it was. Instead of the boy she'd fallen in love with, a man stood before her. A damaged man. And she was a damaged woman.

Danny broke the silence. "I don't know what to say."

Emily traced his cheek.

"Please forgive me," he whispered through her fingers. "For not telling you. I never stopped thinking about you. I never stopped—"

"Every day. Every minute. I tried to dream you alive, but I didn't know how. Still, you came back."

Danny caught her words with his mouth.

38

Daybreak. Emily squinted and rolled over as soon as the sunlight hit her eyes. She sneezed and snuggled closer to Danny, but he felt dead cold when she put her arm around him. She startled awake and reached beneath the sheets to check his breathing. Her fingers touched something soft. She threw back the blankets. Two pillows were arranged beneath the covers, in the shape of a person lying beside her.

Danny was gone.

She stumbled down the hall. No one was in the kitchen. Nor the living room. Nor the bathroom. She pulled on the skirt she'd left on the bedroom floor, buttoned her cardigan, and ran outside. A detached garage stood at the end of an overgrown drive at the side of the house. Danny was sitting in the weeds in front of it. When he saw her, he crushed his cigarette in the dirt. He pocketed the butt and stood.

"Mornin', darling."

Mornin'? Darling?

"Cool-looking shed here. Look at this."

The garage's double doors creaked as Danny opened them. Inside were several shelves and a worktable caked with peeling paint and dust.

"All I have to do is clean it up, seed the lawn, trim the bushes. Then we'll have ourselves a fine place to live, art studio and all."

Emily was about to scold him for making her think he was still in bed with her and for scaring her when she couldn't find him. But here he was, offering to make a nice home for them. With a studio. Emily felt like punching him and kissing him at the same time.

Instead, she studied his eyes. They had the same vacancy she'd seen in the faces of the other POWs. The same vacancy she'd noticed in the photo he'd sent to her in Italy, the one with the radio antennae coming out of his khaki hat. Now, a flesh-and-blood stranger stood before her.

Danny squinted. "Why are you looking at me like that?"

"Because I missed you."

Her lie was also the truth.

Danny cracked two eggs with one hand into a cast-iron pan he found in the cupboard. He stabbed the yolks with a knife and added two slices of toast.

They took their plates out back and sat on the stoop. Their forks scratched against cheap melamine. Neither spoke. Too many stories separated them.

After cleaning up, he pulled an album from a box he'd labeled "Tunes." Dylan's latest: *Pat Garrett & Billy the Kid*. He turned the LP to side two and placed the turntable needle on the second track, "Knockin' on Heaven's Door."

They did the only thing they knew how to do whenever they ran out of words.

"Shit," Danny said, fumbling with the pearl buttons on her sweater.

"It's okay," Emily whispered. She unbuttoned them for him.

She lifted the military clasp on his belt, rugged and industrial compared to the mushroom-shaped belt buckle she so fondly remembered. He used his good hand to slip her sweater off her shoulders. She lifted his T-shirt, nearly transparent against his sharp ribs. A bloom of skin puckered near his left shoulder blade, punctuating a ridge arcing from his back all the way under his left arm and onto his chest. He kissed the hollow of her neck. She touched the tattoo bearing her name, interrupted by his scar.

His skin had soured. It no longer smelled of butterscotch, Jeffrey pines in the forest. He slid her skirt down her hips. She fingered a series of delicate ridges below the nape of his neck with spires reaching a peak in the center. Something else puckered toward the middle of his back. He flinched at her touch. She slipped her hand inside his tattered army pants—real, not the ones so popular in surplus stores. He cupped his hand between her legs.

She braced herself against the wall and tightened her legs and arms around his back, where her middle finger fell into a dimpled wound leading to the track zipping around his side. Her gasp came from a place between pleasure and pain, fear and release. She outlined the trail on his skin as she fought back tears.

Danny lowered her to the floor. He frowned, determined to pull up his fatigues without her help. He turned to grab his shirt.

The size of his scar startled her. Tattoos she'd never seen framed it. A pyramid of intricate symbols had been scored below his neck. At the base of his back, two tigers climbed an abstract mountain.

He spun around, tightened his belt, and nodded toward the pile of her clothes on the floor. It looked like he, too, was trying not to cry. Before she could reach for her sweater, he was out the door.

Emily dressed, slumped to the carpet, and cradled her head.

About an hour later, Beulah arrived, carrying TJ and several boxes of Emily's things. Joseph followed with more stuff in the truck.

"Where'd you unearth all this?"

"Under the house."

She unfolded the flaps of one of the larger boxes while the guys retreated outside. Sandwiched between pieces of heavy cardboard were two canvases: her winged lady and the portrait Danny had painted of her years ago. When she recognized what they were, her chest heaved. She slid them back into the box.

TJ returned and squatted beside her. "I need to talk to you, Em. Not here, though. Joseph's helping Danny clean out the garage. They'll be occupied for a while."

"Sure."

Emily brushed her hands against her skirt and followed TJ to the curb.

"We can walk." He threw a large blanket from Beulah's trunk over his shoulder.

The beach wasn't far. They both stopped to pick up seashells before approaching the shoreline.

"I'm sorry about yesterday. How I acted," Emily said, settling onto one side of the blanket.

"I'm the one who should apologize. I should have told you about Danny coming home and, you know, let you in on how I felt all these years. I should have supported you more. It was hard, Em. I'm not good at this—at least not when it matters. I say the wrong things."

"Me too."

Sitting across from her, TJ drew circles in the sand. "Thanks for the portrait, by the way. It's the nicest thing anyone has ever done for me."

"You finally opened your present. I'm glad. I painted it to capture your mood while you were playing Danny's guitar."

"You captured it, all right." TJ smiled. Then he blushed and added more circles to his sand drawing.

She leaned over and squeezed his arm. "Thank you. For being there for me no matter what."

"I wasn't there that often."

"You were when it counted."

"Okay then," he said after a long pause, "Remember when the POWs came home?"

Emily sat back. "Danny wasn't one of them."

"Actually, he was. On a stretcher. They took him to the hospital at Clark. He was in such bad shape they had to perform two surgeries on him. One to repair a damaged lung, the other to get out some bullets. They cut a nerve or something during the process and had to leave at least one bullet in him. That's why his arm is paralyzed. He went home to New York after going through debriefings and all. He said he needed time to heal before coming to see you."

"Holy shit. He told you this at the gig?"

"Em, I'm worried about him." He searched his pocket. "It'll be tough to go through these. But it's important. You need to know what happened in Nam. That way, we can figure out how to help him." He patted his chest and checked his other pocket.

"The letters?"

"I found them when I was packing Ben's things. I put them on the table where you were painting. Including the letters Danny sent to me."

"Danny sent you letters too?"

"You just looked at all the envelopes and cried. You were so upset. So, I stashed them in our guitar cases. I went through them later and organized them by date. Guess I was mustering the courage to read his letters to Ben."

"Oh, God. TJ. I don't remember—"

"I did a lot of stupid things. I should have told you Danny came to the gig. I got this from him the day after. I have it here, somewhere." He patted his jacket again. "Along with some letters. A few of them, anyway."

"It's okay, TJ. We've been through a lot."

"Danny's been through a lot more."

Emily was silent for a while. Then she squeezed his hand. "I wish Ben were here to help us get through this. I miss him. You supported me, though. Even when I was bitchy. I wish I could be a good—you know, person."

"You are, Em. More than you know." TJ looked up and backed away. "And here he comes."

Emily felt a separation between air and water. She shielded her eyes and searched the horizon. Body surfers. Sea lions. And to her right, Danny. Stumbling toward them.

He kicked the sand as he approached. After reaching them, he struggled to assume a comfortable position next to TJ.

TJ made room. "Sorry, man—"

Danny halted him with his palm. "I know what you're doing."

Emily shifted her weight.

"It's okay, TJ. I get it. Now's as good a time as any to do this. You have the letters?"

TJ searched the pocket inside his parka. "Shit, that's where they are." He pulled out a group of envelopes.

The wind lifted a strand of Danny's hair. He folded it behind his ear. When TJ gave him the first envelope, Danny handed it to Emily. It was addressed to Ben.

Emily pushed it back. "Not here, Danny. Not now."

"Emmie. Here and now is all we've got."

She took a breath and opened it.

No date. It was from Blink.

Dear Ben,

Good and bad news, man. They found Cougar. I guess I should say the Firefly spotted him. Anyway, the important thing is—he might still be alive.

This was unreal. Here was a letter saying Danny was alive. And here was Danny, for real, sitting right next to her.

"Can't you just tell me what happened?"

"Go ahead and read."

"Out loud?"

"To yourself. Please."
A breeze curled the edges of the page.

Turns out the enemy took him and Norris. The Firefly came back to search the area and rooted them out. They were scattering like all get out when the light hit 'em. That must have been when Norris and Cougar got shot. The guys in the Huey saw everything, like in the movies. They dispatched a dust-off. By the time we got there, Cougar was gulping for air. We had to work fast to get him on the litter. We ran him to the perimeter, which was darn close to where we found him. That's when the Firefly zeroed in on the enemy's hideout—a freakin' anthill parked right next to us. We didn't even know it was there. The Huey made sure the entire place was history. But by the time we went to load Cougar and Norris on the bird, Norris was dead, and Cougar had vanished. Along with his litter.

I don't know if you pray or anything, but now's the time to do it. I'll keep you posted when I hear more.

Blink

She searched Danny's face for an opening.
He gestured to the three letters TJ had placed before her.
She lifted the envelope on top.

Dear Ben,

Too weak to hold a pen, so dictating to this guy. Not talking too well right now. Feel like a piece of meat. No anesthetic. Said it would kill me. Think I passed out anyway. Grandfather was wrong about the feather. Things have changed. Tired. Gotta go.

Danny

Emily turned over the letter. Nothing else.
Danny picked at his shoelace.
"I don't understand," she said.

His face was pale. He took Emily's hand when she tried to touch his cheek.

"I wanted to wait until everything was good between us, but —" Danny stopped himself. He released her hand and pointed to the next letter.

TJ leaned in. "I can tell her."

"No."

"I just thought—"

Danny shook his head.

"Okay," Emily said, removing the airmail paper from its sleeve. It was dated May 6, 1970.

This is it! This is the letter Blink talked about. The one you told him to send.

Danny snatched it from her hands. "Fuck it all, TJ. How'd this get in here?"

TJ shrugged.

Danny pocketed the letter with his good hand, grabbed the one beneath it, and checked inside the envelope. "This is it."

"Why not that one?" Emily hated the way her heart slammed against her chest.

Danny rammed his fist into the sand, crumpling the letter. "I'm trying to tell you, damn it." His body began to shudder as he struggled to flatten the envelope against his leg.

"Hold on, buddy," said TJ, touching Danny's shoulder. "It's okay."

Danny shrugged him off. He folded his right arm around his ribs, rocked a couple of times, found a point on the horizon, and fixed his gaze. He ignored the letter as it slid onto the blanket.

A pair of gulls called to each other as they came in for a landing. One seized a small crab and flew off. The other picked around for a while. Nothing seemed worth grabbing.

"I lied to you, Emmie," Danny said.

"What?"

"Remember the owl you saw? The feather I gave you?" He turned to her. "I lied about them. What they meant, that is. I don't know how to say this, Emmie. I wasn't supposed to come back."

"I don't under—"

"The minute my grandfather and I dreamed about the owl that came to you that night, my family knew it was our time. Ben saw the owl in person, like you did. He called me the next day. To warn me something was about to go down. We believe in signs like that. I left the Odin stone behind because it was meant to keep you safe, not me."

"Wait—"

"I know." Danny's nod was long and slow. "You'll never understand our people's ways, Emmie. Or what any of us went through in that damn war. Just read the letter. It took me a long time to write. It's better than anything I can say right now."

She picked up the envelope and checked the postmark. "You sent this from the States?"

"Vets' hospital. New York." Danny outlined a triangle in the sand with his index finger.

"Please, Danny. I don't want to read any more letters." She lifted his chin. *I want to work this out with you—any other way.*

Danny's eyes filled. He turned away.

The letter was addressed to TJ but written to Emily.

She looked at TJ. "When did you get this?"

"Monday."

"Day before yesterday?"

"Yeah."

Danny's handwriting was horrible—a lot of cross-outs and words inserted between the lines. He must have written it with his right hand, the hand he was still learning to use.

Dear Emmie,

Last night I had a dream. I was back in Cambodia. There was this window. It appeared before me as I was lying in the jungle next to my buddy Norris. This voice told me I was looking at the Window of Invulnerability. If I climbed through it, I'd be able to walk out of the war and come home to you. It took a lot of willpower and courage, but I climbed through. When I got to the other side, I wasn't home. I was strapped to a hospital bed. A man was strapped in the bed next to me. An old Cambodian. He said there was no such thing as invulnerability, let alone a window you could climb through to find it. It was a trick to get me to come back to this world. I struggled to turn my head so I could see his face. He wasn't the old villager, after all. He was Grandfather.

Emily glanced at Danny before turning the page.

"Dan," Grandfather said. "You may be on your way home, but I'm going through the Window of Invulnerability. It's okay to be invincible where I'm headed. But not in your world. There, you must know pain. You understand suffering. You know beauty. You must be wounded before you can heal, and you must heal before you can love. You've been through this many times: pain, suffering, healing, beauty. Love. I thought your circle was complete, but I was wrong. You have one more lesson to learn."
   "What lesson?"
   "The one that comes after love."
   "What comes after love?"
   "That's your lesson, not mine."
   In my dream, we both went under the knife. The doc removed a bullet from my back and treated me with the same herbs Grandfather used to use. They didn't do that for the old villager. They just let him die.
   Later I found out Grandfather had died, at that very moment. Along with Ma. They were on their way to a tribal meeting in Allegany. They were never meant to get there. The owl had warned us. Then I found out about Ben.

Emily looked up. Danny's eyes were closed. She blew air from her cheeks, located the next page, and blinked away tears.

I was supposed to die with them, Emmie. In the jungle. That New Year we spent together? In San Jose? I wanted to tell you everything. To prepare you for the worst. But I didn't know how. I thought I'd scare you if you knew too much. That's why I made up the thing about the feather. I guess I wanted to believe the stuff about being alert and seeing in the dark and all that. I wanted to believe the owl meant I'd survive if I paid attention. But Grandfather didn't think a white girl could ever understand the old ways. The owl that came into our dreams was sacred. We had to trust her, he said.

I argued with him. I found the feathers, packed my bags, and came home to you.

It's not a good thing to lie. Ever. But I did then. And I have since. Being scared does this to you.

Emily crumpled the paper. "I never meant to hurt your family. I never meant for the owl to—"

"You're not to blame, Emmie." He met her eyes. "Nor is the owl. There are things in this world that are beyond our reason and control." He took the page from her hands, straightened it, and handed it back. "Please. Just read."

She nodded. It took a while before she could refocus.

When your letters stopped, everything inside me changed. I wanted to end it all. So many of my buddies were dead. So was Ben. So were Ma and Grandfather. I needed to follow my family and the grunts who sacrificed their lives for me. Even if it meant losing you.

While I was under the knife, the old villager located me in another dream. He took me to his hooch. When we got there, it was burned to a crisp. He couldn't bring his family back to life, so he worked his magic on me. He showed me the insects, the plants, and how to navigate by the sun and stars in the jungle. Before the enemy took me away, he leaned on my left arm. It was like he was trying to tell me something. I haven't been able to use that arm since.

Emmie, you were right about the soldier in the mud, the boy under the table, and the same boy in the car. I went off that cliff with you because of our shared dreams. And Grandfather? He was wrong about us. That was what he told me from the other side of the Window of Invulnerability. I know this is all so confusing. And I'm so out of it that I don't even understand my own story. But please. Listen to me. Even if you don't want me anymore, I'll keep you safe. Here. In my heart. That's my promise. I love you. Always have. Always will.

39

Danny didn't want to talk about any of this after that day.

It was New Year's Eve. TJ and Clare came to celebrate at the Santa Cruz home. Everyone squeezed into the kitchen to work—chopping, grating, slicing. Emily placed a pot of brown rice on the stove. Clare lit a candle to keep the onions from stinging her eyes. She and Emily tore lettuce for salad and added wedges of tomato and avocado. Danny threw oil and garlic into the wok he'd bought as a Christmas present for Emily. He added onions, carrots, and broccoli. Emily cubed a slab of tofu and tossed that in.

They ate on the living room floor. TJ pulled Creedence Clearwater Revival's new album from its sleeve and set the needle to "Have You Ever Seen the Rain?"

Clare lifted a glass of zinfandel. "Welcome home, Danny."

"*Cin cin!*" everyone said, toasting in Italian. "To 1974."

Emily smiled at the Christmas tree Danny had purchased from the Boy Scouts. It drooped from the weight of a few handmade ornaments but still looked good in the corner. She and Danny had scattered art supplies around it, promising each other they'd begin painting soon. Danny wanted to make the shed into a perfect studio.

After dinner, TJ placed B. B. King's "The Thrill Is Gone" on the turntable. He passed a joint to Clare, who took a hit and handed it to Danny. Emily gathered everyone's plates and brought them to the kitchen. She savored this alone time as she washed, dried, and put away the dishes.

Clare peeked around the corner. "Finished already? I wanted to help clean up."

"Good timing."

Clare opened the refrigerator and rooted around until she found a champagne bottle. "How about we get a head start on '74? It's almost midnight in New York." Without waiting for a response, she waltzed back into the living room.

Emily heard laughter. Then stony giggles. Then a loud bang.

Danny shrieked.

Emily dropped the towel and ran.

He was rolling on the floor, clutching his chest, gasping for air. TJ and Clare hovered over him.

"You're okay, Danny. You're cool, man." TJ's face pleaded for Emily's assistance. "The cork. We popped it."

Emily knelt by Danny's ear. He looked desperate and scared as he opened and closed his mouth.

"Follow my lead," she whispered.

Her inhale was strong and clear; so was her exhale.

"It's your turn, Danny. Breathe with me. Inhale. Now exhale. Slowly, like this."

Clare and TJ joined in. They breathed in unison until Danny's chest heaved and color returned to his face. Emily escorted him to the bedroom and motioned for the others to curl around him in the bed.

Danny finally calmed. His breathing became steady.

After Clare and TJ left, Danny cradled Emily in his arms.

"Thank you," he whispered.

"I thought you'd be mad at us, fawning all over you like that."

"I was." His eyes were kind. Soft, even.

This was the Danny she knew and loved.

He snuggled closer. "Want to hear a story?"

"Of course." Emily was ecstatic.

"A Khmer folktale—"

"Khmer?"

"Cambodian. About a goddess and a giant. They studied under this hermit."

"Was he the wise and powerful villager who saved your life?"

Danny smiled. "He lived deep in the jungle."

What did they study?

Magic, of course.

"Of course."

"The hermit had a magic ball he wanted to give to his most worthy student, so he challenged the goddess and the giant to collect the morning dew."

"Let me guess. The one who could do it got the ball."

"But they both collected the morning dew. That's the problem. The giant gathered a pile of leaves from the forest, and he let the dewdrops slide from each leaf into his glass. One by one. Like this." Danny clicked his tongue, imitating heavy dewdrops plopping into an imaginary glass.

"Do that again."

Danny exaggerated an O with his mouth and repeated a guttural *tchick*ing sound.

"You're too much, you know that?"

"The goddess was smart, though. Smarter than the old giant. She spread a tablecloth on the grass and left it there overnight. The next morning, she squeezed the dew out of the cloth and into the glass. That's how she won."

"The power of women."

"But it's not the end of the story."

"Typical."

"All the giant got out of the contest was a magic axe, so he used it to stalk the goddess. He flirted with her. Then he threatened her. The goddess was still nice to him because she knew about his tricks. Which made the giant furious, so he threw his magic axe at her."

I thought this was going to be a good story.

It is—

Yeah, right.

"—because he missed."

Emily smiled.

"So, the goddess tossed the ball into the air, creating a bolt of lightning that blinded the giant. He was so embarrassed, he disappeared into the sky."

"Poor guy."

"Not really. He still comes back to confront the goddess every year. In April—"

The month you went to Nam—

Danny shook his head. "—around the Cambodian New Year. Right before the monsoon rains."

As I said, the month you wen—

"The giant is Thunder—"

"—and the goddess is Lightning."

"He's full of noise, but she's the one who has all the power."

"You got that right." Emily hesitated, afraid of spoiling the moment. "Danny?"

"Hmm?"

"Is there a story like this from your people?"

"We don't tell our stories, Emmie. Not without permission. Because they're alive. They let us know how and when they want to be shared."

"Isn't the hermit's story alive too?"

"All stories are. The old man said I could share this one. He thought it might come in handy."

"The man in your dream?"

Danny didn't answer.

"What about these?" She rolled him over and lifted his shirt. She wasn't sure if she should touch the two tigers facing each other near his sacrum—or the series of spires at the base of his neck. "If we ask, will they let you tell me their stories?"

Danny rolled back, pulled her close, and traced a tangled spiral through her hair.

"They helped you dream me alive, Emmie. You had no idea you were powerful enough to answer their calls."

40

"All yours," said TJ the day the shed-like garage was finally ready. He threw his paint-splattered tools into the truck bed, brushed his hands on his T-shirt, and waved out the window while driving down the road.

After lunch, Danny and Emily set up their easels in their renovated studio. They began to paint. He constantly shook his right hand to keep it from cramping around the brush. She could feel his frustration as his left arm dangled at his side. He swore at the botched images on his canvas. She winced when he threw his brush across the room and walked away.

"This place needs music," Danny said the next day.

TJ arrived. Emily stayed in the background as the two spent the afternoon wiring the studio for sound.

For weeks, she heard them working through the night. Not with electrical wires and egg cartons, but on a song the color of strength and fight.

Can you call a raven with a silver coin?

One Saturday, TJ brought Emily and Danny to the Chateau Liberté, the old rock and roll club in the mountains where Wave used to play. He'd arranged to talk with the owner about putting on a solo gig featuring Danny's Firebird. He'd tried convincing Danny to sing the raven song with him, but Danny refused.

As soon as he pulled out the Gibson to continue his pitch, Emily took Danny's good arm, and they stepped outside.

A crowd was forming around a makeshift stage. Charles Lloyd, a jazz musician, tapped a microphone. Emily and Danny leaned against a tree to watch another Charles—Bukowski—step to the main mic. Bukowski grabbed a beer from the speaker behind him, took a long sip, and unfolded a piece of paper.

"Ode to a Blank Piece of Paper," he said in a slow slur after showing everyone the empty page.

The audience laughed. Bukowski closed his eyes and began a long-winded stream-of-consciousness rant about the plumbing in his apartment. Lloyd accompanied him on a breathy flute. Bukowski had begun a new ramble about bathtubs and ants when TJ skipped down the steps from the building. His thumbs-up suggested he'd gotten the gig. Emily hugged him as soon as he joined them to watch the rest of the performance.

That night, Danny was silent throughout dinner. He took a long bath and went to bed early. The next morning, Emily found him standing in the empty studio. He said he wanted to take Beulah for a drive, assuring her he could manage with one hand.

"What about the clutch?"

"That's the foot, silly. The gear shift is on the right."

"What about your driver's license? Do you still have one?"

"Beulah will take care of me."

The following morning, he peered out the car window while Emily drove to her new job at a gallery in Capitola, leaving Danny in Beulah's care.

"They hate us, Emmie," he said as he drove her home that evening. "Everyone hates us. A salesgirl wouldn't even look at me when she escorted me to an interview with her boss. No one wants to hire a vet, especially a left-handed vet whose left arm doesn't work."

Emily tried to reassure him, but he released the wheel and gave her the guillotine gesture.

When he wasn't job hunting, he was sprucing up their home. With his good arm, he scoured the sinks and toilets and vacuumed every speck on the floor. With utter determination, he trimmed the bushes and plucked all the weeds from his newly sprouted lawn.

He inspected every shadow before allowing TJ to help him scrape the siding to bare wood. With the owner's permission, they painted the house and garage in rainbow colors.

Danny religiously adjusted the thermostat. If they were low on milk or butter, he drove to the store. He insisted on going to the Laundromat himself. Emily had no idea how he managed to return with everything meticulously folded. Sometimes, he'd let Emily join him. They'd bring the laundry home in garbage bags and empty everything on the bed. Danny's right hand had become strong and efficient as he smoothed the T-shirts and folded them in thirds. His willpower was bulletproof.

Emily convinced him to try painting again. When he became frustrated, she threw paint at his canvas. He threw paint at hers. It didn't take long before they'd splattered each other from head to toe.

Emily poured leftovers from a gallon of blue house paint on a canvas tarp she'd spread over a small dirt area in front of the studio. She stripped to her underwear and rolled in it, inviting Danny to do the same.

He lifted a gallon of yellow and poured it next to Emily. "For your lightning bolts," he said as he unbuttoned his jeans and slid them off his hips.

Emily got up, grabbed the gallon of red, and poured it onto his naked feet. "Thunder for the giant."

They laughed as they splashed yellow lightning bolts and red thunder across the blue at their feet. Pigments merged, creating spectrums of purple, green, and orange. They smeared the complementary colors over each other's skin and made angels with their four legs and three arms. Then they crumpled the tarp and threw it into the trash. Shrugging, they retrieved it from the garbage can, hung it on the clothesline, scratched their chins, and pretended to be art critics. They hosed each other off. Then they chased rivulets of muddy pigment down the alleyway and into the street, lamenting how thoughtless they'd been for allowing the lawn, the bushes, and the water table to be tainted by toxins. When they realized they were nearly naked, they pointed at each other like horrified kids and raced inside.

Still, Danny searched the shadows. His nightmares multiplied. His criticisms became sharp. Her dress was too short, her neckline too low. He began to grill her about where she was going and when she'd return. When she objected, his foul moods escalated. He yelled. He threw his shoes against the wall. He grabbed her arm and begged her to be strong. He asked her to strike him with her magic ball to make him stop.

"Then stop already, damn it!"

He broke down when she stood up for herself. He apologized. He agonized. He promised. He told her he loved her and didn't want to lose her. He cradled her, and they made sweet, gentle, delicious love.

Then he broke.

TJ, please answer.

The phone kept ringing.

Emily slammed down the receiver, picked it up again, and dialed Clare in San Jose.

"Come over. Now!"

Emily didn't wait for a response. It would take at least half an hour for Clare to get there. She hung up and tried TJ again.

"What's up?"

"Danny locked himself inside the studio. Won't eat or drink. I can see him through the window. He's in the fetal position against the far wall. All he's doing is moaning and rocking."

"What triggered him?"

"He's been having these nightmares. We argued about what I was wearing. He grabbed my arm, and I—"

"How long has he been in there?"

"Two days."

"I'm on my way."

As expected, TJ arrived before Clare. He knocked on the side window of the shed.

"Hey, man. It's me, TJ."

Nothing.

"Have a flashlight?" he asked Emily.

"Tried that. It freaks him out even more."

TJ jiggled the pane. "How 'bout that Swiss Army knife?"

Emily ran to the driveway and pulled it from Beulah's glove compartment.

TJ opened a blade and worked it until he could wiggle the latch. It released, and he shoved open the window.

"Water. Em—" Before he finished his sentence, Emily was already running to the kitchen.

She reached it just as Clare burst through the door, out of breath, unable to speak, and wearing all her questions on her face. Emily handed her the water.

"Take this to the garage. Give it to TJ."

Emily fumbled around in the cupboards until she found a box of Junior Mints. Danny's favorite. She thought it might help.

By the time she reached TJ, he was still holding the glass and humming to Danny. Eventually, Danny's hand appeared, but it didn't look real. Blood gushed onto the sill.

"Shit, man! He slit his wrist!" TJ dropped the water glass, leaped over the shards, and ran to the double garage doors. He crashed his body against them until they gave way. "Call an ambulance!" he yelled.

Danny broke free, blood everywhere. He crouched as if he had a gun in his right hand and threatened to kill anyone who got near. Then he convulsed and collapsed.

41

Too many secrets hid beneath the eclipse of Cambodia's triple canopy. Too many secrets except the ones seared in Emily's mind: the dull click of the hammer; the cold muzzle pressed against Danny's cheek; the sharp taste of his fear.

Blink's letters had informed her that *Firefly* was the nickname for the cluster of searchlights attached to the Huey looking for Danny that night. A rotating mount aimed the beam across an arc twenty to thirty degrees forward and aft, up and down. It blinded everyone. The entire system weighed ninety-nine pounds—more than she did at the time.

Chiaroscuro. Light versus dark. Caravaggio could have painted the scene. Emily pictured the artist working in his dark studio, illuminating Danny's face by shining light through a hole in the ceiling and projecting the image onto stretched linen. *Va bene, li vediamo,* he might have said. *Yes, we see them, his eyes, how they flicker with fear, like Isaac's eyes flashed when his father, Abraham, tried to kill him.* She could see the sixteenth-century Italian crushing luminescent bodies of fireflies, drowning them in white lead, and preparing his canvas with the potion to fix the image in her mind.

The image. The incident. The fear.

Caravaggio had used the firefly's light to express the paralyzing fear Emily was experiencing now.

She was afraid the authorities might put Danny away forever and lock him in the bowels of a psychiatric hospital. She worked frantically to find the number of Dr. Harrison, the man who'd led the rap sessions back east—the talk therapy groups Danny had attended after he was debriefed. It was a breakthrough method recommended by one of the other doctors who'd treated him in New York. Dr. Harrison's secretary referred Emily to a professor of psychiatry at UC Santa Cruz.

To her surprise, Danny wanted the sessions. He'd already benefited from the rap groups back then. Fellow vets were the only ones who'd truly understood the inner hell he was going through. Emily recruited TJ to help her convince the hardheaded officials to release Danny from the loony bin list because they refused to listen to a woman. It was TJ, with all his good looks and charm, who finally persuaded them.

Like Dr. Harrison, Dr. Frazier became revolutionary in his field. He gathered a group of vets and POWs to share their stories. He convinced them of the importance of being candid. No lying —to themselves or anyone else. No semitruths, either.

Blink came to the group after Emily figured out how to contact him in Chicago. He was a divorced schoolteacher who'd grown soft and wore thick-lensed glasses from shrapnel that had virtually blinded him. He'd arranged for time off and booked a nearby motel for almost a month.

"Whatever you do, don't make lasagna," he told Emily the first time she and Danny invited him to dinner. He laughed like it was a joke, but Emily's thoughts placed her on the battlefield with him. Lasagna. The colors. The textures. Images with nightmare-triggering power.

Blink rubbed his belly after finishing Emily's typical brown rice meal. His McGovern T-shirt made her smile. Emily and TJ had celebrated their twenty-first birthdays by voting for McGovern. If Danny had been able to come home in 1972, he could have voted too. If the politicians hadn't been so corrupt, this idealistic patriot might have been able to turn that ugly warship around.

From then on, Blink and Danny spent most of their daylight hours together. They avoided making eye contact if Emily was around, but when they were outside, she spotted them patting each other on the back and laughing before driving Beulah to the sessions. They later walked along the beach and talked all night in Blink's motel room.

After Ford pardoned Nixon and Blink had to return home, Danny went back to punching his good fist through the wall and throwing books across the room. His paints and brushes dried in the shed's darkness. He quit the rap sessions, just like that.

From the kitchen one morning, Emily heard him yell. She tossed the dish towel on the counter and ran to the bedroom.

He was struggling to dress.

"Goddammit, don't sneak up on me like that! Fuck this! Fuck me! Goddammit! Why? Fuck it all to hell!"

She froze.

"Get out! Leave! Now!"

Her heart pounded as she raced from the bedroom and out the front door. She bolted through the empty lot across the street and headed toward the ocean. She wanted the breakers to sweep her away from the truth blinding her and streaming down her cheeks.

She was afraid of Danny.

She spent the afternoon gaping at the surf, aching for the old days when he'd whisper in her ear to calm her during times like this. He'd protected her back then. Now it was her turn to protect him, and she didn't know how.

When she returned, the house was empty. Beulah was gone.

She phoned Clare.

"I don't know where he is or what to do anymore. One minute he's this wound-up cussing mess. Then we make love like nothing's changed. Then the next time, he's so kind. Then he gets this scary look in his eyes, and I—"

"Has he ever hit you?"

"No, thank God."

"You think he misses the war?"

"He misses Blink, for sure—he's the only one who can relate to what he's going through."

"I mean having a mission, a purpose again?"

"You mean, like a—"

"Job?"

"Clare. I just want him to come home safely."

"The army brainwashed him, Em. They told him everything: what to do, how to think, how to act. Then when he was in the jungle, he had to rely on his instincts to survive. That strong intuition of his. And his fast reflexes. He's not using any of those skills anymore. He lost his arm, for god's sake. Music won't do it for him anymore. Painting either. Having a purpose will."

"Clare, you don't understand. No one will hire him. Besides, a job will break him."

"Not a straight job. How about working with the professor? You know, the rap-group guy? It'd be a way for him to support other vets instead of always worrying about himself. Maybe Danny could be an assistant or something."

Clare was brilliant.

Dr. Frazier hired Danny before Danny knew it was a possibility. Danny scheduled appointments, organized one-on-ones, and helped brainstorm the new mentor program. Within a month, he was doing well at work, and his faith in himself grew.

Brush in hand, he pitched acrylics everywhere. The garage became a Pollock masterpiece. Danny painted shirtless, his tattoos glowing. His images were bold, vivid, and terrifying. Rivers of bloody emotions flooded his canvases. His brush cut, devoured, caressed, sighed. Danny's abstract creations reached out, caught hold, and wouldn't let go.

"What are you doing?"

"What do you think I'm doing?"

Emily couldn't look away. There was a new vitality in his face, in his eyes, in the clean line of his jaw.

She grabbed a stretched canvas, placed it on her easel, and selected a brush. Umber. Cadmium red. A touch of cobalt. She glazed layer upon layer of transparent color to reveal the depth of Danny's mood. His body held his pain and tucked it away in his neck, his shoulders, and the scar pinching the flesh around his torso. There was brilliance there too. And levitation. A world of tattoos and pigmented particles. She coaxed them into fluid reflections of light. She caught the sun in his face and released its splendor with her brush. The light made him beautiful. So did the darkness surrounding that light.

She steadied her hand. The act of painting involved pain. The word itself—*painting*—reflected the suffering too many people hid inside. She recognized it in Danny's eyes—and in hers whenever she gazed at her reflection in the mirror.

The act of painting also involved healing. It enabled her to work with her fear of viscosity and coarseness. She wanted everything in her life to be smooth and carefully honed—the way the masters had prepared their wooden panels, polishing them until all texture disappeared. They covered them with gypsum and hide glue and burnished them until there were no irregularities—nothing but luminosity. She tried to mimic this process by creating acrylic glazes so deep she could get lost in them.

Intense emotion buried beneath the illusion of perfection. This was what she sought. But Danny's raw paintings taught her the value of letting go. One moment he'd pour his paint until it pooled in the middle of his canvas. The next, he'd make the most delicate and precise markings. Then, he'd scrape them away with his fingernails, apply thick globs of pigment over them, make a fist, and smear a monsoon of gray across the image.

Their art became their obsession. Their release. Their shared therapy.

Emily's boss at the gallery fell in love with Danny's work and scheduled a special show for him. *The Art of Danny Jackson: From*

Lead Guitar to the Aftereffects of War. Emily's portrait of Danny, "The Artist at Work," would greet viewers at the opening.

Danny wanted her to create an additional portrait for the exhibit. One of Dr. Frazier's clients, also a POW, volunteered to sit for her. Danny believed the man might benefit from seeing his image take shape in Emily's hands. But Emily worried about how the process might affect him and wondered if he'd want his likeness to be shown to the public.

"He's willing to help us," Danny said. "He says our art can show the world what it means to be human—and worthwhile—despite our flaws. If you're up to it, several other guys in our rap group want you to paint them too. It will be our show. Not just yours and mine, but theirs as well."

She found her answer in the POWs' eyes. Beauty in all its coarseness, in all its texture, in all its hostility and suffering. Beauty in all its frustration and fear.

In these portraits and in every work of art she'd created since she was a child, Emily realized she was painting herself.

2001
New York

*We are carrying on a desperate fight,
and we need all our forces.*

— Mary Cassatt

42

EMILY'S FATHER WAS DYING.

Walter had flown him from the West Coast to a Glens Falls nursing home near his residence in upstate New York. A flashy mortgage broker, he seemed to spend more time working in Manhattan than at his home office near Lake George. Emily figured her brother had called her because he was too busy to worry about their dad.

"One of us has to be with him. I've done enough, Emilia."

Danny offered to go with her, even though he hated to travel, especially in September and this close to his birthday. Emily wasn't about to forgive her father's inexcusable actions, but Danny convinced her she had to make whatever amends she could while her father was still alive.

"Try to understand him, okay? War turns you into a monster, Emmie. When that monster surfaces, the ones you love most become its victims."

At the nursing home, Emily looked away as the nurse lifted the bandage from two craters penetrating her father's bony back. The pressure sores looked like bullet holes, black in the center and ringed with red.

No, her dad didn't want a softer chair. No pillow either. He leaned his newly dressed spine against the sparsely covered springs of an old recliner and pointed a shaky finger across the room.

"See those people?" he asked Emily. "Around the piano?"

There were no people, and there was no piano. He must have thought he was still living in his childhood house. It had always been filled with family. Relatives who lived there, died there, were no longer there. He argued with them as he dozed.

"The one at the door wants me to go home," he said aloud. "Sorry. Not yet. I still have stuff to do. Besides, I'm already home." He startled awake and coughed. Several of his teeth fell onto a plate, and he rolled them with his middle finger.

She recoiled. The teeth. The gesture. Ben had done the same thing with the peas on his plate during Thanksgiving dinner decades ago.

Her father reached across the table and tapped at the phone. "Wasn't my dad supposed to call?" His eyes went blank, and then he clicked a remote to the news on TV. "Stupid wars." This from the red-in-the-face career colonel who'd landed on Omaha Beach.

For the first time, he seemed to recognize Emily. He took her hand. "Are you happy?"

She nodded.

From a small dish, he lifted two molars that had fallen from his mouth. He rattled them and tossed them like dice across his lap table.

"I'm glad you're happy." His face collapsed into a grin. His eyes filled. His entire body expressed pain as he reached out for her. Their shared suffering flowed down each of their faces.

"I'm sorry." His voice was so soft.

"Dad—"

"I wish I could take it all ba—" He looked confused. "I'm sorry," he said again.

She crumbled into his arms.

Emily wasn't aware of the Twin Tower attacks until she walked into the nursing home's lobby to meet Danny. She wondered aloud if her brother was okay.

"Call him," Danny said.

"I don't have his number."

"Find it and call him, damn it! Fucking call him!"

Danny's monster had returned.

In their hotel room, he jumped at the slightest shadows. He thrashed in his sleep that night. Long after midnight, the ringing phone startled them both awake.

"What the fuck do you want?" Danny shouted into the receiver, not knowing who was on the other end.

"Just returning Emilia's call. Tell her I'm at Lake George."

"He's alive?" Emily called out from the other side of the bed. She grabbed the receiver and put the phone on speaker. "Walter! How are you? Are you okay?"

There was a long silence. Then her brother broke down. It was the first time she'd ever heard him cry.

A wave of empathy overwhelmed her. She wanted to ask him so many things: How did he get out? Or had he been upstate the whole time? She wanted to know if his coworkers were all right. She wanted to talk about their father's passing. About his last words. About all the wrong and crazy things she and her brother had experienced while growing up. Had he been abused too? Had her father ever told him he loved him? She was embarrassed she hadn't paid enough attention to know. More than anything, she wanted to connect with him, to move through this horrific tragedy and somehow make amends.

"I'm so sorry, Walt—"

"I just lost my whole life," he said while sniffling, "and all you can say is sorry?"

She softened her voice. "I can't imagine what you're going through. I'm just glad you're okay. It's the worst day, and our father just died. Everything feels so unspeakable and devastating and surreal—"

"Didn't you hear? My fucking world is falling apart, Emilia. The last thing I want to do is go broke and become a hopeless loser like you and your boneheaded lover there."

Emily bristled. She took a breath and tried to stay calm. "What about your friends? Your colleagues?"

"What about them?"

"Oh my god. Do you realize what you just said?"

Silence.

"Look, Walt. Maybe this isn't the best time. Is there someone besides me you can talk to?"

"This whole planet is filled with pointless people like you."

Emily covered the receiver with her hand and turned to Danny, now fully awake.

What now?

"Just ask him," Danny whispered.

Her nod was measured. She'd been dreading this conversation. "Walt?" She paused. "What happened between you and Dad?"

Her brother's exhale made a whistling sound. "Oooh, I don't believe it. The world's on fire, and you do this to me? You have no idea. Even if I told you, it'd be more than your stupid brain could handle."

"Try me."

"I gotta go."

"Okay." She didn't want to end the call like this. But she did. She held the phone away from her ear and quietly pressed the receiver button.

"Asshole," Danny muttered under his breath.

"He's definitely alive."

Danny chuckled.

"I shouldn't have asked that. Not now, anyway. I just don't get why he has to be such a—"

"Jerk? Emmie, it's to protect himself from feeling anything. You did what you could. The ball's in his court now."

"I suppose. But what does it take to stay sane through this mess?"

Danny pulled back the blankets and climbed from the bed. "You're asking the wrong guy."

"The whole country is asking that question, Danny. Over and over. Generation after generation. We seem to carry trauma in our DNA."

"Tell me about it." Danny opened a corner of the curtains and scanned the deserted city outside.

43

THE FOLLOWING MORNING, AT THE NURSING HOME, Emily discovered she had no say in her family's affairs. As soon as Walter arrived to sign papers and announce he was in charge, she and Danny had no reason to stay.

All the airports were closed. Chaos, outrage, and endless footage of the disaster charged the news. Gridlock ruled.

A new round of frustration tortured Danny. He cursed and kicked at hotel furniture before grabbing their bags and leading Emily to the train station. They settled into two remaining seats. With her fist, Emily smudged a circle in the window and gazed at the stunned people waiting in line next to the tracks.

She and Danny had planned to go to Red House and circle back to DC. He wanted to kneel before the graves of his ma, his grandfather, and Ben. He wanted to touch the names of his buddies on the Vietnam Veterans Memorial. Now he had to leave them all behind. Again. Without saying goodbye.

It would be a challenging cross-country journey. Shortly after the train began to move, Danny pulled an envelope from his pack, tossed it on his seat, and excused himself. He'd been sick the last few days. Emily assumed he'd spend most of the journey huddled in the train bathroom.

A crescent moon swung from window to window, high, before cascading down and around to the other side of the coach and back again. Emily talked to a few other passengers as they watched it.

A Wisconsin teenager was heading to Silicon Valley to help pack his sister's stuff and take her back home to her family in the Midwest. "It's safer there," he said, drumming on his knee, headphones for ears.

A man from Michigan was on his way to be with his estranged wife in San Francisco. He rested his head on the thin train pillow, hypnotized by the moon. Before the first plane hit, his son had been prepping vegetables in the Windows on the World restaurant on top of the North Tower. "That's what was doing, yes, that was it," he repeated to himself as he struggled to sleep.

A young woman from Manhattan sought refuge in Oregon to be with her parents. She'd lost everything: her friends, her job, the building where she worked. She clutched the only thing she had left: her knitting. She gazed at the moon for a long time before returning to her work. Wool caps, one after the other, to give to the homeless in honor of each friend who'd died.

Dazed refugees, they worked their way west from New York, from Boston, from DC. Castanet rhythms pulled them through windswept fields, red rock canyons, and lightning-bleached deserts. Power spiked all around them, electrifying Emily's lips as she pressed them against the cold window. Rivulets of her breath pooled onto the metal-encased sills. They passed an Amtrak that had derailed a few days before, still on its side next to the tracks. A woman across the aisle told Emily how, just a few weeks ago, a California Zephyr like the one they were on had struck and dragged a man in his car for miles before it could stop. As they passed, Emily pictured the man's spirit rising above Grand Junction, Colorado. If only she knew his name.

It was Danny's birthday once more. Fifty-two. She was grateful he'd made it this long. The swaying moon carried his timeworn furrows. She sensed his anger in the red planet, Mars, as it crested the horizon. And his sadness in every other face taking the long journey on that silent train, curling its way through a ravine somewhere between the shock of war and home.

She touched the folded envelope on the seat beside her. Yellow, faded, and frail, it looked like Danny had been carrying it in his pocket for ages. She picked it up and checked the postmark.

"Oh my God." She sank into her seat, hoping no one had heard her, and turned away from the aisle.

She pulled a tightly folded illustration from the envelope and opened it. The sketch had a musty scent. It was the drawing she'd sent to Danny in Vietnam. A man and a woman reaching for each other, connected by an aura-line of passion. She'd penciled it in Italy when she was only nineteen. Emily carefully refolded it and pulled out the letter she'd been aching to read for decades.

May 6, 1970, New Plei D'Jereng, Vietnam

Dear Ben,

I don't have to remind you of all the villages we've burned, the women and children our guys have ruined, and all the pleading faces we've destroyed. It's nothing but adrenaline, man. We're hooked on the fucking high of it. I've forced my fists into the remains of too many friends to try to stop the bleeding. The guys who killed my buddies were only defending themselves. They're not the evil ones. We are. We're invading their country. We're burning their homes while they sleep. We're executing their babies. None of them deserved to die like that—or to watch their loved ones being massacred. Fuck, it's all about body count to the officials back home.

I shot this old man not too long ago. I'll never forget his face. His daughter, maybe Emily's age, her body spoiled, her dead little boy in her lap. I aimed between his eyebrows. He fell.

That was the moment I killed Grandfather, Ma, you, Emmie. I killed everything and everyone I love. I'm the one who made the sky rain bombs. I'm the evil that Emmie's owl tried to warn us against. So, what do I do now, Ben?

I used to think our family told us those stories to keep us in line, to keep us from straying away from our roots. Maybe they used them to scare us into obeying. They kept telling me I wasn't supposed to be with Emmie. So did you. Shit, I don't want to live through this madness.

Maybe Grandfather and Ma cling to the old ways too much. Maybe the old ways point to the real truth. I don't know what's real anymore.

I keep feeling the jungle's pull. I dream of being buried here, beneath the rot and gore, my bones decomposing with the bodies of those I've murdered. I want to feed centipedes and tree roots. I want my flesh to bring new life to this jungle. I'm not afraid of dying anymore. I know you understand. This place is so beautiful and surreal when you're deafened by mortar shells flaring like fireflies all night.

I told you we're off to Cambodia. I didn't tell you this: I'd rather lay it all down forever than come home a madman. Emmie deserves better than me. So do you.

Once I asked her to dream me alive. It was a time when I felt crippled, but I still had hope. TJ promised he'd take care of her. I know he will. She'll get over me. As for you, dear brother, I should have listened. We could have been in Canada right now. Wish I could look into your eyes and pay more attention to your stories. I don't know what it would accomplish, but I know it'd be better than us struggling alone. Don't show her this letter. It'll shatter her. Just tell her how much I love her.

Love you forever, you know that.
—D.

Emily fought back tears. She picked up the drawing again. On the back, it looked like Danny had scribbled something new.

I've stored this and the letter together all these years to remind me how close I came. Your art means the world to me, Emmie. It kept me alive back then. It still does today.

Her prayers came spontaneously, raw and awkward and real. Instead of calling on a particular deity, she summoned the great mysteries of life. And death. She honored the souls entombed beneath the rubble in Manhattan. She paid homage to the innocents buried beneath Cambodia's canopy. She wept for the animals, birds, and fireflies caught in yesterday's napalm flames and today's toxic ash. She grieved for the scorched lady's slippers and the charred vegetation in Vietnam. She prayed for Danny's buddies and the innocent people trapped in the Towers. She mourned for Ben. Again and again, her heart returned to the fragile man she loved, suffering in the train bathroom, paying the price of a war that had permanently scarred his spirit. She prayed for him. She prayed for herself.

Emily leaned her head against the window and gazed at the moon. Its swaying cadence mimicked the rhythm of her heart. She fell asleep and awoke the next morning to find Danny curled beside her. "Cougar," she whispered. A fitting name.

He opened his eyes and smiled.

Tensions lessened as the train traveled west. At each stop, the engines exhaled like dragons spitting bursts of steam. Weary passengers cheered when their new friends disembarked at their home stations. Across the country, they patted each other on the back for making the journey in one piece. In Truckee, the few who remained hugged Danny and Emily before they climbed down the steps.

They rented a car and traveled to Donner Lake to greet Ben's spirit. They'd done this many times before, but everything felt different today.

Someone had felled a Jeffrey pine and left scattered chunks of wood in the yard of his boarded-up cabin. Emily helped Danny gather the rejected pieces. She lifted a small section resembling a boat and carried it across the road to the water. Danny followed.

He fashioned a sail with a stick and a leaf, secured it to the wood, and set it afloat. "*Nya:wëh*, Ben," he whispered. "Thank you for being my navigator. My North Star."

She and Danny held hands and watched the little vessel disappear behind an outcropping of rocks.

"Thank you, Ben. For teaching me," Emily whispered before returning to the cabin.

After throwing the rest of the wood into the trunk, Danny wiped his good hand on his jeans. "I want to build a box with this tree's gift," he said. "For you to paint. A dream box, like the one your grandfather made for you. To give us hope. And courage. And strength. To get us through all this. TJ can help."

"We can fill it with memories," Emily said.

Danny opened his arm and took her in. "More than that. We can take it to Italy. To thank the countess for her fairy-tale land that gave you the strength to keep me alive."

She pulled away. "You think it might make up for the damage I caused?"

"Emmie, relationships are all we have." He kissed her forehead. "We need to heal as many as possible before it's too late."

2006

Italy

*If you ask me what I came to do in this world,
I, an artist, will answer you:
I am here to live out loud.*

— Émile Zola

44

Danny stepped from the rental car, tucked in his shirt, and grabbed Emily's shoulder bag from the back seat. Emily unwrapped the dream box and cradled it in her arms while he approached the hand-lettered sign on the stone wall. *"Suonare il campanello,"* it read. Following the instructions, he set down the bag and rang the bell.

Before long, Count Giovanni, white haired and dressed in khaki pants and a hunting vest, strode across the courtyard and unlatched the wrought iron gate.

"Emi-lee! You are here. And so early!" He kissed her on both cheeks and held her at arm's length. "Look at you, dear girl. You haven't changed. *Bellissima.*"

He seemed shorter and slightly stooped after thirty-six years, yet his face held the same spirited expression she remembered from 1970. In those days, he'd been a dashing young man. Now he was his mother's heir.

"Is this the surprise you told me about?" Giovanni lifted the box from her hands and exaggerated its weight. "Ah, yes, you paint like an Italian." He nodded at the constellation of fireflies she'd portrayed on its top. "That means you must know about *miniare.*

I see it in the layers of red beneath this blue. *Notevole.* What a remarkable gift. *Grazie mille.*"

His smile broadened as he eased the chest under his arm and shook Danny's hand. "Welcome, sir. It is very nice to meet you. You and I? We are all about color and depth and circumstance, no? Like Umbria itself. Indeed, your wife could paint us both in this vast countryside and call it a work of light."

Emily shaded her eyes and focused on the distant hilltops. Without question, the scene embodied color, depth, and light. It held the kind of beauty that could turn a nightmare into a promise.

Giovanni grinned as if he'd heard her thoughts. He swept his free arm across the landscape. "This is my universe. Treat it like your home. Enjoy the grounds if you would like. You have been sitting in the car so long—I am sure you want to stretch your legs. It will give me a chance to finish my morning business. Please, take your time. You may join me in an hour or so. Do not worry, Emi-lee. You will remember your way. Oh, yes. Pick some grapes for me while you are out. Figs are ripe too. You will need this." He gestured to a basket resting against the well.

Emily placed her hand on her heart and thanked him.

Scanning the courtyard, she noted the double castle doors and their ornate knockers—all recently repaired and gleaming with varnish. The castle's masonry had been scrubbed clean, evidence of the count's renovations after the 1997 earthquake.

The cobblestone well still commanded a significant presence in the center of the court. The earth surrounding it looked like it had been leveled and staked to make way for stonework or perhaps a new lawn.

She approached the ancient structure and rested her hands on its surface. A rainbow of lichens once bloomed on these stones—fungi and algae merging as one, creating a unified force. They must have fought hard, never intending to give up their place in this world.

She leaned against the well's rim, polished by centuries of

similar leanings. When she peered into the darkness, ghost screams of Etruscan soldiers drifted toward her. She smiled, backed away, took the basket, and followed Danny out the gate.

"Look, Gubbio is over there," she said, hop-skipping to his side. Tingling with recognition, she turned and pointed south. "The marquis's castle is on top of that hill. We'll be able to see it once we get to the clearing where the Little Farmhouse is."

Danny gave the handbag to her and took the basket. "I know. You've only told me a million times."

Emily understood why he sounded cranky, especially after the budget flight, the car rental hassles, and the wee-hour drive from Milan. They were both nervous about making this trip. During Danny's quiet moods, she knew not to press. She kissed his ear and whispered, more for her benefit than his, "We can do this, Danny. Everything will be okay."

They walked along a wooded trail near a patch of clover lined with multicolored hives. They paused, transfixed by the foraging honeybees. Then she led him along a path that wound around a cluster of chicken coops. Down the hill, she spotted a familiar terra-cotta roof.

The Little Farmhouse looked like it had anticipated her return. Flowers climbed the rock walls. Table and chairs waited on a green lawn. Emily pictured La Contessa pouring wine from wicker-covered jugs while scorpions scurried into dark crannies. She wished the countess could share this moment with her, but she was gone now. Like so many in this world.

A few paces from the farmhouse, Giovanni's new vineyards came into view. The grapes looked like they'd been sprayed with frost. Emily plucked two burgundy orbs, wiped them on her skirt, and fed one to Danny and the other to herself. Hers tasted of ancient vines and twisted old women begging for atonement. His slight smile suggested a flavor more sublime. He set down the basket and plucked several bunches.

They gathered more treasures from the fig trees down the hill. Then they headed toward the largest outbuilding on the property.

As soon as Emily saw the structure, she slowed her pace, suddenly self-conscious about intruding.

The Big Farmhouse appeared larger than she remembered.

Lanky hounds bayed as she walked toward a tapping sound coming from behind the building. The man she discovered there was lean and wore cutoff jeans. He seemed to be repairing a cement basin. He glanced up. Didn't smile. Didn't frown, either.

She did her best to find the right words as she approached him. "*Ho usato per vivere in questa casa,*" she said. "I used to live in this house. Many years ago. *Molti anni fa.*"

He tapped a chisel with a wooden mallet.

She paused, worried her translation wasn't quite right. Pulling a video camera from her bag, she returned to the language she knew.

"May I take pictures?"

The farmer stopped, squinted, and examined her. He flashed the briefest smile, then looked pained.

"*Dentro?*" He gestured with his tools toward the farmhouse.

"No, no." Emily shook her head. "Not inside." She opened her arms to embrace the view. "Outside. *Con permesso.*"

An awkward silence followed.

She searched for a polite way to inquire about what he was working on. He raised one eyebrow and tilted his head forward as if he were trying to help her speak. She pointed to her camera, then to his project. His expression softened. Finally, he nodded and lifted the mallet above his head like a trophy. She filmed him flexing his biceps in an exaggerated pose as he grinned at the lens.

Something about him seemed familiar, but she couldn't place it. Not knowing what else to do and feeling a bit embarrassed, she bowed, thanked him, and jog-stepped to Danny, who was already rounding the corner toward the front of the building. The farmer didn't bother to call off the dogs barking at her heels.

Out of nowhere, a puppy appeared. He wagged his tail, sniffed her shoe, and showered her hand with kisses. Delighted, she played with him and focused her lens on his adorable face. She slowly relaxed as she petted him. Then she rotated the camera toward a new roof protecting the entryway of the Big Farmhouse and panned over the rest of the building.

The ancient stone steps were gone. In their place lay lifeless cement slabs. As if in defiance, pink and yellow roses scaled the farmhouse walls and crept back to the ground where they seemed liberated, waltzing between doghouses and tractors.

She lowered the camera and stroked the little hound's ear. "You have a nice home here." As soon as she lifted his chin, she took a breath. "Etrusco?" The resemblance was uncanny.

He kissed her nose.

"Thought so." Chuckling, she turned around. "Where are the old olive trees? And that big frog lake your grand-pup loved so much?" When she finally spotted it, she realized it was only a small irrigation pond at the base of a nearby hill.

"So much for memories," she said, massaging the puppy's neck.

"Emmie, let's go!" Danny sounded out of breath as he began climbing back to the castle, his basket brimming with the grapes and figs he'd finished gathering while she was lingering behind.

"Go on home then, little one." She nudged the hound several times until he reluctantly returned to his owner.

Quickening her stride, she watched her footing while navigating the dirt path that looped around a confusing maze of drip lines and misters. When she reached the top of the incline beyond the Little Farmhouse, she stopped to film the valley below. Large machines were scrolling hay like cinnamon rolls in the fields. The scene looked acutely industrial compared to the old days, when farmers used to pitchfork straw into cone-shaped stacks. A warehouse had since sprouted from the poppy-filled meadows. Two men stepped from a cement truck and headed toward the manufactured building. A third man patted the hood of his vintage VW Bug before following the others.

From afar, he looked like Danny when he was young. Emily paused the video and rubbed his image from her eyes. She returned the camera to her bag, reached into her pocket, and pulled out the crumpled picture of the boy she'd loved and lost back then.

    Today was Danny's birthday. They'd planned it this way. A new day of promise. A movement toward change. A brief aria of green and gold before winter hissed at the door.

45

"You are back!" Giovanni said, opening the courtyard gate after Emily rang the bell. He nodded as Danny handed him the basket of fruit. "You chose well, kind sir. *Grazie!*"

He escorted them into a small sitting room and set the basket on a table where a coffee pot and a platter of pastries had been neatly arranged. Patting the cushion of a modest couch, he summoned them to sit while he filled three hand-painted mugs with steaming coffee.

"I have heard much about you, sir. May I call you Daniel? I am happy that you and your lovely wife are able to spend the day with me. There is so much to say and do." He lifted his cup and toasted the air. "To old friends and new."

Emily and Danny toasted in response.

"Tomorrow, you must visit the place that is known for this beautiful pottery." Giovanni selected a pastry and passed the tray. "The art gallery there is worth your time. And be sure to see Perugino's curious fresco of God asking two saints to end the black death in Deruta. I would like to know what you think of it." He took a bite and smiled after clearing his palate with coffee. "It is very different from the fresco in our little chapel here. Do you remember, Emi-lee? It is possible Perugino himself might have painted it."

How could she forget the little Madonna and Child? The fresco had been faded and hard to decipher even back then, but the sentiment was clear. It might have been created to balance the dark energy around the relic beneath the altar.

In those days, before dawn and as everyone slept, she'd sometimes lift the rusty key hanging beside the chapel door and rotate it within the oversize lock. Faith had a slippery flavor. The taste of gold leaf slid over the ridges of her tongue, persimmon-like, forcing all those old stories to slither forth. The slain cardinal. The ruby ring. The knucklebone resting in a box somewhere under the altar. The Madonna's dark voice as she whispered to her tiny child, *Step lightly in this world.*

"I am afraid it is in pieces after the earthquake. It is not yet safe to visit. But there are other works of art I would like you to see. Shall we?" Giovanni placed his Deruta mug on the table and rubbed his back as he stood. "Let us take a tour of this place."

He ushered them across the hallway. They entered the part of the castle where Emily had dined with him and his mother in 1970, but there were no suits of armor in the hallway. Nor were there portraits lining the dining room walls. All that remained were the feasting table and several Savonarola chairs.

Emily remembered La Contessa greeting them all those years ago. How lovely she was in her blue-green outfit which complimented her eyes and graying hair. She'd taken Emily aside after dinner and asked if she spoke Italian.

Emily had shaken her head.

"*Capisci la lingua italiana?*" Do you understand Italian?

"*Un pó.*" A little.

"*Va bene.*" La Contessa nodded. "Okay."

She'd used a medley of both languages to explain how William Steele had written to her in Spanish, as if he actually believed all Latin languages were interchangeable.

"*Un malinteso!* Such a misunderstanding! Twelve choirboys

were due to come here in spring." La Contessa's laugh had been infectious as she gestured to the boisterous students in the dining hall that day. "And here you are, twenty—how do you say? Hippies? In January. *Dove posso mettere tutti?* Where to put everyone?"

Emily remembered how hard it was to understand La Contessa's Italian words and had asked her to slow down several times. It must have been as draining for La Contessa to speak in English, and Emily wondered if it exhausted Giovanni today.

She squeezed Danny's hand as they followed Giovanni up a stairwell and into a spacious living area lined with paintings from the Renaissance and baroque periods. She'd never been in the family's private residence. Giovanni pointed to a large landscape hanging above the fireplace. The panel's dusky varnish created an ominous mood. Shadowy figures crouched under a tree. Pigment peeled. Traces of gloom oozed through the hairline cracks.

"See how the artist tricks us?" Giovanni encouraged them to walk with him to the other side of the room. "Now look at the painting. Everything changes, no?"

Archways and bridges moved as Emily moved. Sunlight replaced the previous despair. There were no shadows, no muffled voices, and the wraithlike figures had vanished.

"Life is like this, no? Things change as we change." He paused in appreciation. "Please, come," he said after a few minutes, as if waking from a dream.

He led them through a doorway and pointed. "All the plaster came down from these ceilings and walls during the earthquake. We had to rebuild the entire structure."

The spiky flavors of fresh paint and varnish prickled Emily's nose. Furniture and boxes lined the corridor where they were standing, evidence of the count's recent move.

They entered a second sitting room, more extensive than the one downstairs.

Giovanni threw his arms toward the ceiling. "Scat! Bad cats!

Bad!" Two yellow tabbies scurried down the hall. "I love them, but they have eaten all our food."

As soon as he said this, a young girl appeared with a dustpan and broom. *"Vi prego di scusarmi,"* she whispered as she cleaned leftover crumbs from the floor.

Giovanni touched her elbow. "No need to apologize, Maria. It is not your fault. Please, let me introduce you." He turned to Emily. "Remember Perlita and Vittorio? This is their granddaughter, Maria."

Little Maria? Or her daughter? Or Lorenzo's?

"Maria, may I present the Lady Emily and Sir Daniel?"

"Piacere." Maria smiled and bowed. Then she quickly left the room. A few minutes later, she appeared again, this time with a fresh tray of hors d'oeuvres.

"You may join us if you like," Giovanni said to the girl. Maria shook her head and pointed to the kitchen. He sighed when she disappeared inside.

"She is lovely, but she is very shy. She lives with her parents in the farmhouse down the hill, where you used to live. They sent her up here to help me prepare for your visit." He lifted a carafe from the table and poured a special late-morning wine. *"Cin cin,"* he toasted. "To old times and new."

"Cin cin," Emily and Danny repeated.

So, the man repairing the basin at the Big Farmhouse was Maria's father. *Lorenzo.* His name lingered on her tongue.

"Please, have a seat." Giovanni pointed to a well-loved sofa. He selected one of the canapés and passed the platter to them. Groaning, he settled into what seemed to be his favorite chair. "Ah, I must apologize. Age is getting to me."

He signaled for Emily and Danny to serve themselves. "These biscuits are from wheat in our fields," he said with the same pride Vittorio and Perlita had demonstrated decades before. "The cheese comes from our goats. Prosciutto from our hogs. The figs and grapes, of course, are those you picked from the trees and vineyards just now." He poised the cracker in the air. His eyes twinkled with mischief. "Now, here is how we eat these in Italy. You place the entire thing in your mouth at once to blend the flavors. Like this, see?" He crammed the canapé behind his teeth and kissed his fingers.

Emily accidentally broke her biscuit into pieces while cramming, and everything on it spilled into her hands.

Giovanni laughed. "Congratulations, my dear. Now you eat like an Italian."

46

After finishing their early *merenda*, Giovanni leaned back and stretched.

"Whatever happened to that so-called professor?" he asked. "In your letter, you mentioned you have a book?"

Emily nodded and searched in her bag. She'd prepared for this. She pulled out a stapled booklet about the size of a poetry chapbook and written by one of Steele's fans. She handed it to Giovanni. He thumbed through it.

Pan was the title. Glued to the cover was a copy of a collage featuring William Steele as Peter: pointy hat, red feather, green tights, and a fairy pasted on his shoulder. One hand gestured to a silver star. The other held a postcard that listed his writings: "Stop the Post," "Glue Man," and "More."

After his firing, followers worldwide contributed to Steele's well-being. They'd printed this small volume to protest his "unfair victimization."

According to the pamphlet, he'd carved his way through a troubled childhood and had chosen music, art, and anarchy as antidotes to the suffering his family had endured after his father was killed in World War II.

"So there was a tolerable reason for his—how do I say? Dreadful behavior?"

"On the next page it gets stranger," said Emily.

After Italy, Steele began a movement called Parodism, a global cult of experimentalists who created work by "Errol Sinfree," a multiple-use pseudonym that anyone could adopt. Errol Sinfree could author a rant about authoritarian systems and the evils of the establishment. Errol Sinfree could pickle sheep in formaldehyde, seal them in acrylic tanks, and display them in avant-garde museums. Errol Sinfree could paint his DNA in blood and mail it to another Errol Sinfree thousands of miles away, someone who might be a woman or a horse or a fictitious character from Neverland. All in the name of art.

"Remember the collaged postcards we found in his room? Apparently, he sent them all over Italy to clog the postal system."

Giovanni leaned forward. "We can now blame him for that strike too?"

"And look at this." Emily turned to the last page of the booklet. "The date on his death certificate is April Fools' Day."

Giovanni rolled his eyes and laughed. "That means he is still alive. A master at deception. This book is too kind. Do you want it back?"

"Not really."

"Very well." Giovanni tossed it across the room. It missed the waste bin. He slowly rose and buried the pamphlet beneath the rest of the garbage. "There."

Emily took a breath. "I'm sorry he came into your life back then. And for all the damage I caused."

"My dear Emi-lee," Giovanni said, returning to his chair. "I am glad you did what you did. 'Flattened him,' my mother said. She was pleased as well."

Danny chuckled and immediately covered his mouth.

Giovanni slapped his knee. "A good laugh at that scoundrel's expense? I like it. But now it is time for you both to tell me what you have been doing all these years. You brought your portfolios, no?"

"I'll get Emily's." Danny lifted himself from the couch.

"Can you find your way, sir?"

Danny smiled.

"He is a nice man," Giovanni said after Danny left the room. "A quiet man. I am glad you convinced him to come."

"It takes a while for him to get used to new places. But brace yourself." Emily laughed. "Once he feels comfortable, he won't stop chattering."

"He chatters?"

"Sometimes."

"Aah, *grazie*!" Giovanni said when Danny returned.

He opened the portfolio, studied each page, and turned to Danny. "Your wife indeed paints like an Italian. Look at these eyes—and the light in them. As I said before, you are a lucky man. This reminds me of a picture I want you to see. It is of Emily and me. But first, I must escort poor Maria home. Her parents must be worried about her return. Look about a bit more if you would like."

As soon as he left the room, Giovanni's two cats leaped into Danny's lap. They purred as he stroked their ears.

Emily kissed Danny on the cheek and excused herself to use the downstairs bathroom. While navigating through the chaos in the hallway, she noticed a series of portraits, showered in amber hues, leaning against the wall.

"I remember these," she whispered to herself.

How ominous and large they'd seemed when she'd first arrived, a row of serious faces glaring at everyone as she and her friends dined at La Contessa's table. And how ironic. Generations of men, once powerful and demanding, were now stashed away in a corridor filled with boxes.

She retraced Giovanni's steps and made her way to a more familiar hallway downstairs. She opened the door to the washroom. It was about half its original size. A small shower had replaced the claw-foot tub. Seamless marble graced the floor. A modern commode and bidet and a contemporary pedestal sink with bronze fixtures completed the remodel.

Curious, she opened the door to Steele's old room. It was gigantic. Workers must have moved the bathroom walls on one side and Emily's closet room on the other to make it this big. Instead of cots with legs in cockroach traps, an antique four-poster clothed in white linens was arranged diagonally across the space. A teddy bear made its home on the pillow, and an embroidered cushion on a wide sill kept the draft from coming through the high window. The wardrobe had been restored. There were no splattered colors to betray her fight with Freya.

"I tell you a secret," Giovanni whispered when he returned. He took Emily and Danny into the courtyard, out the gate, and around the side of the castle. "I do not remember much about the time you were here." He tapped his temple. "I do recall one thing, though. How much my mother loved you kids. As you know, my father died the year before you came. I thought having young people around might lift her spirits. She talked about you, Emilee. She felt for you because you missed your boyfriend the same way she missed my father." He smiled at Danny, then at Emily. "One day she said, 'These young people need something to drink.' I told her, 'Mamma, if you give these kids wine, they'll be drunk all day and forget to study.' 'Gianni,' she said, 'every week, bring them a demijohn. Or two. Or three.' I did."

Emily nearly sank to her knees, laughing. "You were right. We did forget to study."

Grinning, Giovanni pulled a Polaroid camera from his sports vest and fumbled around in another pocket for a skeleton key. "My mother wanted you to be happy, that is all. I would like to show you something." He handed the camera to Danny and unlocked a rotting door. It creaked as he opened it. A cloud of cobwebs greeted them. It was so dark Emily couldn't see the stairs descending to the wine cellar.

"Come, Emi-lee. Help me find that picture." He swept away the webs. "No need to worry. Nothing will collapse. The workers have secured everything."

Danny searched his jacket for a travel flashlight and cast a beam of light across their path. Emily scanned the area for signs of structural reinforcements.

Debris buried the stairway, and gravel tumbled away with each footstep. Emily and Giovanni held hands as they balanced themselves on chunks of plaster.

"Aah, here they are!"

Giovanni released Emily's hand and lowered himself into a small space crowded with mysterious mounds. He lifted a dusty tarp.

Demijohns. A great deal smaller than she remembered. Five of them, still colorful, even after all this time.

Giovanni brushed one off and lifted the heavy jug with both hands. The blue wicker hadn't even faded. He set it aside. Then he sifted through the wreckage until he pulled out a snakelike contraption. He carefully helped Emily descend the rubble and gave her the siphon.

"The camera has a flash," he said to Danny. Giovanni hoisted the demijohn to his shoulder and pretended to drink.

The picture he wanted to show them? It wasn't a painting or an old photo. One click of the shutter, and here it was: an earthquake-ravaged wine cellar, a bright-blue demijohn, a siphon, and Count Giovanni's free arm around Emily's shoulder, coaxing her to pose.

47

"Everyone thinks it is about the lake," said Giovanni as he drove Emily and Danny toward the fortified town of Castel Rigone, near Lago Trasimeno. "Of course, it is a lovely lake. If I were a proper tour guide, I would tell you it is the largest body of water in all of Italy. If I were an artist like you, Emi-lee, I would notice how this pool of water is a vast sheet of radiance. See how it changes with the light?"

He pointed to the left, then swept his hand over the scene. "Milky in the shadows over there, silver in the middle, and look at the intense blue on the right. Painters come from around the world to make this lake their muse."

Danny pushed his hair from his eyes. He simulated the count's dramatic gestures from the passenger seat of the vintage Ferrari, the same red convertible Emily and her friends had swooned over in 1970.

"Yes," said the count. "You are a great artist as well. You know these things. Forgive me if I focus too much on your lovely wife."

From the cramped back seat, Emily hoped Danny might speak up. His abstract paintings were much more candid than her portraits. Though they both were successful artists, Danny had refused to bring his portfolio and was hesitant to talk about his work.

"Ah, sunset," the count said. "To an artist, it is all about the sun. You like to paint it setting and rising so you can use all the remaining colors on your palette. This is right, no?"

Danny laughed.

"Would you like to know what I think?" Giovanni said. "It is about the music. You are a musician, are you not, sir?"

"Used to be."

"Ah, then you still are. Once music touches your soul, it never leaves. You know this. I can tell from your voice."

Danny turned toward the yellow orb bulging on the horizon.

As they approached the walls of Castel Rigone, the count pointed to a sandstone bell tower emerging from a hillside of trees. "This is where I am taking you, my friends: the sanctuary of Maria Santissima dei Miracoli—Saint Mary of the Miracles."

Emily had heard tales about this chapel. The most famous involved a girl drawing water from the public well and the beautiful woman who appeared before her. The lady wanted a church constructed precisely where the girl was standing. It was 1490. The villagers were skeptical and refused to build. After several more visitations and requests, the lady sent the girl home with an inverted pitcher of water on her head. Despite it being upside down, not a drop of water spilled. Out rushed the people of Castel Rigone, instant believers. When they excavated the land to begin construction, they discovered a small shrine with a picture of Mother Mary cradling the baby Jesus in her arms. Amazing things happened after that. Villagers from all around flocked to the site. Word even spread to Pope Alexander VI, who blessed the church and gave it its name.

Giovanni parked the Ferrari under an olive tree. Several people gathered to watch. They seemed to be waiting for him. Hugs and greetings ensued. As he did with Maria, Count Giovanni introduced Emily and Danny as Sir Daniel and Lady Emily, though the three of them, all casually dressed, didn't seem to fit those roles.

After everyone filed into the church, Giovanni halted Emily and pointed to the main portal of the sanctuary. "Do you know who created this doorway?" He winked at her. "Topolino."

"The car?"

He laughed. "Little Mouse was the artist's nickname. His real name was Domenico Bertini da Settignano. A student of Michelangelo." He turned to Danny. "I was saying this to your Lady Emily because Topolino is the Italian name for Mickey Mouse. It is also the name of the Fiat the kids drove back then." He smiled at Emily. "And look at the window above it. It is a wheel of fortune. There is no better fortune than nature. See the fruit and flowers surrounding it? Topolino did these paintings too."

A group of stone angels gazed at the heavens and the turning wheel. Why did miracles seem to take place when nature and the divine merged?

They stepped inside. The painting of Mary and the baby Jesus hung above the altarpiece in the left chapel. On the right, Christ's torture. A graphic image, typical of 1531, when persecution devoured the culture, and memories of Roman tyranny were still fresh. Not unlike today. Not unlike any other era, for that matter. Between birth and death was the great ordeal of life.

The frescoes in the center of the chapel featured animal deities and nature worship, merging pagan spirituality with the church. Images of the surrounding countryside pervaded the space.

A magnificent organ stood beside the altar. "Created by the famous Morettini organ makers in 1768," said Giovanni. "Here, let us sit." He motioned to the empty front pew and insisted Emily take her place between him and Danny.

Two distinguished men set a harpsichord on the floor in front of the organ. Cherubs and doves adorned the top and sides of the instrument. Several more men brought chairs and music stands. The audience fell silent as the musicians took their places and arranged their sheet music. A double quartet: three violins, two violas, one violoncello, and one double bass, with the exquisite harpsichord in the center.

Emily felt suspended in time as the patrons settled in their seats. The harpsichordist poised his fingers over the keys; in unison, the other musicians lifted their bows.

Antonio Vivaldi. *The Four Seasons.*

The musicians began with spring. Flowers, bees, birds. Petals and wings stretching and fluttering through sacred spaces. What better venue for this masterpiece than an Italian chapel? Then festivals. Thunderstorms. The bass's boom. Bows grinding across taught strings. Now silence. Red poppies. Green wheat. A whispering voice: *Little Bird.* Memories of summer. A grandfather's crayon. A dream box filled with voices from the past. An electrifying musician walking onstage. His moon-landing kisses foretelling the season to come. Autumn. A boy mimicking the dance of fireflies. A girl grieving the loss of her mother. A boy painting her portrait to keep her from disappearing into winter's silvery pizzicato. Hallucinating fog. A dusting of snow on the streets of New York. An ancient well. A lady's slipper's promise. Time losing its balance. Emily learning to walk again. An earthquake becoming a celestial pileup. A war turning into a dream.

When the musicians lowered their bows and the harpsichordist rested his hands on his legs, Giovanni leaned his elbows on his knees and cradled his tearstained face.

Emily squeezed Danny's hand. *How long have we been here?*

"For lifetimes," he whispered.

48

"This way," said Giovanni when they returned to the estate after the concert. "I would like to show you something."

"Not the wine cellar again," Emily teased.

Giovanni smiled. "Better than all the wine in the world."

The three of them walked down a well-lit path toward the Little Farmhouse. What used to be the old chicken coop was now an enclosed garage. Giovanni rummaged through several pockets until he found a skeleton key.

"My great-grandfather built this," he said, pulling the door wide and switching the light. In the center of the room stood a rustic wagon carrying a large gray box.

The light machine. Emily's heart began to race.

Giovanni used a smaller key to unlock the doors on each side of the box.

There it was. Polished mahogany. Ceramic levers and knobs. Silver gauges. Copper wiring. Fuse boxes. Cranks. Wheels. Conductors. And two oval plaques: *"Studio Elettrotecnico"* and *"Locomobile Elettrica, per Illuminazione."*

It was a work of art.

"Italy's first electric light machine." Giovanni's face glowed with pride. He addressed Danny. "My great-grandfather built it for Buffalo Bill Cody's Wild West show when it came to Rome in 1890. This generator lit the scene like a circus."

Ben's voice shuddered through Emily's body. *The guy had the gall to name himself Buffalo Bill. But he was good to us. Our great-grandfathers wouldn't have survived if they'd stayed in America.* And then La Contessa's words: *You will understand one day.*

Danny circled the generator, following the intricate wiring with his index finger.

"The entire town turned out," Giovanni said. "Ten thousand people each day. My great-grandfather said it was the best act he had ever seen, especially the Indian attack on the Deadwood stagecoach. It had not been many years since the event took place in America. It became international news." His grin filled his face. "What do you think of this magnificent machine? Is it worth anything?"

Emily frowned. "You're not planning to sell it, are you?"

"No, no. For insurance purposes."

"You can't put a price on a machine like this." Danny ran his fingers over the smooth mahogany. "No more than you can put a price on your ancestors."

Emily touched a plaque bearing the count's ancestor's first name: *Giovanni*.

"I had it restored in Rome. I feel it is quite a miracle it is still with us. I wanted you to know it survived, Emi-lee. You no longer need to worry about the past." Pulling up his sleeve to look at his watch, Giovanni added, "It is getting late. May we return to my home, where it is warm, and we can enjoy some wine?"

In the sitting room, Giovanni steered the conversation away from the light machine and onto the need for the world to move away from gas so electric vehicles might allow the climate to normalize. Then they shifted to discussing the beauty in Vivaldi's music and how it compared to the work of Adriano Banchieri, a composer whose canzonettas might have influenced Caravaggio's most powerful paintings.

Giovanni gestured to the dream box. "Please tell me about the music that inspired this lovely work of art."

Emily cleared her throat. She'd been lost in the medieval world of Banchieri's madrigal comedies and wondered how they might have fit into Caravaggio's dark world.

"It was Danny's song," she said. "About a raven who saved a girl's life."

Animated from the wine, Danny lowered the timbre of his voice to make his words sound dramatic. "It has been said, so it must be true, that ravens make great teachers. As do hermits."

"In this box? First, a raven? Now, a hermit? Like this old count?" Giovanni poured the third round of his finest sagrantino.

Emily lifted her glass. "You're more than a hermit."

He laughed, filling her goblet to the brim. "Young lady, I am proud of my hermitage." He topped off Danny's glass, placed the bottle on the table, and settled into a well-worn chair. "This wine came from Montefalco. My cousin's land. One sack of seeds grew an entire harvest." Giovanni toasted the air.

Emily took a sip. "Mmm. The goddess herself must have harvested this wine."

"I beg to disagree," Danny said after tasting it. "It is so splendid, only a magnificent giant could have picked the grapes." He raised his glass.

"Have I forgotten my English?" said Giovanni. "This is what you put in this box? A goddess and a giant now?"

"And magic."

"Magic?" The count sighed. "You two are confusing me." He took another sip.

"Please open it," said Emily.

He set down his wine, placed the box in his lap, and traced the constellations of fireflies on top.

"For years, we've wanted to thank you for everything you did for us," Emily said. "And to make amends. I apologize for the damage to the wardrobe and the room—and for what Steele and his cohorts did to your light machine. The investigation into that man unearthed so much pain. I never wanted to—"

"Emi-lee. Your professor tried to blackmail my mother over many false claims. I told you before, and I will tell you again. We were happy you brought us justice. He betrayed us all. If it were not for you, he would never have paid a price, no?" Giovanni lowered his eyes and stroked the latch. "I am honored to receive your gift." He touched the night sky before slowly unfastening the lid.

Emily's miniature paintings, inspired by the Khmer legend, adorned the bottom of the box. But the landscape was not Cambodian. It was La Contessa's beautiful estate. The goddess came to life in the olive trees. The giant appeared in the clouds. Carvings on the well stones depicted the face of the hermit. The dew in the wheat fields glistened with images of the magic ball. All showered the landscape with light. A conspiracy of ravens chased each other around the farmhouses. Eagle owls flew overhead. The interior walls of the box replicated the interior of the castle. On one side, the library came alive with volumes of illuminated manuscripts. On another, suits of armor lined the hallway. On a third, portraits adorned the dining room walls. On the fourth, a nightingale sang outside the bedroom where Emily once slept. The chapel's Madonna and Child emerged from the interior of the lid.

The count blinked away tears. "This must have taken many years to paint."

Danny nodded.

"There's more." Emily pointed to an envelope.

Giovanni reached into his pocket, pulled out his penknife, and slid the blade along the seal. Inside was a palm-size book detailing Emily's stories about the beauty of his family's land and how she'd found her voice here. She'd handwritten it in Italian, translated with the help of a language instructor. Eagle owls and nightingales framed each scene, including an intricate illustration of Giovanni and Emily sitting cross-legged on the floor in Steele's old room, surrounded by collages and placards from the protest that heralded the early stages of Italy's terrible Years of Lead. Emily had painstakingly created it to resemble a prayer book from the Middle Ages.

Count Giovanni clutched his chest as he turned each page. A photograph fell from one of them. Danny retrieved it from the carpet and handed it back.

"What is this?" The count put down the book, examined the picture, and took a breath. He rose and showed it to Emily.

It was a faded carte de visite featuring Buffalo Bill Cody and the members of his Wild West show, all gathered around the electric generator. Scrawled across the bottom in a sepia flourish were the words *Roma, 1890.*

Giovanni took reading glasses from the table and motioned for Emily to come closer. They leaned into the image.

Emily gasped.

"Where did you get this?" Giovanni asked.

"My mother gave it to me when I was a boy."

"I do not believe this. Emi-lee, here is my great-grandfather's light machine. And look. Here is my great-grandfather. In the hat." He gestured to a tall gentleman wearing a three-piece suit and proudly standing beside the generator.

"He looks like you," said Danny. When Emmie showed me a photo of you from 1970, I knew I had to give you this picture—and to set the record straight."

"Record?" asked the count.

"About that stagecoach raid—"

"Aah, yes. Many crimes were blamed on the Indians, but they were committed by white men like me to make more reasons to slaughter the indigenous people."

Danny sighed and leaned back. "Imagine being forced to replay that scene—and all the others—over and over every day."

"I regret that. My mother did too." The count pointed to the photo. "My great-grandfather invited all these people to stay at his place in Rome. He got to know them."

"*Oskate wicasa*," said Danny. "Showman. The Lakota label gave them status."

"They were honorable people. And patient. They did much to help us understand their predicament. My great-grandfather took them to visit the Pantheon. They asked polite questions. Always polite." Giovanni pressed the photo to his chest and returned to his seat. "In time, he came to respect them more than he did that swaggering Cody."

Danny's eyes softened, as if revisiting a memory. "Many others joined the Lakota—even a few of my ancestors. Cody paid them well. He even let them speak their own languages. Unusual at the time."

"It is odd," Giovanni said, looking at the picture again. "This feeling that I have—it is like you and I might have been friends if we were alive back then."

Danny set down his glass. "Maybe we were."

"Sir Daniel, if that is so, I am honored to be your friend. I must get brandy to celebrate."

Emily quickly closed her mouth after realizing it had been open the entire time. As soon as Giovanni left the room, she confronted Danny.

"I can't believe you kept this from me."

"I wanted it to be a surprise, Emmie. I was shocked when you showed me photos of Giovanni and his mother. I knew I'd seen him before. Then TJ unearthed Ma's photo when he brought my things to the house in Santa Cruz."

"In the seventies? That was decades ago, Danny."

"I know."

"When did you slip the picture into the—" Emily stopped talking when Giovanni entered with three crystal snifters and a bottle of Etichetta Nera.

He served modest splashes into the short-stemmed goblets and toasted. "Here we are. Three friends. Together."

Danny toasted back. "Thank you for being so good to Emily back then. And for being so generous today." He set down his glass and lifted the photo from the table. "Look at this again."

Giovanni settled in his chair and scrutinized the carte de visite for several minutes. Then he studied Danny's face. "This cannot be true." He motioned for Danny to come over and pointed at the photo. "Am I imagining things? Here. Behind my great-grandfather. This gentleman reminds me of you."

Danny grinned. "As you said this morning, 'We are all about color and depth and circumstance, no?'"

2010
California

*You will find the spirit of Caesar
in this soul of a woman.*

— Artemisia Gentileschi

49

Danny seemed more relaxed after their trip to Italy. His downward spirals were far less frequent now. Emily's anxiety eventually faded too. Each day taught them to be patient with each other. And with themselves. So, this was what "through thick and thin" truly meant.

Emily wanted to keep him with her forever. To watch him as he shook the container of black sunflower seeds, separating the empty hulls from the hearts so the birds could get the best of his offerings. To savor his voice as she listened to him brainstorm with TJ the best way to repair Beulah's brakes. To help him pull the bucket away from a rowan tree's roots so they could plant it in their families' memories. She wanted to walk in the woods with him, to hunt for mushrooms and count bumblebees, to identify wildflowers. She wanted to stroke the down on his forearm, to brush his graying hair, to kiss his ears, to whisper "Dream well" as they closed their books and turned out the light.

It was Danny's birthday once more. She touched his cheek. "How old are you now?"

"A billion years and counting." His voice mimicked the wind.

She opened the covers, crawled into the hospice bed in the living room, and slid beside his wasting form. It hurt him if she touched him the wrong way, so she moved with great care. Still, she wanted to be as close as possible.

For the past several years, his symptoms had become more and more pronounced: nausea, vomiting, shortness of breath, sporadic wheezing. Emily had blamed his increasing distress on the toxicity of the remaining bullet near his lung. The doctor at the veterans' hospital mentioned something about presumptive conditions and cancer, but nothing about Agent Orange or dioxin.

Danny rested his head against her shoulder.

As gently as possible, she pressed her lips to his forehead.

He slept for a while, then roused.

Look, Emmie.

He struggled to lift his finger to point. His eyes reflected the blue-white glow of Rigel, one of the most luminous stars in the night sky. Rigel. Symbol of hope and new beginnings.

No, not Rigel. Look again. Danny managed a smile. His skin pulled against his teeth, accentuating the line of bone along his jaw.

Emily rose from the bed and walked to the window. Beulah's windshield was filled with flickering light—reflections of flashing insects linking sky to earth, earth to sky.

See them?

"I don't believe it! Danny, they're everywhere!"

Go outside, Emmie. It's okay. I'll be all right.

Emily took the flashlight from the table and opened the door. She was standing on the seam of another world, in a faraway fairy tale where she and Danny were still young and burning with desire.

She flashed the light and opened her free hand in disbelief. She knew it wasn't true, but there they were, surrounding her, responding to her signal. She wanted to squeal like a girl, to twirl and dance and follow these tiny diamonds to the brink of time and back. But she knew better. Fireflies didn't glow like this in California.

She turned around, reentered the dark room, and closed the door behind her.

Danny's body was real—not a cluster of pillows lined up to look like a person. It was also unreal. A silent mound. Empty of breath. Empty of pulse. But not empty of heart. Danny had joined Orion and Rigel and all the cycles of nature. He was now the sun and the crescent moon and every firefly in the inky sky. His eyes had filled with shooting stars.

There was a day, long ago, when Emily was a child. She was sitting on a bench in front of her elementary school, waiting for her mother to finish pinning felt storyboards to the walls of her classroom. It was late. Even Clare and her mom had gone home. She fell into a dream.

A man approached her. He looked like he'd been living in the wilderness for decades. He wore loose slacks and a belt that sagged at his waist. His smile was gentle. He knelt on the grass, facing her.

The old man bowed his head and mumbled something that sounded like a foreign language. Finally, he looked up.

"*Nya:wëh sgë:nö*," he said. "It is good to see you well."

His eyes were as blue as the sea.

50

An old Seneca tradition based on the code of the prophet Handsome Lake stated that people should grieve the passing of loved ones for only ten days. If they mourned past the ten days, it tormented those who had died and caused them great suffering. Emily tried to live up to this, but her concept of linear time had loosened long ago. She wasn't even sure if Danny followed the Longhouse Religion.

Of this, she was certain: Danny was no ordinary man. He wore generations in his face. He found strength by cradling the scariest, darkest corners of his fears and helped her find the courage to face hers. Together, they danced in those corners, dreamed them alive, and confronted them with acceptance and love.

She placed her hands on the dream box she and her grandfather had created when she was a child. She slipped her finger along the metal latch and pressed until it snapped. Inside was the velvet pouch containing her Odin stone. It guarded Sammy's Civil War letters, Danny's letters, the owl feather he'd given her, the rice paper envelope containing a disintegrated lady's slipper, TJ's pendant, and the two photographs Danny had sent from Vietnam. Beneath everything was the picture he'd taken of Emily and Giovanni posing with demijohns in the wine cellar.

We are all related.

TJ's first solo album, *Raven Songs*, played on the turntable in the background. Something in TJ's voice reminded her of the tender way he and Clare held her during Danny's ceremony, supporting her to keep her from falling. Was he the third angel her mother had sent long ago to, as her grandfather would say, keep her in this world?

Emily lifted the jacket cover from the shelf and studied the portrait on the front. TJ, his head lowered, his eyes closed, fingering the frets of Danny's Firebird. It was the portrait she'd painted of him as a Christmas present in 1973 before she realized Danny had already come home. On the back of the LP, a small black-and-white photo featured TJ showing Ben and Danny how to play the game of Go.

So many modalities linked their lives. Manifestations of memory more profound than any of them could have imagined.

What is life but a movement of energy?

Danny's voice still visited her.

She dried her eyes and walked to the window. As always, Beulah, lovingly restored, waited in the driveway. Again and again, this little Volkswagen had escorted them to Big Basin so they could walk barefoot along the Redwood Loop trail. Emily would take Danny's hand, lead him to the banks of Opal Creek, and brush her lips against his ear.

Do you hear it?

He'd smile and close his eyes.

Yes. The wind. That's what gives us life. We share the air with everything. We're all common, like a breath. One step inhales. The next sighs.

Emily's voice became that wind: *Fill your lungs with walking.* She slipped her arm around his waist and moved him closer. They synchronized their steps.

They practiced walking through the redwoods.

They practiced walking every day for weeks, for months, for years.

They walked until Danny's knees buckled beneath his weight.

They walked until he could no longer keep himself upright in his wheelchair.

They walked while holding hands in their dreams.

They practiced walking through stars, through space, through all the dimensions of time.

They walked until they were in the breath of something stronger, older, deeper.

They walked until darkness turned to light.

Wings, Little Bird. This is what comes after love.

Luminescence

*We talk to each other with light;
did you know that?*

— Danny Jackson

Acknowledgments

Mating Habits of Fireflies began as a series of poems. Thank you to everyone involved with the late Jibboom Street Writers Group and the Corner Booth Writers for contributing to my growth in this process.

I'm forever grateful for my teachers. Tom Meschery, thank you for helping me find my voice. Floyd Salas, I wish you were still with us. You taught me about rhythm. And energy. And the importance of telling it like it is. Ellen Bass, thank you for encouraging me to compose poems about my Vietnam veteran friends. Anya Achtenberg, your friendship, your courage, and your eccentric workshops sparked my interest in writing out-of-the-box fiction. Michael Croft, thank you for your honest and transformative critiques. To Sands Hall, Louis B. Jones, and everyone at the Community of Writers in Olympic Valley, I'm grateful for your revitalizing support.

Sharon Freewoman, Pam Fritz, Shelley Harris, Sheri Hartstein, Meg Lent, Reina Markheim, Duncan Muffett, Elle Pedri, Esther Sonnenberg, and Mary Zuccaro—thank you for being such indispensable advisors. Bill Back, did you know that restoring a vintage Volkswagen would lead to Beulah appearing on the pages of this book? Jon Robertson, my longtime literary brother, thank you for helping me stay on track. Jean Fournier, thank you for your poet's mind. Clarice Korrison, you patiently scrutinized every draft of this novel, offering invaluable insights each time. You challenged me to dig deeper and to keep going no matter what. A simple thank you only scratches the surface of my gratitude.

It's an indescribable gift to work with excellent editors. Lindsey Alexander, Daniel Burgess, Duncan Murrell, Marcia Trahan, and Margaux Weisman, thank you for showing me how to restructure my manuscript and for helping me simplify a crowded cast of characters. Elyse Lyon, copyeditor extraordinaire, thank you for taking such a deep dive into the nuances of the manuscript and unearthing historical details that I had missed.

Throughout the innumerable incarnations of *Mating Habits of Fireflies*, I've worked hard to stay true to a remarkable group of people: collegemates, companions, friends, family members, and veterans who came of age during an era of assassinations, war, art, free love, psychedelics, and revolutionary music. A few brave survivors of the Vietnam War took the time to share their heart-wrenching tales with me. Tim, Mark, Mike, and Potter, you are no longer with us, but along with others, your energy, music, and art form the heart of this book.

I'm profoundly lucky to have Greig, my husband, as my partner-in-art. Despite my all-consuming passion for images and language, you've nurtured my creative spirit since the beginning of our relationship. *Tha gaol agam ort.*

List of Music
In Sequential Order

"Eve of Destruction" by Barry McGuire
"Crystal Blue Persuasion" by Tommy James & The Shondells
"Universal Soldier" by Buffy Sainte Marie
"Dock of the Bay" by Otis Redding
"Nights in White Satin" by The Moody Blues
"No Man Can Find the War" by Tim Buckley
"I Never Meant to Be Your Mountain" by Tim Buckley
"Goodbye and Hello" by Tim Buckley
"I Shall Be Released" by The Band
"Sunshine of Your Love" by Cream (Jimi Hendrix's version)
"Voodoo Child" by Jimi Hendrix
"For What It's Worth" by Buffalo Springfield
"Salt of the Earth" by The Rolling Stones
"St. Stephen" by Grateful Dead
"Rumble" by Link Wray
"Mountains of the Moon" by Grateful Dead
"Cosmic Charlie" by Grateful Dead
"Whole Lotta Love" by Led Zeppelin
John Mayall & the Bluesbreakers with Paul Butterfield by John Mayall
"Flying High" Country Joe and the Fish
"Superbird" by Country Joe and the Fish
"Section 43" by Country Joe and the Fish
"White Bird" by It's A Beautiful Day
"Fortunate Son" by Creedence Clearwater Revival
"White Room" by Cream
"Nothing Is Easy" by Jethro Tull
"Guinevere" by Donovan
The Who, Buddy Miles, Leon Russell, and "Nobody's Fool" by Poco
"Sookie Sookie" by Steppenwolf
The Progressive Blues Experiment by Johnny Winter
The Best of Muddy Waters by Muddy Waters
"Embryonic Journey" by Jefferson Airplane
"Comin' Back to Me" by Jefferson Airplane
"Knockin' on Heaven's Door" by Bob Dylan
"Have You Ever Seen the Rain?" by Creedence Clearwater Revival
"The Thrill Is Gone" by BB King
"The Four Seasons" by Antonio Vivaldi
Barca di Venetia per Padova, Op.12 (first ed. 1605) by Adriano Banchieri

About the Author

M.C. St.Clair is a writer, oral storyteller, poet, and alumna of the Community of Writers in Olympic Valley, California. This is her first novel.

As a visual artist, she is known as Cathee vanRossem-St.Clair. Her unique approach to miniaturism, inspired by her studies of the masters in Italy, has earned her national recognition. One of her creations, commissioned by the White House, is now in the National Archives.

You can view her work at www.catheestclair.com.

Made in the USA
Las Vegas, NV
12 September 2024

95208002R00208